Beryl Kingston was bor[...]
After taking her degr[...]
taught English and Dra[...]
as well as taking some ti[...]
up her three children. S[...]
husband.

Beryl Kingston's first novel, *Hearts and Farthings*, is also available from Futura.

Also by Beryl Kingston

HEARTS AND FARTHINGS

BERYL KINGSTON

KISSES AND HA'PENNIES

Futura

To. R.D.

A Futura Book

Copyright © Beryl Kingston 1986

First published in Great Britain in 1986 by
Macdonald & Co (Publishers) Ltd
London & Sydney

This Futura edition published in 1987

ISBN 0 7088 3168 0

Reproduced, printed and bound in Great Britain by
Hazell Watson & Viney Limited,
Member of the BPCC Group,
Aylesbury, Bucks

Futura Publications
A Division of
Macdonald & Co (Publishers) Ltd
Greater London House
Hampstead Road
London NW1 7QX
A BPCC plc Company

Chapter One

The young man hurtling down the steep hill of Church Lane in his brand new Morris Cowley was warm with brandy and too full of post-party euphoria to be cautious. It was a dark January evening, and gusts of rain sleeting blackly across his windscreen made it difficult for him to see where he was going, but he didn't let a little thing like that worry him. He'd found from experience that people always managed to get themselves out of the way of his impressive wheels, especially if he sounded his horn to gee them up a bit.

So he was annoyed and puzzled when he arrived at the junction of Church Lane and Mitcham Road to find that his way was inexplicably blocked by the progress of a very solid-looking tram. He clapped on the brakes at once, of course, but the car didn't stop. In fact, it didn't even seem to be slowing down, although he could hear the tyres screeching and his own voice yelling a warning somewhere a very, very long way away from his head. A cocktail of emotions shook themselves together inside his stomach, drunken anger, disbelief, excitement and a tightening knot of fear, and then his lovely expensive motor embedded itself in the side of the tram with a crunching thud that immediately had people running out of the pub opposite to see what had happened.

For a few seconds he sat at the wheel too stunned to move, then he gave himself a shake and climbed stiffly out of his now up-tilted vehicle to inspect the damage. He was so upset he could have cried. The long grey bonnet of his most prized possession was cracked and buckled, water was pouring out of the radiator and his two magnificent headlights were torn out of their sockets like gouged-out eyes. The crowd were enjoying it all immensely, their faces shining with pleasure under their damp cloth caps, but before he could think of the words to rebuke them for their audacity the tram driver had arrived, and the tram driver was furious.

'Why dontcher look where yer going?' he demanded. 'You could 'a' killed someone.' His face was pinched with shock and anger.

The young man drew his drunken dignity around him. 'Look what you've done to my car, my man,' he said. 'Why didn't you get out of the way? You could surely hear me coming.'

'Oh, that's lovely!' the driver said, addressing the crowd. 'Now it's my fault. We 'ad right a' way, mate. You should 'a' stopped.'

'How could I stop?' the young man said plaintively. Really, how unreasonable tram drivers were!

'Driving like a bleedin' maniac!' the driver said to his admiring audience. 'Want lockin' up, the lot of 'em!'

'You've ruined my car,' the young man said. 'Two hundred and fifty pounds that cost me, I'd have you know.'

If he'd hoped to impress the crowd by the mention of such wealth, the ploy misfired. Two hundred and fifty pounds was more than the driver could earn in a twelvemonth, so this careless affluence simply infuriated him. 'I don't give a tinker's fart fer your bleedin' car,' he said, as the faces all round him grinned and growled encouragement. 'You could 'a' killed someone!'

The young man suddenly decided he'd had enough of all this. He would go home. That's what he'd do. He tried to push his way out of the crowd. But the crowd was uglier than it had been when it gathered, and now it wouldn't let him pass. Soon he was being jostled from hand to rough hand and angry faces were mouthing abuse at him, and a new kind of fear was oppressing his chest.

By now, two more trams had arrived and, finding their way blocked, both drivers and several passengers had climbed out to join the fray. And among the travellers on the tram from Streatham were Anna Maria Pelucci and her best friend Pearl. They'd been to a dance at the Locarno and, as usual after such an event, Anna was feeling glamorous and pleasantly excited.

6

'What fun!' she said, gazing rapturously down at the heaving crowd and the two men circling and glowering at one another in the centre of it all. 'It's a fight!'

'Oh lor!' Pearl said. 'I hope they don't get violent.'

Anna dropped a scathing glance at her friend's naivety. ''Course they'll get violent,' she said happily. 'It'll be ripping fun!' This was just the sort of occasion she enjoyed. The kind she conjured up in her dreams. Two strong men, tall, dark, brooding men, fighting to the death, for *her* love. Or not to the death, perhaps, because if they fought to the death there wouldn't be anybody left to love her at the end of it. But fiercely of course, and very, very passionately. And afterwards the victor would take her in his arms and kiss her breathless and tell her she was the most wonderful girl in the world.

'Are we getting off?' Pearl asked. 'It's raining like billy-oh. We shall get ever so wet.'

They were still standing on the platform of the tram and Anna was under the partial shelter of the roof, but Pearl had one foot on the first step down, as befitted her lower status, so she was getting splashed.

'No, don't let's,' Anna said. 'You get a good view from up here.' She'd taken another look at the combatants and neither of them measured up to her dream. One was only a common old tram driver and, although the rich one with the car was young enough, he was horribly ordinary and had a very big nose. But she decided she'd stay where she was, because you never knew with fights. Anything could happen. Absolutely anything. And in the meantime, she'd got herself into a rather splendid position, nicely framed by the roof of the tram and well lit by the street light. She made a very pretty picture in her new red coat and her new cloche hat, with her dark hair springing up on either side of her face and her eyes gleaming in the street light. She was sure they were gleaming. She could positively feel they were gleaming.

'There's your brother Georgie,' Pearl said. 'He's come out the shop to see.'

So he has, Anna thought, without much interest, glancing over her right shoulder at the off-licence on the other side of the road. 'That's all he ever does,' she said scathingly, 'look.' She was quite fond of her brother but really, he was such a dry old stick. Afraid of his own shadow. Well, just look at him now, stooping like that, and pushing his glasses up the bridge of his nose in that irritating way he had, and looking so stupidly worried. Silly boy! You'd think they were going to fight *him*. Really, it was quite an embarrassment to have to acknowledge him sometimes. Why didn't he go back into the shop and get on with his work?

'You gettin' on or orf?' a rough voice said from behind her back. There were two very old men in very damp raincoats trying to push past her. Very damp, smelly raincoats.

'Don't mind me, I'm sure,' she said haughtily, pulling her body away from them as they passed. 'Really! Some people have no manners at all!' One day, when she was married to her nice rich handsome hero, she'd have a car of her own, and a uniformed chauffeur to drive her about, and then she'd never have to mix with nasty common people on trams ever again.

'Here comes a copper,' Pearl said, wiping the rain from the side of her face.

Now that was better! Policemen always looked so nice and some of them were really quite goodlooking. This one was a nice *young* policeman, and he looked impressively tall under his heightening helmet. A nice, young, *keen* policeman, with his notebook already open in his hand. She took action at once. 'Come on!' she said to Pearl. 'Let's go down and see if he'd like us to give him a statement.'

'We didn't see anything!' Pearl protested, but her flamboyant friend had already plunged into the crowd.

'Come the revolution,' the driver was explaining loudly, 'this maniac'll be the first against the wall.'

'Nah then,' the policeman said, massively calm and important, 'which of you two gentlemen is the howner of this vehicle?'

'Perhaps I could help you, officer,' Anna offered, wriggling through the crowd so that she could get her pretty face and her nice eye-catching coat right into his line of vision.

'Are you the howner of this vehicle?' he said, not even looking at her.

'Well, no,' she had to admit, smiling prettily at his bent head and willing him to look up at her. But nobody was paying any attention to her because the rich young man was speaking too,

8

and far too loudly, in his dreadfully posh voice, '*I* am the owner, officer,' so they were all looking at *him*.

'Well now, sir,' the policeman said, 'if you'll just tell me what happened. Take your time.'

I might as well be invisible, Anna thought angrily. 'This isn't going to be a bit exciting after all,' she said coolly to Pearl, who was puffing and panting beside her. 'In fact, if you ask me, it's going to be an absolute *bore*.'

'Let's go home,' Pearl suggested. 'I'm ever so wet.'

'Yes,' she said. 'Let's. There's nothing to keep us here. And this rain is absolutely dreadful. I'll walk with you to the corner of Trevelyan.'

Georgie Pelucci watched her disgruntled departure with affectionate sympathy. That was typical of Anna, he thought, pushing herself in where she wasn't wanted and then getting cross and flouncing off in a temper when somebody else stole the limelight. Personally, he always did everything he could to keep *out* of trouble, but she always went rushing headlong into it. Smiling to himself, he watched until her red coat and Pearl's brown one had disappeared around the bend in Charlmont Road. Then he went back into the off-licence to his nice quiet office and his nice warm fire and the important desk he always thought of as his father's. There were only the accounts to do and then he could go home too.

He'd almost finished when the shop bell rang. He glanced up at the clock, facing him blandly on the opposite wall of the office, and realized that it was well past closing time. Oh dear, he thought. He really didn't want to serve anybody else at this time of night.

But there weren't any customers in the shop after all, only one rather pretty girl who was standing on the doormat opening and re-opening the door to keep the bell jangling. He could see at once that she wasn't a customer, because she was dressed for travel in a long topcoat and wore a pink cloche hat pulled down over her ears and a knitted scarf mounded around her neck and shoulders. There was a battered suitcase beside her feet, tied together with string, and beside that a bulging handbag, scuffed with wear.

'Yes?' he said politely. 'Can I help you?'

His voice made her jump. 'Oh!' she said, 'I'm ever so sorry

to bother you. I can't get no answer to the flat.' Now that she'd turned to face him, he could see that she had a pretty, round face and that her eyes were very blue and very wide apart.

'They're out,' he told her, wondering who she was. 'Mr Chanter plays with a band on Friday nights.' His father's friend, Dickie Chanter, lived in the flat above the shop.

'What about Aunt Tilley?' the girl said. 'She's not out an' all, is she?'

'She's a hat check girl,' Georgie told her, admiring the plump cheeks and bright eyes of his visitor and feeling quite pleased to think she was a relation of Mrs Chanter's.

'When d'they get back?' the girl asked, looking more worried by the minute.

'Late,' Georgie said, and as she bit her lip with anxiety he added, 'I could let you upstairs to wait for them if you'd like. As you're a relation.'

'By marriage,' she explained quickly. 'Sort of cousin really. I always called her Aunty.' She paused, her brow wrinkling with indecision. 'Will it be all right?' she asked. 'Me just barging in like this? I wouldn't want to get off to a bad start.'

Georgie lifted the counter top to allow her to walk through to the door to the flat. 'They won't mind,' he said. But she stopped with one hand on the doorknob and put her heavy luggage back on the floor again, frowning. 'I shan't be on me own up there, shall I?' she said. 'Tell you the truth, it makes me ever so nervous being on me own. Do you leave the shop when you lock up?'

Georgie was alarmed by the turn the conversation was taking. There was a note in this girl's voice that he recognized with growing anxiety. She was making him feel responsible for her, just as his mother did, inching him towards some action he knew he would regret.

'Will they be long?' she asked.

'Quite a time, I should think,' Georgie said, trying to extricate himself from the pressure she was putting on him. 'Why not go home for tonight and come back tomorrow? I'll tell them you called.'

She laughed wryly at this, contracting her eyebrows and spreading her lips wide. Her teeth were small and regular and very white in the shop light. 'Can't do that,' she said. 'I live down Gillingham. I should 'a' come in earlier. It's me own fault. Only I would stop and watch an accident.' She looked quite downcast.

The expression made Georgie feel responsible, as that sort of expression on a woman's face always did. He felt compelled to agree with her. 'You shouldn't be in this place all on your own,' he said. 'You're quite right.' Then he was very uncomfortable because he knew he'd said the wrong thing and his discomfort made him blush.

She didn't seem to notice his hot cheeks. 'Can't think of anywhere else to go though,' she said. 'Oh dear! What shall I do? Are you the manager?' And when he nodded, 'You don't live anywhere near, I suppose. My mum said I was to ask the manager if anything went wrong. I'm ever so sorry!'

He had to admit that he lived a few minutes walk away. 'With your family?' she said hopefully, and now he was beginning to feel pressurized. Surely she didn't expect him to take responsibility for her?

'I couldn't just come home with you, just fer a little while, could I?' she said. 'I'd be ever so obliged. I can't stand being on me own.'

'Well,' he dithered, caught between the entreaty on the pretty face before him and the certainty of his mother's disapproval.

'I wouldn't be a bit of bother,' she said. 'I could sit in a corner somewhere and just keep out a' mischief till they came home. I'd be ever so obliged.'

She was making it impossible for him to deny her. He was beginning to feel panicky. What could he say? He couldn't leave her here to wait all alone when she'd made it so clear she was frightened, but on the other hand, he couldn't go against his mother's wishes, because she would be so patient in her annoyance and so long-suffering in her reproach and that would wear him down beyond endurance. And besides, what would Anna say?

'I shouldn't have asked you, should I?' the girl said, smiling at him as he hesitated. 'Never mind. It's me own fault for mucking about.'

He could feel the pressure of her dependance like an anchor dragging him down. 'No, no,' he said. 'It's quite all right. I'll take you home for a little while. You can't stay here.'

'Thanks,' she said. 'I'm ever so grateful.'

He'd done it now, he thought, looking down at her pretty round face. 'I'll lock up,' he said. 'It's almost time.'

It was very cold out in the Mitcham Road so late at night. The girl wrapped her woolly scarf more closely round her neck and pulled her hat firmly down over her ears. Their breath plumed before them as they stood on the doorstep and Georgie locked up, as carefully as ever. In the harsh street light her eyes looked lustrous. 'You sure your mum won't mind?' she asked, and now he could see that anxiety was etching little lines on her forehead.

Georgie could already hear his mother's disapproval. He looked up at the gold lettering on the lintel, to give himself something else to think about. 'Albert Pelucci and Son. Wines and spirits,' he read. 'That's me. And Son. It'll be all right.'

She was impressed, although she didn't comment. Georgie took her suitcase politely and escorted her across the tramlines.

'Are you Albert Whatever-it-is an' all?' she asked as they set off down a darkened Charlmont Road, past the crashed car, now on the forecourt of The Mitre. It was long past closing time now and they had the streets to themselves.

He told her his name and she approved of that too. 'George,' she said. 'That's nice. Like the old king. My name's Lily. Well Lilian really, but they don't call me that. Well, not at home. They do at school, don't they? Funny that.'

As they walked he found he was observing her closely. He couldn't believe his own behaviour. It was most unlike him to be gazing at anybody, leave alone a young woman. Usually he had to look away after the first fringed glance had reduced him to stuttering and awkwardness. But this girl didn't seem to care when he blushed. She chattered away nonstop all the way home. If it hadn't been for the worrying knowledge that his mother was bound to be very annoyed, it would have been really rather exciting.

'I come up here for a job,' she said. 'You can't get work for love nor money in Gillingham. So my Uncle Dickie he reckons he's got me this job in a big store. Smiths. Linens and cottons an' all. Only on a trial basis, of course. For the January sales. But my mum says, you have a go, she says, do your best, and maybe you'll get took on after. Well, you never know, do yer? Stranger things have happened. My dad's been out of work nine months. There's no life in the shipbuilding, not these days. So I reckon it's up to me. Don't you? Anyway, here I am.'

Despite himself, Georgie was charmed by her. By the time they turned the corner into Longley Road, she had almost warmed him into hope. He was beginning to wonder whether his parents might not approve of what he'd done. After all, he could hardly have left her in the shop all on her own, could he? And she seemed a nice enough sort of girl.

'Here we are,' he said, opening the wrought iron gate between the privet hedges, and looking up at the familiar frontage of his home.

'Oh dear!' she said, abashed by the size of the house. 'You don't live here, do you? Perhaps I shouldn't have ... Are you sure your family won't mind?'

Her awe was extremely flattering, but looking up again at the house, and this time seeing it with her eyes, he could understand how she felt. It really was quite an impressive place. There was such a nice balance about it, with its two wide bow windows on either side of that imposing front door, the stained glass glowing under the triangular porch, and the two carved stone vases moonwhite on their companion plinths. It looked rich and it looked hospitable. 'Come in,' he said.

His mother opened the door to them and he could see at once, from the way she tightened her mouth into a narrow line, that she was not at all pleased. Everything about her was cool and correct as it always was, her straight fair hair pinned into a neat bun, her stumpy figure smoothed and controlled by her corset, the pin tucks in her blouse ironed to knife-edged perfection, but now, because he was seeing her through the eyes of this shy girl, he had to admit she looked unwelcoming and disapproving. Her expression was calm, as always, but her eyes took in every detail of her unexpected visitor, from the home-made hat to the cheap lisle stockings and the patched shoes. 'Really!' she said icily, when he'd finished explaining who she was and why she'd come to Tooting. 'Well, you'd better come in, hadn't you, Miss – er.'

The tone and the query in his mother's voice embarrassed Georgie to frantic blushing. He realized, too late, that he didn't even know this girl's surname. What a fool he must look! But Lily rescued him effortlessly. 'I am sorry!' she said, politely. 'I haven't told you my name. I should have done. Marsden, it is. Lilian Marsden.' And she held out her hand to Alice, as though the meeting was an honour.

Alice smiled politely. 'If you'd like to take Miss Marsden into the dining room,' she said to her son, 'I'll get Minnie to bring you something to eat. Anna's gone to bed.' And with that she swept off to the kitchen, her beaded skirt swishing with displeasure as she went.

Georgie's ears were burning with embarrassment. How silly he'd been to bring a strange girl home to his mother like this. And so late at night too. He might have known she'd be upset. He should have prepared her most carefully for such a sudden change in her routine. No wonder she was cross. But he'd done it now and he would have to go through with it. He set Lily's luggage beside the hatstand and hung up her coat, hat and scarf. 'This way,' he mumbled and, ducking his red face towards the floor, he led his guest into the dining room.

'Oh dear,' Lily said again, as she settled into one of the big leather armchairs beside the fire. 'It's like a palace. What must they think of me, barging in like this. I wouldn't have done it really, if I'd known you were ...'

Georgie was touched by her confusion. He knelt at her feet and made up the fire, balancing the coals carefully across each other with plenty of space between them so that they would burn more rapidly. The room wasn't as warm as he would have liked and, now that they were in bright light again, he could see that she was cold, her nose pink and her ungloved hands a raw, unpleasant red. 'Soon have this going,' he said, as much to encourage himself as to reassure her.

Lily was still sitting on the edge of her chair, awkward with embarrassment, when Minnie Holdsworthy crept into the room bearing a tray on which were two cups of cocoa and a plate full of sandwiches. Georgie was embarrassed too because they had been treated to one of the linen tray-cloths and the second best china, but although Minnie's expression was inquisitive, as least it was friendly. He made his introductions quickly so that she could smile and make the poor girl feel more at home. Dear Aunt Min, he thought, you could depend

14

on her to be kind to anyone. And then he felt ashamed of himself again, because the thought seemed disloyal to his mother, and that wasn't what he'd intended.

'Isn't she kind, your aunt,' Lily said, when Aunt Min had crept away.

'Yes,' Georgie agreed, but then he felt he ought to explain. 'She's not really my aunt. She's actually my mother's cousin. She and her family live in the flat at the top of the house. She helps with the housework and that sort of thing. But I've always called her Aunt.'

'Like my Aunt Tilley,' Lily said, biting into a sandwich. The new coals were beginning to glow and so were her cheeks.

Georgie ate his sandwiches in a dream. It didn't seem possible that he'd actually invited a girl into his home, and yet he had. What an amazing thing! Here they were, sitting one on each side of the fire, eating their supper, like an old married couple. And then that thought embarrassed him terribly too, and he found himself blushing again, and had to turn his attention to the fire to try and hide his face.

As he clipped the tongs together and returned them neatly to the companion set, he heard the rasping click of his father's key in the door, and was frozen with alarm. If his mother, his dear, gentle mother, had been annoyed to see a stranger in her house, then what on earth would his father say? His unpredictable, alarming father, with his sudden passions and his terrifying temper. Why, just the sight of his face was enough to set him into a panic. And, oh God, there he was, standing just inside the dining room door, his black working suit a sombre patch against the red plush of the baize curtain.

Georgie gulped and started to explain. 'This is Miss Marsden, Father ...' But his father was across the room before the words were out of his mouth, one brown hand outstretched in dramatic greeting, dark eyes snapping, thick black hair and moustaches bristling with good humour and well-being and hospitality.

'Welcome to my house,' he said. 'I hear all about you from my wife. My son got good sense to bring you here, eh?' It was all so quick and unexpected that it left poor Georgie spinning between alarm and relief. But there was certainly no doubt about his father's reaction. Albert Pelucci approved. Within minutes he was roaring to Minnie for more sandwiches and urging the rest of the household to join them in the dining room. They would have a hot punch to warm them all up. How would that be?

He was making such a noise and shouting so loudly that his voice could be heard quite clearly even behind the locked doors of the bathroom, where Anna was luxuriating, chin deep in perfumed water, and admiring her nice long legs.

What's he up to now? she thought. If he's yelling for hot punch and sandwiches, ten to one he's brought somebody home. I wonder who it is. It could be somebody exciting. You never knew with Dadda. He was so unpredictable. Like the time he'd come home for Sunday lunch with those two awful tramps and they'd all had to sit round the table and eat roast beef and pretend they couldn't smell anything. Mummy'd been absolutely livid. But she hadn't said anything of course. She'd just looked icy, the way she did. Mummy was so awfully predictable, neat and controlled and tidy and horribly long-suffering. But Dadda was different. Because he was Italian, probably. People who were born and bred in England were so restrained. But he'd spent the first eighteen years of his life in Italy and he was still – well, terribly foreign. It was really rather romantic to have a foreign father, and it made him very easy to love. He was so generous and so full of life. And such fun.

She got out of the bath and dried herself slowly, enjoying the sensation of rough towelling on her heated skin, and deciding what to do. I'll put my new dressing gown on and just drift down and see who it is, she thought. If it's nobody special I can always say I'm tired and drift up again, and if it's somebody really nice I shall look presentable enough to stay. The dressing gown was very presentable indeed, as she was very well aware, being made of soft, brown velvet which was almost exactly the colour of her eyes. It had been her father's gift to her at Christmas and was very expensive. She toyed with the idea of wearing mascara, but decided against it, because she'd never have the energy to wash it all off again before she went to bed and her mother was so acid about marks on the pillow cases. But she brushed her hair thoroughly and arranged it round her face, pressing the neat waves into position with the sides of her fingers. Then she gave her image a beatific smile in the steamy mirror and went downstairs to join the party.

It was a terrible disappointment. After all that noise and people rushing about and everything, there was nobody there except one very ordinary girl. A shop girl by the look of her, in a cheap home-made dress and a droopy cardigan. What a sell!

It was cold in the dining room after the warmth of the bath, so she was quite glad when Aunt Min descended upon her to fuss her into accepting a glass of punch and urge her to sit by the fire out of the draughts. Dear Aunt Min, she was always so loving. Mummy was annoyed. She could see that. Very annoyed. Dispensing punch like a society hostess, with her mouth compressed into a tight, hard line. But she seemed to be cross with Georgie, not Dadda. That was odd! Surely Georgie hadn't brought this silly girl home.

'My daughter, Anna Maria,' Dadda said, leading the girl across to introduce her. 'This is Lily Marsden. Tilley's niece from Gillingham. Come up to Tooting to get a job in Smiths. What you think a' that, eh?'

'How d'you do,' Anna said coolly, extending a nice clean hand to be shaken. What rough fingers the girl had! Perhaps she'd been a charwoman.

'Pleased ter meetcher,' the girl said. And then she looked at Georgie, shyly, as though she was pleading for protection. So it *was* Georgie! Who'd have thought it? The sly old thing!

But Dadda wasn't giving any of them time to think of anything. He was organizing the armchairs into a circle around the fire and telling the girl some long, complicated story about Dickie Chanter in the old days when he worked on the music halls. And Minnie was pressing sandwiches on everybody and giggling. And Georgie never took his eyes off the girl and was looking absolutely gormless. Really, if she didn't think of something interesting or witty to say in a minute, they'd forget she existed.

'There was a ripping accident outside Georgie's shop this evening,' she tried. 'A car went slap bang into the side of a tram.'

'Oh yes!' the girl said eagerly. 'Did you see it too? I thought there was going to be a fight. The tram driver was ever so cross.'

Oh really! Anna thought. Can't I even tell a simple tale without her butting in? But it was too late. She'd lost control of the conversation already. Which was most unfair, seeing she'd started it. But there was nothing for it, she had to sit and drink punch and listen while Georgie and the girl told the whole silly story from beginning to end, with Dadda and Aunt Min hanging on to every silly word.

And after that they talked about Dickie again and the girl told them all a lot of silly family stories about what a 'wild 'un' Tilley had been as a girl. And they were all so cheerful and settled and the fire was so warm, she couldn't interrupt them and get away without looking rude, although it was long past midnight. The evening had been an absolute disaster from start to finish. She'd had hardly any partners at the Locarno and had been forced to spend far too much time sitting at a table beside the dance floor being vivacious and pretending to enjoy herself, and then that policeman had been absolutely horrid. And now this. Life was very hard sometimes.

And then her father made it even harder, ridiculous man. Aunt Min was yawning, surreptitiously of course because she wouldn't have wanted to offend anybody, but her father caught her at it and laughed in that roaring way of his. 'Time for bed, eh?' he said. 'Quite right! We never get up in the morning. I tell you what.' Beaming at Lily. 'Why you not stay the night? We got plenty a' room. What you say, Alice?'

Mummy said of course she should stay and her mouth was tighter than ever. Georgie was grinning like a Cheshire cat. Well, really! What next? They were all being very silly, behaving as if the girl was Georgie's fiancée or something. I'll get up in the morning, she promised herself, and put on my prettiest dress and make her feel really small. Inviting herself into the family like this. Who does she think she is? She stomped up the stairs to bed in a very bad mood.

But Georgie, leading his guest to the spare room with embarrassed pleasure, couldn't believe his luck. He'd actually invited a girl home. And Dadda had approved.

Chapter Two

It was still dark when Anna woke up next morning and sleet was pattering against the windows, but she got up at once, determined to do battle. Aunt Min was already up and about, setting the table for breakfast. She could hear the distant chink of tea cups and a rattling of spoons. It was bitterly cold in the bedroom. Her bare arms shivered into goose-pimples the minute she skinned off her nightdress, but there was too much to be done to let herself be worried by a little discomfort like that. She dressed quickly, choosing her slinkiest frock, a sleek tube made of bright pink jersey. The sleeves were only three quarter length so she would probably feel cold in the dining room, but what of that? It was expensive and looked it, and that was what mattered this morning.

Shivering but determined, she settled down before the dressing table mirror to make up her face. It took a long time because her hands were clumsy with cold and nothing short of perfection would do, but at last she was ready, admirably pretty and looking decidedly wealthy. Her neck looked rather bare perhaps, but that was all, and that could be remedied with a scarf or something. Or her locket. No, not a locket. Pearls. That's what she'd wear. Her nice string of pearls. That would show her.

When she was quite satisfied that she was as near perfect as it was possible to be, she tiptoed across the landing to wake Aunt Phoebe, because she knew the old lady wouldn't want to miss any excitement that was going. She was very fond of Aunt Phoebe, who to all extents and purposes was a grandmother to her. Her real grandmother had died when her mother was born and Aunt Phoebe and her sister, Amelia, had brought her

19

up, because her father was off in India somewhere. He'd died out there, when Mummy was quite small, and Dadda's parents had died in Italy, still in the same village he'd originally come from. So if it hadn't been for Aunt Phoebe she'd have had no grandparents at all.

The old lady was sitting up in bed with a shawl round her shoulders and knitted mittens on her hands, reading a novel by the light of her bedside lamp.

'Guess what,' Anna said. 'Georgie's got a girlfriend.'

'Well, good luck to him, miss,' the old lady said, noting her great niece's band-box appearance and wondering what she was up to. 'It's high time. He's nearly twenty-three, when all's said and done.'

'Ah, but that's not all,' Anna said smugly. 'He brought her home last night!'

Aunt Phoebe's surprise was very gratifying. 'Brought her home? Good heavens above!'

'And that's not all either. She stayed the night! She's here now!'

'Well, well, well,' Aunt Phoebe said and she closed her book carefully and set it on the bedside table. 'If that's the case, I shall get up and come down to breakfast. Tell Minnie to set another place, there's a good girl.' So that's why she's all dressed up. Crafty cat.

Anna went downstairs well pleased with herself. The entire family would be round the table this morning, Aunt Phoebe, and Aunt Min and her gruff old husband Jesse and their great lump of a son, Percy. It was enough to put anyone off.

She was very annoyed when she opened the dining room door and discovered that there was nobody there except her father and Lily Marsden. The room was still stale with the smell of last night's punch and the air struck cold, for although the fire had been lit it hadn't taken yet and was hardly giving out any heat at all. That was unpleasant enough, but there was worse. That awful girl was sitting at the table in *her* place beside her father. The two of them were drinking tea and seemed to be getting along famously.

'Oh,' she said sarcastically, 'are we all sitting in different places this morning?'

'Good morning, lovebird,' her father said, ignoring the

barb. 'My word, you do look a swell this morning. Where's the party?'

That wasn't the way she wanted the meal to start. 'If you must know,' she said tetchily, 'I'm going to the West End with Pearl.' She looked the girl boldly in the eye and spoke directly to her. 'To buy some clothes. Honestly, I'm in absolute rags. Appearances are *so* important. Don't you think so?' She smoothed the rich cloth of the rag she was wearing and was mollified to see that the girl's eyes followed her hands. That's right, she thought, get an eyeful of that.

'My daughter is dreadful spen' thrift,' her father said easily. 'Always she buy new clothes. One day she break the bank.'

Anna poured herself a cup of tea and went to sit at the other end of the table. 'Not much chance of that,' she said coolly, addressing herself to the girl again. 'Not with all the money Dadda earns. He has twelve off-licences, you know, and heaven only knows how many houses. And two cinemas.' Now can you see how far out of your class you are?

Lily was certainly impressed. Her blue eyes were quite round, but she didn't say anything. Good, Anna thought, now you're beginning to understand.

Then Dadda spoiled the effect completely by taking the silly girl's hand and actually patting it. Well, really! And before she could think of anything else to say to redress the balance, Uncle Jesse and that great lump Percy came noisily into the room and had to be introduced. And then her mother and Aunt Min arrived with the porridge, and old Aunt Phoebe came downstairs still in her dressing gown, so the table had to be re-arranged so that she could sit by the fire, and there was so much noise and movement that conversation was impossible. Never mind, Anna thought, Georgie's not down yet. I'll eat my porridge and wait for him. I've made a good start.

Georgie woke up slowly that morning, but with an undeniable feeling of elation. His dreams had been crowded with memories of their impromptu party and images of Lily Marsden, and now he had only to get up and go down to breakfast and he would see her again. He still couldn't believe his good fortune.

21

He dressed with particular care, choosing his very best shirt and the new tie Aunt Min had bought him for Christmas. But, as he stood before the mirror combing and recombing his hair, the image he saw restored his common sense and reduced his excitement to manageable proportions. Not for the first time, he looked at his face and wished it wasn't quite so dreadfully ordinary. His eyes were such a dull grey behind those glasses and his hair such a dull, unremarkable colour, an ordinary mouse brown that no woman in her right mind could possibly find attractive. If only he could have just a little of his father's style. Black hair, perhaps, or a nice thick moustache or eyes with some life in them. He polished his glasses carefully and settled them on his nose, pushing them into position with his right forefinger, and leaning forward for a last glance at his unsatisfactory features. Then he went downstairs, comforting himself that she was only a visitor, after all.

She looked even prettier than he remembered, her eyes very blue and very wide apart and her thick, cropped hair a dark glossy brown. It made his heart contract with pleasure just to see her. But then he noticed that the entire family had come down to breakfast this morning, even old Aunt Phoebe and Anna, and they usually stayed in bed until long after the workers had left the house. Trust Anna to put on a performance, he thought, I'll bet she got Aunt Phoebe up.

As he inched through the door and tried to make an unobtrusive entrance, Anna turned to give him the benefit of her sisterly venom. 'We thought you weren't coming down at all today,' she said. 'Aren't you late!'

'No,' he said, solemnly. 'You're all a bit earlier than usual, that's all.' He bent to kiss Aunt Phoebe's papery cheek. 'Did you sleep well?' he asked her, and his concern, as always, was real and sounded it.

Aunt Phoebe made a kissing movement with her lips as he lifted his head. 'Not badly,' she said, 'dear boy.' She had always been extremely fond of her gentle nephew, and she wanted to show him that she approved of his nice young lady, even if she couldn't speak openly about her yet. There was no call for Anna to be so acid. 'The porridge is very good this morning,' she said, and winked at him with the eye Anna couldn't see.

But Anna wasn't looking anyway. She was too busy thinking up her next remark. 'Yes,' she said, 'you really have to go up West if you want any decent clothes. Smiths is all very well, I suppose, but they don't really cater for people with taste.'

'Good enough fer me, any day a' the week,' Jesse said. 'You seen this in The Herald, Albert?' And then they were passing newspapers backwards and forwards across the table, and Aunt Min was talking nineteen to the dozen with old Aunt Phoebe, and her mother was serving the bacon and eggs and she couldn't get a word in edgeways. Oh, really! Why did they have to make so much noise?

Her father was enjoying himself, eating with gusto, laughing, teasing and talking, his hands gesticulating and his eyes snapping with pleasure. And that horrible Lily sat beside him, and laughed at all his jokes, and ate a second helping because he told her to. Whatever possessed Georgie to bring her home?

'Well,' Albert said, throwing his napkin onto the toast rack, 'time we were off or we shall all be late.' Thank heavens for that, Anna thought. Now you can take her away and we can all get back to normal. Then he and Georgie and the girl went rushing off into the hall and she could hear her father urging them into coats and rooting about in the umbrella stand and roaring because he couldn't find the big umbrella. 'Nothing is ever where you want it in this house!' he yelled. 'Alice! Alice! Where is my big umbrella?'

'It blew inside out on Christmas Eve,' Alice said, patiently selecting a substitute. 'Don't you remember? Georgie, wear a scarf this morning, please. It's bitter out and we don't want you catching another chest.'

Her concern was embarrassing and unnecessary, Georgie thought. It made him sound like a silly child. But he did as he was told, and hoped that Lily wouldn't notice. She was very busy winding her long scarf around her shoulders and cramming that thick hair inside her hat, so perhaps she wasn't listening. In any case, he was glad to be out in the air and on his way to work, even if it was cold. At least now he could walk beside his new friend, and if his father would just stop chattering for five seconds he might be able to get to talk to her.

But there was no stopping Albert now. He was happily describing the day Dickie and Tilley had moved into the shop.

'A' course me an' your uncle Dickie been friendly fer donkeys' years,' he said. 'Me an' your uncle Dickie an' old Harry Jones. Eighteen ninety we met. Think a' that! That's thirty-six years. A lifetime. Not much I don't know about your uncle Dickie, I can tell yer.'

Georgie trudged beside them, carrying her heavy case, brooding and unnoticed. The sleet was stinging his face and his father was irritating his pride. Was it any wonder he lived such a lonely existence? The man was impossible. Like a steam-roller. Didn't he have any sensitivity at all? Thank goodness they were nearly at the shop and then his father would go off to Trinity Road, like he always did on Saturdays, and he and Lily would have a few minutes to talk to one another again.

But his father had other ideas. 'I will pop in to Smiths on my way to the Broadway,' he said. 'I show you where it is, do a spot of business, all the same time. Two birds with one stone. Take the case up to the flat, Georgie.' He was so loud and determined that argument was impossible.

'That's ever so kind of you, Mr. Ploochy,' Lily said. And off they went. There was nothing left for Georgie to do except carry up the case and open the shop. Which he did. In a very foul mood.

To have risked so much and so suddenly and then to be pushed to one side by his father's insensitive ebullience was more galling than he could bear. He lit the fire in the office and put petty cash in the till and set about restocking the shelves, scowling with disappointment and suppressed anger. Even when Frank Hawthorne, his assistant, arrived, limping more markedly than usual because it was raining and the damp always made his wound worse, he found it hard to respond with sympathy, and simply grunted a greeting. Then the early morning customers started to stamp into the shop and work took over and the demands of the day made it impossible to dwell on his difficulties.

An hour later, Lily Marsden came back. She was beaming with success. 'I got took on,' she said. 'Straight away. Just like that. Your dad had a word with a gentleman there, and they

24

took me on straight away. I reckon he's a giddy marvel, your dad. Start this afternoon.'

'I am glad,' he said. 'That's very good.'

'They up yet?' she asked, raising her eyes to the ceiling and the flat above it.

He hadn't heard any sound of them. 'They come down about tennish, usually,' he said.

'I'll go up and get them their breakfast,' she said, happily. 'Give them a nice surprise. One good turn deserves another, don' it?'

It was only after she'd climbed up the stairs to Dickie's flat that he realized how very good her news was. Now she would be staying in Tooting, living in the flat above his head, and working just down the road. He would see her every day. By interfering in her affairs, his father had actually given him exactly what he wanted. He didn't know whether to be pleased or annoyed.

Anna was very annoyed indeed. When her father came home at lunchtime bragging about the way he'd used his influence, it was all she could do not to tell him to his face how stupid he was. Fancy putting himself out for a shop girl! And all because her stupid brother was a bit struck on her. That's all it was. Well, it wouldn't last. These things never did.

'Not in the West End, eh?' her father teased as they finished their lunch.

'No,' she pouted, deciding to let her annoyance show, 'Pearl let me down. Horrid creature! I was *so* looking forward to it, too. I haven't been shopping for ages and ages and there are some perfectly darling dresses in Selfridges.'

'You've got three party dresses,' Alice pointed out, pouring the coffee.

'Oh, Mummy, I can't wear those old things. I'd be an absolute laughing stock. They went out of style years ago.' Trust Mummy to be disapproving.

Albert was in an expansive mood after his success at Smiths. 'Tell you what,' he said, 'you get your hat and coat on, an' I take you up West and treat you. What you think a' that?'

She rose from the table at once to reward him with squeals of delight and rapturous kisses. 'You're the best dadda a girl ever had,' she said. 'I'll be ready in five minutes.'

'You spoil her,' Alice reproved mildly, as her daughter sped from the room. There were times when she felt aggrieved that her dear Georgie should be required to work in the off-licence like any other shop assistant, for the same low wages, when her extravagant daughter was spoilt and petted and allowed to stay idle.

'Only young once,' Albert said, drinking his coffee and smiling at her. But what sort of answer was that?

Oxford Street was crowded that afternoon, because the January sales had begun. The windows were piled with bargains and the shops crammed with bargain hunters, scrambling among the sheets and tea towels, and making havoc with the china. Traffic was jammed bumper to bumper and there were so many shoppers they spilled off the kerbs into the road. Anna felt marvellously happy and perfectly at home from the moment she stepped into the crush. 'Isn't it ripping!' she said to her father. 'Let's go straight to Selfridges.'

There were taxis everywhere, dodging the pedestrians and doing perilous things among the high wheels of the buses. When I'm married to my dreamboat, I shall take taxis whenever I feel like it, Anna promised herself, watching a particularly elegant woman rise gracefully from the wide door of her nice expensive carriage. And I shall wear a coat just like that. I wonder where she got it. She followed her father happily, sniffing the expensive perfumes that wafted past her and uplifted by the sense of power and wealth that all these nice rich people exuded. In fact, there was only one sour note in the entire street and that was a shabby little man with a placard round his neck saying he was an unemployed ex-serviceman, who was standing in the gutter trying to sell matches. She glanced at him without pity. Silly little man. Nobody was paying any attention to him, and really he only had himself to blame. He'd be better off trying to find himself a job instead of standing around in the rain all day.

But the dress department in Selfridges was ripping and the dresses were absolutely darling, just as she'd known they would be. Such gorgeous colours! She spent a long time trying on as many as she could while Dadda read the evening paper, but finally she'd narrowed the choice down to two, an orange crêpe de Chine with absolutely darling trimmings in a lovely pale green, and a very catchy blue chiffon with the latest handkerchief skirt and a rather daring bodice. She decided to angle for them both. 'Oh, Dadda! They're both *so* darling. I just can't make my mind up. What do *you* think?'

But it didn't work this time. He was looking at his watch. 'Ten seconds to choose!' he commanded. 'I got a meeting to go to.'

So she chose the orange crêpe de Chine, and kissed him lovingly and told him he was an absolute darling. It almost made up for breakfast.

Chapter Three

That afternoon, while Anna was busily choosing her party frock, the breakdown van arrived and the battered remains of the Cowley were towed unceremoniously away. Georgie watched the whole business from the door of the shop so that he could tell Lily Marsden all about it when she came home from work at the end of the day.

She was marvellously interested in every little detail, and thought it 'must've been fun' when the running board fell off and got stuck in the tramlines. 'I'd like to see his face when he gets the bill,' she said. 'Did you hear what he said to the tram driver? "You ruined my car, my man!" What a way to talk!'

'The driver hit him though, didn't he?' Georgie felt bound to point out.

'Yes, he did,' she admitted seriously. 'Even so ... I didn't like that young man. He was too stuck up by half.' She smiled shyly. 'Would you like me to make you a cup of tea? It wouldn't take me a minute. I'm all on me own, you see. They're out at a tea dance.'

So for the third time in less than twenty-four hours, Georgie found himself sharing a meal with a pretty girl. It was dizzying good fortune.

Lily thought she was lucky too. 'I've really fallen on my feet,' she said, pouring the tea. 'A job, and a nice room all me own. Well, I tell you, I hardly know meself. I used to share with me sisters before, you see, so it was all a bit of a squash.'

'How many sisters have you got?' he asked, enjoying the tea and the sight of her blue eyes.

'Three,' she said, 'an' two brothers. They had one room and we had the other. So you can imagine what a game it was. And now I got a room all to meself.'

'It's a nice room, too,' he told her. 'I used to sleep in there when I was little boy. You'll get the sun in the morning once the weather's warmer.'

'Fancy that,' she said. 'Fancy you living over the shop. I think that's nice.' And they smiled at one another over the tea cups.

By the end of the week, they had got into the habit of taking tea together in the late afternoon, while Frank kept shop and explained to intrigued customers that young Mr Ploochy had got himself a young lady. By the end of a fortnight, Georgie had decided that this year he would have a birthday party after all, and invite lots of people, and spend the whole evening dancing with Lily. The decision caused a stir among his family, and alarmed his mother into tight-lipped bad temper.

'I can't think what's got into Georgie,' she complained, knowing only too well. 'All this fuss about a party and when we wanted to give him a proper twenty-first he wouldn't hear of it. It's ridiculous.'

'Give him what he want, eh?' Albert said. 'Do us all good. Anna can wear her new dress. That'll please her.'

And Alice had to give in.

Anna greeted the news of a party with squeals of delight. 'It'll be ripping fun,' she said. 'I'll provide the girls, and I'll bet Johnny Ashby would know heaps of boys.' Johnny Ashby had been Georgie's best friend ever since they were at school together and he knew heaps and heaps of people. He might know someone simply super and bring him along. 'I shall wear my new dress,' she said, privately embarking on the most delicious daydream.

'It'll make a lot of work,' her mother said.

'Don't you wory about a thing, Mummy darling,' she said. 'I'll see to the catering. And the dancing, and balloons, and charades, and everything. It'll be fun! You leave it all to me.' It made her feel so good to be helping like this. Valuable and worthwhile, for once. And poor old Georgie deserved a party. He didn't get much fun in his life and she was dreadfully catty to him sometimes.

Her mother smiled at her, thinking how unpredictable she was, and said, 'You're a good girl, Anna.'

And that was praise indeed!

29

Georgie hardly noticed their reactions, he was so full of his own happy dreams. Lily at the party, the prettiest girl in the room, dancing, with him of course, and so close that he could talk to her without anybody else hearing what he was saying, or kiss her if the lights were low enough. But perhaps that was carrying the fantasy just a little too far.

Once he'd decided he wanted a birthday party, the thing had almost organized itself. In the last few weeks, his life had been stood on its head, and although the sensation alarmed him he had to admit he was enjoying it too.

On the evening before the party, Johnny Ashby rang up to say that Eric Barnes had just come back from Paris and wouldn't it be a good idea to invite him too. Georgie hadn't the faintest idea who Eric Barnes was, but by now he was in a state of such recklessness he agreed at once. After all, what difference would it make to invite one more man?

'Good oh!' Johnny said. 'Got a car, you see, lucky devil, so he can bring some of the others. See you tomorrow!'

Georgie's twenty-third birthday dawned cold and grey and unremarkable, but for once he was allowing it to be noticed. The house was unrecognizable with celebration. There were huge fires burning in all the downstairs rooms, and three new servants in black and white had been hired for the occasion and were now deliberately busy setting the table for supper and averting their eyes from their unknown employers. Despite himself, Georgie was excited, and although he kept as still as ever in the middle of all the bustle, the sight of his unaccustomed pile of birthday cards gave him an undeniable frisson of importance.

But the party was for Lily, and for Lily any effort was worthwhile. Or almost any effort. Now that the event was so close, he was in an agony of impatience, his distended stomach growling and gurgling, his palms sweating and a nervous tic making one eye wink in the most embarrassing and ridiculous way. Perhaps, he thought, tying his tie into the fattest folds he could contrive, perhaps I should simply have invited her to tea. But it was too late now. The first guests were already arriving, guffawing and giggling and filling the hall with bright colour and sharp feet and sleeked heads. Leaden with embarrassment, he went downstairs to greet them.

The drawing room already seemed to be full of people, two of Anna's friends, gaudy in their tube-like dresses, their bare arms powdered and their faces bright and false with make-up, and a group of his school friends standing in a long-legged huddle in the corner farthest away from them, Aunt Min in her very best blouse, and old Aunt Phoebe, sitting on the sofa in her party shawl, with her feet propped up on a stool and a glass of sherry in her hand. His father was standing before the fire, warming his backside, and booming happily to his two old cronies, Harry Jones, the gardener, and Dickie Chanter, massive in his evening dress, his bald head glistening in the heat from the fire. Tilley looked thinner than ever in a trailing red dress, with a string of red beads knotted on her flat chest and a red head band tied tightly round her dyed black hair. Glancing at her as he entered the room, Georgie wondered how anyone so gawky could possibly have such a very pretty, very rounded relation. Then, of course, he looked for the relation.

She was standing by the piano, chattering to Harry Jones' son Billy and two of his lanky friends and, wonder of wonders, she was wearing the very latest fashion, like all the other girls, an obviously expensive dress, in pale blue chiffon, with an irregular handkerchief skirt to call attention to her nice plump calves and a cunningly cut bodice to reveal her nice plump breasts. It made him feel quite weak to see so much of her delectable body so openly and happily on show. Tremblingly happy, he crossed the room to welcome her.

Anna was still upstairs in her bedroom, admiring herself in the long wardrobe mirror. She really did look exceedingly pretty. That green headband and the three orange feathers set her new dress off quite beautifully. And all for nothing, that was the trouble. For really, what was the good of it? She'd quite enjoyed herself arranging everything, but now that her limited excitement was over she was privately afraid that the party was simply going to be a bore. Johnny Ashby was a dear old stick, but his friends were all so dull and, anyway, she'd known them all for years. If only she could hurry up and meet her dreamboat. Life would be so different then.

'Heigh ho!' she said to her reflection. 'Better go down and

show willing.' At least the food would be good.

Three of her school friends arrived as she came floating down the stairs and they were all suitably impressed by her appearance and said she looked stunning, so that cheered her a little. And as they were all dressed in shades of green or white, her lovely orange stood out beautifully when they were all grouped around her, like a lovely bright flower among dull leaves. 'Let's all go in together,' she suggested, smiling brightly.

But the smile froze and vanished the minute they all came giggling through the drawing room door. For there was that awful girl, hanging on to Georgie's arm, smiling and simpering and looking silly and, horror of horrors, she was wearing *her* dress, the lovely blue chiffon that Dadda wouldn't buy for her. How could a girl like that possibly afford such an expensive dress? It was absolutely unfair. She drew in her breath so sharply that even Georgie heard it on the other side of the room. Her face was dark with fury.

'What is it?' Pearl asked fearfully. Anna's tempers were always so awful.

Georgie rushed across the room to placate her. But luckily she didn't even have time to think of something cutting to say, because there was a sudden and extraordinary noise behind her. Eric Barnes had arrived, and was quacking his horn at the gate like an angry goose.

'It's Eric, I'll betcher,' Johnny Ashby shouted above the din.

'Let's go and see this famous car, then, shall we,' Georgie said, glad of the reprieve. And they all trooped out into the hall.

The famous car was actually a little Austin 7, but the famous Mr Barnes had decked it out like an ocean-going liner, and now it was docked at the kerb, hung about with ribbons, hooting that incessant horn and crowded with passengers, moon-faced under the street lights. Georgie took one look at the car and its driver and decided that he didn't like either of them at all.

Eric Barnes was a peculiarly personable young man, with hair so sleek and black with Brilliantine that it looked as though it had been lacquered to his skull, and features so even and so empty that he looked like a tailor's dummy come to life.

But there was no doubt that he had come to life. He was the liveliest person at the party and from the minute he set foot in the hall he took the whole thing over. He had a bottle of champagne in one hand and a gramophone record in the other. The champagne, as Georgie was quick to notice, was the cheapest available, but the record was by Josephine Baker, no less.

'He went to see her!' Johnny Ashby said, breathless with wonder, as they all trooped back into the house. 'Lucky dog!'

Anna had remained just inside the drawing room door, still far too cross to join the rabble. Now she turned to mock the commotion, and found herself looking straight into the cool grey eyes of her dreamboat. But he was gorgeous! Absolutely gorgeous! So tall and dark and well-groomed. Just like a film star. Such hard eyes too, masculine and mysterious, giving nothing away, and a really mean mouth. It gave her a shudder of pleasure just to look at it. What a catch! She swept across the hall at once to make an impression. 'Well, introduce us, somebody,' she said, batting her eyelashes at him, and feeling very glad she'd applied that extra layer of mascara.

Georgie did the honours. Rather clumsily, actually, but it didn't matter. 'Oh, I've heard all about *you*,' she said, flirting with her eyes. 'You've got a simply *dreadful* reputation.'

'Lies, lovely lady!' he said, playing up to her. 'All lies!'

The other guests gathered round them, eyes shining, ready to be thrilled too. 'Did you really see Josephine Baker?' they said. 'What's she like? Do tell! How did you manage to get tickets? Lucky you!'

Eric Barnes didn't disappoint them. 'Ripping!' he said. 'Absolutely ripping! That girl's got *it*. Oodles and oodles of *it*. You should just see the way she looks at you when she sings. Ripping!' And as to the problem of getting tickets, why that was easy enough if you were in the know. There were always tickets for all the best shows somewhere in the Embassy. It was one of the perks of the job.

'It must be thrilling to work in the British Embassy, you lucky thing,' Anna said, gazing into his eyes. 'I thought Georgie said you were at the Foreign Office.'

'So I am, pretty lady,' Eric told her. 'But we get shunted across the jolly old Channel from time to time. As replacements, you know, for high ups on leave. It's the sort of thing you have to be prepared for if you work for the Civil Service.'

Then the champagne was opened in an hysterical spray and the record played to general acclamation. The new arrival urged them all on to their feet so that he could teach them the latest craze, the amazing turkey trot, which he'd learned in Paris, at the Embassy, of course. Anna already knew the steps, because the craze had reached the Locarno several weeks ago, but she feigned girlish ignorance so that he would have to teach her, and learned quickly so that he would be impressed by the speed with which she could pick things up. Soon they were dancing together in the middle of the room like two film stars and everybody was watching them. It was ripping! Lily hadn't picked it up half so fast and poor old Georgie had been danced into a corner.

They danced until Mummy arrived to announce that supper was served, and then she made absolutely sure that she would sit next to her dazzling new escort by hanging on to his arm all the way into the dining room. Lily went in with Johnny Ashby, she noticed, and spent the entire meal at the other end of the table, which was the best place for her, even if it did leave poor old Georgie rather on his own.

It was a lovely meal, which was very gratifying. And when her father set down his glass and rose to his feet to make his speech, he beamed at her first, so she knew he was going to thank her for the marvellous way she'd organized everything. Which he did, and everybody applauded her. It was lovely.

'Well, aren't you the clever one!' Eric said, leaning his handsome head towards her as the applause died down. But she couldn't answer him because Dadda was speaking again and he was praising Georgie this time, so she'd better look attentive, because it *was* his birthday, after all.

'Twenty-three years,' her father was saying, 'and always a good son to his mother and me. You can take it from me, as one who knows, this young man has all the good qualities. 'Ardworking, clever, reliable, sensible, steady.' And dull, Georgie thought, cringing with embarrassment. 'A credit to his family! Not many fathers could say that, eh? When he was a boy, I never had to punish him. One word from me, and he do the right thing. One word.'

The faces round the table turned their attention to Georgie like rows of unavoidable spotlights. He knew he was blushing, and he knew too that he ought to respond to them as Anna had done, but he was too tongue-tied with embarrassment to do anything more than duck his head. It was always the same when his father made a speech. It always embarrassed him. Everybody else was swept along in a torrent of charming broken English, and by sentiments that always seemed acceptable or at least suitable to the occasion. But Georgie was left with the feeling that somehow or other, he had been cheated. Or if not cheated, then made to subscribe to a lie. It might have been easier if his sister had shared his disquiet. But she never seemed to see anything amiss. In fact she responded by putting on a similar act, endorsing all her father's extravagant claims with simpering smiles and carefully girlish laughter, like an actress responding too quickly to her cues.

She was doing it now, gazing at her father with that awful assumed adoration. And Albert was acting too. 'My dear wife,' he was saying, smiling at Alice as though he was utterly delighted with her. But it wasn't true, Georgie thought. He never looked at her like that when there weren't people around to see him do it and, although she was smiling back at him politely, her expression was false too. It was the smile she gave to tradesmen when she tipped them.

After supper they played charades, and Anna took all the main parts and was the star of the show. And then it was time to dance again. 'Let's have a nice slow dance,' she suggested, but Georgie's friends wanted to try the turkey trot again, so for once she was overruled. Never mind, she thought, if she couldn't dance cuddled up against her new hero, she would tease him into sitting out with her. 'I'm absolutely baking in this room,' she said. 'Positively melting away. Let's go and find somewhere nice and quiet to cool down.'

'*Is* there somewhere nice and quiet?' he said.

Was that yes or no? she wondered. You couldn't tell from his expression. 'Come into the conservatory,' she tempted. All in among the nice green plants. What could be more romantic?

He allowed her to lead him by the hand. She opened the

French windows and they slipped out into the darkness beyond the curtains.

It was a great mistake. It wasn't romantic at all. It was cold and dark and smelly and grubby. The plants were all dead and there were rusty croquet hoops all over the floor and somebody had moved the garden bench. The only things left to sit on were two very dubious looking deckchairs. Eric looked cross, wrinkling his handsome nose at the smell of damp and rust and rotting vegetation. It was a terrible mistake.

'I gave strict orders that this place was to be cleaned and ready for use,' she lied. 'I shall have something to say about *this* in the morning.'

'You can't trust servants to do anything properly these days,' he said.

'No,' she agreed, happy to have somebody else to blame. 'I'm *so* sorry, Eric.'

'Well, one thing's for sure. We're certainly cool enough now.' It was bitterly cold.

'We'd better go back in, I suppose,' she said. What a sell!

He was on his way back through the French windows already. Oh dear, that *was* a mistake. And what was worse, the cold was having a quite definite effect on her bladder. Now she'd have to go and see Aunt Jane, and one of the other girls might get her claws in while she was away. 'Something to attend to,' she explained. 'Shan't be a minute.'

'I'll save you a place by the fire,' he said, heading towards it.

When she got back he was sitting in the big armchair beside the fire and there was an admiring crowd all round him. He seemed to be telling them a story. 'The tram driver was absolutely livid! Silly fellow! Poor Rollo had a ghastly time with him. Drove his wretched tram straight in front of the car and then practically accused poor old Rollo of causing the accident in the first place. Imagine that! It's what the pater always says, the working men of this country are simply getting above themselves.'

Oh dear, she thought, that sounds a bit political. And she looked round to see where Billy Jones was, because if it was politics Billy would be sure to join in, and then they'd all be arguing for hours and hours, and she'd never get Eric on his own again. She walked briskly down towards the fire, trying to think of something that she could say that would be bright and cheerful and non-political.

But Billy Jones was there before her, already moving into the attack. Even though he knew he had to be on his best behaviour in old Ploochy's house, opinions as biased and ugly as these just had to be challenged.

'Like the miners, fer instance,' he offered.

'Perfect example, old thing,' Eric answered at once, mistaking the challenge for an agreement. 'If the economy of this country demands low price coal, the miners will simply have to take a cut in their wages. That's simple economics. You can't avoid the truth of it.'

'Even if their children starve,' Billy said darkly, looking the debonair Mr Barnes straight in the eye for several uncomfortable seconds.

Now the challenge was clear to everybody in the group, but this time Eric Barnes chose to shrug it aside. 'Alarmist nonsense!' he said with authority. 'Nobody actually starves in England. Not in this day and age. That's all newspaper twaddle. You mustn't believe all the rubbish they print in the papers. Bolshevist propaganda, that's all that is.'

Over on the other side of the room Georgie heard the word Bolshevist and recognized trouble. Somebody's started talking politics, he thought. Now Jesse'll join in. There never was such an ardent socialist as Jesse Holdsworthy. He glanced over his shoulder and sure enough Jesse was on his way over, with Percy on his heels, head perked ready for a fight. I must do something to stop them, Georgie thought, but he couldn't think of anything.

'Since when you been an expert on the newspaper world, son?' Jesse asked, horribly calm and provocative.

Eric saw the trouble he was in, but he wouldn't back down. 'You don't need to be an expert to recognize Bolshevist propaganda,' he said. 'Anyone may do that, with half an eye.'

'Oh, I say, Jesse,' Billy mocked. 'Whatcher been doin' with that rag a' yours? You been printin' pictures a' men on hunger marches, aintcher? How could you tell such Bolshevist lies?'

Oh dear, Anna thought, this is getting nasty. Poor old Georgie looks terribly embarrassed. And she went off at once to find her father.

Eric shifted his feet and lifted his head away from their taunts. The three men watched him with malicious pleasure, as his Adam's apple jerked and jutted nervously before he spoke. 'It's only an argument,' he tried to placate. 'You mustn't take everything so seriously.'

'Not ter me, it ain't,' Billy said, and now his anger was quiet and infinitely more alarming. 'It's my living. I'm a bus driver. One a' the workin' men that are gettin' above theirselves, according to your old man. An' I'll tell you another thing. That tram driver you was being so bloody supercilious about is one a' my mates. Couldn't find a better man the length and breadth a' London. Wounded at Mons, 'e was. Fighting the Great War so's the likes a' you could go shootin' yer mouths off in freedom. Worth six a' your jumped-up friend with the Cowley.'

'There's no need to get abusive,' Eric said huffily. 'Old Rollo's a good chap.'

'Old Rollo's one a' the idle rich,' Billy said.

This was getting worse and worse, Georgie thought, coughing and dithering on the edge of the group. What could he say to stop them?

He was relieved to be elbowed out of the way by his father, who arrived with a dish full of chestnuts in his hands and a determined expression on his face. 'Roast chestnuts!' he said beaming them into better temper. 'How you like that, eh? Min' you don't burn your fingers. Take hold a' the plate, Percy. Why you all standing up, eh?'

Before his cheerful assault, tempers melted and good manners were restored; Jesse took himself off to the piano to find his drink; Billy grinned; Percy handed the plate round; and the young guests sat together beside the fire and ate the nuts and were soothed. And in the new, smooth mood, Anna managed to wriggle in to a space beside her hero and sit at his feet.

Then the party games began again, and they played blind man's buff, and postman's knock and murders, and everything seemed normal and light-hearted and just as it should be at a birthday celebration. And postman's knock gave Anna the opportunity she'd been waiting for.

By peering through the crack in the door when the numbers

were being allocated she managed to choose Eric, and although he only kissed her cheek, and very chastely, that wasn't the important thing.

'Oh, you wicked old thing!' she teased when the kiss had been given. 'I really truly think I ought to punish you, you wicked old thing.'

He looked quite startled, so she pressed on quickly. 'What shall I do?' she asked, looking round as though she was seeking inspiration. 'I know. I'll write my telephone number on your shirt cuff.'

'No, please don't do that,' he said. His mother would be furious if he went home with writing on his shirt cuff.

'Don't you want my phone number then?' she teased him, making eyes again.

'Yes, of course I do.' What else could he say?

'Very well,' she said sternly, still making eyes, 'I'll write it on this little card. Like this. And put it in your pocket. Like that. Consider yourself punished, you wicked thing! Now you've got my phone number and you must promise to phone me. Do you promise?'

'Yes.'

It was a triumph. She went back into the drawing room purring with delight at her cleverness.

'This is a ripping party!' she said to her brother. 'Absolutely ripping!'

But poor Georgie couldn't enjoy any of it now. His system was still so flooded with anxiety after that embarrassing argument that he couldn't respond to pleasure at all. It was a relief to him when the party was finally declared to be over and his guests departed with laughter and thanks, to pile into Eric's car or spill out into Longley Road in noisy excited groups to amble or stagger homewards. Lily went home with Dickie Chanter and Tilley, but that was to be expected. He'd been a fool even to dream of escorting her. He thanked his parents politely for a 'splendid party' and crawled thankfully to bed.

But not to sleep. The night hours plodded past in long church-struck quarters as he lay, tossing miserably, and re-living each humiliating moment over and over again. Why had he ever imagined that he could give a birthday party and handle it properly? He might have known it would all go wrong. No, he decided, as the dawn light finally signalled the end of his long, uncomfortable vigil, the best thing to do was to invite her to the pictures. Somewhere where the rest of his family couldn't see them. Somewhere quiet and dark and safe. That was what he'd do. He'd invite her to the pictures. After a proper interval, of course, and if he could pluck up enough courage.

Over on the other side of the house Anna was wakeful too. She was much too excited to sleep and had too many pleasant moments to remember and re-live. But there was an edge to her night thoughts too. Everything had gone so well, but had he really taken the bait? Would he keep his promise and phone? That was the important thing. Perhaps she'd say a little prayer. That might help. You never knew. She wasn't actually sure whether she believed in God or not, but there was no harm in trying and at least she was in a good position to bargain. I organized that party marvellously, she thought, directing the information vaguely in the direction of the pole-star. I put myself out and I never complained and I was as sweet as pie all the time. Now all You've got to do is make him phone. That's all! Surely I've earned that!

Chapter Four

The telephone was ringing at last, its shrill call stabbing the carpeted silence of the Peluccis' fine hall and sending Alice into her usual state of panic. Even after seven years she still wasn't used to such a self-willed contraption, and nobody could persuade her to go near it when it was ringing, or to speak into that alarming mouthpiece when it wasn't. 'It ruins the look of the hall,' she would complain to Minnie. 'Nasty, black, ugly thing!' If she'd had her way she would have banished it to the conservatory along with the rusty croquet hoops and Georgie's horrible spiky crystal set. But Albert and modernity prevailed.

'Will somebody stop that dreadful thing!' she called from the kitchen door. Anna was rushing down the stairs, her bobbed hair bouncing as she descended. 'I'll get it!' she called. 'Don't you worry, Mummy.' Let it be him, she was praying, as she unhooked the receiver. She'd waited five whole days for this call. It *had* to be him this time.

It was. The voice echoing tinnily along the ether was the one she wanted to hear. At last. 'Why, Eric!' she said, using her good little girl's voice. 'What a nice surprise!'

It took him a long time to get to the point. In fact they had to waste more than five minutes reflecting platitudes backwards and forwards to each other before he ventured the news that there was a ripping film on at the King's Hall, and dared to suggest that she might like to accompany him there to see it. Was she free on Tuesday evening?

'Well,' Anna hesitated, using her most seductive voice. She'd read enough romances to know that a girl should never appear too eager. In the pause she'd created she leaned forward to

41

admire the reflection of her face, framed so prettily in the oval mirror of the hallstand. She was pleased by what she saw, for in the muted light her brown eyes looked soft and her skin peach-coloured. 'Well,' she said again. 'I did promise my mother I would keep her company that evening ...'

'Oh!' he said. 'Oh, I see.' She was delighted to hear his disappointment.

'I could ask her, if she wouldn't mind ...' she offered, sweetly helpful.

'Oh, I'm sure she wouldn't mind,' he echoed. 'Jolly good sport, your mater.'

There was another pause, as neither of them knew what to say next. 'Should I ring back a bit later?' he tried.

'Tomorrow,' she breathed, admiring her eyes again. 'At the same time.' It really sounded as though he was hooked. How marvellous! The other girls would be livid.

Her mother took the news with demoralizing calm. 'That's nice,' she said mildly, and she didn't even bother to look up from the sauce she was cooking. Anna was used to her mother's indifference, but it still upset her and left her feeling belittled. If that had been Georgie, she thought, you'd have been all ears. But you wait, I'll have him eating out of my hand by the time I've finished with him, and then you'll have to be impressed.

So she chose her outfit with particular care, and bought a whole new range of make-up from Elizabeth Arden, and even went to Streatham to have her hair set at the most expensive salon she could find. It was rather a nuisance that they were only going to the pictures, because he wouldn't have much time to notice how very pretty she'd made herself before she was hidden in the darkness. But the darkness could be turned to advantage, as she knew from experience. When they sat beside you in that musty, blanketed privacy, young men were apt to get an urgent need to start kissing and cuddling, silly things, and if you allowed a few controlled kisses, on appropriate occasions, you could soon reduce the poor creatures to slavish dependence and have them begging for favours in the most pleasantly abject way. Since she'd left school four years ago she'd developed the technique almost to perfection, and she used it heartlessly to restore herself whenever her mother had cut her sense of importance.

The evening got off to a most satisfactory start because Eric called for her in his car and they drove to the pictures in style and left the vehicle waiting for them outside the cinema, where all her friends could see it. The ripping film turned out to be one of Harold Lloyd's comedies, which was amusing but rather a disappointment because it made them both laugh, and kissing was a serious business. However, in the interval, when most of her other escorts would have bought her popcorn or an ice cream, he produced a box of expensive chocolates, and told her she was the prettiest girl in the place, and declared himself a jolly lucky chap to have won her company. And that was very gratifying.

When the lights dimmed, she allowed him to put an arm romantically around her shoulders, and as soon as they were comfortably hidden, she began to feed chocolates first into his mouth and then her own, using the seductive mannerisms she'd copied from Clara Bow and which, until now, had never failed to produce an amorous effect. But then the wretched cinema spoiled everything by putting on a perfectly dreadful newsreel, all about the miners and their silly strike. She watched impatiently as an elderly face explained that 'the Commissioners have advocated state acquisition of all coal royalties, and have turned down the proposals of the Miners' Federation and the T.U.C.' How silly they all are, she thought, talk, talk, talk, and all in long words that nobody could possibly understand.

But when the next elderly face filled the screen, she became aware that Eric was paying absorbed attention to it. He was as still as a lizard, and watched without blinking. How extraordinary! Fancy being interested in anything as boring as a strike. 'It is wrong in principle,' the face was intoning, 'that people in other industries should be taxed in order to subsidize the profit and wages of another industry. We see no escape from a reduction in wages in the coalmining industry as a temporary sacrifice. This cannot be avoided except by making that industry a burden on the rest of the community.'

'Quite right!' Eric said. 'Inevitable! My pater always said this would happen.'

Anna tried to distract him. 'Does 'oo want another 'ickle

choc-late, den?' she teased, holding a coffee cream within inches of his mouth.

'No, thank you,' he said politely, and not in the least deterred from his present line of thought. 'It's greed, that's all it is. Grabbing for more and more money all the time. Common working men expecting to live like lords. High time they learnt their place. If the country can't afford to subsidize them, they'll have to take a cut. That's all there is to it.' He spoke with immense authority, as if he were the Prime Minister, and, despite her disappointment at the subject, Anna couldn't help admiring him.

'You're so clever, Eric,' she said, and her flattery was only partly feigned. 'I can't understand politics.'

'No,' he said, smiling his attention at her again, 'of course you can't,' and his tone implied complete approval of her charming, feminine ignorance. 'You just leave stuff like that to us. We'll see you don't come to any harm, no matter what.'

That's more like it, Anna thought, and she offered the chocolate again.

Georgie went to the pictures that week too, but unlike his sister he went alone. After three days trying to pluck up his courage, he had finally gulped out an invitation to the delectable Lily just as she was dashing upstairs to the flat at the end of the afternoon. She stopped at once and thanked him seriously, but the offer came too late. She'd already agreed to go with the girls, she said. She was ever so sorry.

'Never mind,' he mumbled, blushing. 'Another time ... ' And although she said yes, and smiled at him again, he drooped back into the shop feeling a failure and wishing he hadn't made the offer in the first place.

Now, sitting in the sixpennies, he was enjoying the comedy and comforting himself that at least it would give him something to talk about when he saw her again next morning. It was still terribly difficult for him to start a conversation. He usually thought of an interesting topic long after she'd rushed out of the door, and by the time she came home in the afternoon he'd had second thoughts about it and discarded it.

She was so lively, that was the trouble. No, not a trouble, that was the wrong word. Her liveliness was the most attractive thing about her. But it was a barrier. She was always laughing and gossiping with her friends from the draper's, and as they called for her every morning now and walked home with her every night it gave him very little opportunity to talk. I'm pretty useless, he thought. I shall never get married. And the newsreel sounded its trumpets.

The outcome of the Samuel Commission was no news to Georgie Pelucci. He'd been following the proceedings very closely in the newspapers, privately enraged that the miners were to be forced to take a cut in their miserable wages and were probably going to be pushed to work longer hours as well. He and Billy Jones had discussed the strike plans at length and both were convinced that if the triple alliance could only stand firm, the government would have to back down. But they knew it would be a terrible struggle, with over two million unemployed understandably eager to take any job made vacant, even if it meant scabbing, and years of poverty sapping the energy and resolve of even the staunchest. Now, watching the grim, grimed faces of the men trudging home from their 'uneconomic' pits, he felt a pang of angry sympathy and wished he had someone beside him to express it to. If only he'd asked Lily earlier. It seemed so ridiculous that he couldn't even get a conversation going with a girl who'd been to his home and was staying with two of his father's closest friends.

That Sunday, Jesse Holdsworthy and Percy came home from work just before one, bristling with the latest news. Mine owners in Scotland and Durham and South Wales had posted notices at the pitheads declaring that wages were to be cut as from May 1st when the government subsidy ended. It was clear that if the miners didn't accept their lowered contracts they were going to be locked out.

'Then that's it,' Jesse said, when the joint had been carved and dinner begun. 'There'll be a general strike now, sure as eggs is eggs. That's a declaration a' war, if ever I seen one.'

Oh dear, Anna thought, now they'll talk politics all through dinner. What a bore! And Mummy'll get upset, poor thing, like she always does. If only they weren't so dreadfully serious. She listened vaguely as the talk went on – T.U.C. – living wage – owner's subsidy – fight, fight, fight – and she felt left out and ignored and powerless. And sure enough, Mummy was looking more tense and uncomfortable by the minute. I shall have to do something about this, she thought, as voices rose and eyes glared.

'I think it's all so silly,' she said at last, when a break in the conversation gave her a chance. 'Let's talk about something else. Working men can't expect to live like lords, and that's all there is to it.'

'Why not?' Georgie asked. It was a question that had puzzled him a good deal lately. 'Why shouldn't ordinary people be paid enough to live in comfort?'

Trust Georgie to say something she couldn't understand. 'I don't know,' she said. 'But they aren't, are they? And striking won't do them any good. The government is ready for them. They won't get away with it.'

'You'd like that, wouldn't you?' Percy said, rounding on her. 'Hardworkin' men, beaten up by lousy coppers. Troops on the street to fight the working classes.'

That wasn't what she'd meant at all. Oh dear! She'd intended them to see how silly it all was, and now they were all looking fiercer than ever. She glanced at her father quickly, appealing for help, wordlessly, but to his eyes, very clearly.

Anna's right, he thought. Time for a new topic of conversation. He coughed to gain their attention and made an announcement.

'What you think?' he said. 'Nex' week I take Georgie to the wine vault with me. I teach him the tricks a' the trade. How to chose the best wines, straight from the vat. I introduce him to the wholesalers. Time you saw the wholesale trade, Georgie. What you think a' that, eh?' It was the first step to running a shop all on his own, and everybody knew it.

Georgie was impressed and honoured, as his father had known he would be. A slow flush coloured his neck and cheeks as he ducked his head and mumbled an inaudible reply. Alice and Minnie said all the right things and said them at once, 'That'll be a fine thing, Georgie, won't it? Learning the trade. What a help you'll be to your father!' And for the moment the strike was forgotten.

But although Anna was relieved, she was jealous too. She'd gone out of her way to change the conversation and help

Mummy and create a better atmosphere at the table, and somehow or other Georgie had been rewarded for it. How unfair life was! Not for the first time she wished she could go to work and learn to manage a shop and be important too. But girls never had a chance. There was only one way for a girl to be valued and important, and that was to get married. Oh, it really was high time she was married. Life would be so different then.

Chapter Five

There were actually two reasons why Albert proposed to introduce Georgie to the wine trade. The first was the immediate need to improve the atmosphere around his table. The second was because it was spring. Being Italian, he loved the heat of high summer, so the first warm days of the year with their promise of kinder weather invariably lifted his spirits. But when the Tooting gardens were suddenly splattered with the bright butter yellow of daffodil and laburnum, and the cherry trees were tremulous with white blossom, and young grass sprang green and tender from the dust of the city, other and more disquieting emotions stirred in his blood and troubled his memory. The spring reminded him of Queenie.

Years ago, before the Great War, he had met a girl called Queenie Dawson, a skinny, redheaded girl who sang in the music halls, and had started the only real love affair of his life.

He'd met her too late, that was the trouble. Two years too late, when he'd already married Alice and already had a son, a family that he couldn't desert. Although, God knows, it would have been easy enough to desert Alice, because if the truth were told, she'd always been more interested in being a housekeeper than a wife, and had never loved him the way he wanted her to, the way Queenie always did.

When he felt particularly lonely he would try to comfort himself with the thought that at least he and Queenie had had their ten years to remember, snatching what time they could together in the flat he'd rented for her in Clapham. But it was cold comfort because it simply made him miss her more than ever and reminded him that he'd lost her because he'd been too busy with his family and his shops and his cinemas to notice how much she needed him. Even after all those years she'd gone so quickly, marrying some awful wounded soldier and then simply disappearing. He'd searched and searched, asking for her at every music hall, prowling the dark streets where she used to live, but it was as if she'd vanished off the face of the earth. And then just when he'd given up hope and was beginning to find ways to endure his life without her, she'd sent him a postcard from Hastings, a picture of herself and her daughter, and he'd known beyond any doubt at all that the child was his. Then and how frantically he'd searched and re-searched, but all in vain, and after six lonely months of fruitless effort he'd given up hope for the second time.

Nowadays, as soon as spring fever returned to unsettle him, he threw himself into his work with redoubled vigour. The house would be entirely redecorated. He would tour his property, noting conditions, sanctioning repairs, reviewing rents and giving unsatisfactory tenants orders to quit. He would finance a new firm of speculative builders in their enterprises out in the growing villages of Surrey. He would badger the manager of his cinema for balance sheets and reports. Or, most useful of all, he would visit the wine vaults down in the undercroft of the London docks, and there, tucked safely away from sunlight and season, happily choose the stock he intended to sell to his richest customers during the summer. And this was the corner of the trade to which he was now introducing his son.

It was a vast place. Eighty acres of cellerage, where the dank walls were lined with the dark, heaped curves of cask and hogshead, and no light ever penetrated. To Georgie, following his father and the cellarman from one frail gaslight to the next along the chill vaults, it was like descending into the bowels of the earth.

'We got some priceless claret in the tenth,' the cellarman was saying. His voice echoed eerily along the dark corridors, and the sound made Georgie shiver.

'So old Tupman says,' his father answered. 'We'll taste that on our way back, eh, Georgie?'

Georgie couldn't see how anyone would want to taste anything in a place like this, but he said yes, dutifully, and went on picking his way along the slippery floor.

They reached their destination and the cellarman lit four more gaslights that grew slowly beneath the curve of the roof like pale yellow buds opening into flower. Now, by their gradual light, Georgie could see that the whole place was covered in some sort of fungus. It hung from the ceiling in thick webs and trailing strands, and slithered along the stone floor like weed on the sea bed, coating the hogsheads in an eruption of furry white coral and foaming between the slats of the shelves like a colony of blue-white snails. There were even knobs and whirls of it growing on the cellarman's trousers.

Georgie was appalled. What a fearful, filthy place! It was rotting away, foul, putrid, obscene. How could anybody bear to work in such conditions?

The cellarman caught his expression and grinned at him. 'En't so bad as it looks, that ol' mould, Mr Ploochy, sir,' he explained. 'Comes up every year reg'lar as clockwork. Don't never do no 'arm.'

Georgie couldn't help shuddering, and the cellarman grinned again. Then he and Albert settled down to the serious business of tasting the wine. The nearest cask was tapped for two generous samples. 'You'll like this one, Mr Ploochy,' the cellarman enthused. 'You see if you don't.'

The fruity aroma of the wine spread into the air like sunshine. 'Your very good health, Mr Ploochy, sir,' the cellarman said, handing the second glass to Georgie.

It was very good wine indeed, and so was the next sample and the next. By the faint light of their inadequate jet of gas Georgie could see that his father was glowing, his hair and moustaches bristling with enjoyment. 'This is the one for me, Kroxy,' he told the cellarman. 'Best I ever tasted. And that saying something.'

There's no denying it, Georgie thought, sipping his sample happily. 'Now try this,' the cellarman said.

By the fifth glass, Georgie was convinced that there was no mystery to wine after all. He could have managed the entire order by himself. There was nothing to it. Especially with such a very agreeable cellarman to assist him. After the sixth or seventh glass, he wasn't quite sure which by now, he could see that the cellar was really a most charming and magical place. Why, it was just like being under water, in some sort of fairy grotto. He had a vague recollection that he'd spent most of the morning worrying about this visit, but for the life of him he couldn't think why now.

Then his father completed the order and said it was time to go. Georgie set his glass down on the nearest shelf with the elaborate caution of the very drunk, stood up, hiccuping slightly, and promptly collapsed into a giggling heap onto the fungus floor. 'Shorry 'bout that, Dadda,' he said thickly. 'Legsh no shupport at tall.'

'Not used to it,' the cellarman observed sympathetically. 'You should 'a' said, Mr Ploochy, sir. I'd 'a' watered it fer 'im.'

'He will live, Kroxy,' Albert laughed, heaving his giggling son onto his feet again. 'Arm round my shoulder, Georgie!'

''E's 'ad a right skinful, Mr Ploochy, sir,' the cellarman said, supporting Georgie's other arm as he sagged towards the floor again. 'Better get 'im in the air.'

Out in the air, Georgie felt so peculiar that he was obliged to sit on the pavement with his head on his knees while Albert rushed off to find a cab. From time to time he managed to lift his head and smile apologetically at passing shoes and trousers, but he was still feeling extremely feeble and foolish when his father returned, puffing and bad-tempered, to announce that there wasn't a cab to be had anywhere, not for love nor money. 'We walk to the Tower,' he said determinedly. 'Soon get a cab there. Come along!'

Georgie arranged his legs underneath him as well as he could and managed to stand more or less upright. Together they staggered towards the blue risers of Tower Bridge.

It began to rain, first in large, sharp drops that stung against their faces, then in a sleety downpour from a sky grown suddenly grey. Soon umbrellas were being flicked open all around them, and people were rushing to get indoors as quickly as they could. There was plenty of traffic about by the bridge and Albert finally commandeered a cab. It was an ancient growler that rattled and lurched and threw the contents of Georgie's stomach into such a ferment that by the time they reached the Elephant and Castle he was obliged to beg his father to ask it to stop.

He fell towards the pavement just in time to be very sick, publicly, noisily and ignominiously. Although his father and the cabbie took his behaviour with quite amazing nonchalance, he felt completely humiliated, sitting beside the acrid puddle of his own vomit, while heedless strangers trod across his legs and petrol fumes seared his aching throat.

It seemed to take him a very long time to summon up the energy to negotiate the juddering sides of the cab again, and sink into the corner of the seat.

'I'm so sorry, Dadda,' he said weakly. He was overwhelmed by the terrible exhibition he'd made of himself.

''Appen to the best of us,' his father told him cheerfully, opening both the cab windows. 'Don't you worry your 'ead.'

Georgie fought for control of his still heaving stomach. 'Please don't let Mother know,' he begged.

'We go to the shop,' Albert promised. 'You get better there. We won't tell her, eh?' And he winked in a conspiratorial way, as though Georgie's behaviour were actually quite admirable.

Back at the shop, Georgie tottered into the office and lay in his chair in a state of shamed collapse. His forehead was filmed with an oily sweat and his cheeks were tinged green. When Tilley clumped down the stairs to hear how they'd got on, she was most aggrieved by his condition.

'You're a fine one and no mistake, Ploochy!' she scolded. 'Whatcher been and gone and done ter the poor little beggar?' and not bothering to wait for an answer she eased Georgie to his feet again. 'You come upstairs with old Tilley,' she mothered. 'You oughter be lying down, not left in a chair.'

Georgie was beyond argument or reason by now. He followed her meekly up the precipice of the stairs, and obediently drank two glasses of odd-tasting water, and tried to take off his shoes, and failed, and finally fell across the *chaise longue* in her little-used parlour and began to snore.

He woke with a banging headache and a thirst so extreme that it was clawing his throat. The room seemed very dark for mid afternoon and very warm for mid April. There was a strange clicking sound coming from somewhere quite close by and a vague dark shape wavering slightly between his eyes and the drawn blinds at the window. Had somebody moved the coatstand? he wondered, gradually focusing upon it. And why is it making that funny noise? Or is it a dressing gown? In which case he must have gone to bed. Then somebody lit the light outside the shop door and the yellow glow of it rose gently into the room through the gap at the bottom of the blinds to illuminate two strong white hands busily knitting. Two broad, stubby, hardworking hands. As he stared, he realized who they belonged to and shame overwhelmed him again. Lily Marsden. How embarrassing! Smiling so prettily with those frank blue eyes. Looking straight at him. How dreadfully embarrassing! He began to struggle towards an apology and discovered that he was cocooned in one of Tilley's travelling rugs.

She wasn't a bit critical. In fact, she didn't even seem to be surprised. How dreadful, he thought. I hope she doesn't imagine I make a habit of getting drunk in the middle of the day.

'Could you fancy a cup of tea?' she asked.

'Oh!' he said, closing his eyes because he was suddenly and terribly afraid that he might cry. 'Yes. I could. Please!'

She put her knitting down at once and went off to the kitchen. While she was gone he struggled to the mirror and was appalled to see how awful he looked. What must she think of me? he worried, rearranging his crumpled shirt and the rock hard knot of his tie and trying to comb his hair with his fingers. She'll never go out with me now, not after seeing me like this.

The tea was like manna, but although it watered his thirst it couldn't relieve his embarrassment. She was all tender concern, watching over him and waiting on him in a way he'd have given almost anything to achieve a few short, sober hours ago. But now he couldn't bear to be seen, especially by her. He felt unclean, worthy of scorn, abhorrent. He gulped the tea quickly, not meeting her eye, and made muffled excuses and escaped downstairs to the shop.

Frank Hawthorne was polishing the beer handles. 'First time's always rotten,' he said sympathetically. 'Always the worst, the first time. You'll feel chronic termorrer, I can tell yer.'

Georgie didn't doubt it. He felt chronic already and there was still the night and an enraged conscience to face. To say nothing of his mother.

But fortunately Alice had spent the afternoon up in the West End with Anna, buying their new spring outfits, and the two of them were so pleased with their purchases that they paid very little attention to anything else. Anna insisted on modelling her suit and all three of the dresses they'd bought, so that her father could tell her which one she ought to wear for her visit to the theatre with Eric that evening. And Albert, flushed and flattered by her overplayed excitement, chose a red chiffon and enjoyed the display and allowed his shrinking son to sit well out of the light and remain unnoticed.

After supper, Anna sped up to her bedroom to begin the long process of beautification, and Georgie crept to the library to comfort himself with a book. He chose an old childhood favourite, *The Children of the New Forest*, and was soon almost lost in another happy world where unexpected drunkenness could never intrude. But shame still flickered under every turning page and he knew it would have to be faced sooner or later.

Anna's conquest of the dashing Eric Barnes was progressing most satisfactorily. They now had a regular date on Saturday nights and often went out together to a play or a restaurant on at least one other evening during the week. Tonight they were going up West to see the latest smash hit, *No, no Nanette*.

It was a fine, warm evening, Eric was marvellously attentive and the theatre was a most gratifying place, with huge plate glass mirrors all around the foyer, so that you could admire yourself making a splendid entrance up the curved front steps. And then, to her delight, she found that the auditorium was decorated in maroon and gold and made a perfect foil for her new scarlet chiffon. As she snuggled down beside her handsome escort, she felt quite sure that this was going to be a rewarding evening.

As they opened their chocolates and smoothed their hair and waited for the overture, they made small talk in their usual cautious fashion. He told her how beautiful she was and how absolutely gorgeous she looked in her red chiffon, and she said, 'Oh this old thing!' in the deprecating tone that would indicate that she was used to dressing in the height of fashion all the time.

Then, after a handsome pause to alert her to the importance of the news he was about to deliver, he told her he had joined the Organization for the Maintenance of Supplies and had been sworn in as a Special Constable. 'What do you think of that?' he asked, knowing the answer already.

'How brave you are!' she said, to his total delight. 'I always knew you were the sort of man who would turn out to be a hero!' They spent the next few minutes happily reiterating this opinion to one another and, sensing that this was a profitable line of conversation, she made an opportunity to tell him how valiantly she had defended his point of view last Sunday, and how much she'd been made to suffer as a result.

'My poor girl!' he soothed her, flattered that her interest in him was serious enough to have involved her in a quarrel. 'How could they be so horrid, when you're so sweet? But that's the great unwashed for you. No manners and no style.'

The great unwashed! She was entranced by the flamboyance of the insult. It was just the sort of remark that made people notice you. The great unwashed. How stylish he was to think of it!

'That's not the way they taught us to behave at Rutlish,' he said proudly. 'We were taught manners there. How to behave correctly in all circumstances. How to mix with royalty. How to address a bishop. How to treat a lady. The masters were absolute sticklers for good breeding, I can tell you.'

'So much nicer,' Anna said, sparkling at him with approval and encouragement. 'A girl feels so much safer when she's with a gentleman. And a Special Constable too.' Settled against the magenta plush of the stalls, she gazed up at him in her red chiffon, knowing herself attractive as he leaned attentively towards her, his smooth hair gleaming in the spangled light from the high chandelier, his teeth very white and even between romantically narrow lips. He's very like Rudolph Valentino, she thought, and wondered what it would feel like to swoon in his arms.

Then the overture jollied their attention towards the stage and the curtains blazed apart for the opening chorus and they settled down to share the happy fantasy of a world where youth reigned supreme. She didn't get another chance to tease him for compliments until the show was over and he'd driven her right home to her door.

They stood close together under the porch, murmuring their

goodnights so as not to wake her parents. The sky was very high and inky blue and scattered with bright stars like diamonds thrown about in careless profusion.

'Will you come to the King's Hall next Saturday?' he said.

'What if I say no?' she teased.

'It 'ud break my heart,' he told her. His eyes were gleaming like daggers in the bright moonlight.

'Diddums!' she said. 'Would 'oo cry?'

'Buckets!' he admitted. 'Oodles and oodles. Total collapse. Couldn't carry on.'

'Voh-de-oh-doh!' she mocked, pouting at him. 'Then I shall have to say yes, shan't I?' The moon was like a great white plate among all those sparkling stars and the silence was so profound it was making a singing noise in her ears. It was an absolutely perfect night for love. Why was he being so slow?

'See you Saturday then,' he said, and added, allowing himself a touch of admiration, 'pretty lady!'

'Am I?' she breathed, swaying ever so slightly towards his chest.

'Are you what?'

Was he pretending ignorance? she wondered. To encourage her, perhaps? She decided to enlighten him anyway. 'Am I pretty?'

'Very,' he said, and looked as though he meant it. 'Pretty enough to eat.'

That's more like it, she thought, and pouted with deliberate charm. 'Oh,' she said, 'I'm not sure I'd like to be eaten.'

'Well, pretty enough to …' he hesitated, staring at her fiercely.

Surely he wasn't playing now. 'Pretty enough to …?' she encouraged, swaying towards him again.

He seemed to hesitate for a moment as though he were considering. Then he swooped towards her and kissed her once and hard, with his eyes shut.

It didn't do anything for her, which was a distinct disappointment, but she decided to be thrilled, just the same. Just wait till I tell the girls about this she thought, savouring the triumph it would be. 'Good night,' she said softly, like the heroines in the romances, gazing straight at him and fluttering her eyelashes.

He was suddenly in such a hurry to get back to the car that he ran, clumsily and far too noisily, calling goodnight as he went. She was very annoyed with him, although of course she didn't say so. What *is* he thinking of? she thought. He'll wake my mother and then I shall know about it. For a few seconds she almost faced the notion that he was actually running away from *her*. But then she dismissed such an unflattering interpretation and let herself softly into the house and the blandishments of the hall mirror.

Had she known it, her caution was unnecessary, for her mother and father were both still awake and watchful in their separate rooms above the porch.

Alice was much troubled by indigestion these days and although she didn't complain about it, and only discussed it with Minnie, when they were quiet and private and everybody else was out of the house, it was a nuisance, nevertheless. She found it hard to settle to sleep with her stomach in such an uncomfortable, bloated state, although she always made an effort, dutifully, just as she'd done as a little girl, for habits of obedience and endurance were very deeply engrained in her. But after an hour or so, she would get up and sit by the window in her little basket chair, with a blanket wrapped round her, like a baby in a shawl, watching the passing world. She knew all the homing habits of her neighbours and felt sure that the outline of the row of wide houses opposite her own was printed so indelibly on her eyeballs that if she tried to she could produce an after image of them, like a camera.

Tonight she'd heard the Austin 7 rumbling towards the house along the empty road and had watched through the net curtain as it rattled to a halt beside the kerb and Eric handed her fluttery daughter out of the passenger seat. Then, with a certain malicious relish, she'd eavesdropped on their conversation, straining her ears and leaning forward towards the open sash-window. How artfully Anna was teasing her young man, she thought, and what a silly, babyish voice she was using.

Albert had been to the music hall that evening and had come home late as he always did, to a house unlit except for the wall lights in the hall and apparently fast asleep. Alice had left him a plate of sandwiches as usual, carefully wrapped in damp linen to keep them moist, and he had eaten them appreciatively and poured himself one last drink and taken it upstairs to his room. Since the day when Alice had removed him firmly from their bedroom he had furnished himself another room entirely of his own with a comfortable, untroubled single bed and a leather armchair that could have come straight out of a gentleman's club and a fine desk where he could do his accounts and even a drinks cabinet in one corner.

Now he sat by the desk beside the window, smoking his last cigar and planning the changes he would have to make in all his stocks if this strike actually took place. He'd already ordered the cheap beer that would soon be all the strikers could afford and had laid in plenty of cheap spirits too, for when real spirits ran low. Now he was estimating how long it would be before he would have to re-order, and wondering how he would get his stocks back to Balham and Tooting if the carters were out, and considering what extra storage space he could contrive.

He was so preoccupied with his plans that, although he could hear voices whispering and murmuring just below him, at first he paid very little attention to them. It wasn't until his senses recognized the peculiar timbre of sexual teasing that he actually listened to what was being said, and then he was upset and annoyed. It was Anna, his own dear little Anna, behaving like some cheap whore out in the garden, murmuring and cooing and putting on an act. Disgraceful! He put his hands on the window frame ready to lift the window and roar at her, but as he did so he saw Eric running full-tilt down the path and heard him call his frightened goodbye. So there wasn't any point in shouting. At least, not for the moment.

Never a man to waste time in unnecessary thought, Albert returned to his calculations. Whatever the rights and wrongs of the case, when this strike began he intended to be ready for it.

Chapter Six

Rather to everybody's surprise, the great class war began so peacefully that it was more like a national holiday than the outbreak of hostilities. As Albert and Georgie walked down to the shop that Tuesday morning, the thing that struck them most forcibly was the silence. There were no buses or trams running at all, and apart from bicycles and the occasional horse-drawn van the roads were empty.

'Isn't it quiet!' Georgie said, awestruck by the change. He'd never seen Mitcham Road without trams before and their absence made him realize how huge and noisy they were. It seemed very odd to be able to look out of the shop and across the road and actually see the bulging bow window and double gables of The Mitre instead of the blur of a passing vehicle. And although it would probably be disloyal to the strikers to admit it, privately he rather enjoyed the experience.

It didn't please Anna. 'How am I supposed to get up to the West End?' she wailed.

'You're not,' Georgie told her. 'That's what a general strike's all about.'

'Well, I think that's silly,' his sister said. 'They won't get people to feel any sympathy for them if we can't go shopping. And how are we supposed to know what's going on when there aren't any papers? You tell me that.'

'There's news on the wireless,' Georgie offered. 'You can listen to my crystal set if you like.'

But that wasn't any good because only one person could listen at a time.

Albert solved the problem that afternoon by buying a four valve wireless set, which he bore home in triumph ready for the early evening news broadcast. The family gathered in the parlour while he twiddled with the knobs on the front of his new, crackling toy and stood the great brass horn upright on the table where everybody could see it. At first all he could get it to emit were odd squealing noises but suddenly the howls abruptly stopped and the room was filled with the disembodied voice of the newsreader, a calm, suave, upper class voice which assured them that, although the miners and the railwaymen and the dockers had indeed begun their unnecessary strike, there was no need for alarm because the government had everything under control. Food supplies had been adequately safeguarded and there was plenty of coal to maintain all public services. Alice and Minnie were very relieved to hear it, but Jesse snorted and declared that that was exactly what you'd expect from the establishment, and they weren't to believe a word of it.

Albert hustled them all in to supper before they could start an argument and kept them all busy, all through the meal, with stories about his customers. But the difference of opinion was there, just the same, and they all knew he was only deferring the expression of it.

There was a difference of opinion in the Chanter household too, and that one did lead to a row. Lily and her friends had been given leaflets outside Smiths when they left work late on Thursday. They advertised a mass meeting in support of the strike that was going to be held on Clapham Common on Sunday afternoon. Although her friends were dubious about it, Lily decided to attend. Tilley had other ideas. And being Tilley she had them strongly and very loudly.

'No you ain't!' she shouted. In the newly peaceful Mitcham Road, Georgie could hear every word from where he stood behind the counter.

'Yes I am!' Lily roared back.

'You ain't! What would your ma say? I should never hear the last uv it. Out the question!'

'What's wrong with it?' Lily wailed, and now her disappointment was obvious to Georgie's straining ears. 'It's only a meetin'.'

'Oh, come on, girl, it's a strike, fer Gawd's sake,' Tilley said.

'Rozzers all over the place. An' on 'orseback too, I shouldn't wonder. We don't want you off ter the 'orspital with yer 'ead cracked.'

Dickie mumbled something conciliatory that Georgie couldn't hear, and got roared at for his offer. 'Don't you start neither! I got enough on my plate with her!'

'I'd be ever so careful, Aunty Tilley,' Lily pleaded. 'I would. Honest!'

'How many more times?' Tilley roared. 'Out the question! You ain't goin' an' that's flat!'

Feet stamped about, Dickie coughed apologetically and a saucepan was banged down on the table. Then Georgie fancied he could hear the slight sound of subdued sobbing. Poor Lily, he thought, poor girl, and wished there were something he could do to persuade Aunt Tilley.

'It's your day off an' all,' Frank said helpfully. 'Why dontcher run upstairs an' offer ter take her?'

Of course! Of course! How sensible of Frank! He began to smile his agreement, but then doubt entered his mind again. She might not want to go to a meeting with him. What if he embarrassed her?

'Go on, you daft ha'p'orth!' Frank said, grinning encouragement. 'Nothink ventured, nothink gained.' And he took his young, dithering master very gently by the elbow and steered him towards the stairs. Heart pounding, Georgie climbed.

The row was still roaring on as he knocked at the kitchen door. Dickie had joined in and they were all making such a noise that none of them heard him. Greatly daring, he opened the door and peeped in. Oh dear! Lily *was* crying. How awful! She was sitting in the kitchen chair beside the stove with a damp handkerchief in her lap, and she looked so woebegone that he spoke his offer at once out of sheer pity.

The row stopped immediately. 'Well, that's a different matter altergether,' Tilley said. 'If you're goin', Georgie, she'd be properly looked after. Whatcher think, Lily?'

Her nose was red and her hair bedraggled, but her eyes were a quite devastating blue awash with tears like that. She thanked him, as if she meant it, and said she was ever so grateful and what time should she be ready?

He'd done it! He'd asked her out! She'd said yes! It was too good to be true.

It was a long walk to Clapham Common that Sunday but, as Lily was quick to point out, at least they had a nice day for it, and it was lovely and quiet too 'without all them trams clanging'. They walked in happy companionship, past the shuttered shops of the empty High Street and the Sunday dinners of the Totterdown estate and the site where the new shops were being built. She told him how difficult it was to manage when your father was on the dole and how often she and her five brothers and sisters had been hungry back in Gillingham. And he told her how he'd been reading H.G. Wells' *History of the World*, and how much he sympathized with the struggles of the poor.

'And now they're on strike,' she said. 'It's exciting, issen' it?'

Georgie was happy to agree with her, and didn't say anything about the anxieties that had kept him awake for most of the night before. Now that they were out in the sun and on their way he felt almost confident that he could look after her, no matter what might happen. Although of course he would much prefer it if the whole thing went off without events of any kind.

He needn't have worried. Clapham Common that afternoon was in carnival mood, and although the police walked their horses up and down the bridle paths at the edge of the common they were never required for anything more than this gentle and unobtrusive exercise. The crowds ambled about the common and told one another the latest news and bought ice creams from the Stop Me and Buy One and couldn't hear the speeches and didn't really mind. There were babies safely in perambulators and boys cheerful on bicycles and men raucous on soap boxes. But there was no trouble.

Nevertheless, once they'd left the shelter of the chestnut trees and were walking out into that vast throng, Georgie offered his arm to Lily, tentatively of course but with the air of one who is prepared to protect if necessary. And, to his great delight, she took it, and held on to it all through the afternoon.

It grew late and the great crowd began to disperse, drifting amiably away from speeches and allies, but bearing with them the protective sense of the power of their numbers.

'We must win,' Lily said as she and Georgie set out on their homeward journey. 'There's just too much at stake to turn back now. Dontcher think so?'

'Perhaps the government'll see sense,' Georgie said. 'Jesse says he doesn't think they're capable of it.'

'Is that your uncle with the shaven head?' she wanted to know. 'He looked a bit of an old grouch ter me.'

The description made him laugh. 'He is,' he said. 'You've hit the nail on the head.'

'I like your old man,' she said, feeling she ought to say something complimentary just in case she shouldn't have criticized his uncle. 'I think he's ever so nice. Well, look at the way he got me that dress.'

'What dress?' he asked, puzzled.

'For your party,' she explained. 'I didn't know what to wear, an' Uncle Dickie was skint. Well, you know Uncle Dickie. He's always skint, to tell the truth. Anyway, there wasn't any money for new dresses, an' your old man was ever so nice. He wanted to give me the money. But I couldn't have that, could I? So in the end he lent it to me. A business arrangement. I pay him back every week out me wages, a little bit at a time, an' no interest or anything. I think he's an old love.'

Looking down at her smiling face, Georgie thought how typical that was of his father and wished he'd been able to buy her the dress himself. 'He's a very generous man,' he agreed. 'Always has been.'

They were at Bedford Hill already. Soon their outing would be over.

'Oh!' she said suddenly, clapping one hand over her mouth. 'Aunty Tilley said I was to ask you to come to tea with us. I nearly forgot. She'd've skinned me!'

'Thank you,' he said. 'I'd be delighted.' Which was nothing less than the simple truth, and for a moment, as she smiled up at him, he dared to hope that she understood it.

Over at the Elephant and Castle, Eric Barnes was having a very different kind of afternoon. When he'd reported for duty at his depot early that morning, he'd felt pretty sure that he'd be home again within the hour because it was Sunday, and nothing ever happened on a Sunday. But, to his surprise, he was ordered to drive to Hyde Park and pick up a loaded truck. And now here he was in a long convoy heading south to the food stores of David Grieg and the Maypole Dairies, hot and cross and far too frightened for comfort. Even the presence of a solid police constable beside him did little to still his fears, for the streets were packed with angry looking men in cloth caps, and soon he would have to run the gauntlet of the narrow junctions at the Elephant, where even a truck as tall and high powered as this one would be far too vulnerable to a determined attack. Fear was making his palms sweat, although his throat was as dry as a biscuit, and it was difficult to steer properly with sweaty palms.

'Soon be there, son,' the constable said encouragingly. But Eric wasn't encouraged. There was hostility in the air all around him, and he knew too much about hostility not to be alerted by it.

The truck just ahead of him ground to a halt, its tail board juddering. There was nothing for it but to put the brakes on. He could hardly drive straight through a stationary vehicle, although if such a thing had been possible he would certainly have done it. The crowd surged forward at once to surround both vans, and now he could see the hard faces under those awful low class caps and smell the dreadful, dirty, unwashed stink of their clothes.

'Nah then,' the constable said, massively calm, 'stand well back from the cab, *if* you please. We don't want a nasty accident, do we?'

It was a rhetorical question, but the nearest striker answered it. 'Yes,' he said, with determination. 'We do. We'll 'ave this scab out fer a start.' And he grabbed hold of Eric's sleeve and started to tug him from the driver's seat.

Eric wriggled and flailed in a frantic attempt to wrench his arm out of the man's grasp, but other hands rose from the mass to seize him in tight fingers that bruised and pinched. He could barely breathe, he was so afraid. Why had he ever got himself into this sort of trouble? He must have been crazy. He could hear the constable puffing and grunting beside him, and the sound of thuds and gasps, but his head was wedged against the dashboard and he couldn't see anything except his own knees and below them the control pedals. Then he realized with increasing panic that they were rocking the van violently from side to side. Struggling up towards the seat again, he caught sight of the constable on the opposite side of the van, still cool and talking calmly to two ugly faces at the window. What did he think he was doing, the silly fool?

'Hit them!' he screamed. 'Hit them, for God's sake!' He was weeping with fright. But the constable didn't take any notice, and the van rocked more violently than ever.

'Easy on, lads!' someone was yelling. 'We don't want ter kill the buggers!'

'Speak fer yerself Jack!' a fierce voice shouted and a hand came in through the window and seized Eric by the ear, yanking his head down onto the sill. As he fell he could see the policeman's truncheon, fitted into his belt. Christ, he thought, if the fool won't use it, why shouldn't I? He made a grab for it and another and another and, finding it suddenly and surprisingly in his grasp, he hit out wildly at the dark flesh above him. The hand was withdrawn and at last he was able to get back on his feet.

The constable looked across quickly and held out his hand for the weapon. 'I wouldn't use that too often if I was you,' he said. 'Give it back, sir, if you please.' His calm was infuriating, and so was his silly, mild face.

'They've damn nearly killed me,' Eric screamed at him. 'And you sit there doing nothing! Bloody, bloody fool!' Fear had driven him beyond control. He lunged through the window at the men surrounding the van and hit out at them again and again. This time he made contact and heard the hard leather strike home with a crack and saw the face of the man he was hitting and knew he was hurting him and hurting him badly. He was flooded with a marvellous, total joy and hit out again, his face distorted with ugly pleasure. 'Take that, you swines!' he shrieked. 'Don't you ever think you've got the better of me.' He was in control of them. They were trying to get out of the way of his vengeance. They were afraid of him. It was a glorious feeling.

Then that bloody fool constable was wrenching the truncheon out of his hands and actually shouting at him. At first, in the blood-pumping extravagance of his joy, he couldn't hear the words the silly man was booming out of his silly mouth, but then he followed the direction of the fingers pointing in front of his eyes and understood that the convoy was moving again. Obedience triumphed over the joy of inflicting pain. Although he was still more excited than he'd ever been in his life and desperately needed to go on hitting and hitting and hitting, he sat down in the seat again and put the van into first gear. He was surprised to see that his hands were shaking like leaves in the wind.

The rest of the journey passed without incident, and after a mile or so he was sufficiently under control to agree with the constable that of course he shouldn't have taken the truncheon, and to think up the plausible excuse that he'd only done it in order to protect the cargo. But inside his brain his blood was still racing with the same power-giving exhilaration, the marvellous satisfaction of hurting another human being.

He was still swollen with the power of it when he got home to Merton again at the end of the afternoon.

The house where his mother and father had reared him so sternly towards the success they wanted was small and terraced and unremarkable. The decor was an uncompromising and uniform grey, like his father, and the supper, served on a plain white plate exactly on the stroke of six, was cold and unappetizing like his mother. He ate it obediently despite his excitement, for since his earliest years, when they had systematically beaten all trace of disobedience and rebellion out of his nature, he had never once dared to question their authority. But as he ate, chewing each mouthful twenty times in the correct manner that his mother had also instilled into him when he was very young, he was churning thoughts over in his mind too, searching for something to say that would annoy them without giving them cause to tell him off. It was a game he often played, and today he felt he had the strength to play it well.

'Did you have a good day?' his mother inquired politely, allowing her neat mouth the faintest trace of a smile.

'Yes, thank you, Mater,' he said. 'We got the food through. A bunch of roughnecks can't stop the O.M.S.'

'I should think not, indeed,' his father said, lighting a cigarette very carefully so as not to drop ash. 'We don't want mob law in this country, thank you very much.'

'I was wondering,' Eric began, keeping his expression absolutely bland, 'would you have any objection to me bringing home a young lady? For tea perhaps?'

Annoyance flickered onto his mother's face and was immediately controlled. A good start, he thought. 'We-e-ell,' she said slowly. 'A lot would depend on who the young person was, of course.'

His father was scowling at his cigarette. 'Anyone we know?' he asked and his tone was sharp.

'No, I don't think so,' Eric said, deliberately smiling his charming smile at them. 'But I'm sure you'd like her. She's a top-hole girl. Oodles of money. Her father owns a chain of shops and a couple of picture palaces and lots and lots of property. Real estate and all that sort of thing.'

They were hooked. How splendid! His mother was looking down at the carpet to control her expression again, and his father had that awful, eager, barking look on his face, like a dog waiting to be fed. That's right, he thought, be impressed. I'm much further up the social scale than you think.

'What's her name?' his mother was saying, smiling faintly again.

'Anna Pelucci,' he told them and saw at once and too late that he had lost the advantage.

His mother relaxed into her customary acid disapproval. 'Oh,' she said, 'she's foreign!' Her tone conveyed at once and unmistakably her infinite contempt for anyone not born and bred in England. 'Well, my dear, I don't really think you'd find her suitable. Do you?'

'She's as English as you are, Mater,' he said, stung. How very unfair it was that she always seemed to be able to get the better of him. 'It's only her name that's foreign. You'll love her, I'm sure. When shall I invite her?'

'We'll discuss it tomorrow, son,' his father said. 'Time enough tomorrow.' In the wake of his wife's little victory he'd lost all his initial greedy interest, and his face was small and withdrawn again.

Eric felt deflated and realized that he was very tired. One day, he promised himself, as he climbed to his little box-bedroom, I will wipe that expression off the mater's face if it's the last thing I ever do. This wasn't the way he'd intended the day to end. It was very annoying.

And what was worse, as he realized the next morning, was the fact that almost without intending it he'd committed himself to inviting that girl to tea. He wasn't even sure he liked her very much. She was certainly stylish and knew how to dress, and her way of talking and teasing flattered his ego and made him feel both masculine and attractive. But there was something alarming about her just the same, and although he couldn't define what it was he knew he should be warned by it. Now he felt he'd made a mistake.

Anna had had a pretty thin time on Sunday too. Georgie had come home ridiculously pleased with himself and her mother had made an equally ridiculous fuss over him. You'd think he'd done something really clever, when really all it amounted to was a favour for Aunt Tilley. And yet there they all were, saying how good he was and how relieved Uncle Dickie had been, ignoring her and making a hero of him, when even she could see that all he really wanted was to be left alone.

And then as if that wasn't bad enough, they all started again at breakfast the next morning.

'I hear everything went off well at Clapham yesterday,' Aunt Phoebe said, buttering her toast in the slow, painstaking way she had acquired as she got older. 'Such a relief to Tilley, I'm sure.'

'She couldn't never 'ave allowed that poor child to go without an escort,' Minnie said happily, 'and that's a certainty. You never know what might happen these days.'

Alice was pouring out fresh cups of tea, and paused, teapot in hand, to smile across the table at her son. 'She was perfectly safe with Georgie,' she said with approval. 'I'm very glad to say.'

'Oh, really!' Anna said tetchily. 'You talk as if there'd been a battle or something. It was all very peaceful. There wasn't the least bit of danger. Not to anyone. You heard what Georgie said last night.'

'But there might have been,' Minnie said, beaming at Georgie again. 'I think it was lovely of you, Georgie dear, and that's a fact.'

Georgie found he was actually quite enjoying their attention this morning. There was nothing more for him to explain because he'd told them everything they wanted to know already, and they all seemed so happy about what he'd done, even Mamma, which was a great relief. True, his father hadn't said anything yet, but he looked mild-tempered enough, sitting at the head of the table busy with his bacon and eggs. It was really quite pleasant to be praised after all, especially as the most pleasurable part of the day had been entirely his own and entirely private.

'Hm!' Anna persisted. 'It wasn't as if he was actually running risks! Now, Eric puts his life on the line every time he takes his car on the road. I think he's very brave.'

'He's a strike breaker, Anna,' her brother said, mildly. 'If he gets hurt, he's asked for it.'

'He's bringing in your food,' Anna said hotly. 'Without him, you'd all starve, I hope you realize. I think you're very unfair, calling him names.'

'Strike breaker's not a name, girl,' Jesse said. 'It's a fact a' life. And not a pertickerlerly nice one. I told you before, you don't want ter take no notice a' that young man. He's a wrong'un.'

'It takes all sorts, Jesse,' Alice tried. The growing animosity around her breakfast table was alarming her, and she felt she ought to warn Jesse to desist before Albert recognized it too and began to roar. There was only one mouthful of that bacon left to keep him occupied, as she could see out of the corner of her eye. 'What are you all planning to do today?' she said.

'Whatever it is,' Anna said, smiling venomously at her brother, 'I'm sure it's bound to be terribly, terribly brave!'

Albert finished his last mouthful and made up his mind. 'If I stay in this house with all this bickering,' he said, 'I go mad! I will go up the London docks and get more wine. Stocks are low.' He needed the cool, unquarrelsome atmosphere of the wine vaults. He wiped his moustache on his table napkin, stood up and threw the little cloth down onto the milk jug, to Alice's quickly concealed annoyance.

'But how will you get there?' she said. 'You can't walk all that way.'

'I cadge a lift,' he roared. 'I hitchhike. There plenty a' cars on the road. I get there. You'll see. I not stay here with a pack of quarrelling idiots!' And he went, banging the door behind him.

Anna was quite alarmed to see him rushing off like that. 'What if some of them attack him?' she said to her mother. 'They're getting awfully vicious.'

'Don't you worry about your father,' Alice said. 'He can take care of himself. A trip out will do him the world of good, you'll see. He'll come back safe and sound and much better tempered. He always does.'

And sure enough when he finally got back to the house much later that evening all bad temper was quite forgotten and he was singing to himself.

Chapter Seven

When Albert had finally crossed Tower Bridge that day, Big Ben had been striking midday, its long, rich notes reverberating above the quiet capital. It had taken longer than he expected to get to the city, although lifts were easy enough with so many wealthy cars out on the road. At the Oval he'd met up with one of Mr Pennyman's farm carts, off to Hay's Wharf to collect fodder from the dumb barges, and had persuaded the driver that he could easily include six crates of wine on the return journey, for a handsome private fee of course. So he was feeling rather pleased with himself as he strolled beside the fairytale turrets of the southernmost tower.

Below him the Pool of London lay still and idle, like a picture. Four cargo ships rode at anchor alongside the entrance to St Katharine's Dock, but the dock itself was deserted. The strike was having an effect, he thought, whether the wireless admitted it or not. A cluster of Thames barges rested against the south bank, their hatches covered with blue tarpaulin and tar spread on their hulls as thick as blackberry jam, but apart from them the river was empty, its water calm and beautifully coloured by the clear skies and bright sunshine above it. Olive green shimmered against sky blue and the tips of the little licking waves sparkled like crystal. It lifted Albert's spirits just to look at it. He walked on towards the wine vaults whistling cheerfully.

Kroxy had gone off for his lunch, and wouldn't be back for at least an hour, according to his friend, the doorman. ''E'll be in The Pied Piper,' that gentleman said. 'Abbey Street. Over the river. You could cut across and try and gee 'im up a bit if you was in a rush.'

71

But Albert was in no particular hurry and the sun was warm. 'I will take a stroll,' he told the doorman. 'Tell him I come back at half past one.' He would wander down to The Blue Eyed Maid and see if he could find any of his friends in the trade. That would give old Kroxy time to take as much liquid refreshment as he needed. He knew from experience that cellarmen were always much more helpful after an adequate lunch.

There was no one he knew in the first pub he tried and the second was practically empty. But The Rose and Crown wasn't very far away and there was bound to be somebody there. Humming to himself cheerfully and tunelessly, he crossed London Bridge again, heading south.

He never reached The Rose and Crown, because Tower Bridge Road led him to Abbey Street and Abbey Street led him to The Star.

Afterwards he couldn't remember why he'd decided to walk straight on instead of turning right into Tooley Street that afternoon. Idle curiosity? Time to kill? Or plain, old-fashioned good luck? Whatever it was, it changed the course of his existence.

The Star was exactly the same as he remembered it from the old days with Queenie, square, squat and smothered in posters. The brickwork was blacker than ever and the old door chipped and totally devoid of paint, but still ajar. He stood on the pavement and read the posters. 'Support the Miners,' they urged and, 'Rally at Tower Hill,' and stuck askew across several others, 'How to Win – meeting – 12.30 Monday 9th May – speaker Queenie Chapman.'

Another Queenie, he thought, pleased to see the name. I wonder what she's like. Then, because the place was familiar and he had nothing better to do, he went inside to see.

Two burly dockers barred his entrance at once. "Oo are you?' one demanded, looking with great suspicion at his expensive clothes and the gold watch chain decorating his belly.

'Friend a' the speaker,' he lied cheerfully, grinning at them.

'That's different,' the man said, and let him in.

The hall was packed, the lines of tatty chairs set so close together that the audience sat shoulder to shoulder, and with their knees jammed against the backs of the row in front. It was hot and airless and very smelly, but the concentration was intense, for the chairman had finished his introductory remarks and was about to introduce their speaker.

'Yer don't none of yer need me ter tell yer nothink about our Queenie,' he said. 'We all of us know the good work she done fer the committee. Here she is. Queenie Chapman!'

The speaker stood up from among the group of people sitting behind him on the platform, and the sight of her put Albert into shock. It was Queenie! His own dear, redheaded, loving, gorgeous Queenie, bright as a peacock in blue and green and gold, with a cloche hat on the thick waves of her hair, and a long string of multicoloured beads dangling across her dear little breasts, skinnier than ever, but here, here in the flesh, a few incredible yards away from him, found again, at last. Queenie! He wanted to shout and leap about, to run to the platform and hug her till she yelled. His lovely, lovely Queenie!

The audience were cheering and clapping all around him, and he joined them with a total and rapturous abandon. His lovely Queenie! Found at last! When she started to speak he was too happy and excited to understand anything she said. It was enough simply to hear her voice, and to know that when she'd finished and the meeting was over he could push his way to the platform and claim her again. His lovely, lovely Queenie! But after a while her words began to stir in his mind and he found he was listening to her with amazement. How knowledgeable she was! And how well she handled her audience.

'This is a war,' she told them. 'We ain't give out uniforms nor guns, least not to our side, but it's a war just the same. Make no mistake about that. They got armoured cars on the streets an' armed men in Hyde Park an' submarines in the Pool a' London. Oh yes, submarines! And fer what? Ter run the refrigeration plants off their bloomin' electricity so's the rich don't 'ave ter go without their precious red meat. That's fer what. You an' me an' our kids be lucky if we get ter see red meat once a bloomin' month. But you an' me an' our kids don't count in this world. We're the enemy.'

She hasn't changed a bit, Albert thought, watching her as

she threw her words boldly out at the audience. She's still the same Queenie, headstrong, passionate, full of life. I'll bet she still licks her plate.

She brought the speech to a close with a rousing call. 'It's gonna be a long fight,' she said. 'But we shall win it. And fer why? Because they're only fighting fer their rotten money and we're fightin' ter feed our kids. All we got ter do is stand firm and 'old on and never let the buggers grind us down.'

The applause was deafening, but then, oh God, she picked up her bag and turned towards the back of the hall, and Albert remembered rather too late that there was a tradesmen's entrance to The Star. If he didn't hurry she would slip away and he'd lose her again. The mere thought filled him with frantic energy. He shoved his way through bodies and chairs, roaring her name as he pushed.

She turned to face the audience again, half smiling, and then he was on the stage in one bound and had her hands in both his and was kissing her in the Italian style first on one familiar cheek and then on the other. His heart was pounding so hard he thought it was going to burst. But it didn't matter. Nothing mattered now. He had found her again, and this time he would never let her go.

She caught her breath with surprise and the colour drained from her face, but she recovered quickly, more aware than he was of the startled looks and raised eyebrows around them. 'Mr Ploochy,' she said, introducing him generally. 'One a' my friends from when I used ter work the 'alls.' Expressions changed at once, faces relaxed, and the message was glanced from one to the other, 'Theatrical, a' course, might 'a' known.' Then she gave him her full attention. 'Oh, Ploo,' she said, 'ain't 'alf good ter see y' again.' It was a ridiculous understatement and they both knew it. He found he was still holding her hands and thought he ought to let them drop, but she grabbed his fingers in the old way and went on holding him beside her. 'Whatcher been doin' with yerself all these years?'

How could he even begin to tell her? 'You live round here?' he asked.

'Off Cherry Orchard,' she said. 'You can walk me home if you like.'

If he liked? Let anybody try to stop him!

But first goodbyes had to be said and far too many people talked to. Albert stood first on one leg and then on the other, chewing his moustaches with impatience, and Queenie, glancing at him as she said encouraging things to her comrades, noted and was pleased, because although his hair was grey at the temples now and he'd certainly put on quite a bit of weight, he was still behaving in exactly the same ridiculous, impatient way he'd always done. But at last they were out on the pavement and had left the rest of the meeting behind.

'I can't believe it!' Albert said, still stunned. 'I search and search for you at the end a' the war, and now I find you, when I'm not looking.' It felt like a miracle. 'I found your brother one time, your brother Cal, and he said you'd gone away. Did you go away?'

'You still got the shop?' she asked, ignoring his question. Now they were out in the open air, Albert could see that the years had marked her after all. She had changed. There were laughter lines etched around her eyes, and wrinkles of anxiety across her forehead. She was undeniably older but just as beautiful.

'Eight shops now,' he told her proudly.

'An' the cinema?'

''Course.'

'It is good ter see yer!' she said.

They walked along the footpath under the railway bridge where a row of squat Doric columns lined the edge of the pavement like a line of stone dwarves, and then they were in Jamaica Road and heading east towards Rotherhithe. The shops here were very run down and the flats above them grim and uncared for. In fact, as Albert was quick to notice, his senses being sharpened by so many sudden emotions, they were walking into the slums.

At the corner of Cherry Orchard Street, she stopped and looked at him seriously, wearing the determined expression he remembered so well, and with such affection. 'Now,' she said, ''fore we go any farther, there's one or two things we got to get straight.'

'Yes,' he agreed at once, beaming at her. Lovely, lovely Queenie. She might have a few more lines on her face, but otherwise she was just the same as ever. Bossy and beautiful!

She looked at his eager expression and the lift of his moustache and the dark hair bristling with pleasure above that brown forehead, and she knew that he wasn't paying the slightest attention to what she was saying. But she pressed on, nevertheless. It was too important for her to do anything else. 'Listen to me, Ploo!' she urged, tugging his sleeve.

He caught the tugging hand and held it. 'My lovely Queenie,' he said, his face lit with delight.

His pleasure was infectious. She was smiling at him despite herself, remembering how easy it had been to love him in the old days, reckless, extravagant man that he was. 'Never mind all that,' she tried to scold, but it didn't ring true. 'We can't just pick up where we left off, Ploo,' she said gently. 'Too much water under the bridge fer that. I'm married. I got a job. A kid. It ain't the same.'

''Course not,' he agreed, still rapturous. He'd heard the words, but not the meaning.

'So long as that's understood,' she said, but she recognized that it wasn't, even as she spoke. 'Oh, Ploo!' she said fondly, shaking her fingers free, 'you ain't paying me no mind. You're worse 'n a kid.'

'I love you,' he said. 'I always loved you.' What else was important?

'Come on, you soppy thing,' she said, and led the way into Cherry Court.

It was a dark, evil-smelling yard, surrounded on three sides by a terrace of small, single-storey cottages, weighted down by a line of solid brick chimney stacks that were almost as tall as they were and held their sagging roofs in an overpowering grip like the talons of some massive bird of prey. Each cottage had a plain door and one small window, and all of them were in a chronic state of disrepair, the sills heaped with black grime, the doorsteps grey with long wear, long unwashed. One or two of the windows were bravely curtained, their colour daring and pathetic among all that filth, like poppies on a dung heap.

Albert was appalled. 'Oh, Queenie!' he said. 'You don't live here!'

'Don't I jest!' she said grimly. 'Come on.'

They walked over the uneven cobbles of the yard, past an

ugly pump dripping water into a green puddle and across a central culvert clogged with rubbish, coal dust and wood shavings, black rags, damp shit and what looked like broken shards of bone. Albert scowled as he trod through the debris, and made up his mind that he would take her out of this squalor just as soon as ever he could. He'd go down to Fisher's, the Tooting estate agent, first thing tomorrow morning and give him instructions.

The door of the fourth cottage stood open and there were red curtains at the window, rather to Albert's relief. He followed Queenie into the cottage, blinking as they lost the light of the sun.

They were in a small, square room, sparsely furnished and poorly lit. There was lino on the floor, old and chipped and the colour of river mud, and the corners of the room were stained with the black fungus of damp, but one entire wall was bright with music hall posters and programmes and studio portraits. A plain deal dresser stood massively against one wall, littered with an assortment of cheap china and piles of untidy clobber, and in the middle of the room was a small table covered with a bright red cloth, and set beside it two plain kitchen chairs. A third was drawn up beside the stove and there was a little old man sitting in it, tending the fire, a little grey-headed old man.

He looked up as they entered, turning his head towards Queenie and smiling. It was a lop-sided caricature of a smile because one side of his mouth was pulled taut by a long, ugly scar that ran from his cheekbone to his chin.

'Ned,' Queenie said, making introductions, 'this is Mr Ploochy, one a' my friends from the old days, on the 'alls. 'E come in to our meeting. Bit a' luck, eh?'

Ned got up at once and stretched out his left hand for Albert to shake. His empty right sleeve was pinned clumsily to the front of his jacket, and the sight of it made Albert feel uncomfortable, dampening his excitement and bringing him down to reality. A wounded soldier, he thought, and remembered his first meeting with this man, in the flat in Clapham, on that awful day when Queenie had moved out and told him she was going to get married.

'You'll have some tea?' Ned said, smiling his odd smile at

Albert. 'Kettle's on the boil.' He didn't seem to be troubled by memory at all.

Tea was made and they sat around the red tablecloth to share it. It was very strong tea, as brown as boot polish and sweetened by a spoonful of condensed milk. Albert didn't like it at all. But what did that matter compared to the fact that he'd found his lovely Queenie again? He beamed across the table at her and was disappointed to see that she only gave him one brief glance and then turned all her attention to Ned.

They talked about the meeting and the local action committee and the progress of the strike and Ned assumed that Albert was as interested in politics as he was. 'Got a grand council here,' he said. 'Labour majority fer the last four years. Think a' that! They done marvels already, an' that's just a start. You seen the new flats up Salisbury Street? I'll take you down there. Sight fer sore eyes, they are, all new an' clean, electric light an' balconies to sit out on, an' trees planted an' all. It's gonna be a proper garden suburb, our Bermondsey, by the time we've finished with it.'

'An' the babies,' Queenie said, licking the last of the condensed milk from the tea spoon. 'Don't ferget the babies.' Then seeing Albert's puzzled expression, she explained. ''Fore we took over, kids died like flies down 'ere. Specially the babies and specially in the summer, what with all the stink an' all. So one a' the first things we done, once we got control, was ter send midwives out to all the new mothers when they was lyin' in, or supposed ter be lyin' in. See they was properly fed an' clean an' all that sort a' thing. An' in four years we got the death rate right down. Thirty per cent drop in infant mortality. Whatcher think a' that?'

Albert said he was impressed, but he was really more baffled than anything. Here they were sitting in this awful slum, talking about how good everything was. It didn't make sense. Didn't they realize the sort of lives they were leading?

'Time fer our Mary,' Ned said, glancing at the tin clock on the mantelpiece. 'I'll get her, shall I, love? You stay here an' entertain our guest.'

Mary! Albert thought. In his initial excitement he'd forgotten all about the child. Mary! My daughter! 'Where is she?' he asked, trying to sound casual, and annoyed because the question was breathy with renewed excitement.

'School,' Ned told him, and added with enormous pride, 'she's clever. Bein' groomed fer a scholarship.'

That didn't surprise Albert at all. What else would she be, seeing who her mother and father were? He couldn't wait for Ned to put on his cap and go. There were so many things he wanted to say to Queenie, now that he'd got his breath back, so many questions he wanted to ask. And once that husband of hers was out of the way he would be able to kiss her and cuddle her in his arms in the old way and they could begin all over again.

'You're off 'ome now, aintcher, Ploo,' she said as the door closed to. It was an order, not a question, and given too plainly to be misunderstood.

'No,' he said, taken aback.

'Yes you are, mate,' she told him and her jaw was determined. 'I told yer. Things 'ave changed. 'E's a good man, Ploo. 'E's been a good 'usband ter me, and a good father to our Mary Ann. She's the apple of his eye, that kid.' She put the dirty mugs into a bucket beside the stove, and turned to face him squarely. 'You're off 'ome!'

Implacable as ever, he thought, and her green eyes so hard. This time he wouldn't argue. There would be another time, now he knew where she was. The thought made him smile at her in the old, easy, relaxed way, and the smile made her remember, too clearly for sternness or propriety. She put her hands on his shoulders and kissed him once and lightly, but on the mouth. 'Come an' see us again,' she said, 'only go 'ome now, eh?'

He sang and chirruped and whistled all the way home, much to the amusement of the plus-foured undergraduate who gave him a lift. 'This strike doesn't worry you, then?' the young man asked.

'Not a bit!' Albert told him. 'It the best thing that happen for years.'

There was jubilation back at Longley Road too. Jesse and Percy had returned from a union meeting at Clapham fierce with the news that shipbuilding workers and engineers were to down tools at midnight.

'It's spreading like wildfire,' Jesse said happily. 'If we just hold on, we can 'ave this bloody government beat, all hands down. I never seen nothink like it.'

The very next day the T.U.C. General Council announced that the strike was called off. And called off unconditionally. They'd accepted the Samuel Memorandum, wage cuts and all. Somehow or other the government had beaten them.

Jesse, purple with fury, couldn't understand it or accept it. 'They must be out a' their minds!' he said. 'We was winnin', fer Christ's sake. The strike was spreading.'

'I always knew we 'ad lousy leaders,' Percy said sourly, 'but I never thought they'd sell us down the river like this. Them poor buggers in the mines! What's ter become of them now?'

The next few days were confused and miserable. Groups of striking men gathered in Albert's shops to pass on what little information there was, and to argue. Were they supposed to go back to work or not? Nobody seemed at all sure. The employers were already taking full advantage of the surrender, and laying down impossible conditions for workers who wanted to be 'reinstated', as they put it. On the Wednesday there were more men on unofficial strike than there had been the day before when it was official. But on Thursday the railway unions capitulated, and the Railway Companies issued a statement that felt and sounded like a final defeat. The unions had accepted the companies' conditions and had admitted 'that in calling a strike they had committed a wrongful act'.

'There'll be some victimization now,' Percy said. 'They'll crucify the poor buggers.'

'Serve 'em right!' Jesse growled. 'They've put the trade union movement back a hundred years. I never seen nothink so bloody stupid. The only strength they've ever had is to stay out, solid, no scabs, united, till the bosses give in. And they've give it away. I've got no sympathy for them. They deserve all they're going to get.'

The next day the printworkers gave in and accepted conditions and went back to work, and Percy and Jesse went with them.

Anna and Eric went to a victory party at Rollo's house out in Raynes Park, and Anna wore her most expensive dress and thought herself the belle of the ball.

Georgie went to tea with Dickie and Tilley and Lilian Marsden and did his best to cheer them up and was only partially successful.

And Albert bought a huge hamper of food from David Grieg's and took a taxi to Bermondsey.

Chapter Eight

Albert Pelucci's love child, Mary Ann Chapman, had no idea
that she was anything other than the well loved daughter of a
well established marriage. In fact, she was so secure within the
love of her mother and the man she thought of as her father
that it never entered her head to give the matter any thought at
all. There were far too many other things to occupy her mind.
Like most of her classmates, she was eight years old and skinny,
underweight, undersized and for most hungry weeks of the
year considerably undernourished. Nevertheless she was a
lively child with an abundance of reckless energy and an
appetite for adventure and new experiences that was almost as
keen as her need for food. The word that came most readily
into the mind of any adult trying to describe her was 'quick'.

'Will yer look at that kid!' her nan would say proudly as she
watched the matchstick legs of her favourite grandchild
scissoring along the street towards some errand or other. 'So
quick! Just look at her. Like greased lightning.'

And her teachers held the same opinion. Old Miss Wingate
had realized how clever she was before the end of her first term
in the Juniors. 'She's *very* quick,' she told Queenie at the school
gate one afternoon. 'We shall be entering *her* for the
scholarship. No doubt about that.' Queenie and Ned were
swollen with pride for several weeks afterwards, but Mary took
the news calmly. She knew she was clever, but there was
nothing special about the fact or her knowledge of it. It was on
a par with her acceptance that her eyes were brown or that her
hair was thick and curly like her mother's. It sometimes meant
she was teased for being a brainbox when she got all the
mental arithmetic right three days in a row, but as it was easy

teasing, with no edge to it, and there were certainly pleasures to balance against it, she took it philosophically. Teachers liked kids who were quick, and it was warming to be praised. The scholarship was something she rarely thought about. It was all much too far away, in a future too distant to contemplate. Three whole years! A lifetime!

No, there was really only one problem, and that was hunger. And hunger was a perpetual emptiness, sometimes growling, sometimes aching, but only assuaged by some rare and long-remembered treat, like fish and chips, or pie and mash, or the sudden extravagance of a joint on Sunday cooked in the baker's oven. She had learned very young that asking if there were second helpings provoked passionate bad temper from her mother and a subdued and miserable depression in her father, so nowadays she simply didn't ask.

Queenie's tempers held no terrors for young Mary Ann. They might be loud, but they were like dog fights, familiar, harmless and soon over. She could shout back at Ma, and stamp and roar as much and as loudly as she liked. If Pa was at work, of course. Because Ma was tough and rough and didn't mind. They could be screaming with anger one minute and hugging one another the next. She could tell Ma just what she thought, except about food, and Ma wouldn't mind.

Her father's gloom was quite another matter. She'd watched him endure too much and too often, and from a very early age she'd felt curiously responsible for him. Whatever else, she wouldn't do anything that might add to his burdens. They were already too many and too obvious, and the fact that he did everything he could to hide them from his little family only made her obligations greater. She would watch the empty sleeve of his coat and the scars that puckered the right side of his face, and wonder how it must have been to be blown up by a bomb. And when he coughed and couldn't catch his breath, she felt her own lungs straining in sympathy and wished she could breathe for him just for a minute or two to give him a rest. For she loved her father with the protective tenderness of an almost adult compassion. And she knew that however hungry she might be, he wasn't to know.

Nevertheless her hunger persisted, and most of her waking fantasies were concerned with food; cornucopias spilling across her mother's table, sudden banquets descending from the ceiling or the heavens, plates heaped with meat and vegetables and nice thick gravy, newspapers mounded with fish and chips, spiced and succulent with salt and vinegar, dishes piled with the fruit she liked so much and tasted so rarely, strawberries and peaches and pineapples and melons. Imagination fed her short journey home from school, and her imagination was as strong as her hunger.

So when she got home that Friday in May and found that the banquet actually appeared to have descended, she couldn't believe her eyes. For several seconds she simply stood on the doorstep with her eyes and mouth wide open, trying to take it in. It *was* her house, for there was Ma standing beside the table with a huge slice of bread and butter in one hand and a chunk of boiled ham in the other. But the table was transformed. There was food all over it, three loaves and a great chunk of butter, tins of peaches and pineapples and goodness knows what else, a ham with a rough slice hacked off one end (that 'ud be Ma) boiled eggs and fruit cakes and a whole roast chicken and so much fruit it made her gasp to look at it.

'Bli' me, Ma,' she said at last. 'We come into a fortune?'

'All right, innit?' Queenie said. ''Ave a bite a' that!' and she held her makeshift sandwich up to her daughter's mouth.

As she bit and chewed, savouring the salt of the ham and the freshness of the bread, Mary noticed that there was a strange man standing beside the table opening a tin of peaches, a strange, foreign-looking man with very brown skin and an old-fashioned bristly moustache and dark eyes that were sparkling even in the gloom of their dark room.

'Mr Ploochy,' her mother explained. 'Friend a' mine from the 'alls in the old days. Brought us a present. Whatcher think a' that?'

'Is it all fer us?' Mary asked, still scarcely able to believe it.

'Every last mouthful. Whatcher fancy?'

Reason returned. And responsibility. It was like a miracle, but they couldn't just sit down and pig it all by themselves. There were other kids in the court, just as hungry. Fair shares, Dad always said. In the new Jerusalem they were all going to build when the Labour Party got elected it was going to be fair shares all round.

'Sit down! Sit down!' the strange man said, holding a chair for her. 'What you fancy, eh? Peach? Bit a' chicken? Say the word.'

But she wouldn't sit down. 'What I mean is, it's like a party,' she said. 'All that grub. Couldn't we ask Ruby an' the Thompson twins an' them two little'uns at number ten? I bet they never 'ad nothink like this. Never ever! Fair shares, Ma!'

'Quite right!' her mother agreed, beaming at her. 'Fair shares! That's my girl! You nip in an' ask 'em.' And she began to sing, 'There's a party on the 'ill. Will yer come? Bring yer own cup an' saucer an' a bun!'

That was better, Mary thought, as she sped off on her cheerful errand. Sharing good fortune. That was the way. Wouldn't Pa be pleased.

Soon the courtyard was full of scurrying bodies, excited children trotting to the feast with their mugs and plates, aproned mothers bearing chairs, Mrs Thompson with her family teapot and old Mrs Gus with a short plank she said 'would do marvellous fer a bench'. Which, after collapsing three times under the stress of too much climbing and wriggling, it finally did.

It was a lovely party, better than Christmas and Bank Holiday and Empire Day all rolled into one. Mr Ploochy and Ma cut loaves and dispensed food and ate sandwiches all at the same time, and Mrs Gus poured the tea into a long line of cups in one long continuous stream as though she was watering the garden, which was a performance to wonder at, and the Thompson twins didn't scream once because they were so busy stuffing themselves with boiled eggs.

When Pa came home from his afternoon shift at the Cold Store, they were all so busy eating they hardly had time to explain what was happening, but he didn't even seem surprised. 'You're a one, Ploo!' he said to the stranger, as Mrs Gus poured him some tea and Ma handed him a plate and all the kids squashed up on their bench to make room for him. That's funny, Mary thought, Ma said he was a friend from the 'alls. Pa wasn't on the 'alls too, was he? She knew he'd been a docker once, like her uncle Cal, but she'd never heard him say anything about the stage. I'll ask him later, she promised herself, storing the question away in her neat quick brain.

But there was no time for queries now, for a sing-song had begun, and Ma was leading a chorus of 'Down at the old Bull and Bush', and the funny old foreign man was conducting them with his empty tea cup.

'Done us all a power a' good,' Pa said when they were all too well fed to sing or eat any more. 'Just what them littl'uns needed.'

'Bucked us up a treat,' Mrs Gus said, and she leant across the table to tell the foreigner confidentially, 'They been through some pretty lean times this winter, poor little beggars. Through no fault a' their own, neither. It's very good of yer, an' that's a fact.'

'Pleasure!' the foreigner said, beaming at her. How his moustaches stood on end when he smiled. He *was* a funny little man.

And then the party was over, almost as suddenly as it had begun, and the guests were leaving. Mary noticed how shy they were, now that they were standing before their benefactor. As if the relationship between them had been quite altered once they'd left the table. Ma didn't seem to notice. Or was she deliberately looking away? You never knew with Ma. She was quick too.

'Just look at the time,' she said. 'We shall 'ave ter get cleared up pretty sharpish or we'll miss the meetin'.'

The foreigner looked surprised. 'What meeting?' he said. 'You're not going out, are you?'

Ma was busy sweeping the crumbs off the red cloth, and pushing the dirty cups and saucers up to the kitchen end of the table. It was a familiar hint which meant, 'your turn to do the washing up', and Mary knew better than to ignore it, although she would have preferred to stay in the room and listen to their conversation. She poured the water from the kettle and frothed up the soap and dipped the cups and plates as quietly as she could, but even so she missed more than half of what they were saying.

'I'm off ter work. Ned's off ter the Town 'All, meeting a' the Emergency Strike Committee,' Ma's voice said as the water settled in the bowl.

'But the strike's over,' the stranger said. Dip that plate quick. Perhaps 'e's gonna take us all ter the pictures.

'Strike may be,' Pa said. 'Struggle ain't. That's just the beginning. We got a very long fight ahead of us. Made it worse by givin' the first round away. Still, there you are. No good crying over spilt milk.' Ah, Mary thought, the strike. She might have known they'd talk about the strike. That was all grown ups ever did talk about these days. And she wished Pa wouldn't. It only made him sad. She watched a cluster of bubbles slide off the plate she was holding up to drip. 'We got things ter do,' Pa was saying, and now his voice sounded firmer and more hopeful. That was better. 'Them poor devil miners are still on strike and still locked out. Need a lot of help now they will, poor beggars.'

'What will you do?' the foreigner said.

'Start a fund. The poor helps the poor in this world ...' Now there were only the six big plates and she was done. She was very careful with the big plates, because Ma said they came from the 'old days' and she always made a special fuss whenever they were brought out and used.

'I'm off then, Queenie,' Pa said and he came into the kitchen to hug Mary with his left arm and give her a goodnight kiss like he always did. 'See you in the morning, lovey.'

She dried the big plates carefully, as feet scraped and chairs were clomped back into position beside the table and the front door clicked to.

'I shall be late fer work,' Ma was saying, and she sounded a bit cross.

'Where you work?' the stranger asked in his funny broken English.

'Red Lion. Marigold Street. I'm a barmaid.'

'Barmaid and cabaret, eh?' the stranger said, chuckling, as though he was teasing her.

'When the mood takes me.' Why did she sound so cross with him? He was a nice old man, bringing all that food. Ma shouldn't be cross with him. 'You finished them plates, Mary Ann?' Oh Lor, now she was being sharp. There'd be no hope of the pictures if she was in a mood. She carried the clean plates into the living room and arranged them on the dresser. Ma was already in her coat and hat and the stranger was looking at her with the oddest expression on his face.

'Put yer coat on,' Ma commanded.

Mary hated her coat. It was a reach-me-down like all her clothes and it really didn't fit her any more, being tight under the arms and short in the sleeves. 'Must I, Ma?' she asked. 'Couldn't I just carry it? I don't need to wear it. It's ever so warm.'

Ma had her 'you'll do as you're told' look, but the stranger intervened. 'Quite right,' he said. 'Lovely summer evening. You carry your coat, Mary Ann. I carry mine.' And he took up his jacket and slung it over his arm.

'Great daft thing!' Ma said, smiling at him, the cross note in her voice gone as quickly as it had come. 'All right then, carry it.'

'Where you going, eh, Mary Ann?' the stranger asked.

'Aunt Eth's.'

'You remember Eth,' Ma said. 'My sister. Got one a' the new flats just round the corner.'

'You stay the night while your mother work?' he said, lifting that fat moustache in a broad smile.

'She sleeps there most nights,' Ma said. 'On account a' the bugs. They bite sommink chronic when it's 'ot. You don't get 'em in the flats.'

'Oh Queenie!' the stranger said and he looked really shocked. 'Why you not let me get you another place?'

'Don't start that,' Ma said. 'I told yer. Cherry Court's next on the list fer demolition. Matter a' waitin', that's all.'

Does he mean it? Mary was thinking. Could he really get us another house? Why doesn't Ma say yes? A house without bugs! That 'ud be marvellous. She was just opening her mouth to say how marvellous when Ma opened the door, saying, 'Time we was off!' in her determined voice, and the subject was dropped somehow.

So off they went together into the black dust of the courtyard, past the green pump and the culvert full of rubbish, out into the pungent air of Bermondsey, Queenie and Albert with their daughter skipping along between them. Their very well fed, contented daughter.

At the corner of Paradise Street Ma kissed her goodbye like she always did, and then the stranger inclined his head towards her. Am I supposed to kiss him too? she wondered, and she held out her hand hesitantly towards him to show that she would shake hands with him if that would do. Ma had the oddest look on her face. But to her surprise he didn't shake hands. He took hold of her shoulders with his big brown fingers and, bending, kissed her first on one cheek and then on the other, his moustaches rough and tickly. 'I see you again, eh?' he said.

'Yes,' she said brightly, giving him a little nod. 'I'd like that.'

He came back two days later with a shopping bag full of fruit and a big, flat, cardboard box labelled D.H. Evans. 'For you,' he said to Mary, laying it before her on the kitchen table.

He's like someone out a fairy tale, Mary thought as she untied the string and lifted the lid. A fairy godfather with a magic box. There were two sheets of white tissue paper rustling inside the box and underneath them a glimpse of red cloth. Soft red cloth, with a lovely new smell about it, a clean, warm, woolly smell. She lifted it in awe. It was a coat, a brand new red coat with a velvet collar and, lying beneath it, a little hat to match. The sort of coat princesses wore. A brand new coat.

'Try it on,' he urged her and his smile was so wide it was a wonder it didn't split his face.

It was a perfect, perfect, marvellous fit, the silk lining cool against her bare arms, the velvet collar neat under her chin, the unwrinkled cloth absolutely smooth above her skinny legs. Now that she was arrayed she noticed, looking down, how many bruises she had on her legs and how creased and battered her boots were. He seemed to know what she was thinking. 'I buy you a new pair a' shoes to match,' he said. 'An' white socks, eh?'

Ma was laughing at him. 'Oh Ploo, you are a caution! When's she gonna wear a thing like that?'

Mary hugged the coat to her at once. 'Lots a' times,' she said. Ma was going to say it wasn't suitable, and she knew it wasn't suitable, but it was much too beautiful to be given up. 'All over the place, Ma. You'll see. Honest.'

'Well, yer can't wear it ter school fer a start,' Ma said, much too fiercely. 'Be a fine thing sendin' you off ter school looking like Lady Muck.'

'I don't look like Lady Muck!' But Ma was right. What would the other kids say? They'd think she was getting above herself. It *was* a problem. But she coveted the coat now and she

89

wouldn't give it up. It was the most beautiful coat she'd ever seen, and it was brand new, and it was hers. She stood before her mother prepared to do battle for it, her mouth set even though her eyes were pleading.

'You look a beauty,' Mr Ploochy said, and his manner of speaking made it sound as if everything was settled. 'Tell you what, Queenie, I buy another coat fer school. Quiet, sensible, not offend no one. You choose it, eh? And you wear this coat when we go to the Zoo, an' the pictures, an' Madame Tussaud's, an' places like that.'

And it *was* settled. Perhaps the stories were true after all and there really were such things as fairy godfathers.

They went to the Zoo that very afternoon, and on the way there he bought her the new shoes he'd promised, and six pairs of socks. She was still stunned by the opulence of it all when she and her mother got back to Cherry Orchard Court in the early evening, and the coat was folded into its box again ready to be taken to Eth's flat out of the way of the bugs.

'Gaw deary me,' Ma said, kicking off her shoes. 'That was a day an' a half!'

'I 'ad three rides on that elephant,' Mary said, remembering the extraordinary rocking motion of that great, high, gentle creature. Three rides, one after the other, because Mr Ploochy had let her, even though Ma said she'd be spoilt. And the tea they'd had! It made her mouth water just remembering it. Cream cakes and iced buns and meringues that melted away when you put your tongue on them, and you didn't have to eat bread and marg first. It *was* a fairy tale. 'He's a toff, ain't he, Ma.'

''E's all right, our Ploochy,' Ma said. She was coaxing the stove to burn, so Mary couldn't see her face, but her voice sounded soft and dreamy, so she must have enjoyed the day out too.

Perhaps this was a good moment to ask the question that had been puzzling her ever since the day of the party. 'Is 'e rich, Ma?'

''E's not short of a bob or two.'

But was he one of the idle rich? That was the question. Because if he was he'd be killed come the revolution. Everybody said so. Put up against the wall and shot. And she didn't like to think of Mr Ploochy being put up against a wall and shot.

'Is 'e stinking rich?'

Ma turned from the stove and looked straight at her and laughed. 'No,' she said. ' 'E ain't stinking rich. Not our Ploo. 'E's sweet-smellin' rich, that's what. Sweet-smellin' rich.'

So *that* was all right. They wouldn't kill 'im if 'e was sweet-smellin' rich. You could tell that from the tone of Ma's voice. Now it was possible to turn to a less worrying question. 'I wonder how 'e knew the right size,' she mused.

'Got kids of 'is own,' Ma said, 'an' 'e don't miss a trick.'

Lucky kids, Mary thought. Fancy living with a man like that. Why, you could wear nice clothes all the time. And think of the food! I'll bet they're never hungry.

'Come the revolution, will we all 'ave new coats an' meringues?'

'No tellin' what'll 'appen come the revolution,' Ma said. 'Time ter get yer father's supper on.'

But Mary was still thinking about Mr Ploochy. 'I'm glad 'e ain't stinkin' rich,' she said.

Chapter Nine

Anna Maria was being taken to tea with Eric's parents. 'Lucky you!' her friends said. 'He must be getting serious.' But she really didn't know how he felt. It was almost impossible to read the signs, that was the trouble. A mean, romantic mouth was all very well, and undeniably attractive, but it didn't tell her anything. But at least he'd invited her to tea, and that ought to be a good sign, even if he'd done it in such a casual way. And it gave her an excuse for buying another new dress, for she had to look her very best for such an occasion. She was on display.

Her hosts were not impressed. 'A cocktail dress and pearls!' Mrs Barnes said, tightening her mouth with scorn. 'For a tea party! I ask you! Vulgar little thing!'

Mr Barnes, who'd been rather taken by Miss Pelucci's vivacity, looked at her again through his wife's sour eyes and decided to agree. 'Not suitable for our Eric,' he said. 'Not a bit, thank you very much!'

They were squashed together in their little kitchen, doing the washing up in their joyless, methodical way, and Eric was showing their guest round the garden. Or, to be more accurate, he was walking their guest up and down the garden for, as Anna had noticed with superiority, it was a mere six feet from one end to the other, and crowded with ridiculous herbaceous borders and silly china gnomes fishing from stupid little pools of blue concrete. Eric didn't seem to see how common and ordinary his home was, but she had noticed every single little detail, and didn't think much of any of them.

It diminished her hero to realize that he lived in a common, terraced house. And his parents were perfectly awful, sitting at their cheap little table serving perfectly awful food on their thick, common china, as though they were doing her a favour. That awful father saying 'thank you very much' all the time, in such a silly pompous way, and that dreadful mother with her stiff corsets and her mouth so tight and sneering. The two women had disliked one another at sight. It had been a most unpleasant meal.

Eric had talked unnecessarily loudly about his trip to Paris, and his work at the Foreign Office, and how perfectly marvellous it was that people of goodwill had come forward in their thousands and beaten the General Strike; and his parents had said how marvellous it was of Eric to give up his time the way he had, to save the nation; and Anna had looked at Mr Barnes' false teeth and wondered why he didn't bother to clean them.

'The roses look well, don't you think?' Mrs Barnes asked her guest when they were all reassembled in the front parlour, sitting stiffly on uncomfortable moquette.

Roses! Anna thought indignantly. One piffling little rose bush and she talks as if she owned Buckingham Palace. 'It's a nice little bush,' she said, politely disparaging. 'What a pity you don't have room for more. We have a rose garden at home and the smell is absolutely divine.'

Mrs Barnes was annoyed but recovered quickly. 'I always think one rose bush is preferable to a great mass. You get the scent so much better with a single bush, don't you think?'

'I really couldn't say,' Anna told her, determined not to be put down. 'There are so many lovely things in our garden at home, and so many of them scented, we hardly have time to enjoy them all. There's the syringa by the croquet lawn, you remember, Eric, and two lilac bushes, of course, down by the orchard, and a rose arbour. That leads to the vegetable garden, of course, so I don't go down there very often.'

'It must need a great deal of keeping up,' Mrs Barnes said acidly, equally determined to find fault with anything this girl said. 'I wouldn't like a garden that was too big to manage.'

'Well, you don't have that problem here, do you, Eric?' her adversary said, smiling sweetly as she scored the point.

Afterwards, as Eric drove her home through the tidy surburban streets, she wondered whether she ought to tell him how much she had disliked her introduction to his parents. He might want to take her there again and she couldn't bear that. But he forestalled her.

'I must say, you handled the mater extremely well,' he said. 'Absolutely top-hole!'

'Oh!' she said, surprised and gratified by his praise. 'Do you think so?'

'I should say so,' he said. 'She's an old tartar, the mater, don't you know. Most people find her impossible. You were ripping. Absolutely top-hole! You got the better of her. She won't be anywhere near so sharp next time.'

Still glowing with his praise, Anna found she couldn't tell him that she'd never intended there to be a next time.

Georgie was out in the August sunshine walking across Tooting Common with Lily Marsden. It was mid afternoon and the trees on the common were sticky with heat. They'd tried to quench their thirsts with Snofrutes, but with little success. Now they were strolling along the avenue of chestnut trees towards the drinking fountain and he had impressed her by telling her how the trees had been planted for Queen Elizabeth back in the sixteenth century.

'The things you know!' she said admiringly. 'You must have a good head for learning. That's what it is. I couldn't remember half the things they told me at school.'

He filled the metal cup for her and smiled as she drank her fill. It was a Sunday afternoon ritual now, to walk and talk and drink at the fountain. Afterwards they would stroll over to the pond and she would dabble her feet in the water and they would watch the small boys swimming, and talk again.

This afternoon, rather to their surprise, they had the pond to themselves. Two mallards bobbed on the olive water and the island in the middle of the pond was shrill with sparrows but there was no sign of the swimmers.

Lily took off her stockings and began to cool her feet. There was a delightful intimacy about their Sunday afternoons, Georgie thought. They were so easy with one another, talking about everything and anything. He'd never felt so easy with anybody else before, not even old Johnny Ashby.

'Penny for your thoughts?' she said, glancing up at him.

'I think I love you,' he told her, and then blushed furiously, because it wasn't the sort of thing you ought to go blurting out like that.

'Only think?' she queried. What an odd thing to say. His uncertainty was rather unflattering, but he looked so embarrassed and so serious she couldn't help feeling fond of him.

He slid down to the water's edge to be beside her. 'I've never felt anything like this before,' he explained, doggedly honest. 'I'm not sure. It wouldn't be fair to you for me to imply that I was, now would it?' He felt he was expressing himself very awkwardly and blushed again.

'No,' she said, admiring the honesty and sympathizing with the uncertainty. Hadn't she been feeling much the same thing herself? 'It's a big step. You gotta be ever so careful not to make a mistake.'

'That's just it,' he agreed, pushing his glasses into a more comfortable position with a nervous forefinger. 'Just think how awful it would be to get married and promise to love and honour, till death us do part, and in sickness and health and all those other things, and have all your relations there knowing all about it, and then to find out you didn't care for one another after all.'

The idea was sobering, but it didn't stop the conversation. They'd gone too far now, and were breathless with the enormity of the things they might soon be saying to each other. One day. When they were sure.

'I don't think you should ever get divorced, you see,' Georgie went on. 'I think you should marry for life. For better, for worse. For richer, for poorer.'

'So do I,' Lily said, her eyes enormous and exactly the same colour as the sky above the plane trees. Out on the pond the mallards were bobbing like floats on the ripples, and a blackbird was piping its bold, clear song from the top of the hawthorn on the knoll.

'If I were to propose to you,' he said, 'what would you say?' Then seeing her hesitate, he hastened to reassure them both. 'You needn't say anything, of course.'

'I think I'd say yes,' she said, and then she let her smile tell him everything else.

'Oh Lily!' he said huskily, wondering whether he could kiss her now without compromising them both. Her eyes still encouraged him, so he leant forward to try.

It was a clumsy, awkward kiss that left him torn between rising desire and shamefaced embarrassment. His glasses would keep getting in the way, that was the trouble, no matter which side he tilted his head. He ended up banging her nose with them and kissing the side of her mouth instead of landing on target.

She didn't seem to mind his ineptness. Dear girl. 'We need a bit a' practice,' she said. 'Perhaps if you took off your glasses ... ?'

'I can't see very much without them,' he admitted, but he did as she suggested and found that, although the common was a distant blur, her face was in clear focus. This time he found her mouth almost at once and kissed it until they were both breathless.

It was the first of many such kisses.

Ever since the end of the strike, Percy had been unnaturally quiet. Minnie and Alice had spent several anxious hours discussing the change in him, but neither of them knew what to do about it. He'd always been such a loud, active young man, with opinions as strongly held and forcefully expressed as his father's. Now he brooded, withdrawn and perplexed.

'He'll be better when everything's settled down again after that silly strike,' Alice said, trying to reassure her cousin. But work was resumed and the trains ran again and trams and buses filled the Tooting streets, and still he brooded.

In September the underground railway station at the Broadway was officially opened. The event was much discussed in the Pelucci household. Albert thought it was very fine. 'One of the marvels of the age,' he said, quoting the *News and Mercury*. 'A moving staircase to carry you up and down, Alice. You should come down and see it.'

Alice declined the invitation, of course. 'I don't hold with all this travelling underground,' she said. 'It isn't natural. Give me a nice old-fashioned horse bus any day.'

Anna was thrilled with it and took a train to the West End, the very next day, for a shopping expedition with three of her friends. 'Absolutely top-hole,' she said. 'So clean and quick.'

Even Georgie admitted grudgingly that it was certainly convenient. But still Percy had nothing to say.

'I'm beginning to think he's sickening for something,' poor Minnie confided to Alice. 'It's been going on such a long time.'

Then one Sunday lunchtime, when the beef was particularly tasty and the family chatter consequently rather desultory, Percy made an announcement.

'I been thinking a lot lately,' he said unnecessarily. 'I come to a conclusion.' The faces all round the table turned in his direction, interested, intrigued, curious and fearful. 'There ain't no sort a' future fer a young man in this country. Not now the bosses 'ave got the upper 'and. I seen one good man after the other laid off, an' fer nothing more than supporting the strike. We ain't got the liberty we 'ad once, there's no denying it, an' things are gettin' worse an' worse. So I've decided. There's always work in the print, anywhere in the world. I'm goin' to emigrate.'

Minnie's face fell visibly and she covered her mouth with her hand to prevent them from seeing how much it was trembling.

'Things'll pick up, Percy,' she said. 'It's not as bad as all that!'

'I made me mind up, Ma,' Percy said. He didn't seem to be feeling any emotion at all, not even from the sight of her distress. 'I'm goin' to America. I've booked me passage.'

'Good fer you, son,' Jesse said. 'Wish I was. You got some spirit.'

'But America's such a long way,' Minnie said and now the tears were welling out of her eyes.

'It's a young man's country,' Albert told her gently, taking control of the conversation. 'Your Percy will make a fortune, you'll see, an' come home a rich man. How about that? All the best people emigrate at some time in their lives, eh, Percy?'

'I think it's top-hole,' Anna said. 'Such an adventure. New places, new faces. The Wild West and everything.' Mummy and Aunt Min were looking absolutely shattered. Poor Aunt Min! Nothing'll stop Percy, she thought. Not now he's made his mind up. But never mind. *I* shall still be here. I'll never leave England. I'll make a great fuss of her, dear Aunt Min.

She was right about her cousin. He was gone within the month.

Albert fixed everything for him, suitable clothes, strong boots, a travelling trunk, American dollars, even a hip flask full of brandy for the journey. Poor Aunt Minnie followed the preparations in a miserable dream, with Anna hovering protectively at her elbow. It didn't seem possible that in less than a fortnight's time she would be saying goodbye to her son.

'First little Renee,' she said unhappily to Alice, remembering her daughter who had died as a child, 'and now this. I shall be all on my own when he goes. I don't think I can bear it.'

'You've got me, Minnie,' Alice comforted. 'You've always got me.' But she too was distressed by this parting. It made her feel that the family was breaking up, and that was something she didn't even want to think about.

'If he marries,' Minnie said, 'I might never know. I couldn't go to the wedding. I shan't see my grandchildren, Alice. It's very hard!' And she wept again at the thought of it.

'I don't suppose either of us will have grandchildren,' Alice said. 'Georgie will never get married, I'm glad to say. He's got too much sense for that. And Anna is so flighty, I can't see her settling down for years and years. I shall be pushing up the daisies before *she* has any children.' It comforted her to see the future so clearly, and in such an uncompromising pattern. But Minnie went on weeping.

Percy left home two weeks later. They all went up to Liverpool Street Station to see him off. He looked foreign and distant already in his new topcoat and trilby hat. When they'd watched his train until it was out of sight, Jesse went off to the nearest pub and got extremely drunk, and Anna kissed her aunt lovingly and went to Leicester Square to meet Eric, and Albert and Georgie went back to work. But Minnie went home with Alice.

Chapter Ten

When Lily Marsden ran home from work that Friday, with the tears streaming down her face, the shop was crowded with customers. Georgie couldn't even take a minute off to say good evening, leave alone find time to comfort her. She rushed past him, her face averted, and he had to go on pulling pints and exchanging platitudes. He spent the next twenty minutes in a torment of anxiety, straining his ears for sounds from the flat above his head. But what with the din of traffic outside the shop and the babble of voices within, he couldn't hear a thing. As soon as the rush was over, he ran upstairs to see what was the matter.

She was standing by the corner window in the front parlour, quietly looking out at the traffic below her, but the minute he entered the room she flung herself at his chest and began to cry all over again.

'I got the sack!' she sobbed. 'I'm fired! Oh Georgie, it's not fair!'

He patted her hair and dried her eyes and made soothing comforting noises, and felt protective. It took a little while, and a lot of cuddling, to piece the story together, but there was no doubt about the gist of it. Lily Marsden had lost her job. 'They said I was insubordinate!' she sobbed. 'Insubordinate! Me! I never say boo to a goose. Just that one time, that was all. It's that horrid old boot Ladbroke, that's who it is. She's had it in for me from the day I started.'

'What did they say when they gave you the sack?' Georgie asked, trying to be reasonable. 'They can't sack you without cause, you know.'

'They can!' she said, sniffing. 'They have. Oh, it's not fair.

She said I was lippy to the floor walker. I wassen' even talking to her. I said it to Ruby.'

'What did you say, Lily?' he asked as kindly as he could because he could see how unhappy she was.

'I said she looked like a month of Sundays,' Lily admitted. 'Well she does, you've got to admit, all that stringy hair and her cardigan all anyhow.'

The phrase made him giggle, and the giggling dried her tears. 'She does too,' he said. 'Just like a month of Sundays. That's very good.'

'But now I haven't got a job to go to,' she said. 'What am I going to do, Georgie? I can't go home. They're in such a state at home.'

He kissed the top of her head. 'You will stay here,' he said, 'and marry me.' He hadn't the faintest idea how such a thing could be arranged or managed, but it was the obvious answer.

'Oh Georgie!' she said. 'D'you think we can? That 'ud be marvellous.' It would solve all her problems. No more living with Aunt Tilley and her terrible sharp tongue. No more standing behind a counter all day long, pretending to agree with everything the customer said. No more uniform. No more forced politeness. She'd have a home of her own, and the right to do what she liked in it. What a dear, kind man he is, she thought, looking up at Georgie's determined expression.

Georgie knew he ought to be feeling worried or at the very least apprehensive, but curiously enough he only felt slightly elated. Then Frank leaned over the banisters and bellowed, 'Shop!' so he had to go back downstairs and cope with the rush. Any emotion, however good or bad, had to be deferred. He didn't get any peace to consider what he'd done until the shop was closed at the end of the day and he was in the office carefully writing up the accounts.

Then his thoughts erupted like fireworks, and he knew that the step he'd just taken was irrevocable and would be bound to cause ructions. For some unaccountable reason, his mother had never seemed to like Lily. She'd always pulled her mouth into such tight-lipped disapproval whenever the poor girl was mentioned, and she'd never once suggested inviting her to tea. How would she react to this news? he wondered. He would have to break it to her very gently, or she could be very upset. But far far worse than telling his mother was the heart stopping knowledge that sooner or later he would have to discuss it with his father. His palms ran with sweat at the very idea, because it was just a little too easy to picture his father's reaction. He would roar, of course, and say they were much too young, and probably forbid it out of hand. Georgie sighed, passing his hand wearily through his hair, and tried to concentrate on the task under his fingers. But his heart was thudding with anxiety. Why did life have to be so terribly difficult all the time?

As he walked home that evening, slowly, so as to defer the awful moment, he was rehearsing the words in his head. But none of them sounded right. 'Father, I have something to tell you.' 'Father, you remember Lily Marsden.' 'Father, I am engaged to be married.' Oh dear no! That wasn't any good at all. It didn't sound true or likely. When he reached the house he was no nearer a possible formula. But as luck would have it, his father was out, visiting friends in some out of the way place on the other side of London, according to his mother. He decided to wait a day or two and think about it a bit more.

He was still thinking about it on delivery day, and that was nearly a week later.

It was a damp, blustery day, the sort that always disturbed him, even at the best of times. Heavy blue and grey clouds massed and tumbled in the sky above Church Lane and strong gusts of wind blew dead leaves and tattered paper across the road from the churchyard to scurry against the shop window, rattling like mice. It was a restless, unpredictable day, so he shouldn't have been surprised when it blew his restless, unpredictable father into the yard to supervise the delivery.

Fortunately Albert and the drayman were old friends, and the order was just as it should be, so the morning went well. But when the four great shire horses had clopped their van away towards Mitcham, and Frank had gone home to recover with some dinner, Georgie was left alone with his father and his well rehearsed news, and was tongue-tied with embarrassment.

'You doing a good trade here, son,' Albert said, looking at the well stocked shelves and closing the cellar door on the capacity below them. 'Perhaps we should expand, eh? What you think?'

It was a heaven sent opportunity. 'Well, Dadda,' Georgie

said, pushing at the bridge of his spectacles. 'I was thinking of a sort of expansion myself.' Then he realized that the words sounded coarse, in the light of what he was going to say next, and he began to blush furiously.

'Were you?' his father said, noticing the blush and scowling. 'What you got in mind, eh?'

'Well,' Georgie said again, concentrating on the high polish of the counter. 'Well, actually, I was thinking of getting married. Lily and … '

He never got any further, because his father seized both his hands and was shaking them up and down as though they were playing 'Oranges and Lemons'. 'What a piece a' good news!' he said, his eyes snapping with pleasure and approval. 'Wait till your mother hear this! Where is she? I got to congratulate her.'

For a bemused second, Georgie understood that his father wished to congratulate his mother. He looked blankly at the extraordinary, bristling good humour of his father's face as the leaves rattled against the shop window. Then he realized what they were talking about. 'She's gone shopping,' he said.

'We find her!' his father said. 'Shut the shop. Come on!'

They found her in the dairy, buying butter and cream, with a very full shopping basket on the floor at her feet. Albert breezed into the shop, seized her in his arms and kissed her resoundingly on both cheeks, to the amazement of the shop girl. 'I 'ear your good news,' he said boisterously. 'Now you are my daughter-in-law. We make plans, eh?'

What could either of them do but agree? He blew them along in the gale of his enthusiasm. 'First we go to Morden,' he said. 'On the underground. Leave your shopping. We come back for it later.'

They were at Colliers Wood before Georgie had a moment to wonder what they were going to Morden for, and then it was a little too late to ask. And in any case, Lily was enjoying the journey so much, and his father was so happy and full of himself, he didn't think it would be sensible to say anything.

They reached the end of the line and stood on their second moving staircase to be creaked back into the fresh air. 'Here we are!' Albert proclaimed as they emerged. 'Come an' see!'

They were standing in an immense building site. The underground station stood in a very wide, very new road, which was obviously going to be the high street of this new town when it was finished. A parade of new shops was being fitted out immediately opposite them, and there were two smaller parades already occupied on either side of the station entrance. There were builders' vans and carts and gangs of men at work everywhere they looked, but Albert didn't give them time for more than a glimpse. He tucked Lily's hand into the crook of his arm and charged across the road, heading for the nearest unfinished shop, which he entered as though he owned it, only pausing briefly to say, "Ello Charlie!" to the workman plastering the walls.

'I've had my eye on this one since the middle a' summer,' he explained. 'Prime site. Bang opposite the station. Right side a' the road fer trade. They'll all come straight across here on their way home of an evening. What d'you think, Georgie?'

Georgie blinked his way over the scattering of planks and paint pots that blocked the front of the shop and agreed with his father. It seemed to be everything he claimed. Under his guidance, they examined the shop together, the wide plate-glass window, 'Just think a' the size a' that display,' the storerooms and the back office, 'Nice fire, good light.' Then they were bounded up the back stairs to the flat, which was low ceilinged and well lit, a plain, functional, up-to-date dwelling, not at all to Georgie's old-fashioned taste. But as Lily said she thought it was ever so nice, he kept his opinions to himself.

They clomped about the echoing box of the living room, which lay conveniently above the shop, with a grand view of the pipes and trucks of the new road.

'What you think of it, eh?' Albert asked.

'I think it's lovely, Mr Ploochy,' Lily said. 'So modern. And lovely and clean, with the geyser and the bath and everything.' Georgie pushed at the bridge of his glasses and made a murmuring noise that would sound like agreement.

Albert rubbed his hands together, beaming at them both, moustaches bristling. 'I tell you what I do,' he said, enjoying himself. 'I buy this place, and you manage it, Georgie. Run it. Order the stock. Keep the books. Your own shop. We could have it ready to open in five, six weeks. Just good time to fix the wedding, have a honeymoon, be back for the Christmas trade. What you think a' that?'

Lily had been hoping he would say he was going to buy the place for Georgie to run, but the speed of the arrangements he was making took her breath away, and Georgie was so stunned he couldn't even think. Married in six weeks? It wasn't possible. Why, they hadn't told his mother yet.

But his father was rushing them about again, galloping down the stairs and hurtling through the shop. They blundered after him out into the buffeting air and were pushed on, half running, down the newly dug road. The wind was so strong now that it whipped Lily's coat like a flag and lifted her hair on either side of her hat like two brown wings. They tumbled to the end of the parade, where there was a rough wooden hut, labelled Estate Agents, that housed a man with horn-rimmed glasses and a moustache like a small grey scrubbing brush.

Georgie had a vague impression that they all shook hands a great deal and seemed to agree with one another, and then his father signed a massive cheque, and they were out in the wild air again, and he was the manager of his own shop.

'Now,' Albert said, 'we arrange the wedding.'

He's enlarged, Georgie thought, gazing at his father weakly, his spine so straight, chest expanded, hair thickened, eyes sparkling, moustaches standing on end. There was no stopping him now.

They found a hotel in the Merton Road, and Albert ordered steaks for them all and more vegetables than they could possibly eat, and even a bottle of champagne, as though they were already married. Then he settled himself comfortably in his chair, spread his brown hands on the white tablecloth and proceeded to fix what remained of their lives. They would be married in Tooting, of course, in St Nicholas'. They'd like that, wouldn't they? He would pay all expenses, so they needn't worry about a thing. They could go across and see the Reverend Jenkins as soon as they all got back to the shop. No time like the present, eh? He would write to Lily's parents that evening and keep them informed and tell them what a fine daughter-in-law she was going to be. What a marvellous day!

As the coffee arrived in its silver pot Georgie ventured to observe, but very timidly and tentatively, of course, that they hadn't told his mother yet.

'No more we have,' his father said, treating the information as a joke. 'What a surprise for her, eh?'

'Yes,' Georgie said, trying to sound enthusiastic. But he was inwardly afraid that it wouldn't be a pleasant one.

It wasn't. So perhaps it was just as well that Albert broke the news while Lily and Georgie were still quivering with embarrassment in the rectory.

It always annoyed Alice when her family were late home for their tea, and today they were very late indeed, so her deliberate patience was worn as thin as a veneer.

'What kept you?' she asked, as mildly as she could, when her husband finally appeared. 'Georgie isn't home yet, and it's long past his time. Has he been with you?'

'Good news,' he said, beaming at her. 'Our Georgie is going to get married.'

'If that's your idea of a joke,' she told him severley, 'it's in very poor taste.'

'No joke!' he said happily, and he told her what he had arranged.

She went white, and had to straighten her spine and gather reserves of strength before she could speak. 'That's ridiculous,' she said. 'They're far too young for a start. How will she know how to feed him properly? A silly little girl like that! Why on earth didn't you stop them?'

'Stop them?' Albert said, looking at the suppressed fury on her face and feeling that he ought to make an effort to change her extraordinary mind. 'Rubbish! I help them. A marriage in the family, Alice! Good, eh?'

She wasn't persuaded by that. 'Rushing into things!' she said. 'It's the height of folly, Albert. What do they know about marriage? Two silly young things like that. I ask you! It isn't a thing anybody should rush into. It's far too serious.'

'They make a fine pair,' he said, beginning to feel dampened by her disapproval.

'Yes they do!' she said trenchantly. 'A fine pair of fools. Well, I warn you, Albert, it won't last five minutes, and I shall hold you personally responsible when they end up in the divorce courts.'

'Why you never enjoy nothing?' he roared at her, catching

her anger. 'Why you always look on the black side?'

'It's a black world,' she told him, 'so it's just as well one of us has some sense.'

'I not stay in this house a minute longer!' he shouted, and made a dramatic exit, flinging his coat about his shoulders like a cloak, and banging doors behind him as he went.

Anna had been sitting at the tea table all through their furious exchange, keeping quiet, but with her ears straining so as not to miss a word. Fancy Georgie getting married, she thought. Staid old stick-in-the-mud Georgie. Who'd have thought it? And if he was getting married, he must have proposed to her. I wonder how he did it. Or did she inveigle him into it somehow? I wouldn't put it past her. Now, rather belatedly, she wished she'd befriended Lily Marsden instead of pitching into her so much. I might have been able to pick up a few tips, she thought. Because there was no doubt about it, manoeuvring a young man into a position where he'd feel obliged to propose to you was very, very difficult. She knew. Look how long she'd been working on Eric!

He was a charming escort. That she couldn't deny. And they made a very handsome couple. People looked at them everywhere they went. But he never talked about getting married. It was very frustrating.

She'd tried every trick she knew, showing him snapshots of her married friends, loitering beside jewellers' windows admiring the rings, leaving magazines open at suitable pages where there were pictures of brides or wedding cakes, or articles headed 'Your Great Day', but he ignored it all. Or to be more accurate, he simply didn't seem to see it. She couldn't think what to do next.

But something would have to be done. And quickly too. She couldn't have Georgie stealing her thunder. At the very least she ought to be engaged before his wedding. She decided to make a very special effort on Saturday.

They were going dancing at the Wimbledon Palais, and that gave her a head start, because it meant she could wear the red chiffon which was quite the most romantic dress in her wardrobe. And she liked the Palais, with its nice soft art deco lighting blooming on the walls and the central globe dropping sparkles of light all round her as she danced. It was just the right sort of place for a proposal. She would wait till a nice smoochy waltz when all the lights were low and she could cuddle up against him, and then …

It poured with rain on Saturday. Her red chiffon was blotched with horrid damp patches before she even got into the dance hall, and her silk stockings were absolutely wrecked. It was dreadfully upsetting but she controlled herself rigidly and smiled and made eyes and was as charming as she knew how to be. She knew it would be far too risky to let him see her in a bad mood because it might put him off and she didn't want that. So she tried to ignore the ruin below her waist and concentrated on bewitching him with her nice brown eyes and her nice spiky eyelashes. And he said she was the prettiest girl in the place. After a little prompting.

'You dance divinely,' she told him, lisping slightly, because a lisp always sounded so fetching. He smiled, but rather distantly. Perhaps that was because he was concentrating on a rather tricky step. She'd chosen the moment badly. She fitted her heels neatly together and pivotted before she spoke again. Now they were gliding easily down the hall and there was nothing to prevent either of them from giving all their attention to what they were saying.

'Don't you think we make a lovely couple?' she asked, drawling the word 'lovely' because that was a charming thing to do too.

'Yes,' he said, but he was still distant, and gazing over her shoulder.

'A partnership, wouldn't you say?' Come on, look at me. I'm making it really easy for you.

'Well, would you believe it?' he said, and his voice was suddenly bright and relaxed. 'There's old Rollo. Fancy old Rollo coming here tonight. We'll go over and join him, shall we, after this dance?'

So they went over and joined old Rollo. There didn't seem to be any way she could avoid it. And old Rollo told silly jokes all evening and quite ruined the atmosphere, because even during the smoochiest waltzes Eric was remembering the latest joke and laughing. It was hopeless. That damn fool Rollo, she thought angrily, why on earth did he have to come here tonight of all nights? And she laughed girlishly at another boring joke, and tossed her careful curls.

And then to make matters worse the next dance was a ladies' excuse-me, and Rollo's awful girlfriend actually came and butted in and took Eric away from her. That really was too much, particularly as Rollo would insist on dancing the rest of the wretched dance with her, and actually said it was 'to make amends'. How humiliating! Did she really look like the kind of girl who couldn't get a partner, and had to be rescued?

The minute the dance was over she dragged the silly girl off to the cloakroom, and while they were both dabbing powder on their noses informed her carelessly that she was really rather wasting her time on Eric. 'We are as good as engaged, you know.'

'Oh!' the girl said breathlessly. 'How ripping! He's ever so goodlooking!'

'Yes,' Anna agreed. 'He is, isn't he?' And he's mine. So keep off.

'Does Rollo know?'

'Oh no,' Anna said, being very careful not to show alarm. 'It's our secret, just for the present. You understand, don't you? We think it's more romantic this way.'

The girl seemed to accept it. 'Lucky you!' she sighed.

'Aren't I?' Anna said.

But the conversation returned in the middle of the night to worry her. What if that wretched girl couldn't keep a secret? Rollo's friends were all such blabber mouths. What if she went around telling everybody? If Eric heard she'd been saying they were engaged before he'd actually said anything, he'd be as cross as two sticks. He might go right off the whole idea. And that would be absolutely disastrous. Especially now she was getting him used to it. Oh, why was life so unfair? Georgie's wedding was only six weeks away and she *must* be engaged by then. It was the most important thing she'd ever had to accomplish. She must be the next bride. And then Mummy would notice her again and see how popular and successful she was and realize at last what a marvellous daughter she'd always been.

At the moment the entire household revolved around Georgie and *his* silly wedding. Nobody noticed her at all, which was very irksome. It's all very well for Georgie, she thought.

He's got everything he wants now. He's as happy as a sandboy.

Anna was wrong. Georgie was tense with worry and riven with another emotion that really felt far too much like guilt for comfort. He had always been so close to his mother and she had always been so fond of him, nursing him tenderly through all the alarming fits he'd suffered in his childhood and early adolescence, waiting on him hand and foot, urging him on in his studies, tempting his appetite with specially prepared food. Now, although she still looked after him, she seemed withdrawn somehow, and the lack of her loving expression made him feel deserted and a bit afraid. In fact, if it hadn't been for the fact that there was so much to do in the six weeks his father's plans had allowed him, he would have been tempted to call a halt to his wedding. Except, of course, that that would mean upsetting Lily and he couldn't bear the thought of upsetting Lily. It was all terribly difficult.

As the days passed and decisions became more and more fraught, he found he was confiding in Lily more and more often. He was relieved and a bit surprised to discover how very sensible she was. 'Of course, order cheap brands,' she reassured him, when he worried about the stock. 'You just think, all those people moving into new homes. They won't have a lot a' money left over, will they?'

Gradually his confessions increased. He told her he'd had epileptic fits when he was a child and even though he'd grown out of them they might return. She said it couldn't be helped and she didn't mind a bit. He told her how worried he was in case he made a fool of himself at the ceremony. She promised to hold his hand and assured him that she would be blushing so much that nobody would notice what colour he was. He told her how overwhelming his father's sudden passions were. She soothed him that really Albert was 'an old sweetie' and so kind. Why, just look at the way he was arranging their wedding for them. What could be nicer? Or more generous?

And Albert had been generous. That was true enough. He'd furnished their flat, and decorated their shop, and paid for Lily's trousseau, and spent a fortune on the wedding. But somehow all his lavish expenditure only made Georgie feel more guilty than ever. And trapped. As though his feet were caught in some gigantic escalator and he was being pulled down and down at a speed he couldn't control.

He blundered through all the necessary preparations as well as he could, but as the wedding day got nearer he was so punch drunk he hardly knew what was happening. A week before the wedding he and Lily went down to Gillingham, and he was engulfed in the manifold embrace of a family so huge and noisily active that it made his head spin just to look at them. He came home with a headache and the impression that Lily had at least a dozen brothers and sisters, but that her mother and father, although harassed, were friendly and seemed to like him.

And then, with the rapidity of a dream or a nightmare, the weeks were gone and it was the eve of his wedding and somehow or other everything had been arranged. He found himself alone in the house dressing for the stag night he didn't want but knew he would have to endure. His mother and Aunt Min were still in Jack Beard's reception hall arranging flowers, Anna was out with that horrible Eric Barnes, Aunt Phoebe had retired to her bedroom and his father had gone rushing off to get the party underway. There was nothing left for him to do and, as he wasn't allowed to see Lily, nowhere for him to go.

He stood at the window of the bedroom in which he'd hidden for the last fifteen years of his life, and looked out at the November garden, wondering how it would be to live in a flat again with only a back yard. There was enough light from his window to reveal that even in winter the grass of their wide lawn was a rich green and that the cherry tree stood in a pool of golden leaves. There was the old swing, just about discernible among the bare black branches of the apple trees, and there the humped shape of the rose arbour where they sheltered from the sun in summer and the two great lilac bushes that filled the house with perfume every spring. He realized with a pang that he would never share these delights again and that he was missing them already.

This would never do, he scolded himself, and he pulled the curtains firmly to shut out his ridiculous thoughts. He would go and talk to old Aunt Phoebe. She would make him see sense.

Aunt Phoebe was in her bedroom, sitting in an easy chair

110

beside the fire, surrounded by a mound of cushions, and reading *Nicholas Nickleby*. But she put the book aside as soon as she heard her nephew's timid knock, and urged the dear boy to come in at once and see her. 'Mr Dickens can wait,' she said, patting the quilt to indicate that Georgie should sit beside her on the edge of the bed. 'All ready, my dear?'

'As ready as I'll ever be, Aunt Phoebe,' Georgie admitted ruefully.

'And that's plenty ready enough, I'm sure,' she told him, smiling at him over the top of her spectacles. 'I shall miss you my dear. You must come back and visit us as often as you can. I shall want to know how you're both getting along.'

Georgie promised at once, but then he sighed, just a little too heavily. Aunt Phoebe looked at him quizzically and smiled again, her long, ugly face remarkably tender. 'Now what's troubling you, my dear boy?' she asked, in exactly the same tone of voice she'd used to say exactly the same thing to him on so many occasions during his childhood. 'Tell your old Aunt Phoebe.'

'What if I fail, Aunt Phoebe?' he said, pushing at the bridge of his glasses, and gazing at her earnestly through the lenses.

'Then you fail, my dear,' she said calmly. 'And succeed the next time. There is always a next time, you know.'

He smiled, partly comforted by her common sense. But only partly.

'You won't fail, my dear boy,' she told him briskly. 'Work hard. Be sensible. Ask your father for advice. He's got a marvellous head for business. You won't fail.'

But there were other failures worrying her nephew. 'It's a big responsibility,' he said. 'Lily's such a dear. She deserves to be happy, Aunt Phoebe. She really does. What if I ...?' He hesitated, facing his fears, but unable to express them. 'I would like to think Lily and I were going to have a really happy marriage. Something strong and special. And lasting. Love should be strong and dependable and certain of itself, don't you think?'

She looked at him for a long time before she answered.' "In love," ' she quoted, ' "there is always one who kisses and one who turns the cheek." You are the one who kisses. Like your father. There is always a risk in being the one who kisses. That

111

can't be avoided. It is in your nature to offer love, so that is what you will do, my dear. Like your father. I see you very like your father sometimes.'

What an extraordinary idea! It surprised Georgie so much he couldn't think what to say next. Nobody had ever compared him to his father before. He didn't know whether to be pleased or shocked.

Aunt Phoebe leaned forward and patted his cheek. 'You will have a long, happy marriage,' she promised. Her skin was dry and wrinkled and entirely without colour, but her eyes gleamed affection at him, even though their sockets had grown pink with age. It hurt him that she looked so very old, especially when she was trying to comfort him.

Then the doorbell rang, and he knew it would be Johnny Ashby, dead on time to take him off to his ordeal by stag party. He kissed Aunt Phoebe gently. 'I hope you're right,' he said.

'Trust me, my dear,' she said. 'I have an instinct for such things.' And she returned to *Nicholas Nickleby*.

Lily was worried too.

She'd packed her bag with the few items of clothing she'd thought prudent to accept from her future father-in-law, she'd washed her hair and ironed her wedding dress and then, feeling at something of a loose end because Dickie was at the stag night and Tilley hadn't come in from her job at the club, she'd had a bath and gone to bed. But not to sleep.

Outside in the yard the rain was pattering against the corrugated iron roof of the bottling shed, and she could hear the wind rushing and swooshing among the yews in the churchyard. Her wedding dress hung on the bedroom door, no longer thin and delicate and pretty as it had been when Aunt Tilley finished it that afternoon, but ghostly white and heavy and foreboding.

She'd been so busy during the previous six weeks she hadn't had time to rest or think. Now, in a quiet house with the last hours of her single life ticking away from her like sand through some terrible, final hour glass, she began to wonder what she had let herself in for. Georgie was very dear and very kind and very gentle, that was undeniable, but what if they weren't suited?

112

And then there was sex. That was worrying too. What if he didn't like her that way? He liked kissing her, and he said he was happy when he was with her, but what if they got to bed and she did something wrong and he found out he didn't like her after all? It was all such a risk. Why, oh why, had she ever agreed to it? He was such a dear. It would be so dreadful if she disappointed him.

She got up and put her old cardigan over her shoulders, and paced up and down the bedroom as her agitation grew. She was so deep in the worry of her thoughts that she didn't hear Tilley's key in the lock and was quite surprised when her aunt put her hand round the bedroom door and switched on the electric light.

'What's up, mate? Can't yer sleep?' she said and the sympathy in her voice was too much for Lily's pent up emotions.

'Oh, Aunt Tilley!' she wailed, her face crumpling with tears. 'I don't want to get married termorrow.'

Tilley took her outburst with uncharacteristic calm. 'No, my duckie, 'course you don't,' she soothed. 'You 'ave a good cry. Best thing in the world.' And she sat her weeping niece down on the bed and allowed her to cry on her shoulder until the worst of her misery was wept away. And in between sobs Lily told her what a poor sort of wife she was going to be, and how much she wanted to make Georgie happy and how she wished she'd never agreed to marry him in the first place. 'I love him such a lot you see, Aunt Tilley,' she said, blowing her nose and wiping away the last of her tears. 'I couldn't bear to have it all go wrong.'

'Put yer coat on,' Tilley said, 'or you'll catch yer death a' cold. What we need's a nice 'ot milk wiv a nip a' whisky in it. Come on.'

It was odd to be back in a chill kitchen, as if they were starting the day all over again, but from the wrong end, working backwards. They revived the fire with bellows and kindling and warmed the milk, lacing it heavily with Dickie's whisky. Then they pulled their chairs right up close to the little warmth of the rekindled fire and began to talk.

'It's just it's so close now,' Lily said, sipping at her drink. 'I couldn't very well go into that church termorrow an' say "No", could I?'

'Could if yer wanted,' Tilley said quite seriously. 'It's a

straight question, will yer, wontcher.'

'Nobody says "No" though, do they?'

'Be a sight better if some of 'em did.'

The new coals were beginning to glow. They could feel the warmth on their shins. Tilley savoured the brandy again, enoying the heat of it as it spread down her throat and into her stomach. 'I should 'a' said "No",' she told her niece. 'I married a wrong 'un the first time. Never thought twice about it. Jest rushed in. Not much older'n you I was at the time. My hat, 'e *was* a wrong 'un an' no mistake.'

This was news to Lily, who couldn't remember a time when her Aunt Tilley hadn't been married to Uncle Dickie. She went on sipping her milk and listening in wonder.

''E drank,' Tilley said. 'Not till 'e was giggly, like yer Uncle Dickie. No. On an' on, till 'e was downright evil with it. An' then 'e used ter knock me about. Fists, boots, stair rods, leg of a chair, anything to 'and. I stood it four years. Must 'a' been out me head. In the end 'e cracked one a' me ribs, an' that done it. I walked out the same day. Left all me things. Just went. Old Martha Goodyear took me in.' She gazed at the fire, remembering.

Under the impact of such a tale, Lily's fears shrank to insignificance. 'Georgie hates getting drunk,' she said. She was sure of that. And she simply couldn't imagine him beating anybody. 'He's ever so gentle. He wouldn't hurt a fly.' But the doubts niggled still, and her frown revealed them to Tilley.

'So what yer worried about? I'd spit it out if I was you,' Tilley advised.

'It seems silly after all you've been saying,' Lily said. 'It's only ... He's ever so timid sometimes. What if we don't make a go of the new shop? It's a big responsibility.'

'Is that all?' Tilley laughed. ''Course you'll make a go of it. Be a little gold mine. An' anyway, you got old Ploochy behind yer. 'E won't let yer fail. You can always depend on old Ploochy.'

That was reassuringly true. Her father-in-law was a great source of strength. She felt better just thinking about him, and was just about to tell Tilley so when Dickie came giggling up the stairs to regale them both with tales of Georgie's party. Her wedding day was already two hours old by the time they all got to bed, and somehow or other she had decided that she would marry Georgie after all.

Chapter Eleven

The sun shone on Georgie's wedding as though it were the beginning of spring and not the middle of November. Nobody could believe it, but there it was. The wind had dropped, there wasn't a rain cloud to be seen, the sky was as blue as a thrush's egg and the sun shone like a blessing, throwing a solid beam of bright light into Tilley's kitchen as the bride picked at her breakfast and dazzling the groom with the power of its reflection from his looking glass.

By midday, when Lily's father arrived at the flat, awkward in his Sunday best and limping because his new shoes were pinching, it was really quite warm. The flowers were delivered and spread across the kitchen table in a collage of sun-heightened colour, the hired cars, disgorging guests at the church gate, gleamed and sparkled, and Lily stood at her bedroom window in her wedding finery, watching the arrivals and warmed by the sunshine she hadn't expected. Georgie made a self-conscious entrance, of course, shoulders hunched and eyes lowered, careful not to look at anybody, not even old Johnny Ashby, his best man, who trotted along beside him watching him anxiously. And there was her mother, scuttling through the gate but pausing briefly to wave up at the window, and Mrs Pelucci, who would soon be her mother-in-law, stepping down from her car like royalty, in a beautiful new coat with a wide fur collar and fur cuffs, very elegant and fashionable. Mr Ploochy seemed to be everywhere she looked, waving his arms about and talking and talking. There was Uncle Dickie, looking ever so grand, and Mr Jones, the gardener, and just walking in through the lych gate Billy Jones and his new wife, Dora, in a very pretty hat. But who were all those other people? She didn't recognize half of them.

But it was too late for second thoughts or third thoughts or even worries. Her father was outside the bedroom door, coughing politely and wondering whether she was ready. It was time to walk across the road and face the ceremony.

Afterwards, when she and Georgie were finally aboard their train and on their way to Torquay, they confessed to one another that the wedding and the reception had been little more than a confused blur. They were glad it was over, and glad that it had turned out such a beautiful day, but they couldn't really remember much about it. Except for Anna's appearance, and that was something they were both relieved to criticize, because she was so overdressed and had so obviously tried to steal the show and hadn't done it.

As the weeks leading up to Georgie's wedding had rushed past, Anna had made up her mind. If Eric hadn't got around to proposing before the reception, she would make jolly sure he proposed to her then. And whatever else might happen, she would certainly be noticed at the ceremony. So she wore a cream silk suit and a spray of bright red roses to match her bright red hat and persuaded Eric to wear the nice pearl grey suit that she knew would make a perfect foil for her flamboyance. The impact of her arrival was extremely gratifying. All Lily's common relations were positively agape, and her father's friends rushed to tell her how attractive she was.

She spent the afternoon basking in the open sunshine of their admiration and deciding that *her* wedding would outshine her brother's in every possible way. Not for her a simple reception in a pub; she must be seen and admired in the banqueting room of the best hotel in Streatham. As Lily's wedding dress was made of crêpe, hers must certainly be satin, and she would need the support of at least four bridesmaids and a bouquet made of lilies and red roses, particularly if they were out of season. She would have a trousseau full of the most glamorous underwear she could find, no matter how expensive it was, and a fox fur to adorn her going-away suit.

The fact that Eric Barnes *hadn't* actually proposed to her yet didn't deter her in the least from the detailed planning of her dream. She felt sure she could entice him to a declaration sooner or later. One wedding often led to another.

Had she known it, her two most powerful allies had already done everything they could to dissuade her 'itchy coo' from making any kind of declaration at all. In fact, if it hadn't been for one of them, Eric would certainly have declined her invitation to this wedding. When she first suggested it, he had been extremely dubious about it. He was beginning to feel he was being manipulated, and it was a feeling he knew too well and didn't enjoy. Accepting her invitation would look far too much like a commitment, and would give her the chance to introduce him to friends and relations as though he were her fiancé. So he said he wasn't sure what his plans were going to be and muttered something about the Foreign Office and Paris. But he had reckoned without his mother.

Mrs Barnes had been acidly annoyed when her son invited the Pelucci girl back to tea for the second time in a fortnight. After her sixth unwanted visit, she felt compelled to speak.

Eric had come home particularly late and although he crept into the house as quietly as she could have wished, as he tiptoed into the kitchen he was whistling some silly tune. Through his teeth, to be sure, in the hope that she wouldn't hear. He'd learned far too many deceitful tricks since he took up with that girl.

'Ah, there you are,' she said, smiling at him coldly as she closed the kitchen door behind her. 'I thought you weren't coming home tonight. Your father's gone up already.' She spoke her reproach in capital letters.

'We went to the Wimbledon Palais, Mater,' he said, pouring out a spoonful of Camp Coffee. 'The dance didn't end till after midnight.'

'It won't do, Eric,' she said sternly, watching him closely to make sure he put the lid back on the bottle, and the bottle back on the shelf. 'Bring your nightcap into the lounge, if you please. We must have this matter out.'

He saw her agitation and was gratified by it. 'You sound like a dentist, Mater,' he mocked, stirring hot water into the black sludge of his coffee.

She ignored the witticism and led him into the lounge as

though to a court of law. They sat one on each side of the empty fireplace, irritated by the prickly moquette of the best armchairs and their mutual dislike of one another. Eric realized that his mother had scored the first point as soon as he sat down. There was no surface available on which he could rest his hot mug except for his legs, for no one was ever allowed to put anything on the floor, so he was reduced to holding the wretched thing uncomfortably in the air, which looked silly, or lowering it onto his knees, which soon became painful. His mother noticed his discomfiture and gave her little chill smile.

'I only say this for your own good,' she began, ominously. 'You know that, don't you? I would be a pretty poor sort of mother if I didn't warn you when you needed warning, wouldn't I?' She always asked him questions like this, knowing perfectly well he couldn't answer them truthfully. He juggled with the mug and gave her an ingratiating smile. 'I really do think you are being rather, shall we say, unwise, to see quite so much of this Pelucci girl. You probably don't realize how easy it is to encourage girls of her class.'

'And just what *is* her class, Mater?' Eric asked sweetly. She'd made a mistake, talking about class. It might just give him the upper hand again.

'She might have a great deal of money. I'll grant you that,' his mother said tartly. 'But money isn't everything. It can't buy breeding.'

Eric smiled at his mother again and began to list Anna's accomplishments. 'She dresses superbly,' he said. 'She's witty. She's smart. She went to a good school. She speaks well. You could hardly call her one of the great unwashed.'

'She's vulgar!' his mother said, stung. 'If I were you I would drop her. She won't do your career any good at all, you know.'

'Ah, but you're not me, are you, Mater,' he said coolly. 'In any case, I can hardly "drop her", as you put it. Not now. I've just agreed to escort her to her brother's wedding.' Which he had. *Just*.

His mother was marvellously annoyed about it, and the decision was made.

And now, here he was, a special guest at the reception, being made quite a fuss of by old man Ploochy, and wondering whether it might not be to his advantage after all to be a member of this family. The Pelucci wedding presents were all good quality, he noticed. No cheap rubbish here. The food was excellent and the champagne was the best he'd ever tasted. Which wasn't saying very much because he didn't actually get to drink champagne very often, if the truth were told. He sat beside his deliberately attractive partner, and ate well, and drank more than he'd ever done in his life, and knew he was enjoying himself.

The champagne was making him feel light headed and gloriously irresponsible. As the cheerful meal continued, he and his little 'bunny wunny woo' began to toast one another, drinking from the same glass, and sitting thigh to thigh, with their faces so close to each other that they were virtually breathing each other's breath. Ordinarily he would have been alarmed in such a position, but today it didn't worry him in the least. In fact, he was actually enjoying it, particularly as he knew it was making them both the centre of admiring attention.

'How's my ickle itchy coo, den?' Anna cooed between sips, fluttering her spiky eyelashes at him.

'Top-hole, Bunny wunny,' he said happily. 'Never felt better in my life.'

'Let's cause a stir,' she suggested, brown eyes sparkling.

'Um,' he said, drinking his delicious bubbly again. He should have been alarmed by the dangerous note in her voice, but in the haze of alcohol and tobacco the possibility of actually running a risk had become peculiarly enticing.

'When Georgie and that silly old Lily have gone off on their silly old honeymoon, let's make an announcement. Give them all a thrill.'

'What sort of thrill, my bunny wunny brown eyes?' What a very difficult word 'thrill' was!

She pressed her finger tip against his cheek bone. 'Trust me,' she pouted.

The party roared and guffawed all around them, a huge, rough, elemental tide that he couldn't have controlled even if he'd wanted to, and now, dizzy with champagne, he didn't know what he wanted. 'Yes,' he said, and was rewarded with a squeal of pleasure and five little pecking kisses clucked against

120

his cheek. Then old man Ploochy was making a speech, and the gramophone was playing and they were all dancing and, although his anxiety was still niggling away underneath it all, he was swept up in the celebration and found it easy to ignore.

That is, until the bride and groom had been cheered into their car, smothered in confetti and confusion, and the bride's mother was wiping her eyes and the guests had drifted back into the pub again, surprised to find that the air was chill and darkness already descending. Then he saw that Anna had seized her father's arm and was whispering in his ear. Alarm flickered up in his chest, but before he had a chance to say anything Ploochy had boomed for attention, one hand on his daughter's shoulder. 'Quiet please, everybody. My little girl has something she want to tell you. Go ahead, my lovebird.'

Anna managed to look as though she might be blushing. 'I thought you'd all like to know,' she said, using her good little girl's voice, 'one wedding is going to lead to another. Eric Barnes and I got engaged this afternoon.'

No, he thought, we didn't. Engaged? Surely not. I never said anything about getting engaged. But everybody was clapping and rushing towards them both to shake their hands and congratulate them in a most gratifying way. Even Lily's relations said how lovely it was, and that it was always the way. In fact there was so much approval and general acclaim he could hardly argue. It wouldn't have looked right, and besides, with all that champagne befuddling his brains, he wouldn't know what to say. So he smiled and agreed and shook hands, and watched as Anna rapidly became the heroine of the second celebration that afternoon.

Only one face was still and thoughtful in that crowd of smiling mouths and approving expressions. And that was the face of Mrs Pelucci, who looked at him dispassionately, her lips closed and her eyes watchful, as her guests clamoured and exclaimed. 'Not entirely a surprise,' she told them calmly, when they rushed to congratulate her too. 'Not to the family,' hiding her annoyance and entire surprise beneath the control of fifty-two years. She smiled gently at her daughter and her new fiancé, and her guests were charmed, and Eric felt a palpable relief, and Anna smiled back as she tried to calculate what her mother was really thinking.

But Alice kept her thoughts to herself until the guests had all gone home, and Minnie and Jesse were back in their own flat, and Anna had gone off to some dance or other to celebrate, and the long demanding day was almost over. Albert had been watching her all afternoon, alerted by the extreme control with which she'd handled every event. Now, as she stood beside the hallstand brushing the fur cuffs and collar of her expensive new coat and arranging it carefully on its hanger ready to be taken upstairs and put away in the wardrobe, he felt he should say something just in case she was blaming him for the surprising turn the reception had taken with Anna's announcement.

'Our Anna is a naughty little thing,' he said, fondly, 'springing it on us like that. I had no idea what she was going to say, you know.'

'Then you shouldn't have allowed her to say anything,' Alice told him, still perfectly calm, and giving all her attention to the coat.

'She's a naughty little thing,' he repeated, hoping she would follow his lead and make light of it too. 'But young, of course. Very young. Perhaps it just a passing fancy, eh?'

'She's a determined little thing,' her mother said, 'and she's made up her mind to marry this young man of hers. Anyone with half an eye can see that.'

'We could refuse our consent,' Albert said. 'If that's what you would like us to do.' He felt he should try to involve them both in any decision this time.

'It wouldn't make the slightest difference,' Alice said, looking up at him. 'I told you, she's made up her mind. He seems a nice enough young man. A good position at the Foreign Office. Well brought up. Nicely educated. I daresay he'll do. And if he's what she wants.'

'I thought you were worried about it,' Albert said, puzzled.

'I don't worry about Anna,' she said. 'She's far too strong willed to come to any harm. No, no. It's my poor Georgie I'm worried about, taking on the burden of a shop and a wife, and God knows what else. He's never been strong. You know that. And now this ...' She gave the coat a brisk, cross shake and turned to go upstairs. 'Still, talking about it won't help, will it?' she said. 'I'm going up. Goodnight, Albert.'

He laid a hand on her shoulder to delay her. Her shoulder was hard with repressed anger. 'He will be all right,' he said, trying to comfort her. 'Lily's a sensible girl. She will look after him, you'll see.'

But she only snorted. What did he know about her dear, gentle boy? She'd loved him and cared for him all these years, and nursed him through fit after fit, and helped him with his studies. She understood him inside and out. And now, just when he seemed to be growing stronger and healthier, she'd been forced to hand him over to a silly little chit of a girl who wouldn't have the faintest idea what to do if he fell ill, and probably wouldn't feed him properly, and would let him wear damp clothes, and certainly wouldn't make him happy. It was a dreadful, dreadful mistake.

As she walked angrily up the stairs, she realized that she was leaving the warmth of the living rooms behind her, and that the air striking her forehead was very cold.

The hotel Albert had chosen for his newly wed son was a splendid place, with a foyer like the entrance to a palace, the ornate ceiling supported by marble pillars and a grand curved staircase leading horribly obviously to the bedrooms on the upper floors. Lily and Georgie were overwhelmed and embarrassed by it, and Georgie blushed so violently as they were escorted up to the 'bridal suite', that his cheeks were hot for a good ten minutes after the bell boy had pocketed his tip and gone away, whistling saucily.

Left on their own in a huge, foreign room, they felt ridiculous, and didn't know where to look or what to say. It seemed to both of them that their suitcases looked pathetic in such opulence, and that they themselves probably matched their luggage. There were too many mirrors reflecting their inadequacy, and acres of expensive red carpet, and the huge bed, with its silken bedspread and an eiderdown as thick as a mattress, was positively daunting. As they had been told by the bell boy that dinner would be served in half an hour, they decided they'd better dress up for the occasion, because that was what people did when they stayed at hotels as grand as this one. So they took it in turns to disappear into the privacy of the bathroom and then, suitably attired, they made their shy way down that public staircase and into the glare of the dining room.

The meal was a nightmare for both of them. They felt so inexperienced and exposed. The menu was printed in French, so they didn't really have much idea what they were ordering, and Georgie didn't like to admit his ignorance and ask, because the waiter was hovering so. The soup was easy enough, but the main course was an almost insurmountable hurdle. In the end he settled for 'boeuf' because that was one word he recognized. They were both relieved when they were served with little rolls of stuffed meat that actually turned out to be sliced beef.

After the meal, afraid of that high bed and the terrifying initiation that it signified, they wandered through into the ballroom and pretended to enjoy the dance. The band played so loudly that very little talk was necessary or even possible, and the floor was crowded with cheerful strangers who didn't look at them. But at midnight that diversion was over and the dancers drifted upstairs. To stay up any longer would have exposed them to notice and ridicule. There was nothing for it but to retire to the challenge of the night. They were both very nervous and, although neither of them admitted it, they were both afraid.

Georgie thought the bedroom looked bigger than ever. Everything about it was an exaggeration, from the moulding curved around its high ceiling like a series of intimidating surf waves to the blood red carpet and that terrible pink silk bed. How could their little timid love find any place to hide in such magnificence?

They dithered, he beside the wardrobe, she at the dressing table, being unnecessarily busy with their luggage, and avoiding each other with red-cheeked determination. Finally he suggested that they really ought to be turning in, and Lily went blushing off to the bathroom again to change into her nightdress, leaving him to undress in such haste that he ripped three buttons off his shirt and pulled the cord out of his pyjama trousers. Then they were back together again, she swathed in white cotton from her neck to her toes, he trying to tie his sagging pyjamas into some semblance of decency around his middle.

It was all terribly embarrassing, and worse was to follow, for soon they would have to get into that terrible bed, and everybody would know what they were doing, the staff in this terrifying hotel, the guests at the wedding, all those awful men with their dirty jokes at the stag party, even their parents. Oh God, how awful! Even their parents!

With the bad timing of extreme embarrassment, they both tried to get into the bed at the same time and from the same side. 'No, no,' Georgie muttered at once. 'You stay there. I'll …' and he rushed away to the other side, his face burning. They crept beneath the sheets, not looking at each other, and lay side by side, not touching and as straight and still as figures on a tomb.

The electric light hung above them as bright as a tropical sun. They looked at it uncomfortably for several seconds. Then Lily suggested, in a very little voice, that perhaps they ought to turn it off, and Georgie blundered from the bed and shuffled to the switch beside the door, holding his pyjamas up with one hand, and pushing his glasses into his nose with the other. The darkness that descended upon them was unexpectedly total, and he realized with distress that now he had no idea where the bed was. He crashed about blindly, stubbing his toe on a chair and narrowly avoiding the chest of drawers, until Lily took pity on him and whispered, 'Over here, Georgie,' so that he could follow the rustle of her voice until he was able to climb back under the silken counterpane again.

They lay in silence and darkness, smelling the starch on their new, stiff sheets and listening to the unfamiliar sounds of the hotel, footsteps in the corridor outside, thumps of doors, somebody whistling, snatches of conversation. Georgie couldn't think what to say and knew from the state he was in that there was nothing he could do.

Presently she tried to make conversation. 'It's been ever such a nice day, hasn't it, Georgie?' Her voice sounded strained and false.

'Yes,' he said. 'The food was very good.'

'It was a nice band.'

'We'll go for a walk on the prom tomorrow.'

'That'll be nice.'

Then there was a long, dark pause, while the hotel thudded

busily around them. This is dreadful, Georgie thought. We're talking to one another like strangers. Perhaps I ought to kiss her. But what good would that do? What can I possibly say?

Then Lily gave an odd little sound midway between a gulp and a sniff, and he realized with shame that she was trying not to cry. He turned in the bed at once and put an arm around her. 'What is it, my darling?' he whispered. 'What's the matter?'

'Don't you love me no more?' she whispered back.

'Oh yes, yes,' he whispered. 'More than ever. You mustn't think that.'

'But you haven't kissed me or anything. Have I done something I shouldn't have?'

'No, no,' he assured her. 'It isn't you. It's me.' He kissed the tears from her nearest cheek, and the salty taste on his lips made his feel guilty and drove him to confess. 'I can't,' he admitted, glad that the darkness was hiding the state of his cheeks. 'Not in this place. It's ... too public.'

She put her hand to his face and stroked his jaw. 'Oh, is that all?' she said with obvious relief. 'I thought it was me.'

'Don't you mind?' he asked, surprised.

'Not if you don't,' she said.

'Oh, Lily,' he said. 'You are a brick!' He was so grateful to her, the dear kind lovely girl.

She was still a brick four days later. And still a virgin, for the trial they both desired and dreaded had been deferred night after timid night. But at least their demoralizing honeymoon was over and even though they had to struggle to the station against a wind that drove the breath back into their lungs they felt they were travelling in the right direction.

'Soon be home,' Lily encouraged as the train rattled through the sodden fields towards London, and the rain spattered against the windows.

But Georgie was feeling worse than he had at the start of this disastrous trip. Home was no longer his mother's comfortable, well furnished, welcoming domain. It was that small, square flat. It would be empty and cold, and they wouldn't know where anything was. And what would they eat? There'd be nothing in the larder. He grew more depressed by the minute and Lily, discreetly watching his reflection in the darkening window, felt more and more responsible for him. Poor Georgie! She would have to make a great fuss of him once they got home. This silly honeymoon had upset him dreadfully.

It was dark and damp when they finally emerged from the underground station at Morden and walked quickly across the road through the drizzle to the black doorway of their shop. Lily was smiling as he fitted his key inexpertly in the lock, and as soon as they were inside the building she ran up the stairs, almost her old self again. But he followed slowly, weighed down by suitcases and forebodings.

The flat struck warm, and there was a familiar and appetizing smell drifting out to them from the kitchen. They switched on the electric light and discovered to their delight that there was a well established fire burning in the grate, the table had been laid for two, there was a hot pot simmering in the new gas oven and there were two saucepans full of potatoes and Brussels sprouts on the hot plate. Alice and Minnie and Tilley had been busy in the flat all afternoon. There was a note signed by all three of them set under a vase of chrysanthemums in the centre of the table.

Vegetables are parboiled so they shouldn't take long. Apple pie in larder. Fire in bedroom might need attention. Hot bricks in bed. Let the tap run for a bit, the water comes out rusty first time. Love, Mum, Aunt Min, Aunty Tilley.

'Oh!' Lily said, her eyes round with surprise and pleasure. 'Aren't they dears!'

After the first mouthful they both decided that this was the best meal they'd tasted since they got married; after the last they knew it was good to be home. They boiled their new kettle and were soon standing side by side at their new deep sink washing their new dishes. Lily's broad white hands grew rosy in the warm suds and, as she worked, strands of her thick hair escaped from under her hair band and fell forward into her eyes. The sight of them moved Georgie to a tender passion he hadn't felt since he proposed. He lifted the hair very gently and stroked it back into place again, breathing in the lovely combination of scents that now surrounded her body, the musk of her damp hair, the traces of apple pie and hotpot near her mouth, spiced with the sulphur of recent travel and the slight sweat of her busy arms.

The unruly hair fell forward again and this time he put down the plate he was drying and turned her gently, so that he could fix the damp tangles more firmly in place. She smiled her thanks, holding her face tilted towards him, thinking how dear he was and how tender.

And gradually love's magic began to stir in both of them again, mystifying and mesmerizing and sensitizing but, for the moment, holding them still, in a trance of growing sensation, so that they stood, almost in one another's arms, their blood beginning to race, their lips tingling for kisses, gazing with all their senses. Their kiss, when they finally began it, was soft and exploratory and infinitely tender. Now, alone in their own home, away from prying eyes and dirty jokes and other people's smutty opinions, their love could begin, quietly and tentatively and gradually. There was plenty of time, for the evening and the marriage were young.

Chapter Twelve

Anna Pelucci was in a hurry. It was a chill Sunday morning late in February, the kind of day when snow is hourly expected and colour has been drained away from everything. Faces squinting between dark hats and upturned collars were pale as paper, brickwork was damp black and the little strip of sky above the herded houses of Bishopsgate was the colour of sweaty putty. But Anna didn't care. She was warm with exertion and excitement, trotting towards Club Row as quickly as her high heels would allow. She had thought of a spiffing wheeze that would make her wedding the talk of the town. She was going to buy a dog to match her wedding dress.

When Georgie and Lily returned so quietly from their honeymoon and settled into married life like some private obscurity she was delighted. It gave her an opportunity for undivided attention and that was what she'd been yearning for all her life. The stage was empty again, ready for her to occupy with her 'great day'. She began to scheme and plan, wheedling and cajoling and enlarging her delicious day dream despite the annoying lack of co-operation she found all around her. Now, surely, with Georgie safely out of the way, her mother would notice that she had a daughter, a pretty, successful daughter who had made a good match and would have a dazzling wedding.

But Alice remained infuriatingly calm about the whole affair, asking unnecessarily practical questions like where were they going to live, or smiling vaguely at her daughter's extravagant excitement. There didn't seem to be anything Anna could say or do to provoke her. It was a terrible disappointment. And even though she tried to make allowances, reminding herself that old Aunt Phoebe was ill in bed with one of her chesty colds and Mummy and Aunt Min were run off their feet, she still felt aggrieved that they paid so little attention to her when she was trying to prepare herself for the most important moment of her life.

And Eric wasn't much better. It was quite extraordinarily difficult even to get him to talk about it. 'Time enough for that later on, Bunny wunny,' he would say as the weeks rushed from under their feet. He made no effort at all. Why, if it hadn't been for her they wouldn't even have a flat to live in. And he hadn't been the slightest bit interested in the decorations or the furniture or anything. She'd had to see to every mortal thing, and sometimes it made her feel hard done by and irritated. But she kept her feelings under control and smiled a great deal, particularly when she was feeling depressed, and laughed and chattered and did everything she could to appear the happy, excited bride.

The only person who had behaved really well all through the three short months of her engagement was her father. He'd provided the deposit for a lovely new flat in the Grand Parade, right near Raynes Park Station, decided that the wedding would be in April, booked the hotel for the reception and bought her everything she asked for. Even this dog.

'What an idea!' he'd approved when she told him. 'Trust my lovebird to make a splash. We give 'em all something to think about, eh?' And he'd taken out his wallet at once, promising to keep it all a secret from Eric, so that he could be as surprised and impressed as everybody else on the great day.

Anna liked Club Row. It was so splendidly noisy and vulgar, and it made her feel marvellously superior, walking between the hucksters in their rough moleskins and their filthy caps, aware that she looked stylish and wealthy in her clean, fashionable clothes.

But of course what you really came to Club Row for were the animals. Hundreds and hundreds of them and all the cutest little things you could imagine; puppies dangling patiently from lifted fists, or pushing their squashy noses out of hip pockets, or bundling about in their baskets like roly poly puddings; kittens curled in sleep, or washing their tiny paws, or scratching their fleas, or gazing, blue-eyed and mute, from the ruffs of fur the cold was fluffing about their faces; song birds as bright as jewels behind their tiny bars, chickens in crates, squawkingly affronted by every movement; rabbits, dumb and dejected, their bulging eyes as lustrous as the sea under the moon.

But, as far as she could see, no pure white dog. There were dogs everywhere, in every shape and every colour combination of black and white and brown and grey, patched and spotted, mottled and marred, skinny dogs as smooth and dark as liver, and great shaggy heaps like tousled sheepskins. But not a single one that would suit her purpose. She knew exactly what she wanted, a pretty little dog, bridal white and very fluffy so as to match the frills that circled the hem of her dress. A very special animal.

Waving away the offer of a mud-spattered mongrel, she pushed past a group of men who were haggling over the price of a nanny goat, and found the poodle.

She could see at once that it was a noble animal, standing there so still and upright among the dirty straw and all those yapping mongrels. A dog with a pedigree. And a studded collar.

The stall holder noticed her attention and recognized a mug when he saw one. He'd been trying to offload this particular animal for more than three weeks now, nasty, cantankerous little brute, and had already decided that if nobody bought it this morning he'd take it down to Battersea Dogs' Home.

'Pedigree,' he offered, running his hand heavily along the tight curls on its back and bullying it not to snap at him. 'Long as yer arm! Real class, this little feller. Lovely disposition. Jest the thing fer a pretty young lady like you. Whatcher think, Bob?'

His assistant agreed at once. 'Lady's dog, that is,' he assured Anna. 'Come from a very good 'ome. Titled lady.'

The poodle looked more charming by the minute. 'How much?' she asked, trying to appear businesslike.

'Fer you darlin', 'alf a guinea. Ten an' a kick. Cheap at the price.'

It wasn't until the bargain was sealed and Anna had handed across a sixpenny bit and a ten shilling note that he relented enough to warn her. 'Need a firm 'and,' he said as the new pair trotted away.

But Anna wasn't listening. She was back in her fantasy,

imagining herself posing charmingly in the church porch, with her handsome husband at her side and her pretty dog at her feet. She could already see the picture and the caption in the *News and Mercury* waiting to greet her when she came radiantly back from her honeymoon in Paris. 'Film star wedding for beautiful local bride.' Her mother would have to admire her then.

Whether because it was stunned by so many new experiences or because it had decided to match its new mistress and project a good image, the poodle was impressively well behaved on the homeward journey. It sat on her lap in the tube train, occasionally licking her cheek or her nose in a most flattering display of public affection. We make a very pretty pair, she thought, admiring their reflection in the black window opposite them. By the time they reached Tooting she had decided that he was a perfectly lovely little dog and she would call him Rudy, after the late lamented Valentino. 'Who's my booful wooful, den?' she cooed as she carried him up the escalator. 'Won't they just love my booful?'

They didn't.

'What *have* you got there?' Alice said with extreme disapproval as the poodle trotted into the kitchen, its sharp nose raised towards the succulent smell of roasting beef.

'His name's Rudy,' Anna said, realizing with a sinking heart that she would have to brazen this out, after all. 'Isn't he just a little duck? I've just bought him.'

'Whatever for?'

'Because I wanted him.'

'Oh, how silly!' Alice said, mixing the gravy powder to a smooth paste, her hands brisk with displeasure. 'We've got quite enough pets in this house already. We don't need a dog. What were you thinking of? It'll upset Chunky terribly.'

Anna didn't care a bit for Chunky. He was a huge, marmalade cat who tore holes in the cushions and dragged fish heads about the kitchen and was never rebuked. It would do him good to have his nose put out of joint. 'He won't go anywhere near your precious Chunky,' she said. 'He'll stay with me, won't you my booful?' and she picked the poodle up and tried to cuddle it defensively in her arms.

'Where did you get it?' Minnie asked, putting the dinner plates into the oven.

'Only a few more weeks,' Minnie comforted the old lady, 'an' then he'll be gone.'

'Not before time!' Aunt Phoebe growled.

What with Rudy's misbehaviour and her mother's demoralizing lack of interest, Anna grew more and more distraught as her wedding day approached. She fussed over every little detail, checking and re-checking every single arrangement and praying for the sun to shine. Georgie had had a beautiful day, so she really ought to be allowed something just as good or better.

It rained. A steady, pervasive drizzle that darkened the sky and permeated their clothes so that the guests scuttled off to church hidden by umbrellas. Anna was terribly upset. Even the Fates were against her, and today of all days, her own special day when everything ought to go right. She was tearful when the car arrived to take her to St Nicholas'.

'It's so unfair, Dadda,' she sobbed. 'I don't ask for much, goodness knows. Just a little sunshine, that's all! I shall look a perfect freak in all this rain.'

Albert tucked her cold hand into the crook of his arm and patted it encouragingly. 'Never you mind, my lovebird,' he said. 'It will clear. You'll see. Don't cry or you'll make your pretty nose red. By the time you come out the church it will be a lovely day. Come along, Rudy!'

They made a dash along the front path with the poodle cavorting at their heels and Albert's umbrella bouncing ineffectively over their heads. But that only made matters worse, for once they were settled in the car she discovered that her expensive white silk stockings had been spattered with raindrops, and Rudy's ribbon had come undone, and one of his rosebuds was already crushed.

Fortunately there wasn't time for her to be too upset, because the journey to the church only took a couple of minutes and then they were at the church gate and she had to concentrate on being a beautiful bride. But there was another disappointment waiting for her in the porch in the shape of Mr Collyer, the church warden, who explained, very softly and politely, that Rudy would have to wait outside during the ceremony, because animals were not allowed inside a place of worship.

He waited with very bad grace, whimpering and snorting as

the rain dampened his pampered fur and the sodden red ribbon dripped dye across his nose. When the hymns were sung he howled so loudly that they could hear him at the altar rail, and when the congregation finally emerged into the faint sunlight Albert had promised, he was overcome with excitement and started up into such a paroxysm of leaping and barking that Mr Collyer let go of his lead. Finding himself suddenly and inexplicably free, he rushed off at once to cock his leg against as many gravestones as he could manage, knocking down several pious urns and trampling the most recent floral tributes underfoot as he went.

Anna controlled her temper and her tears because the photographer was looking her way, but her thoughts were murderous. She'd give him such a whacking when they caught him, nasty, disobedient thing!

'What a revolting little animal!' Eric said. 'Who brought *that* to my bunny wunny's wedding?'

She smiled radiantly at the camera and didn't tell him. Perhaps somebody would dry the horrid creature and she could have another photograph taken at the reception.

But at the reception nobody was interested in a poodle and, in fact, there were some people who didn't even pay sufficient attention to the bride and groom. For Lily Pelucci was wearing a smock and was more than happy to confess to inquisitive guests that she was eating for two and that the little stranger would be arriving some time at the beginning of September. Anna was pale with anger at such treachery, but she smiled and was gracious, and smiled and was radiant, and smiled again until her jaws ached with the effort.

'I'll never forgive her,' she hissed to Eric when the two of them had cut the cake and were resettling themselves in the seats of honour again. 'How could she be so vile? Nobody looked at me for nearly an hour after she came in in that ridiculous smock. I'll never forgive her! Never!'

But Eric wasn't the least bit interested in the petty squabbles of his two new female relations and didn't even bother to comment. As far as he was concerned the wedding had been a great success. Anna looked like a bride in a Hollywood picture, shimmering in her silk dress with her arms full of red roses and her hair a dark romantic shadow under the expensive lace of her veil. Just the sight of her smiling her way down the aisle had annoyed his mother almost to distraction. And his father was uncomfortably out of place beside the easy wealth of the Peluccis in his cheap suit, with his buttonhole pinned to the wrong side of his jacket. It was a most gratifying sight.

It had taken a week of calculation for Eric to come to the conclusion that the engagement that Anna had wished on him would actually turn out to be rather a good thing. His mother had been speechless with horror when he'd told her the good news, and that was a rewarding start; and then, when he had asked his immediate boss at the office, very politely and tentatively of course, whether it might be possible for him to apply for a higher grade in view of the fact that he was hoping to get married, the idea had been received with a certain cautious approval, which was extremely gratifying.

So he had allowed his bunny wunny woo to go ahead with her plans and had been silently impressed by the amount of money she had managed to coax out of old man Ploochy. The flat in Raynes Park was very grand, twice as big as his parents' poky little terraced house and furnished most expensively and in the most up-to-date style. Even Rollo would admire it, he felt sure, and his mother would be pea green with envy. He was embarking on a completely different life style, higher and richer than anything he'd ever experienced, but fortunately not more cultured. For although Anna was going to bring a comfortable source of income with her to the marriage she had wished on him, she didn't hold all the trump cards. She wasn't intelligent and she didn't know anything at all about art and culture. In that respect at least he would always be able to outshine her and keep her in place. It was one reason why he had chosen to honeymoon in Paris, even though it was prohibitively expensive. He hadn't actually set foot inside the Louvre yet, but at least he knew where it was.

And then, of course, it had made him feel so splendidly superior to be able to drop the casual information into his wedding speech that he and Anna would soon be off to the 'capital of romance'. He'd said it well, he knew, with just the right assurance, as though holidays in Paris were the regular thing with him. Even Mrs Pelucci had smiled. And the chief bridesmaid had said, 'How ripping!' with genuine envy. As he and Anna posed for their last photograph, their faces framed by the window of their splendid car, he could see the caption in the local paper already, 'Handsome couple honeymoon in Paris.'

And then some fool opened the door just as the car was pulling away and everybody was watching and cheering, and dropped that revolting white poodle onto the floor between them.

'Where are we taking the pooch, Bunny woo?' he asked, hoping it wasn't far. He was still smiling through the window, so he couldn't show her how cross he was.

Anna turned and glanced at the dog, who was busily eating the rosebuds on its collar. 'Oh, my poor ickle wickle Wudy,' she wailed. 'Just look at the state of my poor diddums.'

'Yours!' he said, his eyes bolting with horrified surprise.

'Yes,' she said, pouting at him prettily. 'I bought him just for you, my darling. Wasn't that ripping!'

He knew in that instant that this was what he'd been afraid of from the beginning. Foreigners were so unpredictable. Charming and exotic and romantic, yes, but you never knew what they were going to do next. He'd known in some instinctive way that he might have trouble with this girl, she being half Italian. But to be confronted with it so soon was very hard. Why, she hadn't even given him one trouble free day.

'What are you going to do with him while we're away?' he asked, staying admirably calm despite his rising anger.

'Nothing,' she said, smiling deliberately sweetly, because he seemed to be in some sort of mood. 'He's coming with us. Aren't you, my booful?'

'He can't,' he said with relief. 'They won't let him through Customs. There are regulations about dogs.' Trust her not to have thought of it. He felt almost cheerful again at her stupidity.

She didn't believe him. 'They'll let you through, won't they, my booful,' she said to the obnoxious creature. So Eric smiled his superior smile and decided to wait for her to learn the hard way.

The Customs shed at Dover was a great, echoing hangar occupied by a horseshoe-shaped counter and an army of stolid, blue-uniformed officials. It made him feel quelled and obedient just to look at them. She won't get away with anything here, he thought, as he and his bride and their disreputable animal approached for scrutiny. And sure enough, the dog provoked instant inquiry. Was it travelling with them?

'Of course,' Anna said, looking as pretty as she possibly could.

'Have arrangements been made for the statutory six months quarantine on your return?'

'No,' she said, blank-faced with surprise.

'In that case, madam, I'm afraid it will not be possible for you and your husband to proceed.'

This wasn't at all what Eric had expected. If the silly dog was going to hold up their honeymoon it would have to come with them after all. He decided to take the conversation over at once before any more damage was done, and lie their way out of any further delay. 'We don't intend to bring the animal back into the country, officer,' he explained meekly. If there was one thing he really knew about, it was placating authority. 'We're taking it across for a friend.' He could sense Anna's astonishment but mercifully she didn't argue.

'Ah, I see, sir,' the officer said. 'If we could just have your friend's name and address?'

He gave the first name that came into his head and the address of the boarding house in which he'd stayed the last time he'd worked in Paris. Then documents were produced and stamped and fixed inside his passport and with remarkably little fuss they were allowed through and on to the boat.

'How clever you are!' Anna said flatteringly as she tottered up the gang plank behind him. 'Who got my ickle Wudy through, den?' she lisped at the poodle. 'I knew it would be all right, didn't I? I couldn't have left my ickle Wudy behind, now could I?'

More's the pity, Eric thought, looking sourly at their bedraggled travelling companion. Let's hope the stupid thing knows how to behave on board ship. He wasn't at all sure how any of them would behave during the crossing, especially if it was as rough as it had been the last time he came over. He'd been so sick on that occasion he'd been reduced to lying on the deck groaning, and the thought that he might disgrace himself this time too, when he would be on show in front of his new bride, was extremely worrying.

But fortunately for them both the sea was as calm as silk and although the smell of hot oil made them both feel a bit queasy the boat did nothing more alarming than rock them gently as it hissed through placid green waters. And Rudy lay at their feet and slept, and was admired by several other passengers as they passed, which lifted both their spirits considerably. Even in mid channel the rollers were easy and the sunset spectacular enough to take their minds off possible seasickness. Then, as the evening drew in and the lights were lit, they stumbled down the companionway to the restaurant and pretended to enjoy a meal, being very animated and lively, and secretly feeding unwanted morsels to their unwanted pet underneath the table.

It was late at night when they finally arrived at their hotel in Paris, and they were both exhausted with travel and the superhuman effort they'd been making. The Hotel l'Univers, on which Eric had begrudgingly spent so much of his bachelor salary, was a tall stone building that brooded above the narrow pavements of the Rue Saint Michel, dark and shuttered and forbidding. Like a fortress, Anna thought as she gazed up at it, shivering slightly in the night air.

The front door stood ajar and led them to a small, square, ill-lit vestibule where a huge oak counter barred their way and there was nobody to greet them. Three of the walls that surrounded them were painted bottle green and the fourth appeared to be either the side of a long cupboard or the wall of a corridor, since the lower half of it was made of panelled wood and the upper half consisted of impenetrably dark window panes.

They stood together in the gloom pretending not to be worried. Eric struck the bell on the counter with the palm of his hand and shuffled his feet and scowled with annoyance, but neither of them said anything for fear of revealing their feelings.

One of the panels in the fourth wall swung open and became a door. Now they could see that it wasn't a cupboard after all but a little narrow room just big enough to contain a small table, a cane chair and the concierge, who came growling forward, wiping her hands on her long black skirt. She greeted them mechanically and in French, 'M'sieur, madame.'

All through the journey Anna had done her best to convince herself that this honeymoon was going to be a most exciting experience, bohemian and daring and just sufficiently disreputable to impress her friends. She had already decided that she could make an excitement out of most of the unpleasant things she'd had to endure so far, the awful stink on the Metro, for example, and those dreadful wooden benches on the train, even that terrible lavatory at the Gare du Nord, which was really no more than a smelly pit with a wooden seat across it. But the concierge took her breath away.

At the very least she had expected some comfort and courtesy once they reached their hotel, even if it *was* foreign. They should have been greeted by the manager, in evening dress of course, and speaking impeccable English. Not by this extraordinary woman. Why, she was positively vulgar, so short and squat, with whispy grey hair that looked as if it hadn't seen a comb for days, and the most dreadful teeth, little more than stumps really. And she didn't seem to understand English at all, but just went on gabbling at them in some sort of low class French, and far too quickly, so that they couldn't understand a word she was saying. Eric did his best, speaking very, very slowly and shouting at her so as to help her understand, but she just looked straight through him and continued to speak in her own incomprehensible language, sounding the words through her nose, and not smiling.

The duologue went on for several unproductive minutes but finally the old lady shrugged her black shoulders, opened the register with a determined slap and said a word that Eric recognized. 'Sign.'

'Why didn't you say that before?' he asked huffily and signed the book in his carefully elaborate handwriting, 'Mr and Mrs Barnes, Raynes Park.' The concierge studied the entry, her jaws working. It seemed to satisfy her, for she snapped the book shut again and unhooked one of the huge keys that hung on a greasy board behind her.

It was labelled No. 10, but she didn't hand it across to them. Instead, she opened another door in that odd panelled wall and led them out through a short corridor into the chill of an inner courtyard, where the hotel frowned down upon them on

141

all four sides. But they hardly had time for more than a glimpse at it before she had trotted them across the cobbles and into the far corner of the building, where they found themselves standing at the foot of a steep spiral staircase.

'Deuxième étage,' she said, slapping the key into Eric's palm. Then she switched on an inadequate naked light and was gone.

They had no idea where room 10 was, and were both aggrieved at being treated so curtly. As they climbed the stairs, with Rudy whimpering behind them and their suitcases banging against the walls in that narrow space, they told one another how cross they were and said they would certainly complain to the management in the morning. Things got worse when they reached the first floor, because the light suddenly switched itself off, leaving them in total darkness, and just at the moment when they were setting off along the corridor. It took them a long time to find another light switch, and even longer to convince one another that room 10 wasn't on the first floor. Anna felt fairly certain that *deuxième* meant two, but she didn't want to point that out to her new husband, because that would have been a bad way to start and not at all romantic.

By this time Eric was feeling more disagreeable than he cared to admit and Anna was beginning to wonder whether a honeymoon abroad was really such a good idea after all. Room 10 turned out to be at the very end of a long corridor, but at least the great key fitted the lock, and then they were in their bedroom at last, and romantically on their own together. If they didn't count Rudy, who scrabbled into the room, his claws scraping the linoleum, and settled down at once in the middle of the bed, arranging his body in an undignified squat with one hind leg swinging stiffly in the air below his chin, and proceeded to bite his toes.

The bed made Anna feel romantic at once. For this was the moment she'd been looking forward to ever since Georgie's wedding, the marvellous moment when she would make her glamorous entrance in her beautiful new negligee and Eric would take her in his arms, like Rudolph Valentino, and kiss her until she saw stars and wanted to swoon. She took her night things out of her case, and found her dear little dolly bag

142

of make-up and swept off to find the bathroom. 'I shan't be a half a minute, Itchy coo,' she promised, encouraging him with her eyes.

She was over half an hour, for although she undressed in a few minutes, it took a long time to arrange her hair in just the way she wanted and to make her face up to perfection. Because, of course, nothing less than perfection would do. After all, this was her wedding night. The greatest night in a woman's life.

Left on his own, Eric beat the dog off the bed and unpacked his clothes, hanging them neatly away in the hideous wardrobe that bulged in one corner of the room. Then he undressed and donned his new pyjamas and admired his reflection in the dressing table mirror. Now that his very first sexual encounter was so close, he felt ill at ease and needed to reassure himself that he looked good, and that what he was about to do was perfectly natural and nothing to be alarmed about. Like masturbating, only inside a female. His female, who'd promised to love and obey him, and was now committed to his pleasure, available for his use any time he wanted. Better than masturbating, probably, because it didn't have all those unpleasant consequences, like premature baldness and bad breath and moral decay.

The odd thing was that when they'd first got engaged this was the moment that had been most pleasurable to contemplate. It had made him horny immediately just to think about it. Now, as the minutes shadowed past and Anna still didn't reappear, he began to wilt and worry.

The light switched itself off for the second time, and he walked across to the window in the darkness and opened the shutters so that he could look down into the courtyard. But there was no comfort for him there. It looked so dreadfully foreign. He only had one cigarette left, and he'd been saving that to smoke afterwards, but he decided that his nerves were too finely strung and his present need too great. He lit up and was annoyed to notice that his hands were trembling.

But eventually Anna drifted back into the room, taking care to switch on the light so that she would stand revealed in the middle of the room in her exotic negligee. It was a well staged entry and Eric found that he could rise to the occasion after all.

'Darling!' he said, nipping out his cigarette between finger and thumb and burning himself in the process. 'You look ripping!'

'Do you really truly think so?' she breathed, drifting towards him, negligee outstretched and thinking, now he will take me in his arms and kiss me and we will sink together towards the bed, like they do in the pictures.

He received the impact of her travelling body just as he was shifting his weight from one foot to the other. Caught off balance, he toppled backwards with her heavy perfume clogging his nose and her trailing draperies obscuring his sight. They fell together, not gently and gradually into the feather mattress, but awkwardly across the corner of the bed. He kissed her, nevertheless, when he'd disentangled himself, and tried to roll her over onto her back, because it was really rather ignominious for her to be on top.

'Does 'oo love me den?' she asked, reminding him of the things he ought to be saying.

'Oodles and oodles,' he said as the light went out with a click. He was trying to lift all her flowing clothing out of his way. What on earth had she got on? There were yards and yards of it.

She began to help him, but discreetly, of course, hauling at the silk with her free hand. She could understand how he felt. Passion was driving him frantic. 'Are you really truly mad with love for me?' she said.

He tried to force her legs apart with his knee. 'Don't talk!' he commanded sternly. Her cooing was making it difficult for him to concentrate on his pleasure, and he was afraid he might wilt again if he didn't hurry. Where was he supposed to put it? There might be a wrong place where it could go by accident. How was he going to put it in the right place with this stupid nightdress all over everything? He jabbed at her crossly and found, to his relief and surprise, that he was inside.

'Ow!' she said, shocked into honesty by the violence of his attack. 'You're hurting me!'

He took no notice at all, but went on banging into her, thump, thump, thump, like a great sweating machine. She didn't like it at all, but couldn't think how she could get him to stop. The weight of his torso on her chest was making it difficult to breathe and she was extremely uncomfortable down there. This is vile, she thought. Not a bit romantic. He worked away in silence, a trick he'd learned since randy adolescence had made him aware of his mother's sharp hearing. This is the life, he thought, concentrating hard. If he kept on like this for just a little longer he'd be there, and it felt as though it was going to be a big one.

But at that moment the poodle became excited by the smell of what they were doing and trotted to the side of the bed, brightly lecherous and eager to join in the action. Eric's bouncing buttocks were massively attractive and so was his right pyjama leg, which was flapping that erotic smell straight towards him. He seized a mouthful of jerking cloth between his teeth and gave it a tug, and then another and another, growling happily. At first neither the sound nor the movement were enough to break through Eric's determined concentration, but what happened next certainly was. Now fully aroused, the poodle leapt upon the leg, seizing it firmly with his forepaws, and started to perform his own act, thrusting away at the hot flesh underneath him.

Eric swore and tried to kick him away, but the dog held on, eyes glazed, rump jerking convulsively. 'Jesus!' Eric said, still thrusting, but weakly and with very little effect. 'That bloody dog of yours! Why d'you bring a bloody silly dog on honeymoon? Stupid fool. Get off! Get off! Bloody thing!'

'*I* didn't bring it,' Anna said, trying to struggle free. '*You* were the one. You got it through customs.' She couldn't see anything round his heavy body but she could hear the poodle panting and knew that something very odd was going on. Her struggle was Eric's undoing. He came at once, and most unsatisfactorily, with the dog still pounding at his leg and his concentration completely gone.

Weeping with humiliation and disappointment he rolled away from Anna and tore the dog from his leg, flinging it against the wardrobe where it lay whimpering and still jerking. Then he sat on the edge of the bed and glowered at it, willing himself to regain his breath and his composure.

'What are you doing?' Anna demanded, feeling a momentary spasm of pity for the poor thing despite her frustration. 'You'll hurt it.'

'I'll kill it,' he said viciously. 'If it jumps on me again I'll kick it to bloody death.'

'Oh, that's nice, I must say,' she said, afraid and angry. 'A poor, dumb, defenceless animal ...'

He flung himself down on the bed, turning his back on her and pulling the covers firmly under his chin. 'Shut up!' he said wildly. 'I've heard enough from you for one night.' Then he closed his eyes and escaped into sleep, refusing to have anything more to do with her, or the dog, or the wretched honeymoon. They could all go to the devil.

Anna felt she had been left all alone. For a long time she lay in the odd-smelling darkness trying to cope with her disappointment and wondering whether sex was always like that and how on earth they would behave to one another next day. When she finally drifted into an uncomfortable sleep, she dreamt that she was being gored by a bull and all her friends were laughing at her. She woke in a sweat and put out a tentative hand to her new husband, hoping he would open his eyes and comfort her. But he slept on, in the most aggravatingly peaceful way, and wouldn't be woken.

When she woke for the second time it was morning. Shrill French voices were shouting in the courtyard below her, and Eric was up and dressed. He seemed to be quite himself again, sitting at the dressing table brushing his Brylcreemed hair neatly down onto his skull.

'Good morning, Bunny woo,' he said cheerfully. 'Lovely day!'

'Hello, Itchy coo,' she said, relieved that they were back in their easy baby talk again.

He shone his film star smile at her, briefly, but with the air of a man bestowing forgiveness, as though she had been in the wrong the night before. It was horribly irritating but she couldn't run the risk of being annoyed about it, not now that they were behaving in their usual way. So she got up instead, rubbing the sleep out of her eyes, and realized from the traces of mascara on the side of her fingers that her make-up must have smudged and run during the night. She'd better get down to the bathroom pretty quickly before he took a close look at the mess she was in. 'Shan't be a jiffy, darling,' she said and ran from the room, her streaky face averted.

When they emerged to the cultural delights of Paris an hour or so later, they had carefully restored their precious necessary image. They were bright and happy and attractive, the very picture of honeymoon bliss.

'Let's go to the Louvre, shall we, Bunny wunny?' the bridegroom said, feeling cultured and superior and manly.

'Oh let's, let's!' the bride gushed, hoping it wouldn't be too much of a bore. 'That'll be ripping fun!'

They had established their pattern.

Chapter Thirteen

Time was catching up with Mary Ann and pushing work and perplexities upon her. So much had happened during the last three years she'd hardly had time to notice how the months were skidding past, yet here she was, in the top class of the Juniors with the preliminary of the dreaded scholarship only a few weeks away, struggling with the two exercises from the Wheaton Scholarship Book that old Miss Wingate had set for homework that night.

The arithmetic was easy enough, but grammar was a constant puzzle. Why should there be a right and a wrong way of using simple words like 'was' and 'were', for instance? And if everybody she knew used the wrong way, how did that come about? There wasn't any sense in it. 'Proper English,' Miss Wingate explained, over and over again, peering at her special pupils over the top of her glasses in her odd, owlish way, 'proper English. The language of Shakespeare. And if you want to go to grammar school, my dears, that's the way you'll have to speak.' She was right about most things, Mary thought, so she was probably right about this, but it was annoying, just the same. Was Ma's English improper then? Improper, like a fraction. Only a part of what she ought to be. As though there was something lacking in her. That couldn't be right. Ma was such a love and so clever. She understood things quicker than anyone, even Miss Wingate, who was usually very ponderous despite the propriety of her English. It was a puzzle and it was a nuisance, because it meant she had to think about every single word before she wrote it, and that slowed her down and made her feel frustrated and irritable. Like she was now, sitting at the table before the stove, struggling with 'was' and 'were'.

Outside, rain was falling in monotonous sheets from a sky as grey and threatening as a battleship. It had rained off and on for nearly a fortnight and Bermondsey was sodden, the drains clogged and the gutters a muddy torrent. Roofs leaked, kitchen walls ran with moisture and in the sparsely heated upper rooms black mould grew on the ceilings and the furniture was damp to the touch. All the old people in the Court sniffed and spat and complained that they were 'that bunged up' they couldn't breathe, and the kids had chesty colds and runny noses, despite being greased for the winter. It was January, and the year and the population were at their lowest ebb.

The Thames, on the other hand was in full spate, its waters a swift running current, oily khaki in colour and devastating in impact. On the Essex marshes it bit at its banks like a voracious snake, scooping out handfuls of soil and churning them off into the midstream torrent; and in the mean streets that crowded beside the docks, worried councillors watched its width and its growing aggression and made what plans they could in case they had to cope with a flood.

A group of them had gone down to Cherry Orchard Pier that very morning to watch the high tide. 'Wouldn't take much,' they told each other soberly as the angry water slapped against the black sides of the warehouses, and tossed the anchored boats like corks, 'wouldn't take much to 'ave that lot over the side an' in the streets. Only need a strong wind an' high tide ter come tergether an' then God 'elp us!'

Ma and Pa and old Ploo had been quite worried about going off to the pub and leaving her on her own tonight. Silly things. They all made such a fuss over her. It was like having three parents. 'You run along,' she'd said to them. 'I shall be all right, you'll see. Old enough and ugly enough ter look after meself. If there's a flood I shall swim round the Red Lion and tell yer. Promise.'

'Don't yer think you'd be better wiv Eth?' Ma had said, her forehead all wrinkled up with concern.

'I'm nice an' warm in 'ere by the fire. Go on, you go. You'll be late fer the meetin' else.' It was the management committee tonight, upstairs in The Red Lion, as she knew because she'd had to do her piano practice in the bar because they were getting the room ready. And Dr Salter, their nice Labour M.P., was going to be there, too. 'Go on, you mustn't miss it.'

So they'd gone, leaving her to get on with her homework in peace. Which was just what she wasn't doing. She'd done the sums, but now she was sitting with her feet on the fender, just thinking. There'd been so many changes in the last three years. It was as if the pace of her life had been altered. Quickened somehow. So now and then she needed to pause and think things through. To make sense of what was going on.

They still lived in Cherry Court, and the bugs still bit furiously especially in warm weather, and there were still black beetles in the outside lav. And the cops still came marching down in pairs to make arrests and then got set upon by everybody in the street, which was fun. And the place still stunk of Peek Frean's biscuits and Sarson's vinegar and all the rotting debris in the Thames. But at least they could get a decent bath nowadays or go for a swim in the new Municipal Baths in Grange Road. Best municipal baths in the whole of England they were, and very nice too. And she *could* swim. Ma had taught her. They'd had six whole days at the seaside, two every year, and Ma had taught her to swim on the very first one, and she'd got such a tan in the bright sunlight she'd come home with her skin almost the same colour as old Ploochy's.

He was so much a part of her family now she could hardly remember a time when he hadn't been there. And with the maturity of her eleven years she could now see how good he was to them. She and Ma weren't nearly so skinny, for a start, and they had much better clothes to wear and didn't catch nearly so many coughs and colds in the winter time, which Ma said was all on account of being better fed.

And then there was the piano playing. She'd been having piano lessons for more than two years now, and that certainly wouldn't have happened if it hadn't been for Ploochy, because Pa could never have afforded the fees, no matter how much he might have wanted to. 'An excellent decision,' Miss Wingate had said when Pa told her about it. 'Good per se, and then of course it will give her the edge when she comes up for interview. They like our pupils to offer something extra. It shows they've got what it takes.' She always spoke with such confidence, as if Mary was bound to pass the scholarship and be called for interview, almost as a matter of course. It was very reassuring to her. And she enjoyed playing the piano.

Especially now that she'd learned to sightread. Every afternoon, as soon as school was over, she took her music case to Marigold Street and knocked at the side door of The Red Lion, and Mrs Oxbury let her in to practise, sometimes upstairs on the best piano, sometimes in the bar where the piano was tinny with spilt beer and didn't sound half as nice.

Now and then, Tom Oxbury would come in and listen for a while. The first time he'd done it she'd been rather embarrassed and played an awful lot of wrong notes, because he was a big boy, in the third year of St Olave's Boys, and he looked very grown up. But after a few weeks she got used to him, and now he was really quite useful because he knew the way they went on in grammar schools and she was beginning to feel she ought to find out. Just to be prepared. She'd spent quite a lot of time just recently discussing the vexed questions of pronunciation and grammar with him, and he'd made her secretly rather cross because he agreed with Miss Wingate and assured her that she'd have to speak proper English once she got to St Olave's Girls so the sooner she got used to it the better. But he was a kind boy and he'd been ever so nice to her that horrible time when the kids called Pa a gargoyle.

She'd been red-hot with anger, and trembling at the unfairness of it. "'E ain't!' she'd yelled, over and over again. "'E ain't!'

'You an' your stuck-up pa! 'E is too.'

'Shut yer face!'

'Cry baby, cry! Stick yer finger in yer eye!'

"'E ain't! 'E's the best man in the 'ole a' Bermon'sey. Better'n your mouldy ol' dad, any day.' Her chief tormentor's dad was in the Scrubs.

They'd rushed from abuse to blows very quickly after that and soon she'd been kicking and screaming and quite beside herself. It had been Tom Oxbury and his friends who had pulled them apart, and Tom had taken her off to The Red Lion to clean her face and get over it before she went home. And while she bathed her eyes, he'd talked and talked. Reasonably and calmly and sensibly, just like his old man.

'No shame in bein' ugly, Mo,' he'd said. 'We can't help what we look like. None of us can. It's what we do that counts. Look at my Dad. Now he *is* a gargoyle if you like. And nobody thinks none the worst of him, now do they?'

And it was true. Mr Oxbury was terribly ugly. He was well over six foot tall and built like a prize fighter, with massive shoulders and ham fists and knotted muscles that made his neck look like a column of cabled ropes. And his skull was grotesque. It wasn't rounded or egg-shaped, like everybody else's, but looked as though it had been moulded by a pair of butter pats, being curiously rectangular, flat on the top and with long straight sides in which his ears whorled like deformed shells. He had so little forehead and such a great deal of jaw that he looked as if his head has been fitted on upside down. His eyes were pig small and pale grey but his nose grew heavier and fleshier as it descended and his mouth was as wide as his brow. Locally he was known as the Ox, but it was an affectionate nickname, that was all. Nobody would ever have dared to call him really rude names.

And that was another thing, Mary thought. How was it some children looked so much like their mothers or their fathers, and others didn't resemble either of them in the least? That was very odd. Tom didn't look a bit like his father, except that his face was a bit sort of chunky, and his hair was the same sort of mousy brown, and he really wasn't much like his mother either. And she didn't look a bit like Pa. Once she'd tried asking Ma about it, but for once she didn't get an answer. Or to be more accurate she'd got two answers, one in words and the other in looks, and they didn't match. 'That's how it is,' Ma had said, and it had sounded casual, as though it wasn't worth bothering about. But when she looked at her mother's face, there was that odd expression, a withdrawn, unfocused sort of expression as though she was thinking of somewhere a long way away, a private, distant, dreamy expression with a touch of sadness about it in the droop of her mouth. She couldn't understand it, but it alerted her and made her feel quite sure that she'd asked an important question after all.

She was beginning to realize that the looks people gave one another often said far more than words ever could, and said it very quickly. Ma could warn her at once that Pa wasn't well and shouldn't be troubled. All it took was a warning glance, quick as a blink, slid from the corner of her eye when Pa wasn't looking. And that was another thing. There was them other looks, straight, significant looks that she'd seen so many times, sort of hanging between Ma and Ploochy. Now they weren't quick looks at all. They lasted quite a long time and seemed to hold them together as though there was an invisible string running between their eyes.

Last spring she'd seen the look again. It was holding Jamie McTavish and Babsie Pullen together as they went ambling along the street with their arms round one another's waists. And Pa said they were courting. She'd thought and thought about it, and finally she'd asked Tom Oxbury, because she couldn't think of anybody else, and she knew he'd give her a straight answer if he could. He'd seen Jamie and Babsie Pullen too, and he said he knew what the look was all right, and he didn't think much of it. 'Pretty soppy, if you ask me,' he'd said. 'It means they want to get married and have babies.' It was a staggering piece of information. Surely Ma and Mr Ploochy didn't want to do that! Eventually she'd asked Ma. Not straight out, but in a roundabout sort of way. Subtly. 'Was yer thinkin've 'avin' any more babies, Ma?' And Ma had roared with laughter, throwing back her head and showing her teeth the way she did, and then she'd given her an answer where the words and the look were a perfect match. 'Good God, no! I've got quite enough wiv you, kid. Whatever put such an idea in yer 'ead?' So that was all right. Or was it …?

There was a sudden unfamiliar movement behind her and cold air was driving against her shoulders. She just had a second to think, someone's opened the door, and then a torrent of black, evil-smelling water was swirling into the room, knocking her feet from under her. The stove went out with a long, angry hiss and then the gas, plopping and sighing, and she was left alone in an ugly darkness with heavy water rushing and pushing all around her. For several crazy minutes she clung to the table, spreadeagled across it, with her heart pounding, too shocked to think, as the air pounded and roared in the little room and the water froze all feeling from her feet. Then she took herself in hand and decided to be sensible.

The Thames must have overflown, that's what it was. Now that she was calmer she could recognize the smell of the water. Now what was the best thing to do? If the gaslight had been blown out she ought to turn off the tap or she'd be gassed unconscious. As the water wasn't pushing against her legs quite so much now and there didn't seem to be any more of it washing into the room, at least for the present, she eased herself off the table until she was standing up again. She was knee deep in icy water, but she wasn't being knocked over. So that was something. She waded to the wall and groped her way along it until she'd found the gas tap and turned it off. Now what? It was wickedly dark with no light and no fire. Like the back yard when she went out to the lav and forgot to take the torch. The torch! Of course. Up on the mantelpiece, next to the clock.

It was only a pocket torch, with a Number 8 battery and the cone of light it dropped into the darkness wasn't much bigger than a tuppenny icecream, but it showed her enough. She stood by the table examining the room a slice at a time. The front door had been knocked askew and black water was still washing in, quite quickly too, for the heaving surface was peaked into sharp little waves. Her new winter coat hung on the kitchen door a mere six inches away from the wet, so she waded over and put it on top of the dresser out of harm's way.

Then, through the roar of the wind, she heard a faint tapping from next door. Poor old Mrs Gus! 'You all right?' she yelled, but the wind was making too much noise. She'd have to try and wade in.

The water was very weighty and it took her a long time to push her way against it and out of the house, her little cone of light pointing her onwards like a white arrow. Mrs Gus had burnt her front door for firewood earlier in the week, so it was easy enough to get in. The old lady was sitting on the table with her cat on her lap and the poker in her hand. 'Bleedin' Thames!' she growled.

'You all right?' Mary said, wading through the dirty water.

'Knocked me off me feet. Bleedin' Thames. They got the boats out?'

'Not yet,' Mary said. So that's what they did. Got the boats out and came and rescued you.

'We oughter get blankets,' Mrs Gus said. 'Only I shall never get through ter the bedroom. Not wiv my legs!'

'I'll go!' Mary said, glad of the chance to be moving, for the water was bitingly cold when you stood still.

There were three blankets and a dilapidated eiderdown on Mrs Gus's bed and she soon had them piled round the old lady on the table. 'Now what?' she asked.

'Wait, I expect,' Mrs Gus said. She seemed quite happy among the blankets and the cat was purring. But Mary was too cold and too excited to stay still. 'I'll go an' see how the others are,' she said. 'You'll be all right, wontcher?'

Out in the courtyard the water was swirling round and round as though it was going down some enormous plug hole. She reached the pump and clung to it gratefully while she got her breath back. The sky was full of falling water and there wasn't a light anywhere and no sign of any boats. The rain was falling in such heavy squalls she was soon as wet above her waist as she was below her knees, but as her eyes grew accustomed to the darkness she found she could see a shape standing in the empty doorway of Number 10. Mrs Patterson, was it? No good calling out, she'd better go and see.

She was just starting her push to Mrs Patterson's door when a light flickered in the blackness at the end of the courtyard, and she fancied she could hear voices shouting into the wind. It must be the boat, she thought. And so it was, a small filthy dinghy rowed by Teddy Thomas, who lived next door to the pub, and wading beside it three solid figures with torches.

'Over 'ere!' she yelled as she struggled towards them. 'Over 'ere!' Now she could hear the creak of the oars and thought it was the most protective sound she'd ever heard. 'Over 'ere!' She was almost on top of the waders before the light of her little torch revealed who they were. Pa and Ploochy and Tom Oxbury. Well, fancy that! And she'd thought he was a man!

'You all right kid?' Pa said, peering at her anxiously as his torch swung towards her. His face looked most peculiar lit from below, like a skull, with huge black sockets for his eyes and pale, gleaming skin, at least on the unscarred side.

''Course,' she said proudly. 'We ought ter get Mrs Patterson out first, 'cause a' the kids.'

Mrs Patterson had wrapped her two snuffling boys in blankets and packed all the food she possessed in one of the deep drawers from her dresser. The sudden beam of light from Pa's torch made her squint, but she grinned when she saw who

155

her rescuers were. She didn't seem at all put out that her living room was a foot deep in water. 'Just got that fire going lovely,' she told Pa as she paddled beside him out of the house, 'and then in it all came. What a life! Bring the clock, lovey,' she called back to Mary. 'I wouldn't want nothink to 'appen to me clock.' Laden and cheerful, they waded back to the boat, Pa carrying one boy and Ploochy the other. Mrs Gus was already sitting in the stern, with a tarpaulin over her head and her cat still on her lap. 'What price this fer a lark, Ned?' she said, and the torchlight revealed three discoloured teeth and a grin. Now the boat had come it was beginning to be an adventure.

By the time the last precious object had been retrieved from Mrs Patterson's dark, drowned hovel, a second boat had arrived with the news that all the homeless were to be taken to Farncombe Street School.

'You go in the other boat, kid,' Pa said.

But that wasn't what Mary wanted to do at all. 'Let me stay, Pa,' she pleaded. 'I can fetch an' carry. I don' mind. We ought ter get the kids out first.'

So he gave in and let her work with the rest of them, and for the next hour and a half she struggled from house to boat with blankets and clothes and babies in improvised cradles, and rabbits in hutches and, on one occasion, even a bird cage. And at last the court was clear and Teddy Thomas was rowing her and Tom Oxbury and little Mrs Morton out into the running river that had once been Cherry Orchard Gardens. Then, because the effort of rescue was over and she was sitting still, she realized that she was extremely wet and very, very cold.

The upper hall of Farncombe Street School was full of slime-stained scarecrows wandering about in ancient blankets or sitting on their haunches beside a pile of dishevelled belongings telling the tale to one another. There were improvised beds for the little'uns, made out of two school chairs and a pillow, and wet clothes were hanging to dry on the backs of chairs set at haphazard angles all over the room. A huge fire was burning in the grate and the gaslights were all on, and that made the scene acceptable somehow, as if it could pass for normal if it tried. But the smell of river slime and wet dirty clothes was all pervasive. Ma was making tea, pouring out water from the big school kettle into a massive tea pot, but when she saw Mary she put it down at once and rushed across the hall, all hands, to strip her of her wet clothes and rub her down with a blanket and get her into something warm before she 'caught her death'.

'What was you thinking of?' she said to Pa. 'Keepin' 'er there, all in the wet. She should 'a' come back on the first trip.'

'She's been a reg'lar brick, ain't yer, kid?' Pa said proudly. 'I don't now what we'd 'a' done without 'er, an' that's a fact.'

'Chip orf the old block,' Mrs Gus said. 'Gor, I could go a cup a' tea.'

It was two o'clock in the morning before Mary felt really warm again, and by then news had come through that the high tide had passed and the water was beginning to go down. Ma rolled her up in a blanket and put an old coat under her head and told her to try and get some sleep. 'You won't be fit fer nothin' in the morning else.' But she was really too excited to sleep much, and anyway the floorboards bruised her hips and the place was full of alerting, unexpected noise with all those people coughing and snoring.

At daybreak she woke for the umpteenth time to see that Mr Ploochy was putting on his wet shoes. The sky outside the window was smeared with bloodshot cloud and she could hear a tram clanging away from Jamaica Road.

'I'm off 'ome,' he said. 'No need to wake yer ma.'

She remembered the question she'd been meaning to ask him. 'Mr Ploochy,' she said, propping herself up on one elbow, ''ave yer got kids of yer own?'

'Yes,' he said seriously. 'I have.'

'How many?'

'Three. Three very good ones.'

'D'yer want any more? Babies I mean.'

'Not at my time a' life!' he said, and he looked up from his shoe-laces and laughed at her. 'We got enough excitement in our lives without that, eh, my Mary Ann?'

Chapter Fourteen

Alice had had a disturbed night, her sleep broken by indigestion and anxiety and bad weather. It had always been her habit to stay awake until she was sure that all the members of her family were home safely for the night and now, even though Albert was the only one left for her to worry about, the habit persisted. She drifted in and out of a sleep she really didn't think she ought to allow herself as the wind roared down the chimney and threw rain at the windows like sharp pebbles, and still Albert didn't return. It was most unlike him. Or at least, it was most unlike him now. When they'd both been young of course, he often used to stay out all night, coming home with the milkman, tired and sheepish and full of silly excuses about staying with Dickie Chanter. As if she ever believed such rubbish! He'd been with that dreadful redhead, as well she knew. But now he was older he was more settled. Liked his creature comforts too much to go gadding about after silly girls. So as the hours passed and still he didn't return she grew more and more concerned. By five o'clock in the morning she had decided that he must have met with an accident somewhere. She made up her mind that she would get up as soon as it was light and go down to the police station and find out what had happened.

She was dressing when she heard his key in the lock. She buttoned her blouse quickly and sped downstairs, taut with anxiety and fatigue. 'Where *have* you been, Albert?' she demanded as she trotted down towards the hall, but then when she saw the state he was in, 'Oh Albert, my dear! What is it? What's happened?' Gusts of foul-smelling air pulsed from his every movement, damp and dirt, rotting vegetation, river slime, the sour decay of Cherry Court.

He told her quickly, to stop her worrying, and proudly because he wanted to be admired. She was very interested and instantly full of a wifely concern that satisfied them both. 'You must take a warm bath at once,' she said, 'and get out of those damp clothes. I'll go and cook breakfast. You mustn't catch a chill.' They both knew how unlikely that was because Albert was one of the healthiest of men. But it was pleasant to be able to fuss. 'What a dreadful thing to happen!' she said as he squelched upstairs. 'Was anybody drowned? Will it be on the wireless, do you think?' It was quite a relief to see him home again and another to realize that his news would give them something to talk about over breakfast, and something to tell Anna when she came to visit them that afternoon. It was getting more and more difficult to talk to Anna these days. She was always bright and cheerful, but distant somehow.

She arrived late, of course, and looking very elegant in a new camel hair coat with the collar turned up to frame her face and keep her ears warm. Her father fussed her into the parlour and sat her by the fire, beaming with the pleasure of the news he was going to tell her.

'Guess where your dadda was last night.' It had been in all the evening papers, as he knew because he'd bought them all.

She shook her head, smiling at him brightly.

'There!' he said, holding out the *Standard* so that she could see the headline. 'Thames flood. That where I was!'

She was most impressed. 'What excitement!' she said. 'I wish I'd been there with you. It must have been thrilling.' It was the truth. She was growing bored with her little flat and finding Eric more and more difficult to handle with every passing day. Or, to be more honest, with every passing night. To have been involved in a flood would have been really fun. Especially a flood like this, with just enough danger to make it exciting and not enough to make it really dangerous. 'Did anyone get drowned?'

'No!' Dadda said triumphantly. 'We got 'em all out. You should 'a' seen all the boats! Sight worth seeing, that was.' And he plunged cheerfully into his story.

'What a brave old dadda I've got,' she said, when he finally paused for breath, and her admiration was genuine even if she was laying it on a bit thick.

But then Mummy left them to go and make the tea and he went and spoiled it all by embarking on a long, unnecessary tale about some wretched little slum kid, and how she'd carried people out of their houses when she wasn't much bigger than they were. 'Never saw such a kid! So brave, and only a little scrap of a thing. Little thin wrists.' And he circled an imaginary little thin wrist with thumb and index finger.

The story and the gesture made Anna suddenly and powerfully jealous. There was no cause for it, but it grew in her belly and altered her expression just the same. If any girl's wrist ought to be circled by those brown fingers it was hers, not some silly little thing from the slums. 'Fancy!' she said, acidly. 'I wonder she wasn't in the papers. A heroine like that.'

Dadda's eyebrows shot up, the way they did when he was surprised or angry, and she realized that she was revealing too much. But she couldn't help it. She really couldn't. Eric was being so beastly, and the awful thing was she couldn't tell anyone how beastly, because he was being beastly in bed and all that sort of thing was a dark secret and never to be talked about, as she knew only too well. His lovemaking was still as crude and brutal as it had been on their honeymoon, and it was beginning to make her feel used and worthless. It was always the same and never pleasurable, jumping on top of her without a word and then banging away for several minutes with his eyes shut and then jumping off again and going to sleep as though somebody had switched him off. It left her feeling frustrated and miserable and – well – dirty. And that, in some obscure way she didn't understand, made it peculiarly difficult to control her feelings and keep a bright face on things.

Fortunately Mummy rescued them with tea and toast and they all started talking about the dangers of another flood and what would happen if the river overflowed at Wandsworth, and Mummy remembered the time they'd had a cloudburst in Tooting and the High Street had been like a river. So she got through tea quite charmingly, and subdued her ruffled emotions, and felt she was doing quite well after all. Then Dadda said it was time he got back to work, and there was only Aunt Phoebe to see and her weekly duty call would be safely over.

Aunt Phoebe rarely came downstairs to tea these days, especially in winter time. She preferred a nice tray in her nice warm room where the gas fire gave out a nice steady heat and she could lie on the bed snug under her eiderdown and read or doze as she pleased. But it was always interesting to see the children and to note how they were getting along, so she was glad when Anna put her head round the door.

'You look very swell,' she said to Anna as her great niece bent to kiss her. Anna always wore such pretty clothes, and that pink dress looked warm as well as fashionable. But how hard her face was becoming, hard and withdrawn, with discontented lines beginning to pull down the corners of her mouth. 'What have you done with your little dog? Did you bring it with you?'

'Oh no,' Anna said, lightly pushing away an uncomfortable suspicion. 'We had to leave it behind in Paris, you know, because of the quarantine regulations. Eric took it out for a walk and found such a nice lady to adopt it.'

'Humph,' Aunt Phoebe said. Anna decided to change the subject.

'How are you, Aunty?'

'Keeping warm. How are you?'

'Oh, I'm thinking of having the lounge redecorated.'

'Whatever for?' the old lady asked sharply. 'You've only just moved in. And anyway, that's no answer. I want to know how *you* are.'

'Oh I'm fine,' with a toss of her curls and an artificial smile.

Aunt Phoebe lifted Anna's hand from the eiderdown and held it firmly. The child was unhappy. That was plain. Even her fingers were tense. 'You remind me of your grandfather,' she said.

Anna was very surprised indeed, because she couldn't remember any of her grandparents ever being spoken about. 'Do I?' she said. 'In what way?'

The old lady thought for quite a long time before she answered. 'Being married,' she said. 'That's what reminds me. He married twice, your grandfather. Married twice and died young, and never got the hang of it. There's an art in being married, you see. A knack.'

'Oh, Aunt Phoebe, how do you know? You've never ...' But the words died on her tongue because she knew they were going to sound rude, even if they were right.

Aunt Phoebe was unperturbed. 'Been married,' she finished. 'True, my dear. But when you watch a race, you may see who are the better runners, even if you've never sprinted anywhere in your life. It's a matter of observation. The watchers see more than the runners, if the truth be told.'

That was right, Anna thought. The runners were too busy running. Perhaps this trenchant old lady really did know something about marriage. 'What have you seen, Aunt Phoebe?' she asked, and although she didn't know it her face had softened.

'It takes time to make a marriage,' Aunt Phoebe said. 'Time and patience and gentleness. It's a knack. Your brother's got it. You just watch him. Watch his hands. So gentle, holding the chair for Lily to sit down, helping her into her coat, washing little Johnny's face. He's very gentle with that baby.'

Anna had a vague feeling that she and Eric were under attack, and she sprang to the defence at once. 'It's all very well for Georgie,' she said, 'he's not ambitious. You can't be gentle if you're ambitious. If you want to get on in this world you have to be hard.'

'Your young man's sharp,' Aunt Phoebe said, looking inwards and seeing him clearly. 'Sharp enough to cut you to the quick, I should say.'

How does she know these things? Anna wondered. What else has she seen? Oh, if only I could tell her all about it. But you could hardly talk to a maiden aunt about sex, could you? No matter how wise and knowledgeable she seemed to be. That was the one thing she certainly wouldn't know anything about. The sense that she was very near the help she needed and still couldn't reach out for it made her irritable again. 'It's all very well for Georgie,' she said. 'He isn't aiming high. Eric's aiming high.'

'Pity!' And it was a sneer. How hurtful!

'And besides, he's got such a common wife. You must admit that. I mean, what is she? A shop girl, that's all. A common shop girl.'

'Hoity toity!' Aunt Phoebe said sharply. 'We are all common, Anna. Common clay. All the lot of us. It doesn't do to get jumped up ideas about yourself.'

I've made a mistake, Anna thought miserably. 'I didn't mean …' she tried. 'It's just …'

'I know what it is, my dear,' Aunt Phoebe said and her face was so full of affectionate understanding that Anna suddenly felt as though she was going to cry. But the conversation wasn't going any further. The old lady was calling a halt to it. 'Come and talk to me again next week, child. I need my nap.' And she gave Anna's hand a dismissive pat.

So she kissed her aunt goodbye, and went out onto the freezing landing and down the chilly stairs, her emotions boiling. Was it possible Aunt Phoebe understood? Could she really talk to her? Really, really talk? I'll spend longer with her next week, she promised herself, and we'll see what she says then. And then, as another thought chilled her even further, I hope she doesn't say anything about it to Mummy.

She needn't have worried, for Aunt Phoebe was always the soul of discretion. In any case they all had the flood to talk about. It kept them all amused for days, for there was nothing the old lady enjoyed more than a disaster. 'Worse will follow. You mark my words,' she said with immense satisfaction at breakfast the next morning. 'If it's flooded once, it will flood again. And think of all the diseases. Troubles always come in threes.' And she munched her bread and butter vehemently, her odd sausage curls bouncing against her forehead.

And although it annoyed Albert to admit it, she was proved right before the week was out. Two days later, while the inhabitants of Cherry Court were still trying to dry out their sodden belongings, the Thames overflowed again, and the next day Queenie sent a card to the Tooting shop to tell Albert that Ned had been taken to Guy's Hospital. 'His lungs,' she wrote in her hasty scrawl. 'He's very bad. Visiting time 6.30.'

Albert set off for the hospital that evening wracked by very mixed feelings indeed. Ever since he'd found Queenie again his desire for her had grown and grown, infinitely pleasurable of course, but infinitely painful too, because it was never gratified, and as far as he could see it never would be. He knew beyond any doubt now that the only way he would ever be able to live with his darling again was if Ned were to die. But Ned was a good man, a patient, loving husband, a devoted father, the sort of friend you could admire and trust. It was impossible to wish him ill, and unthinkable to wish him dead. Torn by conflicting passions, he bought lavish presents for the invalid, and rushed into the quiet ward blazing with concern.

Ned was lying in a small, white bed, yellow faced and still with exhaustion, with Queenie sitting as close beside him as she could get, holding his hand. The harsh, dry cough that usually punctuated everything he said was more noticeable in this hushed environment, and the shadows under his eyes looked blacker against the cleanliness of the pillows mounded behind his head, but his lopsided smile was as warm as ever and he greeted Albert with affection. 'Nice ter see yer, mate. Our Queenie says they been cleaning out The Red Lion this morning. Soon be back ter normal.'

'What about you?' Albert wanted to know. The Red Lion was unimportant.

'Oh, I'm coming along all right. Mustn't grumble. Just me chest's a bit troublesome, that's all.' And he coughed into his hand, looking apologetically at them over the tips of his fingers.

Queenie flashed one quick warning glance at Albert and then plunged into a dramatic account of all the local news: how the fire brigade had pumped out the police station, and how the school was still being used for all the people from the courts, and how Eth and Charlie had put a big bed in their living room for her and Mary Ann and got the leg of it stuck in the fireplace. Albert would have liked to know more about Ned's condition but she deflected all mention of illness and kept the conversation on light-hearted things, making them both laugh and deliberately entertaining them. Poor Ned, he thought, he must be bad.

But at last the ward bell was rung and a soft-footed nurse rustled them out into the corridor. Queenie's shoulders were hunched with effort, but now she dropped them and her bright smile together, and Albert could see how drawn and anxious she was. He put an arm about her at once, scooping her into his side for comfort just as he always used to. 'What is it, my darling?' he said.

'Consumption,' she said shortly. ''Ad it two years nearly, poor beggar. 'Is lungs was left weak after the war, they reckon, bein' blown up.'

'That's dreadful!' he said, appalled. 'We must get him to Switzerland. Anything. We must *do* something.'

She smiled at him wryly, close to tears. 'Nothink we can do Ploo, or we'd 'a' done it. It's in both lungs. Too far gone to cure. An' a' course 'e made it worse carryin' people about, an' gettin' isself soaked.'

'Does he know?'

'Oh yes,' she said. 'You can't fool Ned. 'E knows right enough.'

'If I got him a place in a clinic somewhere,' Albert tried, biting the ends of his moustache with distress, 'would he go?'

'Doubt it,' she said. 'You know Ned. You can ask 'im, if yer like. When 'e's got over this lot, a' course. 'E ain't in no fit state now. You can see that. 'E was coughing up blood yesterday morning.'

Worse and worse, Albert thought, as they walked out of the hospital and down into the bleak chasm of Tooley Street. 'I will find a clinic tomorrow morning, first thing,' he promised. 'Fresh air. Good food. Make all the difference, that will. You'll see!' But Queenie smiled at him wearily, as though he were a child, and he knew he hadn't comforted her or persuaded her at all.

Nevertheless he made inquiries the very next morning and found an expensive clinic on the shores of Lake Geneva which, according to its agent, would be more than willing to accept a new patient as soon as he was well enough to travel. Hope renewed, he rushed off to Guy's again clutching their brochure.

Ned wouldn't even consider it. 'You're a good bloke, Ploochy,' he said, putting the booklet down after the briefest glance. 'One in a million. Best friend we ever 'ad, an' that's a fact. Ain't it, Queenie?'

'Then you'll go?' Albert said.

'No,' Ned said, slowly and quietly. Then he gazed away from them, his eyes unseeing, gathering his reasons together so that he could explain them properly to this boisterous, generous friend of theirs without hurting his feelings. Albert and Queenie waited for him, Queenie gently, Albert with appalled impatience. Finally he turned his head towards them again and smiled in his lopsided, affectionate way. 'I been living on borrowed time, you see,' he said. 'Ever since Wipers. Should 'a' gone then, if it hadn't been fer the Ox. So what I mean ter say is, it's a sort a' gift really, bein' alive. Not ter waste or run away. A gift. Ter make the most of. Ter use. Ter make my part the world a better place. Now we done a lot already, flats an' new gardens an' all, but that don't mean ter say we can just sit back. That's just a beginning. Next year we ought ter see all them courts come down an' new going up in Wilson Grove. Gonna be lovely, that is! So we got a lot ter do, me an' Queenie, ain't we, gel?'

'But if you go to the clinic and get well, really fit, you'll have more energy,' Albert tried.

Ned smiled at him again. 'I got the consumption, Ploo. You know that, dontcher?' he said. 'That ain't the sort a' thing they can cure. Least, not yet. Some a' the young 'uns might stand a better chance. Be worthwhile sending them away. Not me. I shall never make old bones. We all know that, don't we gel?' There was no self-pity in his tone, only resignation. And patience. ''Sides,' he said, grinning again, 'if I ain't got so long as the rest a' yer, I can't afford ter waste me time in some foreign country. I want ter be here with my Queenie.'

It was unanswerable.

'Told yer!' Queenie said as they walked back to Bermondsey together when the visiting hour was over. The streets were dark and damp, but the trams rattled past them as bright as ocean-going liners, all warmly lit windows and purposeful noise. ''E belongs 'ere, you see. No good uprooting him. Not now.'

'I don't understand it,' Albert said, perplexed and disappointed. 'If that was me, I'd go anywhere, do anything.'

'It's not you though, is it?'

'Does Mary know?'

'Not in so many words. I ain't said nothink. I daresay she's worked it out. She's a clever kid. Don't miss much.'

'Will you tell 'er now?'

'Wouldn't do no good, would it? Only worry 'er, an' get 'er worked up. Time enough fer all that when 'e …'

But for once in her life she'd misjudged her daughter. Mary knew well enough that her Pa was very ill indeed. She'd seen the blood stains on the sheets that morning, and knew why her mother was pushing them into the laundry bag so quickly, but

166

it never occurred to her that he was a dying man. Other people died of consumption, sickly children and gaunt men and women with grey faces and racking coughs. Pa wasn't like them. Pa was indestructible. He'd survived the Great War, and got a job, even with one arm. And even though he coughed and coughed, he always got his breath eventually. He was a good man, and a strong man, and it wasn't possible that he could die. The fact that her mother never spoke about his illness made it more acceptable and less serious. If it had been really bad, Ma would have said so. So she wrote him a long, cheerful letter, commanding him to get well, and put all fears of death firmly to one side of her busy brain.

And to prove her right, after seven more days of rest and nourishment he was considered fit enough to be allowed home, and life in Cherry Court returned to its normal pattern, except that the place was dirtier and more dilapidated than ever. But even that had its good side, as Pa was quick to point out when the letter arrived from the council, at last, to tell them that the court was due for demolition at the end of May and that all the inhabitants were to be offered dwellings in the fine new buildings in Wilson Grove.

'There you are, Mary,' Ma said in triumph. 'Watcher think a' that?'

'You can milk some good out a' most things if you try,' Pa said. 'If it hadn't been fer the flood we might 'a' been 'ere much longer.' His optimism was unquenchable. This wasn't a man to be killed by consumption.

But there was still the rest of the winter to get through. And, as old Aunt Phoebe pointed out ghoulishly and repetitively every New Year, January and February were nasty, treacherous months, not to be trusted for a second. She did determined battle with them every year, wrapping herself in thick wool from her neck to her ankles, and sitting so close to her nice gas fire that her legs were soon permanently mottled and her slippers scorched brown. Alice and Minnie cosseted her with stews and soups and brought her a nice hot cocoa to settle her every night, and encouraged her to take to her bed at the first sign of the snuffles, but nobody really worried about her health because she was as tough in her old age as she had been in her

167

youth, determined and forthright and apparently indestructible.

So it came as a dreadful shock to Alice when she went to wake the old lady late one grey February morning and found her lying still and peaceful among her pillows, with her eyes closed and her hands clasped patiently together and the chill of death already upon her.

'A lovely way to go,' Minnie comforted as she and Alice waited in the parlour for the doctor to arrive. 'No pain or anything. In her sleep, peaceful as anything. A lovely way.' Her eyes were full of tears but she was being reasonable and sensible in her loss.

But Alice was beyond reason. 'First Georgie marrying that silly girl, and then Anna, and now this,' she said, her face fierce with her determination not to cry. 'Just when everything's settled and life is how it ought to be, everything goes wrong. I can't bear it, Minnie! She was all the mother I ever had! She and Aunt Amelia. My only relations!'

'You've still got me,' Minnie said lovingly. 'And Anna and Georgie.'

Rather to her mother's surprise, Anna seemed genuinely upset by her aunt's death. She wept freely and often, and without thinking what she looked like afterwards. 'I do believe she was fond of the old lady after all,' her mother said. 'I never thought she'd grieve like this.'

Anna hadn't expected to be so overwhelmed with sorrow either. But the truth was this death was like a door being shut in her face, and she was lost and bleak and angry and desperate at the mere thought of it. Since their extraordinary conversation, she'd visited her Aunt Phoebe every week, and every week they'd talked vaguely of life and marriage, and although they never said anything that was really important or helpful, Anna felt they were moving gradually and carefully towards the moment when such things might be said and heard at last. And now the moment was lost for ever.

When she stood beside the grave watching the coffin, which didn't seem to have anything at all to do with old Aunt Phoebe, thinking how cruel and meaningless it all was, she was numb with disappointment and misery. Small flakes of snow were falling softly and silently from a white sky, and there wasn't a sound except the murmuring of the priest as he mumbled the burial service into his cassock. Why couldn't you have lived a little bit longer? she mourned. We could have really talked to each other if only you'd lived a little bit longer. Now she was all alone again with no one to confide in. Dadda was always too busy to listen these days, rushing off here there and everywhere, making money all the time, and she'd never been able to talk to her mother. Grief and the chill air were making her shiver and she knew she was terribly lonely.

Chapter Fifteen

Spring took a long time to arrive that year, almost as though it had been delayed by grief and illness. Over in Raynes Park, Anna was yearning for it. Warm weather and new leaves springing up. Just what she needed to lift her spirits again. But the cold continued and so did her misery. In March she was annoyed to hear that Lily was expecting again. She would be, she thought furiously. Now Mummy would make a ridiculous fuss like she did last time, and start throwing out hints at *her*. Which was most unfair because it wasn't her fault she didn't have a baby. Why, oh why, didn't the spring come?

In Bermondsey things were even worse. New life was always hesitant down by the docks, deterred by cramped streets and huddled brickwork and an almost total lack of nurturing earth. There were no flowers in Marigold Street and no trees in Cherry Orchard. The back yards were sour with too much use and too little air, and what little soil they possessed, exposed in odd corners between dustbins and coalsheds and outside lavatories, was as black as ashes and equally lifeless. But at last it was April even in Paradise Street, and the sky was china blue above the grey slates and the clouds as white as new lambs, and even though dirt and debris still bobbed against the black sides of the old warehouses, out in mid stream the Thames was free running and as green as glass. Over in Southwark Park lilac bushes grew shaggy with scented blossom and in the newly planted trees beside the newly built flats in Salisbury Street blackbirds lifted yellow bills to flute their bright fountains of song out into the sun-touched air, and flocks of finches fell from bough to bough in a golden shower. At long, long last work could resume on the building site in Wilson Grove.

Mary had lived through the winter in a passion of impatience. She'd passed the preliminary and sat the scholarship, but that wasn't what was important, not now. What was important was moving out of the bug-hutch into a nice clean flat.

Ma and Pa were getting excited because there was a general election in the offing and they hoped there'd be a Labour majority this time. 'You just think how we can get cracking then,' Pa said, 'with a government on our side. Make all the difference, that will. We'll 'ave the slums cleared in no time.'

'Perhaps they'll put a jerk on with this lot,' Ma said, looking at the chipped walls of their cramped front room.

The houses in Wilson Grove weren't finished yet although the foundations seemed to have been laid for well over a year. Ma and Pa had got into the habit of taking her for a stroll down into the site of a Sunday afternoon to watch progress, which Ma said was much too slow. Pa was more patient. 'Slow but sure,' he said. 'You can't work slapdash if you want a good house. Last for years they will, once they're up. We shall feel the benefit after all's said and done, Queenie. It's worth waiting for.'

But at last, at last, the new season began and the new flats were roofed. Wallflowers opened in sweet-scented, tawny profusion beside all the newly laid greens around the estate, the plasterers moved in to Wilson Grove and the official letter arrived with its excitingly sober news that they would be moving into their new flat at the end of May.

'We go shopping,' Ploochy said, the minute they told him. 'I treat you to something for your new home. How about a sofa, eh? For old time sake! For old friends!' What a funny generous man he was.

'We can manage,' Pa said, and he sounded rather stiff. 'Ta all the same, Ploo. We got neighbours ter think of.' Was he embarrassed because old Ploo was so generous?

'The neighbours won't say nothink,' Ma said, diplomatically. 'They all know 'e's from the 'alls. More money than sense, they reckon. Nice new bed fer Mary, p'rhaps. Be good ter get a shot a' that rotten ol' truckle bed, won't it, lovey?'

Mary loathed her truckle bed but she said she didn't mind it a bit really, because it wouldn't have done to upset Pa. But her eyes were shining at the thought of a room of her own, and a bed that didn't have to be packed away each morning. 'I could put all me books on shelves,' she said, 'all in the one place like a little library.' The possibilities there'd be at the new flat!

'I buy you a bookcase,' Ploochy promised at once, 'chest a' drawers, wardrobe, dressing table, all to match. How about that?'

'It's council flat, remember,' Ma said, laughing at him. 'Nothink too extravagant, fer Gawd's sake.'

'You'll spoil 'er,' Pa warned, but his face was signalling excitement and pleasure now. So that was all right.

'No fear a' that!' Ploochy said. 'She much too nice. I will go to Waring and Gillows tomorrow, as ever is.'

He went up to the West End the very next morning. It was a fine day, the sky busy with bright cloud above the imposing frontages all along Oxford Street, and the huge windows even busier with spring fashions.

The shop assistant at Waring and Gillows was a most obliging young man. It didn't take him long to establish that satisfying this particular customer would mean a nice fat commission, so he treated Albert like a lord, smoothing him from one richly polished suite to another all through the resinous length of the showroom.

'Weathered oak is all the rage this year ... Macassar ebony, very smart ... Indian laurel wood, just the thing for a young lady, very feminine, don't you think? ... Walnut, very acceptable,' he murmured, his head tilted watchfully to one side like a sparrow alert for pickings.

As Indian laurel wood was just the thing for a young lady, Indian laurel wood it was, with two glass-fronted bookcases to match. By the end of the transaction both men were well pleased with themselves. The assistant took himself off to the shadowy end of the showroom to calculate his commission and Albert walked out into the spring sunshine whistling happily and tunelessly.

There was just nice time to get down to Streatham for the meeting of the cinema consortium he was a member of. He wasn't really looking forward to it because he felt pretty sure his timid associates were going to take the wrong decision. So it was pleasant to be buying presents in the meantime.

The tram made good speed and he got to Streatham with half an hour to spare and decided to fill the time with some more window shopping. It was an idle decision, nothing more, and having made it he walked idly, admiring his reflection in each shop window as he passed, glimpse by satisfactory glimpse; his head and shoulders perky among the haphazard ranks of spring hats; his watch chain winking brightly against the dark cloth in the bespoke tailors; his legs bouncing briskly through the fiddles and flutes and stands and stools of Fisher's music shop, to disappear altogether as a particularly solid grand piano obscured their way. A very fine piano indeed, he thought, stopping before the window to admire it. Just the sort of thing for Mary Ann. What a capital idea! A piano for Mary Ann, in her own flat, where she could practise whenever she pleased. He was in the shop almost before the thought was through his mind.

For the next half hour he listened as Mr Fisher's assistant demonstrated the splendid tone of a variety of instruments and lifted lids to display the pristine gleam of their strings and finally applauded the entire suitability of Mr Ploochy's choice, which was of course the most expensive baby grand in the shop, as both of them had known perfectly well that it would be right from the start.

'I will send you details for delivery, date and place and such like, as soon as I know them myself,' Albert said, patting his cheque book back into his inner pocket. It had been an inspiration, nothing less. He went off to meet the consortium singing aloud with happiness.

The meeting began late, which was no surprise to anybody, and gave Albert a chance to talk business with Mr Whiting, the estate agent. He was thinking of buying another shop. 'I was considering Dulwich,' he said, swinging his brandy from side to side in its wide bowl.

'You could try Peckham too,' Mr Whiting suggested. 'Good class of customer there. Quite a thriving town, Peckham, these days.' He drooped beside the fire, his long, thin, round-shouldered body curved towards the coals, like a heron watching a pool. He was enjoying the warmth on his knees, which were large and bony and horribly prone to rheumatics. 'We've got a branch in Peckham Hill, corner of Peckham High Street. Might be able to help you.'

Albert said he would give it thought, but really he was only making conversation, toying with the idea just as he was toying with his brandy. But by now all six members of the board had arrived and Mr Chalmers was coughing the meeting to attention.

There was really only one matter on the agenda, he said, glancing nervously at Albert, and that was the offer from the talking picture company which had been mooted at their last meeting. The company offering to buy their two sites in Tooting was one of the giants of the motion picture industry. They intended to pull down both the old cinemas and build a really splendid new one equipped to show the new talking pictures and in the very latest, luxurious style. And, of course, being a big company they had the money to do it. He had to admit they had made a very tempting offer, and if he were asked to advise he would certainly think most seriously about acceptance. It would undoubtedly cost a great deal of money to adapt their present premises for the new talking pictures, if indeed it could be done at all. The figures were on the table before them, and on the blue paper they would find complete details of the offer.

'Can't see any sort of future in talking pictures meself,' Mr Wainwright said, paying great attention to his cigar, which wouldn't draw properly. 'All right for musicals, that sort of thing, pictures with a lot of noise and nonsense, but it wouldn't do for drama, you mark my words. Nobody would want to hear a lot of talk in a drama.'

'Quite right,' Mr Whiting agreed nodding his long sharp nose at the table to emphasize his agreement. 'Flash in the pan. That's all it'll be. If they want to risk their money on it, then let them. It's a good offer. I say we sell out.'

Albert put down his brandy and sat well back in his chair so as to get the best view of all their faces. 'I say, take a risk,' he urged. 'That the essence a' good business, risk an' hard work. This could be just the thing. We could make a fortune.'

'Loose a fortune, more like,' Mr Wainwright said gloomily. 'Have you seen the estimates for wiring The Regal? Where would we raise money like that?'

'Risks are all very well, providing they're not too risky,' Mr Whiting agreed. 'We're certain of a profit if we sell the site.'

174

There was no denying that, as four of the other five members were quick to agree. Albert argued on but he had already lost his case, and by the time a vote was taken his was the only dissenting voice. The company that had run two local cinemas and made a comfortable profit for all six of them over the last ten years would soon be sold out and disbanded.

He went home in a thoroughly bad temper and spent the rest of the evening banging every single door that was capable of being banged and re-living the whole stupid meeting, remark after asinine remark, for the unwilling benefit of poor Alice, who was pale with fatigue and wanted nothing more exciting than a nice warm hot water bottle and her nice quiet pillow.

'I'm sure it will all turn out for the best,' she said, trying to bring the diatribe to an end. 'You've said yourself the pictures aren't as popular these days as they used to be. Perhaps you'd all be well out of it.'

'Best! Best!' Albert roared. 'What do they know about business? You got to take risks. You don't make money being cautious. Fools! Where would we be if I'd been cautious? You tell me that. I never saw such fools!'

He was still in a towering temper when he finally agreed that they ought to go to bed, so he spent what was left of the night tossing and turning and kicking the mattress. But to Alice's great relief the news in the papers next morning was dramatic enough to take his mind off his disappointment. The expected general election had been called. The country would go to the polls on May 30th, and the editorials were full of speculation as to the difference the new flapper vote would make to the outcome.

Albert didn't approve of giving the franchise to young women, and neither did Alice, so for once they were in agreement. 'Time enough for them to vote when they've learned a bit of sense,' she said sternly, pouring him a second cup of tea. 'It's downright silly giving such responsibility to little bits of girls.' Even Anna and Lily would be going to the polls. It made her feel most annoyed. 'They're barely out of the cradle. If I could wait till I was forty-four I really don't see why they shouldn't wait until they're at least thirty.'

'They won't have the sense to vote properly,' Albert agreed

rustling the paper into the folds he required. 'Anyone can see that with half an eye.' He didn't have the vaguest idea what voting properly would entail this time, but he liked the sound of the sentiments. He usually voted for the Liberals, because that was what his friends on the Chamber of Commerce did, but now that he'd discovered a new circle of socialist friends in Bermondsey he wasn't sure of his affiliations at all. He would read the papers and go to one or two meetings and then he would make up his mind. The indecision of it was really quite exciting.

For Ned and Queenie there was no indecision at all. By the time Albert joined them in The Red Lion that evening they had already formed a local election committee and were busy making plans for a thorough canvass of every single house and flat in their crowded ward.

'We got ter get 'em all out,' Ned explained earnestly. 'Every vote's gonna count this time.' He was warm with enthusiasm, sitting in the centre of a group of local party members, scheming and dreaming, his dry cough barely noticeable in the babble of voices around him.

'*Should* he be doing all this?' Albert asked Queenie when he had her undivided attention for a moment, later in the evening.

'Try stopping 'im,' she said, cheerfully wiping the bar with a sloppy rag. 'It's what 'e lives for, this is. No! Be the breath a' life to 'im. We're gonna change the world this time. You wait an' see!'

He grinned at her determination, and she grinned back, flicking her untidy red hair out of her eyes. 'Got another bit a' good news this morning too,' she said. 'We move in on the twenty-seventh. Three days 'fore the election. Whatcher think a' that?'

'Be a busy week,' he said.

'Sommink out the ordinary anyway,' she agreed. 'Bit of excitement'll do us all good.'

'I will come up in the afternoon and give you a hand,' he promised. And then he had to turn his attention quickly to the political meeting at the other end of the pub because he had suddenly realized that what he really wanted was to be moving into the flat with her, and he couldn't even tell her.

She noticed the abrupt downturn of those bushy moustaches, and the way he averted his eyes, and was torn with pity for the need she couldn't answer. 'It's a rum old world,' she said to Mr Oxbury, with a sigh.

'In with a chance though, ain't we, gel?' he answered, thinking she was referring to the election like everyone else in his pub that evening.

She smiled at him but kept her thoughts to herself. For what chance did any of them have, tied by loyalties they couldn't avoid and responsibilities they'd taken on for life? Her dear old Ploo, taking himself off to the other end of the pub like that because he couldn't speak his thoughts. She watched his dark head moving among the cloth claps, the flecks of silver above his ears bright in the half light, and his moustache lifting and stretching as he spoke; and those dear tender hands talking too, as clearly as any words, swaying rhythmically like two brown cradles, chopping fiercely right against left, picking meaning out of the air neatly between middle finger and thumb, dancing and caressing, and she was suddenly consumed with desire for him, so swift and so strong that it made her feel quite weak and she had to walk about among the tables collecting empties in order to still it a little. They were both growing older, she thought sadly, and their love was wasting away unused.

177

Chapter Sixteen

Moving day was a very long time coming. Mary had had all her things packed in cardboard boxes for weeks and weeks. And ever since the letter had arrived she'd kept a calendar stuck to the wall beside her bed, and crossed off the days, one by one, with a weird blend of excitement and impatience.

'Watched pot never boils,' Ma said. But the sight of the growing mass of crossed out days was a comfort as the plaster fell and the cockroaches scuttled, and the mould grew black and spongy in the corners of the room. Soon they'd be out of all this, in a clean house, with an indoor lav, and a bath of their own, and electricity, and a little balcony. It was like dreaming of paradise.

Ma said she wasn't looking forward to it. She'd moved too often and she remembered last time. It 'ud rain, she said, sure as fate. She'd just be glad when it was over and done with. But Mary was buoyant with optimism.

And it didn't rain. It was a lovely, sunny day and marvellously exciting. Everybody was on the move at once, Mrs Gus and the Thompsons and the Pattersons and all four of the families in the corner house. Uncle Cal arrived with the cart, and they all set to and had it loaded in no time and then they were off.

There were six other families moving into the new flats on that day too, as well as all the people from Cherry Court, so the nice new courtyard was jammed with carts and tea chests and a cheerful muddle of aproned women and unwashed children. Two scraggy mongrels had joined the action just for the fun of it, and were busily inspecting every box and chest and every crumpled scrap of newspaper they could get their noses into, barking incessant encouragement and getting under every-body's feet. And the whole place smelt so new, with sharp new bricks and damp plaster and the resinous scent of new wood. It was smashing! And they were going to live in it. Mary stood beside the new lawn and enjoyed it all as she scanned the rows of uncurtained windows and empty balconies above her head and tried to work out which one was theirs.

Presently Ma emerged onto one of the balconies on the first floor. She was wearing one of the Ox's black aprons and had tied up her hair in a frayed cloth that looked like a bit of old curtain, but she was cheerful enough now they'd arrived. 'Door's open, so let's get cracking,' she commanded. 'They've done the lino.'

Soon the living room of their new flat was full of furniture and tea chests and cardboard boxes. 'We'll get it all in 'ere first and then we can sort out where we're going ter put it later,' Ma had said, and although Mary would have preferred to put things in their correct places straight away she knew better than to argue with her mother on moving day.

'Now,' Ma said surveying the muddle. 'Where shall we start?' And the doorbell rang.

'Our first visitor,' Mary said, thrilled at the idea. 'I'll go, shall I?'

It was the bedroom furniture Ploo had bought for her, and it took her breath away. 'Bli me, Ma!' she said as the delivery men struggled in with a dressing table padded with cardboard. 'Bli me!'

Ma was cross. 'It'll all 'ave ter go straight in your room,' she said. 'There ain't room fer it 'ere. Bed, it was s'pposd ter be. Not all this lot. You'll 'ave ter see to it.' So she did and was very proud to be allowed to do it.

It was lovely in her bedroom, high and quiet, with an amazing view of the river. Her very own room, with her very own furniture. She couldn't wait for the men to finish bringing it up so that she could unpack it and see it properly. Such lovely furniture, the wood so glossy and clean and new, and such a lot of it, a bed and a wardrobe and a chest of drawers and a dear little dressing table with a stool to match, and two lovely bookcases. She felt like a film star. Perhaps if she asked him nicely Uncle Cal would come in and help her lift it into position.

But when she got back into the crush of the sitting room, Pa was sitting on the floor with his back against a tea chest, drinking tea from a chipped enamel mug, and Aunty Eth was handing out fish and chips.

'Time fer a break,' Ma said. 'There's yours.'

It smelt smashing. 'Our very first meal,' she said happily. And Ploochy put his head round the door. He was in his oldest clothes and had his sleeves rolled up all ready for action.

''Lo mate,' Aunt Eth said. 'Fancy a cup a' char?'

It was thick, dark brown tea, flavoured with condensed milk, and Mary knew he didn't fancy it at all, but she noticed that he took it and pretended to drink it.

'You bought enough stuff fer our Mary Ann, didntcher?' Aunt Eth said, grinning her approval of his extravagance.

'Bed it was supposed ter be,' Ma said, licking her fingers. 'We got any vinegar?'

'Still packed,' Pa said, tossing the information over his shoulder. 'D'you ever see such a pickle, Ploo?'

'Soon 'ave it sorted out,' Ploo said cheerfully. 'Where d'yer want me ter start?'

Pa went back to the Cold Store when he'd finished his fish and chips, which Ma said was just as well, considering, and Cal went off to his shift, so Ma and Mary and Aunt Eth and Ploochy were the only ones left to do battle with the furniture. By the time they'd arranged everything, they were filthy dirty, and aching with exhaustion, and the flat seemed full to capacity.

And it was just at that moment that Fishers delivered the piano.

Mrs Gus brought the news. 'There's a bloke in the Grove says 'e's got a pianner fer you,' she told Ma. 'You made a clearance in 'ere, aintcher?'

Ma rounded on poor old Ploochy. 'What you been an' gone an' done now?' she said, angrily. 'You ain't never bought a pianner, 'ave yer?'

'It a very good pianner,' he said, and his anger matched hers at once. 'Don't you want your daughter to 'ave a pianner, you foolish woman?'

'A pianner!' Mary said entranced. A pianner of her very own. It was like a dream. Only Ma didn't seem to think so.

'You ain't got the sense you was born wiv!' she said, flouncing to the balcony to see what was going on. Aunt Eth gave Mary a sympathetic grimace as they both followed her, but when she saw the size of the piano, still filling the entire bulk of Fisher's largest delivery van, she began to laugh.

'Oh, Ploo!' she said. 'Look at it! How d'you ever imagine we could get a thing like that inside a flat like this. Oh my dear good God! You are a caution an' no mistake.'

'Caution my eye!' Ma said, scowling at the van and thumping her hands down onto her hips with a gesture of impatient anger that Mary recognized only too well. 'You don't never stop ter think, do you? You want yer bloody 'ead examined.'

'Ingrateful woman!' he roared at her. 'I buy this for you. I come 'ere all this way to 'elp you. I work 'ere to 'elp you. You don't deserve it! You don't deserve *me*. That the truth of it. You just ingrateful!' Now that he'd unleashed it, he was enjoying his anger, the way he'd always done when they used to row in the old days.

'Damn silly thing ter do!' Ma growled, undeterred by his temper. 'Where d'yer think we'd ever put a thing that size?'

Mary was still on the balcony gazing with undisguised longing at the musical magnificence that was still filling the delivery van. 'It's a lovely pianner, Ma,' she said. 'Couldn't we make room fer it, some'ow?'

'No we could not,' Ma said with horrible determination. 'Don't you start! It'll 'ave ter go back. That's all there is to it!'

'No that *not* all there is to it!' Ploochy shouted. 'You come with me, Mary. We fix it!' And he seized his coat and hat from the tea chest where Ma had flung them and charged out of the building. And as Ma didn't say she wasn't to, Mary trotted down the stairs after him. It looked like a lovely pianner. Surely they could make room for it somehow, particularly now Ploochy'd bought it. You couldn't go wasting a pianner.

The two delivery men were still examining the flats and scratching their heads over the impossibility of the job they'd been sent to do. And now that she was out in the warm sunshine and facing the enormous bulk of the piano Mary could see that Ma was quite right. It would never fit in the flat. But it was a lovely, lovely pianner.

Ploochy was talking to the delivery men. 'Of course,' he was saying, 'I tell you what you do. You return it to the shop and I will ring Mr Fisher with instructions later. You've had a lot of trouble for nothing. Treat yourself to a drink before you go back, eh?' and he gave them both half a crown apiece. What extravagance! But it certainly restored their good temper immediately.

'Ta very much,' the driver said, and he climbed into his seat and inched the van out of the Grove, while his mate waved goodbye to all the children who had gathered on the green to watch the fun. Mary watched too, standing quietly at Ploochy's side, but her face was withdrawn into disappointment.

He put out a hand and drew her fingers into the crook of his arm, patting them comfortingly. 'You shall have your piano, Mary Ann,' he promised gently. 'I will fix it.' He didn't have the faintest idea how it could be done, but he was determined to do it. Particularly after Queenie had been so abusively angry with him. She was standing on the balcony now, looking insufferably smug. 'Told yer!' she shouted at him, and his anger rose again despite the hand holding his elbow.

'I'm off!' he shouted back. 'An' serve you right!' But his face was glowing, with love as well as temper. 'Come on Mary Ann,' he said, 'we go for a ride eh?' and he stomped off across the new green following his anger wherever it led.

She had to run to keep up with him, he was pounding along so quickly. They reached Jamaica Road in record time and he jumped onto the running board of the first tram he saw.

'Where we going?' she asked breathlessly, clambering up after him.

'No idea!' he said, and asked the conductor.

It appeared they were going to Peckham Rye. What an extraordinary man he is! Mary thought. Fancy getting on a tram and not knowing where you're going! What'll 'e do next?

Peckham Rye was dozing in the afternoon sun. It was a very posh place. Not a bit like Bermondsey. All the shops and houses were different from one another and none of the streets were straight. They curved and turned abrupt corners as if they were rivers. Right in the middle where the tram stopped there was a triangular space where the High Street was joined by Peckham Hill and Rye Lane in a tangle of tramlines and traffic and wandering pedestrians in very smart clothes. On the corner of Rye Lane stood Jones and Higgins department store, where Ma was going to buy her uniform if she passed the scholarship. It had a high clock tower on one corner with a gilded weathercock on top and there were golden numerals on the clock face. It looked impressive and prosperous and so did the shops that fronted the High Street, where Ma had bought her some chocolate once.

'Come on!' Ploochy said and he went bounding off across the street towards the parade. One of the shops was empty of everything except dust, and a board above the front door proclaimed that H.A. Whiting, Estate Agent, was offering it for sale.

'What you say I buy this shop?' he asked.

She didn't know what to say. People didn't just walk in and buy shops, did they? Like a pound of apples or new boots. 'I'll 'ave this shop. Send it wrapped!' The idea made her giggle, and he laughed too, his great, roaring laugh, slapping his thigh with one dirty, brown hand.

'Come on!' he said again. 'Estate agent just round the corner.'

Mr Whiting's estate agency was terribly posh, and the clerk behind the mahogany counter was a most superior person. He wasn't at all pleased to see them when they came barging into his nice quiet office, as Mary could tell from the way he looked down his nose at her dirty dress, but he was extremely polite.

'Can I help you, sir?' he said.

'You have a shop for sale in the High Street,' Ploochy said brusquely. 'I wish to buy it.'

The clerk looked pointedly at their dirty clothes but then he noticed that Ploochy had a thick gold watchchain dangling across his waistcoat and that there was a fat diamond embedded in the gold signet ring on his left hand. He decided that this man was either an impoverished con artist or rich and eccentric, but that either way he ought to be handled with care. 'Well actually, sir,' he smoothed, 'that particular property is being handled by Mr Whiting. Would you like me to call him for you?' That'll settle him, he thought, if he's not the genuine article. And he went away, looking smug, and left them standing in the quiet office.

Mr Whiting was a long, thin gentleman with a stoop. When he entered the office he had a rather worried expression on his face, but when he saw Ploochy he cheered up at once. 'Get a chair for Mr Ploochy,' he ordered the clerk, 'and one for the young lady. And look sharp about it.' That was nice! 'The young lady.' And it was a lovely chair too. The seat was made of velvet. She sat on it cautiously, hoping she wasn't making it dirty, and waited while the two gentlemen talked.

'You've come at just the right time, Albert,' Mr Whiting said. 'We've got some splendid properties. Suit you to a T.' He reached behind him for one of the folders that stood in ordered ranks on his neat shelves, all carefully labelled and full of papers. 'No, not that one. What am I thinking of? That's houses. You don't want houses do you?'

'Houses?' Ploochy said, thinking about it. 'Bless me, yes! That *is* what we want, issen' it, Mary. A nice big house fer a nice big piano. Somewhere between the High Street and St Olave's Girls. What you got?'

Mary knew that her mouth had fallen open but she couldn't help it. Was he really going to buy a house just for the piano? People didn't do things like that. In fact, the people she knew didn't even buy houses to put themselves in. They simply couldn't afford it.

Mr Whiting was more skilled at hiding his feelings than she was. He didn't reveal his surprise even by the merest flicker of an eyelid. Six suitable houses were chosen at once. 'We could inspect them now if you'd care to,' he said. 'I could take you there in my new motor.' The car was his most recent acquisition and he was inordinately proud of it. It would be marvellous to show it off to old Ploochy.

Soon the three of them were bouncing over the tramlines and on their way towards Camberwell, following the tree-lined curves of Peckham Road, and being admired by all the passers-by. It was very exciting, sitting up so high above the road, and on leather too, that gave off a lovely warm, horsy smell in the strong sunlight. But Mary didn't know what to think. It was the first time in her life she'd ever seen a rich man in action, and although it was extraordinary and undeniably exciting, like something out of an adventure story, she couldn't help feeling a bit – well – ashamed of the way he was going on.

It wasn't right that one man should have so much money that he could buy up shops and houses whenever he felt like it, while others couldn't even earn enough to feed their families.

But she didn't say anything because it wouldn't have been right. Not then. And presently they arrived at the first house.

It wouldn't do at all, Ploochy said. It wasn't big enough. So they drove on. The second was tall and chill and dark and the third detached and disapproving. But the fourth was promising. It was one of a pair and had been built in the expansive style of the eighties, with large windows and an imposing front door and a bold gable above the main bedroom window, its bargeboards painted white and elaborately carved. It stood in a small, quiet square off Lyndhurst Way facing its neighbours across a railed garden of green lawns and unexpected trees, pale limes and silver birches, a horse chestnut heavy with foliage and a eucalyptus with delicate *eau-de-nil* leaves and ginger bark as shaggy as hemp.

As they stopped the car outside the house, a blackbird began to sing his evening song from the branches of a may tree in the front garden and, looking towards it, Albert noticed to his great satisfaction that the garden also contained a fine laurel bush and a laburnum and that there was a wisteria plant covering the left hand wall of the house with grape clusters of pale lilac blossom. Mary thought it was the most magnificent house she'd ever seen. A house for a toff.

'We will see it,' Ploochy said.

They walked up the garden path, Mr Whiting stooped and stalking, Ploochy bounding with excitement, and Mary following on tiptoe, in awe of the quiet and the grandeur. 'In very good condition,' Mr Whiting promised, fitting the key in the lock. 'Well maintained. Been in the same family since it was built, you see.'

The hall reminded Albert so strongly of his first house in London that he felt at home at once, for it contained the same elaborate hall stand and a similar aspidistra and was even decorated with the same wallpaper. Mary was overwhelmed by it, looking first at the Turkey carpet and then at the wallpaper and then at him, her eyes round in her dirty face.

Mr Whiting took them on a tour of the downstairs rooms, noting the capacious cellar, the well equipped kitchen, the convenient scullery, the dining room with its oak table and a dazzling overmantel to reflect the light, and finally they arrived at the drawing room. It ran the full length of the house, from a wide window overlooking the square to French windows leading through a conservatory full of overgrown plants into a back garden lush with roses and honeysuckle. It was everything Albert now knew he was looking for. Not a huge barn of a place like his great house in Tooting, nor a common little flat like the one he'd shared with Queenie in Clapham, but just the right size, a secure, solid, comfortable, dependable house. The place where he and Queenie and Mary Ann would live together like the family they really were. 'I buy it,' he said.

Mr Whiting was purring.

'What you think, eh, Mary Ann?' Ploochy said. 'You'd like ter live in a house like this now, wouldn't you?' He sounded ridiculously pleased with himself.

'No,' Mary said, and was perversely pleased to see his face fall. But really, what a silly thing to ask, just when they'd moved into their lovely flat and she'd got her nice clean, square room with its view of the Thames and electricity and a bath and everything she could possibly want.

He bought the house, there and then, with a cheque. And after that they went back to the office and he bought the shop too, because it had interested him and it was in a good position, and because it would give him an excuse for frequent visits to Peckham.

Then he took Mary to a slap-up tea in a very posh restaurant where all the waitresses called him Mr Ploochy and one of them took Mary off to a palatial washroom so that she could wash her dirty hands and have a tinkle.

And when she'd eaten all she wanted and they'd had two pots of tea, he told her they were going to make a bargain.

'Can you keep a secret, little Mary?'

'Of course,' she said. That was a matter of honour.

'Then I tell you what. We keep this house a secret, eh? Just between the two of us. We not tell no one. Not even your ma.'

She'd never kept a secret from Ma in the whole of her life. 'For always?' she asked.

'No,' he said laughing.

'How long?'

186

'Six weeks. Eight maybe. Then we surprise 'er, eh? What you say? We bring 'er down 'ere and show 'er the 'ouse an' surprise 'er.'

The idea of surprising Ma was very tempting. So although she knew it would be impossibly difficult, she agreed.

'Now I'd better take you home,' he said, flashing his brown eyes at the waitress for the bill.

They got home just in time for her to help Ma cook the supper in their nice new kitchen, and for the next two days they were all so busy she forgot about the house and her promise. But on the third afternoon, while Ma and Pa were out knocking people up to vote in the general election, she remembered and wondered. And it all seemed a bit silly really. Why should Ma be excited because Ploochy'd bought a house? If only Pa wasn't so busy with the election she'd ask him what he thought, but she knew she wouldn't get a chance. Not now.

The general election was something of an anticlimax to Albert. He voted for the Liberals again, but out of habit and not because he'd given the matter very much thought. And when his newspaper analysed the muddle of the results and proclaimed that with Labour winning two hundred and eighty-eight seats and the Conservatives with two hundred and sixty, the Liberals with their mere fifty-nine were actually holding the balance of power, he didn't really care.

It was mid July before contracts were signed on his new house and he was able to take possession, but for once in his life he managed to keep a secret. He told his business associates about the shop, and Alice, of course, but he kept the house hidden like a private pleasure, having the piano delivered, hiring a gardener and a firm of decorators, and even a cook-housekeeper, but waiting, with a quite amazing patience, until everything was exactly as he wanted it to be.

And Mary kept her promise and her secret, because she'd almost forgotten about it, and because there were more important things in her life. She won her scholarship to St Olave's, just as her teacher had predicted, and Ploochy gave her a splendid party when the results came through. And on the very next day he took her and Ma to Peckham to buy her new school uniform.

When they emerged from Jones and Higgins, laden with parcels, it was mid afternoon and the streets were crowded with shoppers. 'Now,' Ploochy said to Ma, 'Mary an' me got something we want you to see.'

She was suspicious. 'What sort a' thing?'

'A house,' he said, hailing a cab. 'Come on. We show you.'

'What you up to, Ploo?' she asked as the cab headed west. 'You never said nothink about no 'ouse. What's 'e been an' gone an' done now?'

'Nothing!' he said, but his face was wrinkled with smiles and devilment.

It's all very well him looking like that, Mary thought. She's cross. I knew she wouldn't be excited. It's nothing to do with us.

But they went to the house just the same because he was so happy and so insistent. And it *was* a nice house. Even Ma thought that. She could see. He ushered them into the drawing room, and there was her lovely pianner standing in the sunlight. It made her sigh with longing just to look at it.

'Would you like to play it?' Albert asked, beaming more widely than ever.

'Wouldn't I just?'

'Then go ahead.'

So she settled herself on the leather stool and lifted the lid cautiously and began to play.

'I show your mother the rest a' the house,' Albert said, encouraged by the way things were turning out. And although Queenie gave him a quizzical look, she followed him out to the kitchen, and was introduced to Mrs Midgeley, the housekeeper, and admired the view from the window, and agreed that the garden was very pretty.

'Roses and honeysuckle,' Albert said with satisfaction, as if he'd created them specially.

'Daft ha'porth,' she said.

'Wait till you see upstairs.'

She took a peep at the bathroom and said the front bedroom was very grand, and then followed him into the back bedroom which was beautifully decorated but empty, because this was going to be Mary's room and he'd bought her furniture already.

'What you think?' he asked.

'It's yours, ain't it?'

'Yes,' he agreed happily. 'What you think?'

She laughed at him. 'You beat cock fighting, Ploo, you really do. Whatcher want ter go an' buy another 'ouse for?'

'I bought it for the piano,' he said, grinning at her.

'No you never,' she said lovingly. 'You bought it fer us. This is Mary's room. That's why it's empty.' She turned away from him, sighing with disappointment and frustration. 'I can't leave Ned. You know that, dontcher?'

'I know,' he said gently, putting his hands on her shoulders to turn her back towards him again. 'I won't persuade you. I promise. It's here when we need it, that's all.'

His tact and patience overwhelmed her, and his touch was too tempting to be borne. She gave a little moan and swayed towards him. And then they were in one another's arms and kissing with the anguished intensity of great affection and long frustration. Somewhere behind the riotous pounding of their long subdued blood, Mary's cool music rose to serenade and remind them, but they kissed with abandon, forgetful of everything except the pleasure of the moment. Soon he was fondling her breasts with his thumbs in the old delightful way, and she was biting at the lobes of his ears and rolling her belly against him, and the pattern that neither of them had forgotten was carrying them along again towards stronger and stronger sensation.

The music stopped abruptly, and the lack of it brought them suddenly to their senses. They drew apart, listening almost fearfully, because footsteps on a well carpeted stair were difficult to detect. 'Quick,' Queenie whispered, 'make yerself respectable. She mussen' see us like this.'

They straightened their clothes guiltily, and by the time Mary put her bright face round the door they were standing at the window admiring the view of the garden. 'There's a lady downstairs says tea is served,' she told them, and to their relief she didn't seem to notice anything amiss.

'We mussen' do that again, Ploo,' Queenie whispered as they followed the child downstairs.

'Why not?' he whispered into her hair.

'Have some sense,' she hissed at him, and now she sounded cross.

'I love you,' he told her. They were nearly at the bottom of the stairs.

'Oh, Ploo,' she said. 'I dunno what's ter become of us!'

As they settled to their tea in the posh dining room with its dark furniture and its thick red wallpaper, Mary noticed that her mother *was* pleased by the house after all. She looked so happy, and she was licking the jam off her fingers. How weird grown-ups were sometimes!

Chapter Seventeen

In August Georgie's second baby was born. She was a plump little girl and they christened her Margaret. Albert was thrilled with her and went charging off to the West End to buy her extravagant toys and more pretty dresses that she could possibly wear.

Then it was September and time for Mary to start her career at St Olave's Grammar School for Girls. She wore her full winter uniform on her first day, like all the other first formers, and came home swollen with pride and heat as a consequence. It *did* make her feel special, Tom was right, setting out in the morning in her smart blue coat and her neat velour hat with its superior badge. Proud and special and set apart. A grammar school girl. But the feeling soon wore off as she got used to her new style of life, and by the end of her first year she hardly noticed the uniform at all because she was so busy. During her second year, she started violin lessons. By the end of her third she was in the school orchestra. In the evenings she stopped off at Ploo's house in Lyndhurst Square for an hour's piano practice, and his housekeeper gave her tea and sent her home with a bunch of flowers from the garden. It was a very good life even if she did have to do homework every evening.

In her modern flat in Raynes Park, Anna continued to endure. Eric was just the same as ever, going off to work every morning as neat and smart as a rolled umbrella. She kept herself cheerful, tidying her flat every day and going to tea dances to relieve the boredom. But privately she felt that life was passing her by. It was another New Year now, 1933, and what had she got to show for it? She longed for excitement and yearned for love. If only something would happen to change things.

Her mother on the other hand had noticed a change and didn't approve of it.

'I reckon Albert's got a woman somewhere,' she said to Minnie as the two of them sat by the fire busy with their embroidery. She'd had her suspicions for more than three years now, ever since he'd bought that shop over in Peckham, but this last week had confirmed them. Staying out all night once a month was one thing, but twice a week was quite another.

'Oh not Albert, surely,' Minnie said, finishing off a French knot, and looking up hopefully for more.

It was a very cold night, even for mid January, and the two women had barricaded themselves into the little front parlour, with the curtains drawn and the draught excluders mounded against the door, and had settled down beside their nice warm fire for an evening of wireless and embroidery and gossip. Now that their children had all left home and they no longer had to care for an old lady, their evenings had taken on an almost luxurious indolence.

Percy's latest letter had been read and re-read, and three snapshots of Georgie's children had been much admired and then stuck carefully into the current photograph album, they'd enjoyed 'Those were the Days', and now they were into the third and most satisfying phase of the evening, the criticism of their husbands.

'It wouldn't be the first time,' Alice said, starting on the centre of a large blue daisy. 'He had quite an affair when the children were little. A horrible, skinny actress with red hair she was. Dickie used to see them out together at Luigi's, you remember, that old restaurant in Clapham. And Tilley used to tell me. He thought I didn't know what was going on. But I knew right enough. And I know now. Men are such fools!'

'But he's sixty, Alice,' Minnie protested. 'He's a grandfather!'

'And whatever makes you think a thing like that would stop him?' Alice said, jabbing her needle into the linen cloth with unnecessary fierceness. 'No, you mark my words, he's got a woman. All this stopping overnight in Peckham. He doesn't fool me.'

Minnie was really eager now, for there was nothing she enjoyed as much as the vicarious thrill of a romance, especially if it was illicit. 'I'm sure you're wrong,' she said, encouragingly. 'Your Albert's such a nice man, even if he does have a paddy on him sometimes. Look how generous he is. Perhaps he's just staying overnight to help someone out.'

'The only person he's helping is himself,' Alice said scowling at the daisy. 'I haven't said anything about it to the children. This is just between you and me, you understand.'

'Of course,' Minnie agreed, but feeling rather disappointed because it looked as though this fascinating topic was being closed. 'They've got lives of their own to worry about.'

Which was certainly true of Anna, who took one of her worries to a doctor the very next morning. It was a very delicate subject and they were both pink with embarrassment to be discussing it.

'If I were you, my dear lady,' the doctor said, trying to find an escape, 'I should go in for a nice little baby. That's what I would advise. That would solve all your problems.' He smiled benignly at her over his long white fingers, wishing her anywhere but in his surgery.

'But in the meantime, isn't there something you could do to stop the pain?' Anna said, pressing on despite her embarrassment. 'Surely it isn't natural to have such a lot of pain. Not month after month.'

'Have you tried aspirin?' the doctor offered. These women with dysmenorrhoea, under-employed neurotics, the lot of them.

'Of course!' Anna said scornfully. The man was a fool. 'It *is* very bad pain, doctor. Aspirins don't have any effect on it. I'm creased in agony, don't you understand.'

'A baby,' the doctor said firmly, edging away from the note of hysteria in her voice. 'That's the answer. You go away and think about it, and if you're not improved in three months time come back and see me again.'

Anna left the surgery in a bad temper. How could she possibly get pregnant, even if she wanted to, when Eric only did it once a week? She wondered what the doctor would have said if she'd told him that. Called her names probably, like Eric did on the rare occasions when she actually felt she might enjoy it and tried to encourage him to start.

She walked miserably away from the doctor's fine house, wondering whether she would ever get pregnant and whether other women had quite so much pain with their periods or quite so little fun in bed. The heroines in the novels she read always seemed to enjoy whatever they did, although of course, none of them were ever described doing 'that'. But they were always swooning with bliss and being kissed till their heads spun. It was horribly unfair and horribly difficult. Particularly as there was nobody she could ask about it. It had taken her weeks to gather up enough courage even to tell a doctor about her cramps, and now she knew she'd simply wasted her time. Oh, why did life have to be so terribly difficult?

She decided she would make a special effort that evening, cook a very special meal and wear her most daring dress and plenty of make-up. If a baby was the answer, perhaps she ought to try. Georgie and Lily had babies easily enough, and Georgie was a dull old stick. Unless he had hidden talents. The bawdy thought cheered her and made her plans more acceptable. A special effort, and perhaps that would do the trick. She wasn't really sure whether she would know how to cope with a baby, but everybody else had babies and seemed to manage all right, so she would probably be the same. And goodness knows, she needed something to give her life some purpose.

Eric enjoyed the meal and said his bunny woo was the cleverest cook alive and looked absolutely ripping in her new dress. But when she suggested an early night he said there was something on the wireless he wanted to hear. It turned out to be a dreadfully boring talk about some silly man called Herr Hitler, who'd just been appointed Chancellor of Germany, or something like that, and was the leader of some silly political party called the National Socialists. Eric listened to every word, nodding and approving and looking wise, but it very nearly sent her to sleep. Nevertheless, she sat it out and managed to keep her eyes open. But it was well past midnight before they went to bed and Eric turned off the light and settled himself on his side ready for sleep the minute he got between the covers.

'Aren't you going to kiss your booful goodnight, Itchy?' she cooed, pouting prettily at him even though she wasn't sure he could see the full effect in the darkness.

He kissed her forehead, chastely, as though they were brother and sister. 'No, Itchy coo,' she said. 'Not like that! Kiss me properly.' And she put her hands round his waist and tried to tug him into a better position.

He resisted solidly. 'It's very late, Anna,' he rebuked. 'Time we were asleep.'

'Don't you love your ickle bunny wunny?' she tried, still tugging his unyielding ribcage.

'Of course I do,' he said, angrily patient. 'Now go to sleep, there's a good girl.'

'I don't want to be a good girl,' she lisped, snuggling up against his side so as to give him the idea, 'I want to be a bad bad girl. Wouldn't 'oo like 'oo's bunny to be weally bad?'

'No!' he said, horrified. 'I would not.'

'Come on, come on,' she urged, snuggling even closer as he tried to edge away from her. Pursuing him like this was making her feel very sexy. She slid her hands artlessly down his belly, wondering whether she could get close enough to feel what sort of state he was in.

He sprang out of the bed as though she'd given him an electric shock. It was cold outside the covers, but he simply couldn't stay in a bed with a woman who was acting like a nymphomaniac. Pawing at him like that! Grabbing at him! It was disgusting! 'It isn't Saturday!' he shouted at her, his eyes bolting out of his head.

'Oh, what does that matter?'

'Saturday is when we ...'

'I know that. But why not now? Or can't you manage it?'

'You're abnormal,' he said, shaking with fury at the implication of what she'd just said. 'Once a week is quite enough for anybody.'

'But I don't always want it when you do,' she said.

He covered his ears with his hands. 'Filth!' he shouted. 'You're talking like a street walker.' He was very frightened. The book he'd bought just after they were married, with great daring and because he was afraid of his ignorance, had made it quite clear that too much of 'that' was positively dangerous. It drained you of energy and made you unfit for work the next morning. Once a week was what the author advocated and once a week was what Eric accepted. On Saturday night, after they'd been to the pictures, so that he could sleep it off the next morning and nobody at work need be any the wiser. Not now, in the middle of the night!

'You can't do it, can you,' she said taunting him.

'Shut up!'

'You can't do it! You're not a proper man!'

He was shivering, and even though it was dark in the bedroom he felt sure she could see. 'I'm not staying here to listen to this filth,' he said, and was annoyed to hear that his voice was shaking too. He ripped one of the blankets off their bed and wrapped it round him like a protective shield. 'I shall sleep on the sofa,' he said, stumbling across the dark room.

'Coward!' she shouted after him. But he'd already gone.

She was tense with anger and frustration and the demoralizing knowledge that somehow or other he'd made her look dirty and unnatural. Sleep was out of the question now, but it was too cold for her to get out of bed, so she stayed where she was and felt sorry for herself and cried a great deal and listened to the wind howling outside the window, until it was dawn and the street lights came on again and the sky turned muddy pink. Then, although she didn't notice it, she must have fallen asleep, because the next thing she knew she had just woken up and it was nearly ten o'clock.

Eric had got up and made himself breakfast, and left for work without a word or a note. Well, she thought, if that's the way he's going to behave I shall go out and buy myself a new hat, and he can have bread and cheese for his supper and see how he likes that.

But he came home in his most charming mood, smiling his film star smile, as smooth as a tailor's dummy, all baby talk and chocolates. So they went out to dinner and billed and cooed all through the meal and were the envy of all the other courting couples in the restaurant. And Anna resigned herself to the fact that she would never be pregnant and sex would always be a bore.

Fortunately she was very late coming on that month, and that was cheering because any delay in the onset of that creasing pain was a blessing. Two weeks passed, and then three, and still nothing happened, although her breasts were sore enough for it to start at any minute. But still the days passed, and she got used to the soreness, and now it was more than two months since she'd seen anything. Surely he couldn't have managed it after all. That really would be too funny! She consulted her encyclopaedia, which didn't help her and finally, when eleven weeks had gone by and still nothing had happened, she went back to that objectionable doctor. He was horribly condescending, of course, beastly man, but he confirmed her pregnancy. This time she laughed all the way home.

She didn't tell Eric, because he didn't deserve it and anyway she wasn't really sure how he'd take it, and she didn't want to provoke another scene. Besides, she had a much better idea. Easter was approaching, and at Easter her father and mother always gave a special dinner for all the family. She would wait for a suitable moment during the meal and then surprise them all. Eric would have to be charming and Lily would have to stop being so beastly superior, and Mummy would have to admit that her daughter was every bit as good as her daughter-in-law. She decided she would dress in pink because it was such a feminine colour and it would make her look frail and interesting. The more she thought about it, the more delightful it all seemed. It would be a triumph for her.

Georgie and Lily were trying to make up their minds whether or not to go up to the West End and see *42nd Street*, the latest Hollywood musical, which by all accounts was really good. Now that little Johnny was at infant school and Margaret had grown into a most amenable three year old, they sometimes left her with Madeleine next door and sneaked off to the pictures for the afternoon when the off-licence was shut. But they'd never been up West before, and Lily wasn't at all sure whether they ought to.

'Go on!' Madeleine urged. 'Spoil yerselves. Do you good. She'll be as right as rain playing with my Joanie. Won't you, lovey?'

So it was settled. And although Lily couldn't help worrying a bit, because Margaret was only a baby really, it was certainly very pleasant to be on her own with Georgie for a few hours, especially now, and especially on such a nice afternoon, with the sun shining and the days lengthening and spring on its way.

They dodged across the road to the tube station, holding hands and as happy as kids hopping school. After six years of marriage and the demands of two lusty babies their delight in one another was stronger than ever.

During Lily's first pregnancy, well meaning school friends had warned Georgie that a baby would 'soon take the gilt off the gingerbread.' Johnny Ashby had been horribly pessimistic. 'You'll be up all night teething,' he said. 'You'll never have a moment's peace. It'll yell all the time and there'll always be nappies on the line, and she'll be too tired for anything. They're the very devil, babies, I'm telling you!' His own was three months old and he was heartily sick of it.

But Johnny Pelucci had turned out to be a plump, placid baby with a mop of dark, curly hair and big blue eyes and a smile that was so delicious and so direct that he bewitched them both. Lily hadn't read any books on how to bring up babies, so she simply fed him when he was hungry and cuddled him when he cried, exactly as her mother had done. She quickly established a rapport with her infant that was quicker and more profound than anything she had ever experienced, even with Georgie. And although Georgie wasn't sure that his son really ought to be feeding at all hours of the day and night, because, of course, he *had* read the books, as it didn't seem to be worrying Lily and the baby was obviously thriving on it, he didn't criticize. In fact, as the months passed and Johnny grew into a splendidly self-confident toddler who ate anything he was offered and slept peacefully at nights and didn't seem to be the least bit spoilt, he even began to wonder whether the books were wrong.

By the time Margaret arrived, two years later on a beautiful morning in October, and was fed within minutes of her birth, he had forgotten that he ever had any doubts. The nurse was an earnest lady who was a firm believer in the methods of the great Dr Truby King. She lectured Lily about the need for four-hourly feeds and strict discipline, and suggested that the new baby should be put in a room by itself during the night so that it could cry itself out without disturbing them. 'You've got to let her know who's boss,' she said, fastening her bag with a brisk snap. 'It doesn't do to spoil these little creatures.'

Lily, secure in her own experience and Georgie's support,

didn't attempt to argue. She said yes, and smiled at the nurse over her new baby's delicious dark head, and waited until her visit was over and Georgie had seen her out and come back into the bedroom with little Johnny. 'We know who's boss, don't we my darling,' she said to the warm head nuzzling into her neck. 'Come and see your little sister, Johnny. Isn't she a duck? As if we could leave her on her own in the night, and not feed her when she's hungry, the pretty dear.'

'She *very* little,' Johnny said, fitting a forefinger inside the baby's grasping fingers, and beaming with delight when she held on. 'Oh, look, Daddy. She holdin' my hand.'

'Who's my very best, lovely boy?' Lily said hugging him, and at that Georgie had to cuddle all three of them because he thought they were all so marvellous and he felt so supremely happy.

'No bouncing on the bed!' Lily said mimicking the nurse to perfection. 'Fat lot she knows about beds!'

'It's the best place in the house,' Georgie said tenderly. And so it was. A place for love and birth and suckling babies. For pleasure and happiness and security. The centre of their lives.

The daffodils were in bud in Leicester Square, and there were two flower sellers outside the cinema offering 'Lovely vi'lets' so Georgie bought a little bunch for Lily to pin on her coat. And the film was lovely too, although Georgie would have found any film lovely just for the pleasure of watching it in the dark with Lily cuddled up against his side. When the mighty Wurlitzer rose from the depths in its effulgent pink light and the organist began to play 'In a Monastery Garden' fortissimo and with a lot of frantic footwork, he was quite dreamy with contentment.

'Look down there,' Lily said squeezing his hand. 'There's our first. Third row. Holding hands.'

'So they are,' Georgie agreed. 'Six out of ten, I should say.'

It was a private game they'd started soon after they were married, spotting other loving couples, and assessing the strength of their affection. 'They're not looking at each other much,' Lily said. 'I'd only give them four.'

'Couple behind us,' Georgie said. 'Seven. Her lipstick's smudged.'

'Oh yes,' Lily agreed after a surreptitious glance, 'and he's got his arm round her. I wonder if we'll find a ten.'

They were still lover spotting when the lights dimmed for the second half, and the best they'd found was an eight. 'Perhaps we're the only tens left,' Georgie said, kissing her in the darkness.

But they weren't, for as they were leaving the foyer at the end of the performance they saw a lovely couple just ahead of them, an obvious ten. They were quite old, the man's dark hair greying at the temples, and the woman's face lined, and they were both wearing very old-fashioned clothes, but they were a lovely ten nevertheless. The man had just put an easy arm around his partner's waist and scooped her body against his side. It was such an experienced, contented movement, and she had answered it so readily, swaying towards him and turning her head to smile straight into his eyes. There was no doubt about the strength of this affair. 'Ten!' Georgie said, delighted with them, and hugging Lily in the same way. Then the couple turned as they reached the entrance and with a sense of sudden shock and disbelief, Georgie recognized the man. It was his father.

'Oh my goodness!' Lily whispered, standing where she was beside the sweet kiosk. 'Whatever shall we do?'

'I don't think they saw us,' Georgie said.

'But we saw them. How awful! Who is she, Georgie?'

'I don't know,' Georgie said. 'But whoever she is, she loves him.'

They worried about it all the way home. 'We're going to dinner Easter Sunday,' Lily said. 'I shan't know what to say to him. Perhaps we shouldn't go this year, Georgie.' She'd never been really at her ease in her mother-in-law's house, and this looked like an excellent excuse to break with tradition.

But Georgie wouldn't hear of it. 'It would upset Mother dreadfully,' he said, 'and it's not her fault he's ...'

'It might be,' Lily said, greatly daring. 'It takes two, when all's said an' done. I wouldn't rate your parents one out a' ten. I always thought they were too old for it.' Then she was almost afraid of what she'd said, because it sounded so rude.

Georgie was stunned for a second, because she'd never been so outspoken before, but then he gave it thought and decided

200

he liked this uncharacteristic boldness, even if it was shocking. 'You're right,' he said lovingly, 'you dreadful woman. But we must go to dinner. It would upset the children if we didn't. *They* enjoy it, even if we don't.'

And that clinched it, because it was true. Whatever else Lily might think about her mother-in-law, she had to admit that she was very, very fond of her grandchildren, petting them and spoiling them at every opportunity, with mounds of presents for them at Christmas, and Easter eggs beside their plates on Easter Sunday and a Bank Holiday outing in August that was organized almost entirely for their amusement.

'It'll be ever so awkward,' she said, but the resignation in her tone told Georgie that she had agreed.

'We shall manage,' he said, giving her a brief hug to show her how much he appreciated the effort she was going to make. 'We always do, don't we?'

And so the family gathered for the feast, Anna in her new pale pink dress hanging on to the arm of her smooth, pale pink husband; Lily in her old blue cardigan, smiling as her children hopped from toe to toe with excitement; Alice and Minnie in their new Easter blouses and Albert presiding at the head of the table, noisily cheerful, just as he always was. There were daffodils on the table and Easter eggs on the sideboard and the sun was shining.

'There you are,' Georgie whispered to Lily. 'It's all going to be all right. What did I tell you?'

The roast pork was borne in, sizzling on its dish, and the crackling was carefully detached and distributed, and the very nicest pieces of oven-browned meat were cut off the joint for Margaret and Johnny.

'Nothing but the best for our darlings, eh?' Albert said, beaming at them from the top of the table.

'Pretty dears!' Minnie said. 'And so good. They're the best behaved children I've ever known,' and she gave her smile to Lily.

'Quite right!' Albert boomed. 'A credit to you both. Don't you think so, Alice?'

Alice was busy cutting Margaret's meat into tiny pieces, and the child was watching, leaning affectionately against her arm as she worked. Johnny watched too, waiting his turn patiently and quite confident that he would be the next to receive her attention. She smiled lovingly at them both. 'You're my little darlings,' she said. 'Your old grandma can't think of anything nicer than having grandchildren round to dinner.'

And at that, Lily and Anna both opened their mouths at the same time and spoke their news together.

'What would you say if I told you …' Anna began and then hesitated, realizing that Lily was speaking too.

'… another baby,' Lily said, and then looked at her sister-in-law with amazement. 'You too?'

This wasn't how Anna had intended it at all. She was very put out. Wasn't that just typical of Lily! She couldn't even allow her to have a baby on her own.

But Albert was roaring with delight and had sprung out of his chair and rushed around the table to hug his two delightful, breeding daughters. 'When will it be?' he boomed at Anna.

'October,' she said smugly. At least she'd got that in first.

Lily smiled at her. 'I'm ever so glad for you,' she said. 'Just think. We shall be carrying together. Our's is due in August. Won't that be nice?'

'Ripping!' Anna said, hiding her chagrin with commendable control. Then she caught sight of Eric's face and realized that she'd stunned him into shock, and felt pleased with herself again.

'We go shopping!' her father promised happily. 'All three of us. How about that, eh?'

'Ripping!' Anna said again, smiling stiffly. But it wasn't how she'd planned it. There wouldn't be any fun in sharing a pregnancy. Oh, how dreadfully unfair life was! She never got anything she wanted. Not ever!

202

Chapter Eighteen

Pregnancy was a miserable disappointment to Anna Barnes. It was true that her father took her up to the West End and bought a crib and a pram and a most expensive layette for his latest grandchild, and made his usual fuss doing it, but his mind was focused almost entirely on the baby, which was most unfair because the silly thing didn't even exist properly yet, and she did, and needed attention so much. And her mother was worse, because although she spent a great deal of time talking to her during that ghastly, swelling summer, their conversation was either about babies and how delightful they were, which was a sentiment she didn't share, or worse, and more often, about birth and how painful and difficult it was, which was something she would have preferred to ignore.

Eric had been perfectly beastly about the whole business, but really that was no surprise to her. Not now. When they got home after that disappointing Easter Sunday he had ranted at her for over half an hour, telling her what a fool she was, and how she'd humiliated him in front of her parents and how he certainly had no intention of being tied down to some awful child and finally ordering her to get rid of it. She had agreed, not because she had any intention of obeying him, she wouldn't have done that even if she'd known how to, but because it was the only way of shutting him up. And he'd shut up at once, and spent the rest of the evening silently reading an article about National Socialism and looking insufferably smug.

He didn't mention the topic again for weeks and neither did she. Spring burgeoned into summer, and a very hot summer at that, and the baby became steadily more noticeable and more uncomfortable, but he went on ignoring it. Which was more than she could do. Soon the horrid little thing was interfering with her sleep, wriggling about and squirming just as she'd got herself settled and then banging its head on her bladder so that she had to get up in the middle of the night to go to the lavatory. It was almost as unpleasant as Eric's ridiculous Saturday night exercises. And it had ruined her figure, absolutely ruined it. No matter how many yards of expensive material she draped around the bulge, she still looked grotesque, especially among all the lovely boyish figures of the happily unpregnant all around her. Even her face had grown fat, and her eyes looked as though they were bolting out of her head.

As the baby enlarged, their flat diminished. By the end of July it was ridiculously small. She seemed to be bumping into the furniture all the time, and the kitchen was little more than a box. She began to throw out hints to Eric that they ought to move to something more commodious, but he only grunted or smiled his empty smile, depending on his mood.

Fortunately the *Evening News* was more helpful. They ran a whole page of advertisements for homeseekers every Saturday night and very tempting some of them were. It didn't take Anna long to discover just the place she wanted, a nice new, modern house on the nice new, modern estate at Stoneleigh Park, right on the edge of the country and yet near enough to the new station for Eric to get to Waterloo in twenty-five minutes. She went down to the estate the very next day, despite the heat, and came back with her mind made up. If pregnancy wouldn't earn her the attention she deserved, she would try moving up in the world. The estate agent had been absolutely charming, telling her all about the residents association and the marvellous social life she would lead as a member of 'the Stoneleigh Set', and clinching the deal by remarking casually, as he escorted her gallantly out of the front door, that she was exactly the sort of forward-looking young lady that the estate had been designed for. She arranged to return on Saturday with her husband and assured the nice young man that it was really only a question of deciding how big the deposit ought to be, for they would certainly buy the house.

Eric refused to consider it. 'You're out of your mind!' he

yelled at her. 'How could we possibly afford a place like that? Have you any idea what the repayments would be? No, of course you haven't. You wouldn't think of anything like that, would you? One pound nineteen and sixpence a month! That's what they'd be! I'm not made of money, you know. I'm not your father!' His face was distorted with anger, pinched and elongated as though it had been put through the mangle. His eyes get so small when he shouts, she thought, small and hard, like nasty little grey pebbles. 'I'm not your father!'

'I know you're not,' she said and was pleased with herself for keeping calm even though he was shouting loudly enough to make her shake. 'My father is a gentleman.'

'Your father is a low grade foreigner,' he said. 'A low grade, jumped-up foreigner. He might have a lot of money. I don't doubt that. I'll grant you that. But that's all he's got. Apart from his money he's got nothing, no class, no culture, no education, nothing.'

'And of course your father's so marvellous,' she shouted back at him. 'I don't think! What can *he* afford? A poky little house, in a nasty, common street, with a garden like a pocket handkerchief. And now you want me to live in a nasty, poky place too. Well, I won't! I'm not used to pigging it! I'm a cut above that.'

He was grey with rage, and shaking visibly. 'You bitch!' he said. 'Don't you dare talk about my father like that!'

'I'll talk how I please,' she said, tossing her head. But she was inwardly afraid, because he looked so threatening.

He lit a cigarette to steady his nerves and give himself time to regain control of his voice. 'I'm not listening to you,' he said, and he turned the wireless on very loudly to drown her out, sitting beside it with his head as close to the speaker as he could get it, so that he didn't have to look at her. It was a concert from Radio Luxemburg, and the noise made his ears ring, but that was infinitely preferable to the awful things she'd been saying.

Anna toyed with the idea of switching off the set and really annoying him but decided it might be too dangerous. 'If that's how you're going on,' she said to the racket, 'I'm off to bed.' It was only nine o'clock, but there didn't seem to be anything else to do.

205

The next morning she stayed in bed and pretended to be asleep until Eric had left the flat. Then she got up and telephoned her father, who was rather surprised to hear from her so early in the morning but agreed to meet her for lunch at Pratt's, providing she was there 'spot on one o'clock.'

For once in her life she was early for an appointment. This was so important she was prepared to obey her father in every particular. She dressed discreetly and hardly wore any make-up at all, so as to look pathetic, and she waited with superhuman patience for the right moment to present itself, while her father ate a good meal and inquired after her health and wondered what she really wanted. After four years in Queenie's astringent company he saw his daughter with much clearer eyes and could recognize, now, that her deliberately artless charm was a sure sign she wanted something. But he was taken aback by her businesslike approach when she finally plucked up the courage to tell him what it was.

'I simply can't stay in the flat,' she said, batting her eyelids. 'Not once the baby's born. It wouldn't be fair to bring up a baby in a flat, now would it, Dadda?'

Allbert said he supposed not, and then, after he'd said it, remembered that Georgie and Lily were bringing up a family in a flat. But his daughter was ploughing on with her set speech, and working very hard to charm him.

'So we must move. You can see that, can't you? The only trouble is the silly old mortgage. It's *so* difficult for poor Eric. He'd buy a new house for me like a shot, if he could only afford it, the dear boy. So what I thought was this ...' She took a deep breath and closed her eyes briefly, rehearsing the line she was going to take, just to be sure she got it right. 'You've always looked after me and Georgie so well. We couldn't have had a better father. Everybody says so. Buying that shop for Georgie so that he could get married and keep a family. And I know you won't want to do anything less for little me. Especially now I've got a baby coming.'

He had to admire her boldness. She was a chip off the old block and no mistake. 'What you want, lovebird?' he asked, feeling fond of her despite the act she was putting on.

The old nickname encouraged her. 'If you could let us have a really nice big sum so that we could put down a big deposit ...'

He could see the desperation behind the charm. 'How much?' he said.

'Three hundred pounds?'

What cheek she had! He grinned at her. 'I tell you what I'll do,' he said. 'I paid three hundred and twenty pounds for the shop, and you've already had the deposit for your flat, which was nearly a hundred pounds, so I'll make up the difference. You can have two hundred and fifty pounds for the house. How will that be?'

She got out of her chair and, blundering towards him, flung her arms about his neck in relief and gratitude, to the consternation of the other diners.

'Oh, Dadda! You are good to me,' she said. 'We could go down to Stoneleigh Park this afternoon and settle it.'

So by the time Eric came home that evening, he was well on the way to becoming a member of the Stoneleigh Park Residents Association, although as yet he didn't know it. The deposit had been paid, the mortgage applied for and solicitors instructed. The only thing missing was his signature, and Anna had spent the last few hours of that hot afternoon working out how to persuade him to provide it.

Fortunately they lapsed into baby talk as soon as he walked through the front door, and baby talk always made things so much easier for both of them.

'How's my poor ickle itchy coo den?' she cooed as he hung up his coat and wiped the sweat-band inside his hat before putting it neatly on the hatstand.

'Hot,' he said, and he sounded genuinely weary. 'It's like an oven in Whitehall. A good job my bunny wunny doesn't have to go off to the naughty city every day like I do, eh? It's enough to make a saint weep.'

'I got my itchy coo something super dooper,' she told him. 'A nice big jug of lemonade to quench his nasty wasty thirsty.'

It was appreciated and gulped greedily. So far, so good. 'Dis is a nasty old flat for my poor itchy coo,' she said as he set down his glass and took up the evening paper. 'Wouldn't it be super if we could just open that door and walk through and find a nice little garden just outside, waiting just for us.'

He joined in the fantasy at once. 'We could have our nice lemonade sitting on the terrace …'

'… in a hammock …'

'… with a wrought iron table and four chairs to match …'

'… painted white …'

'… and a nice smooth lawn … we wouldn't have any nasty old weeds in our garden … and a nice sun dial … and my bunny wunny woo with a lovely suntan …'

'… and all the neighbours thinking, they must have been to the South of France!'

'And all for less than ten shillings a week.'

'What?' he said, jerked out of his dream by the abrupt change in the tone of her voice, and the unlikely price she'd just quoted.

'Ah,' she said, tickling him playfully under the chin. 'Who's got a clever little wifey then?'

'What are you talking about, Bunny?' he asked, and although he was still baby talking he was more guarded now.

'A chalet in Stoneleigh Park,' she said quickly, 'with three bedrooms, and a dining room with a lovely bay window overlooking the most classy road you ever saw, and a living room with French windows to the garden, and we can make the garden just how we like, and all brand new, and with the nicest neighbours, really classy people, and it won't cost us a penny more than ten shillings a week, because Dadda has given us a lovely big deposit. What do you think of that?'

Her eyes were bolting with anxiety. She looked really grotesque, he thought, all swollen up like that, like a great brown toad, but she'd got him a bargain and no mistake. He'd be a fool not to accept. He beamed his filmstar smile at her. 'Who's a clever little bunny woo?' he agreed.

'It'll make all the difference,' she assured him, 'living on a classy estate.' Perhaps he won't be quite so cross once he's in a proper house, she thought. And it'll certainly give them all something to think about on Bank Holiday Monday. And take Lily down a peg or two, which she richly deserves for being pregnant at the wrong time. Her spirits began to perk up, despite the heat and the wriggling weight of the baby. This drought can't go on much longer, she promised herself. It'll have to rain soon and then we shall all feel better. And in the meantime there was a triumph to look forward to.

It was still hot and sticky when the holiday arrived. Even at seven o'clock in the morning the butter was runny almost as soon as she took it out of the brick. She opened the kitchen window to let in what little cool air the night had left behind and made their sandwiches as quickly as she could. The paint on the window sill was flaking away from the wood.

'We'd do better to stay at home in the shade,' Eric grumbled, feeling aggrieved at the thought of the long, hot day ahead of him.

'Oh come on, Itchy,' she tried to jolly him. 'You'll enjoy it once you're there. You always do, you know.'

But he seemed determined not to enjoy anything and drove them to Wimbledon Common in silence, his face cross and closed. It was an uncomfortable journey, what with his horrible silence and the petrol fumes making her feel sick. I shall be glad when we get there, she thought to herself. Dadda'll buck him up. He always does. He could make any holiday go with a swing. Thank God for Dadda!

As they bumped across the burnt grass of the common towards the little roped off enclosure where they usually parked their car, she could see the whole family waiting for them. Georgie and the two children in their white sunhats, and Lily, sitting down already she noticed, and looking marvellously fat. And there was Mummy with the same old parasol, and Aunt Min talking to Em and Harry, and Dickie Chanter mopping his bald head, and Tilley, skinnier than ever. But where was Dadda?

'Gone off to visit some friend of his in hospital, if you please,' her mother explained crossly. 'Wounded soldier, so he said. Anyway, he had a telephone call just as we were all going out the door and off he rushed. You know how he is. There's no stopping your father once he's made up his mind.' She was very put out.

Anna was so disappointed she didn't know what to say. How could he do such a thing? Especially now, when she needed him so much. He *always* spent the Bank Holiday on Wimbledon Common. Always. 'Do you think he'll come on later?' she asked.

'Don't ask me,' her mother said sourly. 'We should have given the whole thing a miss this year. I told him so yesterday.

But he would press on. It's not the weather for gallivanting about in the open air. No good'll come of it. You mark my words.'

'Who's for a game of cricket?' Dickie said, doing his best to lift the gloom.

'It's too hot for cricket,' Mummy said tartly, and then, as she saw that the children were running forward and eager to play, 'Well, don't blame me if you all get heatstroke, that's all.'

It was a desultory game, despite having Eric as umpire and Dickie and Harry as captains. Margaret fell over and grazed her knee on the rock hard ground, and Em got stung by a wasp. They decided to walk to the pond and bathe their injuries, but even beside the water it wasn't a great deal cooler. They looked absolute wrecks already, Anna thought, and it wasn't midday. Dickie was puce in the face and still breathless from the cricket match, and Tilley was cross with him. 'Ain't got the sense you was born wiv,' she grumbled. 'Man a' your age rushin' about in all this heat. Give yerself 'eart attack, that's what you'll do. Look at the state of yer, fer cryin' out loud!' Oh dear, Anna sighed to herself. They wouldn't have been carrying on like this if Dadda had been here.

'Time for the picnic,' Aunt Min said when hands and feet and wounds had all been washed. But the picnic wasn't a success either, because the sandwiches were as limp as they were, and the lemonade almost as hot, and the chocolate bars had melted away and looked absolutely revolting. She offered her news while they were eating what little they could, but it fell very flat. Lily did say, 'That's nice,' but Tilley said she already knew and Harry only went 'Um', as though he wasn't listening at all.

Feeling horribly pregnant and thoroughly demoralized, she propped her bulk against the side of a tree and closed her eyes against the heat and the dust and her overwhelming disappointment. Eric was being charming somewhere down at the water's edge, talking to Em and Aunt Min, but the sound of his false cheerfulness and that awful booming voice of his only made her feel worse. It was too hot to breathe. Even the birds weren't singing.

She drifted into an uncomfortable doze, and woke to find that the sun had moved and a strong beam was flooding her eyes with painful red light. The same listless conversations were still going on around her and the children were splashing down at the water's edge. She blinked the unwanted colour away and presently she could make out the dark shapes of the paddlers silhouetted against bright blue water. A little wooden jetty extended into the lake just to the left of where she was sitting and Johnny was balancing along it as though he was walking a tightrope. That's dangerous, she thought, he might fall in, and she looked across at Lily, who was fast asleep against a beech tree. Nobody seemed to be watching the child. I'd better keep an eye on him, she thought, just in case.

He was almost at the end of the jetty and balancing easily, moving forward with a gliding, dancing rhythm. Very graceful for a boy, she thought, and was wondering idly whether her baby would be graceful too when the body she was watching suddenly became rigid, its feet scuffling the boards, its spine folding forward like a jack-knife. Then it flung its dark arms into the air and fell backwards into the water. 'Oh my God,' she yelled. 'Quick! Johnny's drowning!'

Then everything happened at once and confusingly. Lily woke with a start and lumbered to her feet and set off at an ungainly trot, calling, 'It's all right, Johnny, we're coming!' and Harry was yelling, 'Find a pole!' and they were all running down to the water's edge, and Georgie was already wading in. But in amongst it all Eric was running in circles, panicking, with his mouth open and his eyes bolting, shouting ridiculous things. 'Oh, Anna, what shall we do? What shall we do? He's drowning, Anna! Oh my God, what shall we do?' As she pounded towards the pond he was suddenly right in her way, bleating and looking absolutely useless. 'Shut up!' she yelled, elbowing him in the chest. He was just a nuisance. Worse than a child. 'Shut up!'

And then, just as Georgie was halfway out towards him, little Johnny stood up, and they realized that he was standing in little more than a foot of water and wasn't drowning after all. Relief exploded into laughter and they all began to talk at once, scolding Johnny for giving them a fright, and saying what a bit of luck it was, and would you ever believe that, and the crisis was over.

'Well, he won't catch cold. That's one blessing,' Mummy

211

said, rubbing him down with the tablecloth. 'You bad boy, Johnny. We thought you were drownded.' Her voice was full of love for him, the way it always was when she talked to Georgie or his children.

I wonder whether she'll talk to my baby like that, Anna thought enviously. Then she remembered how stupid the father of her baby had been, and looked round to see what he was doing. He'd retreated to the other side of the lake and was sitting stony faced at the water's edge, brooding and smoking. She'd hit him, hadn't she? Pushed him out of her way. Now she'd cop it. He did look cross. But he'd asked for it, she thought, panicking like that. Everybody else was being sensible and helpful and he was just running about, asking somebody to tell him what to do. It was childish. Pathetically childish. Looking across at his dark face as he brooded with anger on the other side of the lake, she realized, with the clarity of strong sunlight, that she didn't like him at all. I've swapped my lovely father for that, she thought. And now I'm stuck with it. It made her miss her father more than ever. Why, oh why, hadn't he come with them today?

Chapter Nineteen

The City was lethargic with heat. Tar melted, wheels stuck, boats were becalmed and the sky bulged with sunlight in a pale yellow blaze like newly lit gas. Cobblestones and pavements burned underfoot, so hard and hot that even the short walk from the tram stop to the hospital gates was decidedly uncomfortable. The streets were almost empty but down on the blue river two coal barges inched lazily upstream, creaking through the water with so little effort that they scarcely made a ripple. Pigeons moped in the guttering, too fatigued to stir, and the few horses still toiling their carts across London Bridge were black with sweat and dragged their hot hooves painfully. It was a horrid day, Mary thought, as she followed her mother towards the hospital. The air was so heavy and still and hard to breathe, even with healthy lungs. Poor Pa. Poor darling Pa.

She knew he was desperately ill. There was no avoiding it this time. The ambulance had come so quickly and Ma had looked so awful. She'd dressed in such a rush too, flinging on the first things that came to hand, a faded brown cotton frock and a straw hat the colour of long-dried mud. Her eyes were red-rimmed, although they both pretended not to notice, and her lovely, bold hair had been pinned back off her face. The lack of it made her features look defenceless and exposed and gave her an air of strained dejection that frightened her daughter.

Mr Ploochy was waiting for them inside the hospital portico. Ma seemed pleased to see him but his presence annoyed Mary Ann. It was nothing to do with him. This was a private anxiety, hers and Ma's, not his.

'How is he?' he asked Ma, and he annoyed Mary even

further by chaffing her mother's cold fingers between his hands. I could have done that she thought. Leave her alone.

'Going,' Ma said, expressionlessly. 'Terrible, it was. I never seen so much blood.' The words reminded Mary too terribly and she had to look at the stone column beside her for a little while so that she didn't cry.

'He will pull round,' Ploochy was saying. 'Like last time. He pulled round last time.' His concern only irritated Mary. What do you know about it? she thought. He was chewing his lips with concern.

Ma didn't say anything, and Mary knew how she felt. She was too worried and upset for words. She simply led them into the hospital and along a maze of shaded corridors into a pale green ward. Pa was in the end bed, lying with his eyes closed, his hair and skin grey against the pillows. The scar tissue that covered the right side of his face was more horribly noticeable than she'd ever seen it, like an old leather mask, stiff and brown and unyielding. The rest of his face seemed to cower behind it, the flesh shrunk back onto the bones.

For a moment, she thought he was already dead, but then the muddy eyelids fluttered and his eyes looked up at them all with the familiar rueful expression he usually wore when he had to succumb to the nuisance of illness. 'Not much cop!' he said hoarsely, and Ma rushed to take his hand and assure him that everything was all right.

'I've brought Mary with me,' she said. 'An' 'ere's old Ploochy come ter see yer.'

Pa's eyes acknowledged the visit but then he began to cough, weakly and insistently, and he couldn't say anything. The silence that followed embarrassed them all. Ploochy was chewing his moustache and fidgeting, and that annoyed Mary. I wish he'd go away, she thought. She wanted to talk to her father even though she hadn't the remotest idea what she could say. And then Ploochy opened his silly mouth and said something so crass it made her gasp. 'Soon be better, eh?' It sounded falsely hearty and cruel. Ma looked at him as though she couldn't understand what he was saying. Her face was strained, the flesh taut across her cheekbones and her eyes loose in sockets grown dark since yesterday.

'No,' Pa said calmly when the coughing fit was over. 'Not

this time. On the way out this time.'

'You mustn't say that,' Mary implored, anguished by such appalling acceptance. She stood beside the bed, silently willing her father to put up a fight. Just to give up would be obscene. 'Pa, please!'

'I been 'ere before,' Pa said, still totally calm behind his terrible mask of scars. 'Wipers. Should 'a' gone then. I know, you see. Been 'ere before.' He closed his eyes again as if he were going to sleep, and the ward was quiet except for coughs and harsh breath.

"'E's going,' Ma whispered, reaching out blindly for Mary's hand.

But the eyes opened again, bright and alive in that odd dead face. 'Take care a' my girls, Ploo,' he said.

'I promise,' Ploochy said.

The eyes flickered a smile. 'Shall sleep,' he said and turned his head to one side like a child.

They watched over him all that day, taking it in turns to go out into the corridor for a break, and once leaving him for ten minutes while they all went to the canteen for a cup of tea. Speech was superfluous. What could any of them say, caught in that terrible limbo of powerless inaction, enervated by heat and grief?

Nurses came and went, a meal was served to those well enough to eat it, and towards three o'clock a doctor walked through the ward and paused long enough beside Pa's rattling sleep to tell Ma that they had done all they could, and to give Ploochy some gentle advice, whispered at the foot of the bed. 'If I were you,' he said, 'I would take Mrs Chapman home for a little while. A rest. A meal perhaps. I don't foresee much change before evening.'

It's nothing to do with him Mary thought resentfully, but she was too miserable to protest. So they went back to Peckham and the quiet of Lyndhurst Square. The air in the house was oppressive with accumulated heat, even though Ploochy opened all the windows. So they sat in the garden until the sun went down and a cool breeze sprang up to rustle the leaves of the cherry tree. They were too grieved to talk and too exhausted to move.

A robin was singing from the topmost branch of the furthest

apple tree, its trilling piccolo ice clear among the jaded leaves. Behind its perky body and the thrilling feathers of its busy throat, the sky misted with hazy lilac. They were coming to the end of another perfect summer day, but what was the point of it?

Mrs Midgeley had cooked a light supper for them all and she served it to them in the garden on individual trays as though they were invalids. Everything was unreal, the green garden, the unremitting heat, even the food. Mary ate without appetite and with no knowledge of what she was putting into her mouth. She was living in abeyance.

The heat was still brooding over the city when they went back to the hospital later that evening. It was very quiet in the pale ward and there were only two other visitors, sitting protectively beside a bed right at the far end of the long room. Most of the other patients were asleep and there were screens all round Pa's bed.

'D'you think 'e's asleep or what?' Mary whispered, daunted by the silence and the unfamiliar routine.

Ma couldn't say, and Ploochy was chewing his moustache. They stood together in the middle of the ward, hesitating, as the sufferers snored and stirred around them.

'If there's anybody in there, doin' things, they'd be out be now, surely,' Ma was saying, when the ward sister suddenly appeared beside them, neat in her dark blue and white, with her face just a little too composed and contained for comfort.

'Would you come into my office for a few moments, Mrs Chapman,' she said, and the tone of her voice betrayed the news she had to give them. Ma followed her at once, awkward with distress, but Ploochy had the good sense to stay where he was and after a second's hesitation Mary left him and went with her mother.

Nothing was said until they were safely inside the office and the door was shut behind them. Then Ma cut through any possibility of softening preamble.

''E's gone,' she said flatly.

'I'm afraid so,' the sister told them. 'Just after six o'clock.'

'Was 'e bad?'

The sister looked Ma in the eye for a long second, and Mary knew she was estimating her strength. Then she told her the

216

truth. 'I'm afraid he was,' she said. 'Very bad. He had another haemorrhage. We did all we could.'

'I'm sure a' that. Did 'e suffer long?'

'Yes. He was very brave.'

''E always was.'

'You'd like to see him?'

They saw him, neat and still behind the screens, washed and laid out and already unapproachable. But it didn't matter, because without his wry, self-mocking expression and with his eyes shut so tightly on the world, this body wasn't Pa. It was an effigy, no more, an image of wax and crumpled leather. But it wasn't Pa.

They stood for a few minutes, looking down at the body, without speaking. Then Ma began to shake. There was no expression on her face, and she didn't cry, but she shook as though she was standing in the full force of a terrible gale, and was powerless to move. I ought to help her, Mary thought but she was numb, unable to think or speak. Then Ploochy was at her elbow.

'We go home,' he said to the Sister. 'I come back tomorrow and make all the arrangements.' And he put one arm firmly round Ma's trembling shoulders and took Mary gently by the hand, and led them both away.

They went with him, without a word, obedient and withdrawn, and sat beside him in the cab, frozen and silent. Ma's shaking fit gradually subsided, but she still didn't speak, and from time to time a shudder would engulf her again. And so they drove back to Lyndhurst Square.

The night sky was completely cloudless and surprisingly blue, the stars glimmering like scattered sequins and the moon so clear and white that the face was bold on its surface. All along the main roads the streetlights shone like strings of amber beads, and the empty pavements were the colour of polished tin. It was all so beautiful Mary thought, and Pa had loved it so much, and what was the good of it now he was dead?

The next morning Pa's body was returned to lie in state in Wilson Grove, and all day long people trailed in and out of the crowded flat to pay their last respects and to commiserate with

Ma. It was soon obvious that his funeral was going to be a public occasion, no matter what Ma's opinion might be, and no matter how much she wanted speed and privacy.

By the end of the afternoon she was distraught with the pressure of so many people and so much sympathy, and Mary was huge-eyed with grief and bewilderment but Ploochy stayed with them all day long, solid and dependable like a shield. 'We will see you at the church,' he told the last of the day's mourners, edging them firmly out of the house.

'There's so many!' Ma said. 'We'll never get 'em all in, after. I can't see how we'll ever manage, Ploo.' The problems that this funeral was creating seemed totally insoluble. And it was so hot! Too hot to think straight.

'I find somewhere else,' he promised. 'Don't worry. It all be all right. I promise.'

Mary was drifting about the flat, drumming her fingers on the drawn blinds, and moving cushions unnecessarily from chair to chair. She looked lost and bleak in the half light of their muted rooms. 'Pack your things,' he said, 'and we all go back to Peckham. It no good for you to stay here.'

'I can't leave Ned,' Ma wailed.

'Yes you can,' he told her firmly. 'He wouldn't want you to stay here an' be miserable, now would he? And you can't do him any good if you stay.'

Put like that she saw the sense of it, and although she argued on for several minutes, eventually she and Mary drifted away to their dishevelled bedrooms to gather a disorganized collection of odds and ends, because they were still too numb with grief to know what they were doing, and Albert called a cab and took them away to Lyndhurst Square.

But it was still unreal. Like living in a dream. Mary ate another meal, and washed herself and lay down as if she was going to sleep, in an unfamiliar bed, in an unfamiliar room, in a house she didn't care for. None of it was really happening. Or at least it wasn't happening to her. She had become somebody else, living inside her skin, but feeling nothing. She didn't care where she was really, for what was the point of anything? She'd stay here in Ploo's house for the time being. What did it matter?

The heat continued, and now each new day was more sticky and debilitating than the last. The Thames smelt as though it was full of rotting vegetation, and Bermondsey was breathless under the increasing oppression of a heavy, cloudless sky. At the best of times the place was rank with the stink of the cargoes it handled and the local industries they engendered; now it was overpowered by them, the meaty decay of the tanneries, Sarson's vinegar, pungent and pervasive, and the sickly sweetness from Peek Frean's biscuit factory. It was almost impossible to find a patch of air unsullied enough to breathe in comfort. Quite the wrong time for a funeral.

They were all too hot in their heavy mourning clothes, and they looked as uncomfortable as they felt, walking with awkward, unrhythmical slowness behind the coffin as the bearers shuffled it through the churchyard of St Mary Magdalen, past the scorched lawns and the blaze of bright roses in the flower beds and the ragged children clustered about the four white gables of the drinking fountain. Mary had insisted on wearing her school uniform because it was suitably sober in colour and Pa had been so proud of it, and now the rough serge of her gym tunic chafed her bare legs and her velour hat was making her forehead sweat. Ma was no cooler, even though she was wearing an old cotton frock she'd dyed black for some other long forgotten occasion and a glazed straw hat that at least kept the sun out of her eyes. She looked subdued and foreign and quite unlike herself, her bright hair as shocking as nudity among all that black material.

It was easier when they were all inside their unassuming church and the ginger wood of the pews could obscure their unseasonable clothing and give them some cover for unpredictable emotions. The building was full of summer flowers, roses, pink and red and yellow as butter, orange marigolds, cloud white marguerites and clusters of forget-me-nots as blue as the sky, piled in vases at every corner and heaped on the coffin in scented profusion. The sunlight pouring in through the high, plain windows magnified their perfume and drew their colours into rich focus. They were so innocent and potent and joyfully alive that soon and almost despite themselves the grieving congregation began to relax.

As the service progressed heads began to nod approval of

the priest's honest eulogy, and the second hymn, 'When wilt thou save the people?' was sung with fervour, because it was one of Pa's favourites and expressed a sentiment they endorsed and shared. 'Not thrones and crowns, but men,' they sang. 'From want, oppression and despair, God save the people.'

Then the Ox lumbered into the pulpit and took the edge of the lectern in his huge, blunt hands and spoke his simple address. 'Me an' Ned, we was a right pair a' gargoyles,' he said, and his audience smiled, remembering how often they'd heard him say it. "E used ter say we could scare the livin' daylights out've anyone. His joke, that was! I never known 'im scare a soul. 'E was too busy workin'. Fer the party, fer Socialism, fer the council, fer 'is neighbours. Never knew no one like 'im fer workin' an' that's a fact. Always thinkin' a' someone else, that was our Ned. We shan't see 'is like again. We all know that. 'E was a good man.'

It was the theme of the reception afterwards. As the guests crowded into the long upper room at The Red Lion, they kissed Ma and hugged Mary and told them, and one another, over and over again, that Ned had been one a' the best, a fine man, and nobody would ever forget him, not ever, not in a million years. It soon became a loud boisterous party. 'He'd a' loved it,' they said. 'I'll bet 'e's lookin' down now enjoyin' 'isself.' It was extraordinary and it was reassuring.

But it upset Mary dreadfully. As the laughter increased and the limited food was eaten she retreated farther and farther down the long room, in a miserable attempt to get away from it all. By the time Maisie Oxbury noticed what was going on and sent young Tom to rescue her, she was beleaguered among the hats and coats, her back pressed against the wall and her face pale with grief and disbelief.

'It's horrible the way they're laughing,' she said as Tom sat down companionably beside her. 'I can't bear it, Tom.'

'It's only their way,' Tom tried to explain. 'They don't mean disrespect. They were all very fond of him, you know that, don't you?'

She nodded miserably, knowing but not accepting. 'Poor Mo,' he said. 'I do know how you're feeling. You want to hide away all on your own and cry where no one can see you.'

'How d'you know that?'

'If I can feel it, I'm sure you must.'

He means it, she thought, looking at his kind, rugged face.

'It's like a nightmare,' she said. 'I keep thinking I ought to go home, because he'll be there and wondering where I am. I don't really feel any of this is true.'

'I know,' he assured her.

She gave him a wry smile as laughter bubbled up again from the group at the other end of the room. 'You're the only one here who does,' she said.

Then and without any warning, she suddenly put her head in her hands and began to cry, terrible, wracking sobs that shook her chest and couldn't be controlled. 'I can't bear it,' she sobbed. 'I can't bear it.'

Queenie was down the hall and by her side in a second, cradling her in her arms, murmuring and soothing. But this was a pain that couldn't be kissed away. 'Oh,' she groaned. 'Why did he have ter die? I can't bear it.'

'Get her home,' Maisie said. But that caused more weeping.

'No, no, no,' she cried. 'Not ter the flat. That's where 'e … Not ter the flat. I couldn't bear it.'

'To Ploochy's, then.'

The tears became screams. 'No! I won't. Never, never, never!'

'She's hysterical,' Queenie said, looking up at the circle of anxious faces around them. 'Stop it, Mary! D'you 'ear? Stop it!' It was dreadful to hear such anguished sobs. She looked around desperately for someone who could tell her what to do. And Eth took over.

'You come 'ome wiv yer Aunty Eth,' she said. 'How'd that be?'

By now Mary was incapable of speech, but at least she didn't say no.

'But you're off ter Dunton on Sat'day,' Queenie said.

'She can come an' all. Can't yer duck?' Eth said. 'Do 'er good, Quee. Take 'er out of 'erself. You'd like ter come ter Dunton, wouldn't yer?'

And Mary gulped back her sobs for long enough to say that she would and the matter seemed to have been settled. But it took another ten minutes and a lot of cuddling before she was sufficiently in control of herself again to stand up and dry her eyes.

'I'm so sorry, Ma,' she said. 'I didn't mean …'

'You cry all you like, lovey,' Queenie said. 'Get it out yer system.'

'Ready?' Eth said, taking her arm.

So Mary found her hat and kissed her mother and went off with her aunt, and the funeral was over, the other guests departing suddenly and all at once. Albert and Queenie were left behind among the trestle tables, surveying the wreckage of squashed sausage rolls and half eaten sandwiches and dirty glasses, and feeling drained of all emotion. Somewhere to the north of the river they could hear the distant rattle of thunder.

Maisie Oxbury was stacking glasses on a tray. 'Storm coming,' she said, lifting her head to listen to it. 'Hark at that. Leave all this to us, Quee. I'd cut off 'ome if I was you. You've 'ad enough fer one day.'

The thunder rumbled and rolled in the distance as the cab took them south, and by the time they reached Peckham Rye dark grey storm clouds were gathering ominously over their heads. A spattering of hot raindrops stung their faces as Albert paid the fare and thunder crashed above their heads, so loudly that it made them both jump.

'I wish it would really rain,' Albert said. They'd been waiting for rain for such a long time. A downpour would be such a release. It would wash away the funeral and Ned's suffering and Queenie's misery, and leave the way clean and clear for their affair to begin again, like the marriage it really was. But the grey sky lowered over the parched garden and the air was as hard and hot as a furnace and there was no release.

They sat at the table beside clean plates and glasses that they had no intention of using and talked as a slow dusk gathered to fold them both in gentle shadow.

'D'you think she'll be all right wiv Eth?' Queenie worried.

'Best thing for her. Take her out of herself.'

'I dunno how we shall make out now 'e's gone.'

'You will live here with me. I look after you. Both of you.'

'Take a bit a' gettin' used to,' she said. Her body was dropping with languor and there were heavy shadows under her eyes.

'Mary's used to it already,' he said, hoping it was true.

'Be different now though, Ploo. If we live 'ere, what'll she think?' Under the burden of too much immediate grief, problems all seemed insurmountable.

'Better to be here than in the flat. Think how she'd feel in the flat.'

'An' that's another thing. If we don't keep it on, it'll all 'ave ter be cleared out.'

'Me an' Eth'll do it.'

'No,' she said with a terrible, weary sadness. 'Ta, all the same, Ploo. I must see to 'is things meself. Wouldn't be right else. An' then there's all the work 'e was doin' fer the Party.' Burdens pressed upon her. 'I shall 'ave ter take that on too, Ploo.'

'You do what's right, my lovebird. I won't stop you, I promise. If you want to work, you work. If you don't, you don't. Time enough fer all that later on. You don't have to decide now.'

'No,' she agreed. 'You're right. I don't. I should miss The Lion if I gave that up, specially of a Sat'day.'

'Then you stay on. It will all work out, you'll see.'

The room was very dark now, and in the back garden beyond the window, the foliage looked quite black against the blue grey sky. The storm had passed without amounting to anything and it was hotter than ever.

'Come to bed, Queenie,' he said. 'You're all in.'

Even that was a problem too difficult for her to solve. 'Where am I supposed to sleep?' she wailed. 'I can't sleep with you. Not now. Not after …'

'Yes you can,' he said firmly. 'You can come to bed with me, an' I'll cuddle you if that's what you want, or you can talk all night, if that's what you want, or you can go straight to sleep an' not cuddle or talk or anything. It's entirely up to you. Come on.'

Even in the depths of her present misery his tenderness warmed her a little. 'You're a good bloke, Ploo,' she said.

'I love you,' he said, holding both her hands in the old way.

She felt she ought to warn him. 'You'll 'ave a long wait, if you're gonna wait fer me,' she said. 'I don't think I shall be capable a' feeling anything fer anybody, not fer months and months.'

'Oh, my dear, lovely Queenie,' he said. 'It will all be all right in the end, you'll see. I've waited seven years. I can wait a few more weeks. You're worth waiting for.'

Chapter Twenty

Mary was drifting again, back in abeyance, feeling nothing, like a leaf being swept downstream by the river. Her terrible tears had watered her grief, but that was all. Now it returned in all its numbing unreality. On Saturday morning she went to Liverpool Street station with her aunt and her two rowdy cousins like someone walking in a dream. And the journey down to Laindon simply took her farther away from reality. It was no surprise to her when she arrived at Laindon station to find that she was in another world.

They walked from the station to Dunton along an empty, dusty pathway through fields of prickly stubble and harsh corn standing as high as her waist and burnt loaf brown. Strange birds carolled in the hot bushes and in the distance a harvester was chugging through another field taking leisurely bites out of the crop as it went. There were no houses anywhere in sight. No shops and no buses and no life. Just a long, low landscape stretching to very distant, low hills somewhere to the north and, above her, a sky so vast and blue she felt it was pressing down upon her like some huge weight. Purgatory could be like this, she thought, as she trudged beside her chattering cousins. A great empty, waiting space.

When they first left the shade of the little railway station they'd walked quickly, eager to get to the bungalow and start their holiday, but the day and the landscape gradually slowed them down and soon, although they didn't realize it, they were strolling. Aunty Eth was telling her about the bungalow and how Uncle Charlie's brother and sister-in-law had built it. She listened amiably without hearing very much.

'Five pounds that bit a' land cost. Ter start wiv they used ter put up a tent weekends. And then Spud reckoned 'e could build a little place for 'em. Well, you know yer Uncle Spud. They used ter come out wiv bits a' plank from the buildin's an' slate an' nails an' putty, an' things like that. Tucked under their arms. All the way down in the train. They're a pair a' cards! Took 'em best part a' two years.' She spoke with great pride of the achievement.

Mary had never been to the bungalow, although she'd heard all about it because Aunt Eth and her four cousins spent most summer weekends down there. And once every year Spud let them have a whole week's holiday. Uncle Charlie and his two working children came down for both Sundays, and Aunty Eth and the kids lived there.

'Home from home,' Aunty Eth said. 'There it is!'

It was exactly what she expected, a low, ramshackle wooden shed with a corrugated iron roof and a tin chimney. It sat on its haunches in a dusty field alongside an untidiness of tents, a tacky caravan and several other equally peculiar dwellings, like a mongrel dog, cocky and dishevelled and hopeful. The windows were all different shapes and sizes and the front door was squiffy, but there was a painted sign over the lintel proudly proclaiming its name, 'Home from Home'. A lean-to, which turned out to be the second bedroom, had been propped against one side wall and there was a large green water butt beside the front door.

'Whatcher think!' Aunty Eth inquired.

'I think it's smashing,' Mary said, and it was nothing less than the truth.

The Tids were already rushing round the field looking for old friends among the other plotlanders. 'They're off!' Eth said affectionately. 'Little beggars. Shan't see them fer an hour or two.' It was quite a relief because the Tids were hard work. They'd been christened Robert and Anthony when they were born ten and eleven years ago, but nobody ever called them anything other than the Tids because they were very much alike and totally inseparable, two shaggy, mischievous, freckled boys with a taste for practical jokes and, according to their mother, 'far too much damned energy'. On that first Saturday afternoon they annoyed their next door neighbour by pinching his bicycle and riding it round the field, went birds' nesting and got their legs scratched to ribbons, and finally broke one of the camp beds they were supposed to be sleeping on by jumping up and down on it. 'Serve yer bloomin' well right,' their mother said, surveying the wreckage. 'You'll jest 'ave ter sleep in the one bed, that's all.' But that didn't worry them a bit. It was a treat.

And so their extraordinary holiday continued, and because everything about it was so different from life in Bermondsey, it did take Mary out of herself, just as Eth had promised. There were so many odd and unexpected pleasures in it, milk bought at a farm where the people spoke in a slow baaing drawl, like sheep, bread fresh out the oven and tasting doughy and thick, sunsets that blazed above their heads for hours, flooding the horizon with red and gold, and tinting the sky pale green. They washed in rain water from the water butt, and cooked over a primus stove that smoked and spat and left soot in their hair, and at night when the Tids had finally been persuaded to go to sleep they lit two little oil lamps and set them on the cottage table, and talked about Pa in the comfort of their yellow light.

Remembering like this was the greatest comfort of all, for it brought him back to life again. 'You jest think of all the good 'e done,' Eth advised. 'The work 'e put in fer the Party. Them flats'll stand fer years. Good strong 'omes fer the people. An' the Baths. Best in the country. That's the way ter be remembered.'

Back in Bermondsey Queenie was faced with a decision. There was a lovely young couple on the list, needed a flat, and there was her flat going begging. 'I oughter give it up, Ploo,' she said. 'It's selfish 'anging on to it.'

He couldn't see the problem. ''Course,' he said. 'Give it up. Save yerself the rent. Move in with me.'

'What about Mary? She's the one I'm thinking about. We oughtn't ter rush 'er, poor little thing.'

'She's fifteen.'

'It'll upset 'er.'

'She'll get used to it. No good fussing over kids. It makes 'em worse.'

'I don't know ...'

'Give it up,' he said firmly. 'Move her furniture. Get her

227

settled in the minute she gets back. The longer we let things drag on, the worse they'll be. If you 'ad a bandage stuck to a cut you'd rip it off quick, wouldntcher? Get it over with all in one go.'

'No,' she said. 'I'd ease it off bit by bit. You know me. I'm a coward.'

But she was persuaded, because it *was* the sensible thing to do, and the tenancy of the flat was handed over. Albert had the furniture moved on Friday morning, and in the evening they spent a bruising hour arranging it. Which was very difficult indeed because Queenie was so anxious. It was very hot again, with another storm brewing, and by the time they'd finished they were sticky with sweat.

'I could do with a nice cool bath,' Queenie said.

'Good idea!' Albert said, hopefully. 'Give me a shout and I'll come up and wash your back for you.' If only she'd say yes, it could be like old times again. Surely they'd waited long enough now.

She gave him a thoughtful look. 'Dunno about that,' she said. 'We shall 'ave ter see.'

'You please yourself, my lovely darling,' he said, anxious to do the right thing, even though he was crawling with desire for her.

'I'll put some spuds on first,' she said. 'Then we can 'ave cold meat an' pickles.' She kissed him lightly and went into the kitchen.

Albert waited in the dining room, impatient but determined to be controlled if that was what she wanted. It was such an opportunity, with Mary out of the house, but he didn't want to spoil things, not after he'd promised to be patient. Presently he heard her clomping up the stairs and then the geyser lit with a whoosh and the bath water ran noisily. Outside the window the sky brooded into darkness and thunder rattled in the distance. It was impossibly hot and he was impossibly impatient. But finally, after ten splashing minutes, she actually called his name. It *was* like old times after all, marvellously, rewardingly like old times. He ran up the stairs two at a time.

Her clothes were slung on the bathroom floor and his lovely, naked darling was luxuriating in the faintly steaming water, her red hair pinned on the top of her head, her green

228

eyes lazy and her lovely white body openly on display, her breasts blue veined just as he remembered them and her belly curved like a soft white egg above that endearing triangle of rough red hair. 'Oh, Queenie,' he said, kneeling beside the bath so as to get as close to her as he could. 'I love you so much.'

'I don't think we should,' she said, but she kissed him back, holding his face between her wet hands, and when he began to stroke and fondle she didn't stop him. The bath water chilled and they were still playing. 'You was supposed ter be washing my back,' she teased. So he sponged her back, just to show willing, and she washed her feet, covering them with a white soapy lather, and while they were both decently busy they became aware of a faint smell of burning rising to them from the kitchen.

'The spuds!' Queenie said, clapping her hand to her mouth in alarm. 'We've gone an' burnt the spuds. My Lor'! Mrs Midgeley'll 'ave sommink ter say!'

He ran downstairs to rescue them, and presently she appeared beside him, draped in a dressing gown, and they dished up the unburnt remains and put the wrecked saucepan in the sink to soak, giggling like naughty children. 'That's a judgement,' she said, 'fer bad behaviour.'

'Serve us right, eh?' he said. But he felt rewarded, not punished.

'Just as well it's a cold meat,' she said, laughing. 'Least we couldn't burn that.'

They couldn't eat much of it either, for the potatoes tasted burnt and the meat was dry and neither of them had much of an appetite. They were both flushed and bright eyed with a desire they might deny but they certainly couldn't hide, especially from one another. Eventually they gave up the effort, and followed their instincts and went to bed.

But the consciences they'd ignored returned to plague them in the midst of their pleasure. It took Queenie a long time to come, as though guilt were an anchor weighing down her senses, and when she did it was with an ecstasy so strong and sharp that it was almost painful. And Albert, following her almost at once just as he used to, was pained too and then ashamed. As she lay in his arms, recovering her breath, she began to cry. 'We shouldn't 've,' she said, over and over again. 'We shouldn't 've. An' Ned barely in 'is grave. Oh Ploo, we shouldn't 'ave.'

'Hush! Hush!' he soothed, kissing her hair. 'It's all right. Ned wouldn't mind. Really.' But she sobbed on, and it took a long time to comfort, 'We shouldn't 've. We shouldn't 've.'

Her bare arms were chill to the touch, and he pulled their blanket up to cover her again. The air in the room was definitely colder. 'Look,' he said. 'It's raining, Queenie.'

And so it was, in vertical rods of white water falling before their dark window, as straight and thick as a bead curtain. Queenie dried her eyes and sat up in bed beside him to watch and listen. It fell with a steady pattering rhythm, like a reward, or a blessing, and presently the clean fresh smell of newly watered earth rose from the gardens of the Square to fill the room with its peculiar fragrance.

'We waited a long time fer that,' she said.

'Yes,' he agreed, cuddling her, 'we did.'

Chapter Twenty-One

Oh to wake in a warm bed, breathing the lovely, salty scent of his darling again and happily aware of the weight of her sleeping body sprawled against his side. It was a moment of total happiness. Then he realized that they had overslept. Mrs Midgeley had arrived before they were awake. He could hear her downstairs filling the kettle.

'Wake up, my lovely,' he said. 'Mrs Midgeley's here.'

Queenie threw the sheet over her head and groaned. 'Oh my good Gawd, Ploo, what'll she say? Us bein' ...'

'She won't say nothing,' he said ungrammatically but as it turned out accurately. 'We employ her. Come out of it, Queenie. Don't be daft!'

'It's all very well fer you,' she said, emerging from the sheet to give him a rueful grin. 'You don't mind livin' in sin.'

'You didn't mind it in the old days.'

'It's different now. What'll Mary say?' The thought was really alarming.

He made up his mind. 'Soon as breakfast's over I will go to Tooting and tell Alice I want a divorce. Then we'll get married. How's that?'

'It ain't the best proposal I've ever 'ad,' she said laughing at him, 'but I s'ppose it'll 'ave ter do. If yer mean it. I've 'eard all this before, don't ferget.'

'You'll see,' he said.

So they dressed and went downstairs.

Mrs Midgeley served them a full English breakfast with a deliberate, watchful politeness that Queenie ignored and Albert found disquieting.

'Was there anything else?' she inquired as she put a fresh pot

231

of tea and even more toast and marmalade before the hearty appetite of her employer.

Albert smiled his thanks and shook his head, hoping she would go away and take her unspoken question with her. But she persevered. 'How many will there be for dinner?' she said.

'Three,' Queenie told her, and found that it was easy after all. 'Mary'll be back ternight. Anythink you like. Only nothink fancy.' Leg of mutton was agreed to and the housekeeper gave them one last quizzical look and left them alone.

'Now,' he said, 'I go to Tooting and tell Alice.'

'Oh, Ploo!' she said. 'I don't believe it! Are yer *really* gonna do it?'

He kissed her sticky fingers. 'Should 'a' done it years ago,' he admitted ruefully. 'I know. Don't tell me.'

'You're an old love,' she said, happier now that she'd faced the housekeeper. 'Better late than never.'

So they went their separate ways, she to Peckham Rye to do the shopping, he to Tooting for his long overdue confession.

Now that the moment had finally arrived, he was surprised to realize that he was totally calm about it. In one rather distant part of his mind he was aware that Alice would probably make a scene, but the knowledge brought no reaction, not even the slightest twinge of conscience. He felt he was impervious to any emotion now. What was to happen would happen. He simply had to live through it.

There was nobody in the house except an elderly charwoman who was on her hands and knees sweeping the stairs with a dust-shovel and brush. The hall was full of dust, despite the fact that the stair carpet was liberally sprinkled with tea leaves. 'No,' she said supporting her kneeling weight on the brush, 'The missus ain't in. Gone ter market wiv Mrs Holdsworthy, she 'as. Won't be back jest yet awhile. I'm jest ter get on while they're out, y'see.'

It was demoralizing. She had no business being out when he came home. He stomped off to the shop in a bad temper to see how Frank Hawthorne was getting along now he was the manager, and gave him a difficult hour while he inspected the books and grumbled because trade was down for the second week in succession. He was still cross when he got back to the house again.

The stairs were clean, the charwoman had gone and Alice was alone in the kitchen peeling potatoes.

'You're back then,' she said, sourly and unnecessarily. 'We've only got cold meat and pickles.'

'That'll do,' he said crossly, waving the idea of cold meat and pickles away from him as though it were a fly buzzing round his face.

'It'll have to,' she said, reaching for another potato and then moping the sweat from her forehead with the back of her hand. It was very hot in the kitchen and he realized that the stove was alight, and was annoyed. 'You're surely not cooking on that awful stove in this heat!' he remonstrated. 'Why don't you use the gas oven?'

'Nasty, new-fangled thing,' she said. 'I'm not lighting that up just for a panful of potatoes.' She liked the old stove. She was used to it.

Albert took a chair and set it underneath the open kitchen window. Her pig-headedness had made him crosser than ever but, worse than that, it had also made him forget the way he'd planned to start this conversation.

'Did the funeral go off all right?'

'Oh, yes.'

'That's good then.' So why was he chewing the ends of his moustache and scowling so? There was something the matter. That was very plain.

He bit his top lip, settled his mouth, and then spoke again, rapidly and without looking at her. 'To tell you the truth, Alice, I've only come home to pack my clothes, then I'm going back to Peckham.'

She sat perfectly still with both hands in the water among the potato peelings. 'Oh yes,' she said calmly. 'How long for this time?'

He took the opportunity she'd given him and made rapid use of it. 'For good,' he said, brusquely. 'I've bought a house in Peckham. I'm leaving.'

Her face froze into a listening mask, almost without expression. 'What do you mean, leaving?'

Now he found the courage to look her full in the eye. 'I'm

233

leaving *you*, Alice,' he said. 'I want you to divorce me.'

'It's some silly little girl, again, isn't it?' she said.

He wouldn't be drawn. 'I shall take my clothes, and my desk,' he informed her. 'That is all. Nothing else. I will pay for the upkeep of this house, and you can have your housekeeping the same as usual, but I shall live in Peckham. It all settled.'

'Don't be ridiculous,' she said, still frozen, 'It's out of the question. We're much too old for such nonsense.'

Her apparent complacency made him cruel. '*You* are too old,' he said. 'I am not. I have a life to lead. A life of my own.'

'Your life is here, with me,' she insisted. 'I'm your wife. Or have you forgotten?' There was a new, sharp edge to her voice now, and a dark red flush suffusing her neck. She's an old woman, he thought, looking at her closely and seeing her with a stranger's eyes. An old woman, with jowls on either side of a bumpy chin, and faded eyes and grey hair so thin it no longer covered her skull, a barrel-shaped old woman with false teeth and sagging breasts and nothing about her that was the least little bit attractive.

'No point talking about it,' he said, standing up. 'I've told you. Now I'm going.' And he went upstairs quickly while he was still in control.

His bedroom looked bleak and unloved, more like a hotel room than a dwelling, with its bachelor bunk too small and too empty, and the desk closed and polished and so little evidence of his occupation that for a few stupid seconds he wondered whether he'd ever actually lived in it at all. He dragged two suitcases out of the wardrobe and began to pack his clothes at once, throwing them carelessly and quickly into the cases. Now that he'd begun it he wanted to get this particular job over and done with as quickly as possible. He worked so rapidly he was almost finished by the time Alice followed him upstairs.

'I suggest you stop all this nonsense and come downstairs and eat your dinner,' she said, cold and deliberately calm, although her neck and cheeks were still flushed with anger.

'Good God, woman!' he roared in exasperation. 'How many more times I got to tell you? I leave you. I leave this house. I live in Peckham. It all settled.'

'Oh no it's not,' she said fiercely. 'You may live where you

234

please. I can't stop that. But if you think you're going to rush off and marry some cheap little tart, you've got another think coming. I shan't divorce you. Never in a million years. And you can't divorce me because I've never given you any reason.'

'Reason! Reason!' he roared. 'Fifteen years we've lived in this house like plaster saints. You 'ave never love me once in fifteen years. Don't talk to me a' reasons.'

'Oh well, if you're going to talk dirty …' she said. It was always the same with him. That's all love ever meant to men.

'It's not dirty, Alice,' he tried to explain, but her face was closed, and he could see she would never understand. 'Oh, do as you like,' he shouted at her. 'Divorce. Refuse. It make no odds. I not stay here to sleep on my own. Never again. I'm off!' And he pushed past her and charged down the stairs and out of the house, banging the front door after him with a great deal of noise and satisfaction.

Minnie had been listening at the top of the second flight of stairs. Now she put her head over the banisters, avid for scandal.

'Did you ever hear the like of it?' Alice said.

'What did he say?'

'He only thinks he's going to leave me and marry someone else.'

'No!' Minnie said, thrilled and appalled.

'Well, he's got another think coming, that's all I can say,' Alice said with massive determination. She had got her breath back after the initial shock and now she was planning her campaign. 'I've got the right on my side, Minnie. The very idea of a man his age leaving his wife and family! I've got the right entirely on my side. Well, we'll just have to see about it, that's all.' She stamped down the stairs, her spine rigid and her face set, and for the first time in her life picked up the receiver of that dreadful telephone as Minnie watched, her mouth wide open with amazement. Even when the operator's horrible, disembodied voice rose from the earpiece she was undaunted, and asked for Georgie's number, without a tremor.

Mary came back to Lyndhurst Square just before twelve o'clock, and as she was happier now and the house was empty, except for Mrs Midgeley, she settled down to play the piano. If

235

she had to wait around in the house until her mother came home she might as well make good use of the time. Soon rippling notes were rising like birdsong through the open window and into the front garden. She'd chosen a Beethoven sonata, and a difficult one, so she was concentrating hard, the tip of her tongue between her teeth.

It was an immense relief to Queenie, a nice normal sound to hear as she walked up the garden path with her basket full of shopping. The holiday'd done Mary good. What a blessing!

'All right?' she asked, putting her head round the drawing room door to smile a welcome at her daughter.

'Yes.' Still concentrating furiously.

She sounds all right, Queenie thought. 'D'you have a good time?'

'Yes. The Tids were little beggars.' She was on the last page of the second movement.

'I'll go an' see 'ow Mrs Midgeley's getting on with the dinner. Ploo'll be back at one o'clock.'

The rest of the movement could wait. 'When are we going home, Ma?' she said, closing the piano lid and standing up.

Her mother looked uncomfortable. 'We are 'ome,' she said.

'Home to the flat, I mean.'

'We're not going back ter the flat. I've give it up. We're going ter live 'ere, wiv Ploochy.'

Mary didn't know which piece of news to respond to first. They both made her equally angry. 'You can't give up the flat,' she said. 'That's our home.'

'Not no more, it ain't.' She looked apologetic, but she was standing her ground.

'I ain't livin' 'ere, Ma, so you can just get that straight.'

They were standing in front of each other like gladiators ready to strike, eyes glaring and already panting, Mary with anger and grief, Queenie with anger and apprehension.

'Don't you talk ter me like that. You'll live where I say.'

'I won't.'

'You will.'

'I'll go back to the flat an' tell 'em we've changed our minds.'

'Won't do no good. The other people've moved in. I told yer. It's settled.'

'Moved in? Already? They can't 'ave. What about the furniture. What've yer done with my furniture?'

Ma looked more embarrassed than ever. 'We 'ad it moved,' she said. 'It's 'ere.'

'Here! Here!' Mary yelled. This really was the limit. 'How dare you bring it here! It was *my* furniture. Well, I tell you I won't live here. You can move what you like. Heaven and earth. It won't make no difference.'

'Oh, come on, Mary,' Queenie tried. 'It's a lovely place. Best 'ouse we've ever 'ad. You oughter be glad, not carryin' on like this.'

'Glad!' Mary yelled. 'You move in here. You don't ask me. An' I'm supposed to be glad!' She couldn't credit her mother's stupidity. 'Don't you understand? I don't want to live here. This is Ploochy's house, not ours. I want to live in our own house, just you an' me. That's not much to ask, surely to goodness.'

'Just fer a little while,' Queenie lied, caught because she couldn't tell her daughter what was really going on. 'While we get ourselves straight.'

'An' how long's that going to take?' She was still hot with anger but she could see that Ma was trying to placate her.

'Not long. You'll see.'

'An' then we'll get another flat an' go back to Bermondsey?'

'Well … I don't know about that.'

'You're not going to move,' Mary said understanding the embarrassment. 'You've moved in with him, 'aven't you? You've moved in with that wretched Ploochy, and Pa not dead five minutes. How could you?'

'It's a good 'ome,' Ma said stubborn with distress. 'It's the best 'ome we've ever 'ad. Don't you value a good 'ome?'

'It's Ploochy's home!' We've said this before, she thought. We're going round in circles not getting anywhere.

'Come an' 'ave some dinner,' Ma suggested. 'You'll feel better fer a meal.'

'It'ud choke me!' Mary said furiously. 'You haven't understood a word I've been saying. I won't stay here! I won't live here! This is Ploochy's house! I'm going back to Aunt Eth's!' And she stomped off into the hall to find her panama.

As she jammed her hat firmly on her unruly hair, Ploochy

put his key in the lock, and glancing up she could see his broad shadow through the coloured glass of the door. As he came in, she went out, head held high and cheeks blazing. And she went without a glance or a word.

'Oh dear,' he said, when the door slammed after her.

'She's in a mood,' Queenie said. 'Took it bad. I knew she would, didden' I? She's gone back to Eth's. How did you get on?'

'She took it bad an' all,' he said.

'Perhaps we shouldn't 'ave.'

'Yes, we should 'ave,' he assured her, cuddling her in her dejection. 'And anyway, we can't put the clock back. Not this time. This time we stay together no matter what. It'll be all right, my lovely Queenie. You'll see.'

Mary was still cross when she got to Jamaica Road, but she took some of her anger out on the pavement, banging her feet all the way to Aunt Eth's flat. But there was no answer and when she peered through the letter box the place looked empty. All right, she thought, I'll go to The Red Lion. There's always someone there.

Mrs Oxbury let her in. 'Hello, lovey,' she said. 'Go on up. D'you 've a good time wiv Eth? Tom's in the kitchen.' And so he was, reading an important looking book. The sight of it reminded her that he was waiting for the results of his Higher Schools so she put her anger aside for a moment to ask him if he'd heard.

'No,' he said. 'Not yet. How did you get on at Dunton?'

'Oh *that* was all right,' she said.

'Then what's up?'

She told him. 'If it wasn't for Pa,' she said when she'd finished, 'I'd leave school and get a job and set up on me own.'

He considered this seriously. 'I wouldn't do that if I was you,' he said finally. 'That would be a wicked waste, with your brain. You ought to go on and take your Lower Schools, and then Highers and then university if you can. You owe that to all the people who've helped you. And think how we need trained minds in the Labour Party. No, I don't think you should give up.'

She didn't either, but it soothed her anger to threaten.

'If I go on,' she said, 'I shall have to stay in that house with that man. All on me own.'

'You could visit us,' he offered.

He *was* a kind boy. 'It's not the same though, is it?' she said. 'A visit now and then. It 'ud be a help. An' I daresay I could go to Eth's now and then. But all the rest a' the time I shall be on me own. Oh, I wish I had some brothers and sisters, Tom. Like me cousins. There's always such a lot of them.' There was safety and comfort in a crowd of siblings. And a lot of fun too, as the last week had shown her.

Then Mrs Oxbury came upstairs and asked her if she'd like to stay to dinner with them. 'Only pot luck, but you're welcome.' And she realized that what with her anger and her journey she was feeling very hungry.

'Ta,' she said, 'if it won't put you out.'

'Go down and phone Mr Ploochy and tell him,' Mrs Oxbury said to Tom. And he gave her a grin and went. Maisie looked at her visitor's tearstained face. 'You'll feel better for a meal,' she said.

When Georgie answered *his* telephone call, he was so surprised to hear his mother's voice on the other end of wire that for a moment or two he didn't know what to say to her. He felt sure that there must be something terribly wrong, but his mind was spinning in such confusion he couldn't focus it long enough to think what it might be. She didn't enlighten him. 'Can you come and see me this afternoon?' she said, and while he was still catching his breath and trying to think she assumed he'd agreed. 'As soon as the shop's shut,' she said.

'Yes,' he answered at last, but she'd already hung up.

He went back to his shop puzzled and upset. It was most unlike his mother to give orders in that detached, peremptory way. But then it was entirely unlike her to use the telephone. He had no customers, so he went to the bottom of the stairs and called for Lily, who presently appeared at the top of the first flight, her hands covered with flour and her apron ballooned by her pregnancy. 'What d'you want?' she asked mildly.

He told her about the phone call. 'Fancy!' she said. 'I'll just get this pastry finished and then I'll come down.'

But even with a plateful of warm jam tarts to assist them and their daughter sitting chattily between them they couldn't make any sense of it.

'It must be something pretty important or she'd never have used the phone,' Georgie worried. 'But then again, if it was serious Dadda would have dealt with it.'

'You'd better go and see what she wants,' Lily said at last. 'Don't stay too long though, will you?' The baby was due in ten days' time and she was nervous about being left alone.

'I'll be as quick as I can,' he said, kissing her.

It was more easily promised than achieved, although at first, because his mother opened the door to him and was calm and controlled, he relaxed and thought it couldn't be anything very much after all and that whatever it was he could probably deal with it quite quickly. Then she led him into the front parlour, sat him beside the empty grate and dropped her news into his head like a bomb.

'Your father's left me,' she said, sitting still and stony faced before him.

He was suffused with sympathy for her. 'Oh, poor Mother,' he said. 'I *am* sorry.' His emotion undid them both, for the sight of his crumpled distress broke her control immediately.

'How could he do this to me?' she wailed. 'I've been such a good wife to him all these years. Such a good wife. I worked in that shop till I could hardly stand, I was so tired. Not that he ever noticed. I've kept this house spotless for him. Absolutely spotless! Always clean clothes whenever he wanted them and good hot meals no matter what time of the day he got home. Well, you know that, Georgie. I've sat up all hours waiting for him, worried sick in case he'd had an accident and I never said a word. Not once. Not a word. Plenty of other wives would have said something, that I do know. Especially knowing what I knew. But I never did. Not once. I've scrubbed and cleaned and washed and ironed. And never one word of complaint. Oh, it's not fair, Georgie! What did I ever do to deserve to be treated like this? Cast off like an old boot. After all I've done for him!' And she wept uncontrollably, the tears running off the end of her nose and into her mouth.

Georgie was terribly embarrassed. Strong emotions always upset him, because they made him feel so exposed. He'd always been timorously sure that emotions had to be kept firmly under control, private and hidden, not rushing all over you in broad daylight like this. But he did his best, kneeling at his mother's feet and holding her tear-damp hands in both of his, and trying to find the right words to say to comfort her.

'Don't cry, Mother,' he pleaded. 'You'll make yourself ill if you cry like this.' It was so out of character, like something happening in a nightmare. 'I'm sure he doesn't mean he's left you for ever.'

'Oh, you don't know the half of it,' she wailed. 'You think your father's such a good man. Well, he's not. He's not. He kept some awful woman for years and years when you were little, and now he's got another one. Some cheap, dirty little tart. I know the sort! Street walkers, that's all they are. That's the sort of creature your marvellous father consorts with. I don't know how I've borne it all these years! I've lived with filth, Georgie. Filth!'

'I'll make you a nice cup of tea,' Georgie said quickly, terrified by this new tirade. He had to stop her before she said anything worse. The heat in the room was overpowering and glancing over his shoulder he saw that the windows were tightly shut. 'You'd feel better for a breath of fresh air,' he said and disengaged his hands as gently as he could.

'Air!' she said wildly, grabbing at his coat as he stood up. 'What good is air? You haven't been listening to a word I've said. Your father's leaving me! Oh, Georgie, what am I going to do? You must help me, Georgie, please, please.'

He turned to face her again although her distress was making him squirm with embarrassment. 'Of course I'll help you,' he promised earnestly. 'I'll do anything for you. You know that. Now let me go and make you a nice cup of tea.'

She clung to his jacket like a lifeline. 'Go and see him, Georgie,' she pleaded. 'Talk to him. You could talk to him, couldn't you? Make him see sense. He can't just walk off and leave me like this. You'll talk to him, won't you, Georgie?'

There was no way he could refuse her. Somewhere underneath all the turmoil of these ugly emotions his reason was telling him quite clearly that he shouldn't have anything to do with this, but he was caught. 'Yes, yes,' he said, 'I promise.'

And then Minnie came bustling into the room with the tea

trolley, so promptly on cue that he couldn't help thinking she'd been listening outside the door. 'There you are, Alice my dear,' she said, administering tea. 'I told you our Georgie would know what to do. Did you ever hear the like, Georgie? Your poor mother! It's a wicked old world and no mistake. Would you like a bit of cake with your tea?'

Lily was not pleased. 'You keep well out of it,' she advised. 'Nothing to do with you.'

'She *is* my mother, Lily,' he said mildly. He had to open the shop again in a quarter of an hour and now he was at the kitchen sink, washing his face and hands in a vain attempt to cool down.

'It's entirely their own affair,' she said. 'I knew this'ud happen the minute we saw your father in the pictures. Keep out of it. There's nothing you can do, anyway.'

'I gave my word,' Georgie said miserably.

'I've drawn a tree,' Johnny said, looking up from the kitchen table where he was covering a large sheet of brown paper with bold colours. 'What shall I do next, Mummy?'

'Do that dog we saw in the park,' Lily said, kindly but vaguely. 'No. Not that brown. That's Meg's.' She handed brown wax crayons to both her children before they could start a quarrel. 'This hot weather's making everybody cantankerous,' she said, looking back at her husband again. 'Leave it till it's a bit cooler, Georgie.'

'I'll see if I can find out where he is first,' Georgie said, slowly patting his face dry. 'That's bound to take a bit of time.' The thought of an excusable delay cheered him up. 'I won't rush into anything,' he promised.

But his father removed the excuse on Monday morning by sending a printed card to all his employees giving his new address and telephone number, and the terse information that this was where he could be contacted, if necessary. And of course, it *was* necessary. His mother had seen to that.

'I'll go next Sunday,' he said to Lily, handing her the card to read. 'Get it over with.' He was weary with foreboding.

Chapter Twenty-Two

Mary was planning a campaign. Somehow or other she'd got to get Ma to accept that she couldn't go on living with Ploochy. Reasoning with her was useless because she didn't listen, and rows didn't work either. They'd had four already, real slanging matches, and all they'd done was upset one another to no purpose. Ma was being really obstinate. She wouldn't give way. 'Shout all yer like,' she'd said. 'We're staying 'ere, and that's flat!'

So she would have to change tack, find a more subtle approach, outwit them. She'd got a very good brain. Everybody said so. Now she must use it.

She started by trying to examine their situation dispassionately and coolly, and the first thing she had to admit to herself was that from her mother's point of view it was undeniably attractive; the most comfortable house they'd ever lived in, a housekeeper to cook delicious meals and keep the place clean and tidy; and a man to dote on her. For whatever else she might think of Ploochy, his affection was too open and too strong to be denied. So if she wanted Ma to see sense and leave it all, she'd have to start by convincing her that they could be just as comfortable living somewhere else, on their own. What was needed now was a practical demonstration that she could cook and keep house every bit as well as Mrs Midgeley. And a little bit of steady propaganda, of course. About the sort of money she could earn when she started work, and how much nicer it would be to live near Nan and Aunt Eth. That sort of thing. Ploo was such a buffoon, clowning about and playing silly games all the time Ma 'ud be bound to go off him in the end.

She put her plan into action the very next weekend, cooking Sunday dinner for them and doing all the washing up, all by herself, because she knew how much Ma hated washing up. Ploo declared it was the best dinner he'd ever had and even Ma said it wasn't too bad, so she felt she'd made a good start. Then she went back to the kitchen to bake a batch of fairy cakes and twelve maids of honour. She was just putting the cakes in the oven when the front door bell rang. Little Miss Fenston from up the road, she thought, come to chat and borrow. 'I'll go,' she called to her mother, for she'd decided to be butler as well as chief cook and bottle washer.

It wasn't Miss Fenston, but a strange young man with mousy hair and glasses who blushed when she opened the door. 'Yes?' she said, wondering who he was.

He pushed his glasses firmly onto his nose. 'Could I see my, er, Mr Pelucci, do you think?'

'You'd better come in,' she said and called over her shoulder. 'It's fer you, Ploo!' And Ploochy came bounding out of the door behind them.

'Well, bless my soul!' he said with obvious pleasure. 'Look who's here, Mary! It's my son Georgie.' And he introduced her, 'Queenie's daughter, Mary. What's brought you here, Georgie? Come on in. Have you come ter tea? Mary's making cakes.' He sounded ridiculously proud, silly man. She wondered what he'd say if he knew what her real motives were. 'Come on in!' and without waiting for any kind of answer, he seized his son by the hand and dragged him into the house.

Mary went back to the kitchen to finish the tarts, her mind as busy as her hands. She was very surprised by Ploochy's son. How washed-out he was, with his mousy hair and his pale skin and his anxious expression. They weren't a bit alike, she thought, except for the big nose. But perhaps his harassed expression was because he was finding it difficult to visit his father and Ma. That was probably it. She spooned the last of the almond mixture into the maids of honour and licked the spoon thoughtfully as a fascinating idea grew sharply in her sharp mind. I'll bet *she* sent him, to tell his father to come back to her. I know *I* would if my husband ran off with another woman.

As she put the tarts in the oven and removed the cakes, she

was grinning to herself. Perhaps Fate had sent her an ally. The tarts could be left to their own devices for a few minutes. If this really *was* the situation it had to be exploited.

But when she got into the garden, Ma and Ploochy and the pale young man were deep in a conversation about the old days, and she couldn't compete with that, or even get a word in edgeways. They were sitting under the shade of the cherry tree, and Ma was telling her visitor how she remembered him as a little boy, hiding under the table during some sort of party in the garden in Tooting. 'You was only a nipper,' she said. 'Don't suppose you'd remember. 'Ouse warming or some such, wassen' it, Ploo?'

'Can't remember,' Ploo said, watching Mary as she settled herself on the hammock beside her mother.

'No,' the young man said, 'neither can I, but I think I can remember you. In a pantomime once. You were the bad fairy, I think. Anyway, you wore a red dress and sang a song sitting in a swing.'

'Sounds likely,' Ma said. 'I was always the bad fairy. They didn't reckon good fairies should 'ave red 'air.'

'Type casting,' Ploo said smiling at her with an affection so open and easy it simply couldn't be missed. Horrid man!

'I remember going to Fuller's after the show,' the young man said, smiling, 'for tea and cakes. Old Aunt Phoebe and me and Anna. And Mother, of course.' And he suddenly looked terribly embarrassed and coughed to clear his throat and pushed at his glasses with his forefinger.

I was right, Mary thought. She has sent him. 'How is ...' she began. But Ma was too quick for her.

'That reminds me,' she said. 'If you're staying to tea we'd better get the table set. And them cakes should be done be now.' And she took Mary by the hand and removed her from opportunity.

The cakes turned out beautifully, which in an odd sort of way was rather a nuisance, because it gave Ma and Ploochy a chance to talk about her and how clever she was and then she couldn't change the subject without appearing rude. And that meant she couldn't give Georgie the chance to explain why he'd really come visiting.

After tea, she thought, when we're all sitting round in the

drawing room, I'll ask him about his family. That should do it. She knew Ploochy had a family, because he'd told her. Three children he'd said. Well, they could start by talking about *them*.

But Ploochy was forearmed. He rushed them from the table straight into the sort of activity that would preclude talk. 'Leave the dishes! We do 'em later. Come an' hear our Mary play the pianner.' 'Our Mary' indeed! If she hadn't been putting herself out to be pleasant she'd have given him such a piece of her mind! But she had to be charming, all the time, if her plan was to work, so she smiled and played, choosing a Debussy prelude because it was impressively difficult and Ploochy didn't like it much.

And Georgie was very impressed and told her he'd always wanted to play Debussy's preludes himself, but he'd never been able to get his fingers to handle the notes delicately enough.

'Miss Templeton says everything depends on the angle of your wrist,' she said. 'Look, I'll show you. If you keep it high you get more power.' Despite herself, she rather liked this young man. He was so slow and gentle. I'll bet he wouldn't leave his wife and run off with someone else's, she thought as she played.

'Why dontcher try a duet?' Ma suggested when she came to the end of the prelude. Sly thing!

'He might not want to,' she said dubiously, glancing at him, but it was obvious that he found the idea very attractive, although he was too shy and polite to press for it.

So she found a set of Spanish dances, and soon they were playing duets together, and Albert was humming bits of the tunes and grinning at them and Georgie was feeling guilty because he was enjoying himself so much. After the fourth piece he remembered Lily waiting in that hot flat with the children, and said he really thought he ought to go home. 'Lily hasn't got long before the baby,' he explained, blushing.

''Course,' Ma said easily. 'You cut along. You can always come again, cantcher. Now you know where we are. Bring the family.'

They all went to the door to see him off, and to his surprise and delight Queenie kissed him goodbye. 'It's been ever so nice ter see yer,' she said.

'Come again,' his father said, thumping him on the arm,

and Mary smiled and was furious because he was leaving and he hadn't had a chance to say anything. It was too bad! Almost as if they'd seen what was coming and prevented it. But they needn't think they were going to get away with it. When the two of them went cheerfully back to the drawing room, she slipped out of the back door and gave chase.

She caught up with him halfway down Lyndhurst Way and her arrival made him look anxious again. 'Oh dear,' he said. 'Have I left something behind?'

There wasn't time for diplomacy. Ma mustn't miss her, so she'd got to be quick. 'Look,' she said, 'I know why you came 'ere this afternoon. *She* sent yer, didn't she? Ploochy's wife.'

He looked desperately embarrassed. 'Well, no. Not exactly. I mean, I wanted to see him.'

'I don't blame her,' she said trenchantly. 'I'd do the same mesself. If she sent yer, good luck to 'er. 'E ought ter go back.'

'You don't like him,' he said, fiddling with those wretched glasses again.

'No, I don't. So next time you just tell 'im ter go home. I shan't mind a bit.'

He settled his glasses slowly, squinting at her in the sunlight. 'I don't think it's our business to tell them what to do,' he said. 'I wouldn't like my children to tell me what to do. I can see that now. You're right, of course, she did send me. But I was wrong to agree. There's nothing I can say to persuade them. And anyway I don't think they'd take any notice if I tried. They love each other, you see.'

'They're too old for all that nonsense,' she said angrily. 'And somebody should tell them.'

'I can't help you,' he said, and he smiled, as though he pitied her.

She was furious. 'What's the good of her sending you if you won't say anything?'

'No good at all,' he said, 'and that's the truth.'

'Oh!' she said, scowling with anger, and turned on her heel and stomped off. She's just like her mother, he thought, watching her go.

It wasn't until he was on the train and steaming away from Peckham Rye that he remembered that he'd have to report this mission to his mother. What on earth would he say to her?

And even worse, what on earth would she say to him?

It was a relief to be back in Morden. As he climbed the familiar narrow staircase to his flat above the shop, he knew he was relaxing again. He felt at home and he felt safe, back in his own territory where life was predictable and straightforward.

The kitchen was empty, and so was the living room, empty and tidy and curiously deserted. Somebody was walking quietly about the bedroom and he could hear the children splashing in the bathroom but as he listened he realized that they were murmuring to one another and sounded subdued. Then Madeleine from next door opened the bathroom door a crack and mouthed the word 'baby' at him as she beckoned him in with a sideways nod. 'Bein' ever so good, Daddy,' she assured him once they were all crammed inside the little steamy room. 'Mummy's got a little headache and gone to lie down. Don't you think they're the best children out?'

Oh my God, Georgie thought to himself, I was out when it started. How dreadful! Just when I ought to have been here to help her with the other two. His guilt was so extreme he felt weak at the knees and had to sit down on the edge of the bath to recover. But he told his children how pleased he was they were being so good, and sponged Meg's back, and listened to them while they sang the Ovaltineys' song, very quietly of course, so as not to wake Mummy, and for a few minutes tried to pretend that everything was as it should be.

Meg didn't seem at all put out by the change in her routine, but Johnny was quieter than usual and watchful, his blue eyes anxious. Finally he tackled his father with this new puzzle. 'Mummy had a headache yesterday and she didn't lie down then,' he said. 'Why is she lying down now?'

'I expect she's tired today,' Georgie said. 'It's been very hot. It makes you tired when it's hot, doesn't it? I'll go and see how she is, shall I?'

That satisfied, and the boy's anxiety lifted a little. 'Yes,' he said solemnly, 'you go and see how she is.' And they smiled the same serious smile at one another and Georgie was released.

His first hesitant tap at the bedroom door went unanswered and so did the second, but he was much too embarrassed and ashamed of himself to knock any louder. He could hear the nurse's voice, giving instructions, but Lily didn't seem to be saying anything. Coughing with nerves, he knocked again.

The midwife was her usual efficient self and brisked him inside the door for a brief glimpse at her labouring patient. 'Everything going according to plan,' she said confidently. 'Try not to disturb her.' But Lily was already profoundly disturbed and in private depths of disappointing experience that the midwife couldn't begin to fathom.

'You weren't here,' she said accusingly to poor Georgie.

'I'm so sorry,' he said, pushing at the bridge of his spectacles and blinking at her with distress.

She turned her head away from him. 'She means more to you than I do,' she said, wearily. 'That's the truth, issen' it? When it comes down to it, she means more than me an' Johnny an' Meg all put together.'

'No. No,' he said. 'She doesn't. You mustn't think that. You're more important to me than anything in the whole world.' It was the truth and he was desperate that she should understand it, but she wasn't listening. She had closed her eyes and was breathing in an odd, unnatural rhythm that he remembered and recognized, puffing the air out of her half opened mouth in a series of deliberate gasps like a horse blowing. A pain, he thought, watching her labour through it. We shouldn't be quarrelling at a time like this. And he felt more ashamed than ever.

She opened her eyes as the pain receded, but her face was still withdrawn, concentrating on the rhythm of this birth. Then recognition swam back and she looked at her husband again. 'Oh, do go away!' she said.

He crept from the room like a beaten child, knowing the enormity of his mistake and powerless to begin to put it right. The long hours of the birth passed minute by apprehensive minute and there was nothing he could do but wait. Madeleine put the children to bed and went back to her own family, promising she would 'look in' at breakfast time, and the nurse creaked about the bedroom and Lily panted through pain after pain and George prowled and worried and waited. Soon his stomach was aching with guilt and anxiety.

After midnight, the air grew cooler and the children slept more peacefully. But the baby still wasn't born. Georgie opened the window in his dark living room and stood looking down at the empty width of the Parade, gradually and painfully thinking things out. Lily's words had stung him to a guilty realization. His mother dominated him. He had to admit it. She dominated him. He'd made a mistake, and a very bad one, and now he had to do something to put it right. Somehow or other, he decided, he must find some unanswerable way to say no to his mother. It simply wasn't fair to Lily and the children to let her dictate to them the way she did. They had lives of their own. And besides, he liked Queenie. She was warm and welcoming, and anyone with half an eye could see how much she loved his father. If he took his mother's part in all this he wouldn't do any good, and he'd probably lose his father's company and support. 'Come again,' they'd said. 'Bring the family.' And why not? Or perhaps, on second thoughts, he'd better keep out of trouble and avoid them all. It was very difficult to know what he ought to do for the best. If only Lily wasn't … If only the baby would …

The midwife rustled at his elbow. 'You have another son, Mr Ploochy,' she whispered. 'You may go in and see them if you're quiet about it. Not too much excitement, mind.'

He'd forgotten how overwhelming the impact of a birth could be. Lily was sitting among her mounded pillows with their new baby cradled in the crook of her arm, rosy in the halo of light from their bedside lamp, and smiling so tenderly first at him and then at the dark head of their new infant that he was quite overcome with emotion and felt the tears start into his eyes. The midwife, for all her no-nonsense approach to her trade, knew when to make herself scarce. 'Eight o'clock, Mrs Ploochy,' she said, and left them on their own.

'You clever, clever, lovely, beautiful girl,' he said, awed and grateful and shamed and repentant.

'Isn't he a little duck?' she said, proudly, stroking the child's miniature fingers. 'And so pretty, aren't you, my darling.'

'I'm so sorry I wasn't there,' he said, but she was smiling forgiveness before the words were out of his mouth.

'Shush! Shush!' she said. 'I was an old grouch an' all.' She was wrapped in a trance of contentment, gazing at her baby.

'You're more important to me than anything else in the whole world. My dear, lovely, beautiful, clever Lily. You do know that, don't you?'

They both knew it. Now.

So they cuddled their baby, and Georgie named him, and Lily fed him, and the sky grew lilac with dawn. 'I've decided something,' Georgie said as the dawn chorus piped and warbled below them. 'Mother must fight her own battles. It's not my affair. My place is here with you. You're my family.'

'That's right,' she said, drowsy but approving. Sleep and contentment were washing her away, but she was smiling at him even though her eyes were shut.

My family, he thought, my life, my way, not my mother's. The decision was made, and it was irrevocable, and it was right.

Alice telephoned at half past seven.

'Georgie?' she said. 'How did you get on?'

He was still stupid with sleep and emotion and breathless from his rush downstairs to take the call before it could wake Lily. 'She had a little boy,' he said. 'Seven and a half pounds. We're going to call him Norman.'

'What?'

'A little boy,' he said patiently. 'At four o'clock this morning.'

Understanding caused a short pause. Then his mother spoke again. 'Very nice,' she said. 'How did you get on with your father?'

Now he must tell her. Now while his courage was high. He settled his glasses firmly on the bridge of his nose. 'He won't come back,' he said. 'He *has* left you, Mother.'

He heard her catch her breath. Then there was another pause, as the earpiece sizzled and they were both afraid.

'How can you possibly say that?' she demanded at last. 'You've only seen him once. You must go back again and make him see sense this time. I'm depending on you, Georgie.'

'I can't move out of the house till Lily's up and about,' he said reasonably. 'You wouldn't expect me to leave her on her own with a new baby.'

'She wouldn't be on her own. You could get somebody in to sit with her, surely.'

'No,' he said, angered by her selfishness. 'I couldn't. And even if I could, I wouldn't.'

'Are you refusing?' she asked. She sounded amazed. 'Your own mother?'

'I can't help you, Mother,' he tried to explain. 'I've told you. He won't come back.'

'We'll see about that,' she said grimly. And put the phone down.

Upstairs, Meg and Johnny were awake and chattering together in their high fluting voices. Georgie wiped the sweat out of his eyes, shook his mother's voice out of his ears and went back up the stairs to the flat to introduce them to their new brother.

In the cool shadows of her quiet hall, Alice looked at the disagreeable reflection of her face in the little oval mirror on the hallstand and stamped her foot with anger and frustration. This was all Lily's doing, of course. She'd always been a sly, treacherous little thing. Look at the way she inveigled poor Georgie from his family. Oh, how unfair life was! And there was Albert's umbrella in the stand. He'd be yelling for that the next time it rained.

At the edge of the mirror she could see Minnie tiptoeing down the stairs behind her. 'Was there any news, me dear?' her cousin asked, her face wrinkled with anxious concern.

'He's being very stubborn,' Alice said, cryptically. 'There are others, fortunately.'

The first of the others presented himself at the kitchen window for her instructions just over an hour later. Harry Jones, come to do the garden, as usual on a Monday morning. They exchanged the usual domestic courtesies, inquiring after grandchildren and relations, Alice announcing the birth of her new grandson, and Harry glad to say that Billy's Dora was well again, and little Harry 'a right little beggar' these days, plaguing the life out of his brother. Then they agreed that the onions were dry enough to plait, and that the grass needed watering, and there was always plenty of weeding.

'Terrible disappointment, them ol' onions,' Harry said.

'We all have to face disappointments, Harry,' she told him. 'I'll be out presently to look at the rose arbour. That's been a disappointment this year too.'

But when the washing was on the line, still and straight as becalmed sails, and the lawn was dry as straw again, it wasn't the rose arbour she talked about.

'Didn't know where ter put meself,' Harry told Em later that morning as they sat in their back kitchen eating their midday meal. It was making him hot with embarrassment just to remember. 'It ain't my affair what old Ploochy gets up to, now is it? Not when all's said an' done.'

'Fancy 'im runnin' off an' leaving old Alice,' Em said. 'After all these years. I'd never 'ave believed it. Poor Alice.'

'Be ever so awkward,' Harry said, scratching his head with both hands. 'What'll 'e say on Wednesday, I wonder. Be ever so awkward.'

But he needn't have worried because Ploochy turned up at Jack Beard's that Wednesday just the same as ever, and they talked about work and the weather and the state of the world and enjoyed themselves just as they always did. Which, Dickie said, was much the best way.

August burned on, dry and breathless and enervating. Georgie's new baby seemed to have been born with an insatiable thirst, and Johnny and Meg were hot and sticky and quarrelsome, cooped up in their stale little flat all morning. As soon as the shop was shut for the afternoon, Georgie took them both off to the park to breathe some fresh air, but what they all really needed was a holiday somewhere nice and quiet beside the sea. Eric and Anna had gone to Herne Bay for a fortnight, and sent back regular postcards bragging about how lovely it was and how much they were both enjoying themselves.

'Next year,' Georgie promised his family, 'we'll have a holiday too. I'll hire someone to look after the shop, and we'll all go away.' He was full of plans for the future, another shop, in Worcester Park to catch the cocktail trade, a house with a nice private back garden on one of the new estates just round the corner. It all seemed perfectly possible now. Stepping out from under the weight of his mother's intensity had given him an extraordinary sense of purpose, as if he had suddenly undertaken some long voyage of exploration and was solely and confidently in charge of it all. 'As soon as the weather breaks, we'll all go to Peckham and see Dadda about the new shop,' he said. 'We shall see some changes by Christmas, I promise you.' It was rather exciting.

'Not just yet though, eh?' Lily begged, drooping over the baby in her lap. What with the heat and young Norman's non-stop feeding, she was feeling worn and exhausted.

'When you're ready,' Georgie promised lovingly. 'It's too hot for anything just at the minute.'

It wasn't too hot for Alice. Anger impelled her onwards day by furious day. There was nothing else in her life now but her one terrible compulsion. Albert must be forced to return to her. She didn't care how it was done, but she wanted it settled before the neighbours began to notice. She wrote two long letters every day, one to Georgie outlining his duty to her, the other to Albert, explaining with the monotony of obsession that he simply couldn't leave her, that she would never divorce him, that his cruelty was making her ill. She wrote with such anger that the nibs buckled and crossed under her fingers, and the more her letters were ignored, the longer and more querulous they became.

Finally she wrote to Anna.

Chapter Twenty-Three

When Anna left for her 'ripping' holiday at Herne Bay, she was a plumply pregnant brunette. When she returned, she was a plumply pregnant, spectacular blonde.

It was all Eric's fault. He'd been perfectly beastly all the time, making such a fuss if he didn't get his stupid newspaper in the morning, lying about in deckchairs all day long as if he were a hundred and ninety, and then jumping on top of her all night and every night. Horrible. Especially now, with the baby making her so uncomfortable. No consideration at all. Not that he worried about the baby one little bit. 'It's your own look out,' he said heartlessly, when she dared to complain. 'You would have it. I told you not to.' And to make matters worse, there were so many pretty girls about. Slim, pretty girls parading on the beach in the most feminine dresses and the most delicious swimsuits. The fashions this year were darling. She'd have looked really stunning in them, if only it hadn't been for the baby. Life was very hard. It made her feel so out of things, sitting in a deckchair, all swollen up and ghastly. Why, nobody gave her so much as a second look. She simply had to do something about it. So she had her hair dyed.

The girl in the salon had been perfectly ridiculous about it, saying it wouldn't take because her hair was so dark. Making excuses, that's all it was. But she'd insisted, and of course it had taken, not quite the colour she'd wanted, she had to admit, because she'd been thinking in terms of a nice light gold, like the film stars, and this was a bit on the heavy side, more like butter really, but gold certainly, nobody could deny that. It made her eyebrows look rather coarse and heavy, which was an unexpected side effect, but one that was easily remedied. Ten minutes determined plucking soon reduced them to the merest line, and although the plucked flesh looked rather angry, she was sure the red patches would soon fade and they were easily disguised by make-up. By the time she'd finished, she was transformed.

It absolutely shattered Eric. When she made her entrance to the hotel dining room that afternoon, his face was a positive study.

'Good God, girl,' he spat at her, but quietly of course and between his teeth so that the other guests wouldn't hear, 'what have you done?'

'Ripping, isn't it,' she said gaily. All eyes had turned her way, which was very gratifying. So if he didn't like it, he could lump it.

She didn't really have second thoughts about it until they were in the car and driving back to London. It was raining and the holiday was over and she had a very definite sensation of coming down to earth. She wondered, with some trepidation, what her mother would say, and began to think that perhaps she ought to go to the hairdresser's and have it toned down a bit before her visit on Tuesday.

But the letter put paid to that.

There was the customary bundle of bills and circulars lying on the doormat awaiting their return. She picked them up at once because Eric got so cross if the flat looked untidy, but she didn't pay much attention to them. At least, not at first. Bills were always so horrid and there were always so many of them these days. But then she suddenly noticed her mother's neat handwriting on one of the envelopes and her heart gave a little jump of surprise and foreboding. It was most unlike Mummy to write a letter. Whatever could it be?

'My darling daughter,' Alice had written, 'I don't want to upset you just when you have got back, especially with the baby, but I thought you ought to know your father has left me for another woman. It is a great shock to us all. Nobody can help me. I've asked Georgie but he can't do anything. Neither can Mr Jones or Mr Chanter. Your Aunt Min has been very kind. I am very unhappy. Please come and see me as soon as you can, darling. I hope you and Eric are well. Your ever loving Mother.'

The news lifted Anna into a state of such happy intoxication that she wanted to jump in the air and dance and leap about. At long, long last her mother was noticing her, writing to her for help, turning to her in her hour of need. Not to Georgie or Aunt Min or anyone else, but to her, to her, to Anna Maria, her daughter. At last! She stood in the hall for a long rapturous minute, clutching the letter with both hands, her eyes blazing. Then she grabbed her handbag, and ran precipitately out of the flat.

Eric was already unpacking their luggage in the bedroom, following his mother's instructions even after six years of married life, but when the door banged he ran out into the hall, and then out of the flat, to see what was going on. She was already halfway down the second flight of stairs. He could just see her ridiculous yellow hair below him. 'Where do you think you're going?' he demanded.

She didn't even look up. 'Mummy needs me!' she called gaily and trotted off from the foot of the stairs.

He could hardly believe his ears. What was she thinking of? Rushing off the minute they got in, when there was a meal to cook and clothes to unpack. Selfish bitch. He ran to the window of the lounge and flung it open, determined to call her back, and there she was, in the middle of the road, climbing into a taxi! The very idea! A taxi! Such extravagance was beyond endurance. He could feel his veins swelling with an intolerable anger. He'd have something to say when she got back and no mistake.

The taxi drove as though it had wings. It was a fairy coach carrying Anna, the knight in shining armour, to the rescue of her distracted parent. She sat, straight-spined with importance and pleasure, with the precious, precious letter still in her hands, planning all the marvellous things she would say to her mother and all the marvellous, grateful things her mother would say to her, savouring them in advance, word by long overdue word. As they passed Merton Garage, she caught sight of Harry Jones standing beside the dusty entrance, leaning on the handle bars of that battered old bicycle of his. He was talking to his son Billy, who looked very tall and solid in his driver's uniform, even if he was only a working man. You couldn't help my mother, could you, she thought, gloating

257

inside her head as the taxi bounced on towards the soot black walls of the old paper mill and the oily waters of the river Wandle. She was the one pure, true, valiant creature in this whole sordid landscape.

It was an amazing success. Almost as good as her fantasy.

'My poor dear, darling mother!' she said as Alice opened the door, and then she had her arms about her mother's neck and the two of them were clinging together like lost souls, and she was promising to do anything, *anything* to get her father back home again. This time when Alice explained what a good wife she'd been and how little she deserved such shabby treatment there was a child at her side who agreed vociferously with every word, and then said all the right comforting things.

'It's disgusting! A man of his age! He ought to be ashamed of himself. Don't you worry about a thing, Mummy darling. I'll soon sort all this out for you. You leave it to me. I'll go over there and give him such a talking to.'

'She will too,' Minnie said admiringly, patting Alice's arm. 'Didn't I say Anna would be the one?'

'I know how to handle Dadda,' Anna bragged. Hadn't she always been able to wheedle things out of him? Even as a little girl. 'I can twist him round my little finger.'

'You mustn't upset yourself,' Alice counselled, enjoying the bombast immensely. 'We've got to think of the baby.'

In the warmth and well being of this marvellous upsurge of righteous indignation Anna had forgotten all about the baby. 'Don't you worry about a thing, Mummy darling,' she said. 'Now I'm home everything will be all right.'

It was a wonderful homecoming. Mummy and Aunt Min made such a fuss of her, with a special lunch in the garden and a Wall's ice cream to pamper her, just as though she was a little girl again. And neither of them said a word about the colour of her hair.

At least, not until after she'd gone off to Peckham.

Albert was concerned with colour too that afternoon, but in his case it was the colour of a motor car.

Ever since he'd moved Queenie and Mary Ann into Lyndhurst Square he'd been toying with the idea of buying himself a motor car, transport of his own, as the salesman said, to take him anywhere he wanted at any hour of the day or night without having to wait for public transport. Funnily enough it was a visit from Georgie that had finally persuaded him make up his mind, his sober son suddenly offering to manage another shop out in Raynes Park and sounding amazingly confident about it.

'Who'd have thought it?' he said to Queenie.

'I would,' she said cheerfully. 'Always said 'e was a good 'un.'

'Very well!' he said. 'I buy him the shop an' I buy us a car.'

He bought a red racing car, an Alpha Romeo Pescara, because it was expensive and dashing and Italian and had a very loud engine and an even louder colour. And that afternoon he took delivery, a splendidly exciting moment.

Queenie and Mary were summoned from the garden at once. Now what's he up to, Mary thought. Was this the chance she'd been waiting for? Was he going to make a fool of himself?

'Whatcher think a 'that?' he said proudly.

'Like a bloomin' fire engine,' Ma said, as pleased and excited as he was.

'Bit bright,' Mary said. She sounded just sufficiently disapproving for her mother to believe her and her delight to be hidden. Go on, she willed him, show yourself up. Let her see what a fool you are.

'Hop in,' he ordered. 'We go for a spin.'

'All of us?' Mary queried. She hadn't expected that. 'There's only two seats.'

'You can sit on the buggy seat at the back,' he said, happily donning his dashing leather helmet and a huge pair of driving goggles.

'But you can't drive,' Queenie protested, grinning at the extraordinary frog-like apparition he had become.

'Its easy,' he said, masterfully. 'Nothing to it. Hop in.'

So they hopped, and after a short interval while the starting handle was crashed and cranked and one or two curses uttered their new toy sprang into juddering life and off they went, out of the square on their very first jaunt.

Negotiating corners was more difficult than he'd antici-pated, especially as he really couldn't see very well from behind his goggles. In fact, the first three weren't so much turned as trampled, to the consternation of passers-by, who were a little aggrieved to be roared at by a frog-headed lunatic in a large car. One or two shook their fists at his retreating wheels and called him a road hog. But he wasn't deterred in the least. ''Aven't got the hang of it!' he explained cheerfully to them over his speeding shoulder.

'Slow down, Ploo, fer Gawd's sake,' Queenie begged, laughing at him. 'You'll knock somebody over.'

Don't laugh at him Mary thought, and despite herself her face revealed her disapproval. He's acting like an irresponsible idiot. But it wasn't the right time to say anything. That would come later.

'No I won't,' he yelled back at her. 'They can 'ear me coming. They're all right,' and as he careered round his third corner, 'Mind yer backs! Make way!' This time he only drove across a few feet of pavement before bumping down onto the road again, and the elderly couple who had been forced to lean into a hedge to get out of his way merely looked bemused. 'Soon get the hang of it,' he said and began to whistle, happily and tunelessly, as he always did when he was pleased with himself.

He took the next corner in style, and found himself in Highshore Road, hurtling at a quite ridiculous speed towards the crowded street market, a confused mass of striped awnings and stained canvas, stalls piled with everything edible, fruit and vegetables, fish and fowls, whelks and winkles, a litter of crates and baskets, boxes and barrels, an impassable roadway crammed with fast-moving activity, boys on bicycles, men on the make, dogs on the rampage and an army of overweight women with baskets to match.

'Stop! Stop! Stop!' Queenie yelled, and Mary Ann hid her face in her hands, and Albert struggled to remember what he was supposed to do to work the brakes. Startled faces gaped towards them as the tyres squealed and the car slewed across the width of the road and came to a halt a few inches away from the nearest stall holder.

'Cuttin' it a bit fine, aintcher?' the coster shouted sarcastically. 'Sure you wouldn't like ter park it in the stall while yer at it?' And his customers applauded and jeered.

'Where's 'e think 'e is? Brooklands?'

'What you on about?' Albert said, unabashed. 'Never touched yer.'

A happy crowd gathered to offer advice and cheerfully pessimistic comment. ''E'll never get it out a' there.' 'Need a tow, that will.' 'You wanna put it in reverse, mate.' 'Need a push?' The coster glowered, Queenie scowled, Albert held the gear stick and the car trembled and juddered like a thoroughbred at the off.

'It'll 'ave ter go backwards, Ploo,' Queenie said.

'Don't tell me what it'll 'ave ter do,' Albert shouted. 'We're *going* backwards. Hold tight.' And he pushed the gear stick down as though he knew exactly what he was doing, and the car shot forward like a rocket, straight into the side of the fruit stall. For a split second there was a stunned, delighted silence then everything happened at once. The coster swore, the crowd converged, the stall broke in two pieces and fell away from the car, apples rolled in all directions and the awning collapsed in delicate slow motion, like a sail losing the breeze, and came to rest covering stall, coster, car and Queenie in a confusion of canvas. Only Albert emerged from the chaos calm and self-possessed. He removed his goggles and stood up on the driver's seat. 'Everything is all right!' he ordered.

'All right? All right?' the coster shrieked. ''Alf my bleedin' stock gorn ter wrack an' ruin, an' you say all right.'

'I pay you all the damages,' Albert said coolly, producing one of his cards and handing it down to his irate adversary. 'I take responsibility. It all right.'

'That's all very well,' the coster told the crowd, only partially mollified. ''Ow do I know 'e's a man of 'is word?'

Hands were pulling the awning away from the wreckage and several of the faces above them frowned and agreed. 'It's a cryin' shame,' one woman said fiercely. 'You've took 'is livin', I hope you realize. Just 'cause you've got a posh car don't give yer the right ter take away 'is livin'.'

Mary Ann scrambled out of the buggy seat and climbed onto the running board. She didn't want to be publicly associated with reckless driving. After all, the stupid man was nothing to do with her. There was going to be a row, so she would leave them to it. 'I'm off for my piano lesson, Ma,' she said. 'It's almost time. I can catch a bus from Peckham Rye.' And she went quickly before Albert could argue with her or do anything even more embarrassing with his awful car. Ma chose him. Let her sort it out. I hope someone hits him on the nose. He won't be quite such a hero to her then.

But unfortunately, as she left, someone in the crowd was yelling recognition. 'It's Mr Ploochy! 'E'll pay yer, Binzey. It's Mr Ploochy from the orf-licence.'

She looked back angrily over her shoulder. What bad luck. The crowd was calming down and the man called Binzey was listening and nodding his head and seemed to be agreeing. He was going to get away with it. She stomped off to catch her bus in a very bad mood. Why was the luck always on his side?

So honour was satisfied, the card accepted and Albert, having marshalled the crowd to disentagle his car, finally discovered how to put it into reverse and drove ebulliently away.

'Honest ter God, Ploo,' Queenie said in disbelief, 'it beats me 'ow you get away with it.' There were times when her Ploo really annoyed her with his thoughtless complacency. He was so sure money was the answer, that was the trouble. 'That poor bloke!'

But Albert wasn't paying any attention. He was whistling again.

Chapter Twenty-Four

Anna arrived in Lyndhurst Square a few minutes after her father's dramatic departure. Little Miss Fenston from two doors up was still sitting beside her drawing room window, lace curtain in hand, and eager for the next event. When the Pelucci family had moved into her quiet square, they had brought a touch of much needed excitement into her circumscribed existence, and now she was making the most of it. She'd been such a quiet, subdued little thing all her life, obeying her parents, behaving properly and waiting, in the most ladylike way, for the proposal of marriage that never came. Now that her mother was dead she shared the house with her father, who was elderly and cantankerous and bed-ridden. It was like living in a morgue, although she was much too meek and subservient ever to say so. The comings and goings of Mr Pelucci and his family were the breath of life to her.

Now she watched as the young lady with yellow hair rang the bell and waited impatiently on the doorstep, tapping her foot and occasionally peering through the stained glass, her nose pressed right against the pane. A fine young lady, very fashionable, and undeniably in the family way. She rang again and Miss Fenston heard the bell jangle and wondered why that nice Mrs Midgeley didn't come to answer the door. Then she remembered that it was Saturday, and knew that the house was empty, and she felt sorry for the young lady standing there in the hot sun. Greatly daring, she tiptoed out into her front garden to see if there was anything she could do.

'They've just gone out,' she said, her voice quavering a little because she was nervous and self-conscious.

The young woman looked tired. 'Will they be long?' she said.

'They've gone for a ride in their new car,' Miss Fenston said. 'Would you care to come in and wait for them in my house?'

So they returned to the shade and clutter of Mr Fenston's Victorian drawing room, and Miss Fenston sent her 'little maid' to make tea and after a discreet interval, in which the two women introduced themselves they settled to the tea cups, each secretly determined to glean as much information from the other as they possibly could.

'You are a friend of the family I daresay, Mrs Barnes,' Miss Fenston offered.

'Oh yes,' Anna decided to agree and then sipped her tea delicately to avoid having to admit anything else.

'He always seems such a very busy man, Mr Pelucci. Business, I daresay.'

'Oh yes. He owns about a dozen shops, you see, and oodles of property.'

'Have you known him long, if I might make so bold as to ask?'

'A good many years, yes.' That was vague enough. Nosy old thing. 'Long before he moved here.'

'Oh, a very long time.'

'Yes. It has been a long time. I can't remember now what year he moved. Silly me!'

'Nineteen twenty-nine,' Miss Fenston said at once. 'Just after the election. I remember thinking, we shall see some changes now, and then, bless me, there he was.'

'Of course. Fancy me forgetting that. Four years ago. I had the vote then, you know. My first vote. It was ripping.'

Miss Fenston wasn't the least bit interested in the franchise. Gossip was much more entertaining. 'And then this year he married Mrs Pelucci. So nice to see him with a family of his own, so to speak, after all these years. But no more than he deserves. Such a charming man. Always so jolly. We've grown quite fond of him here.'

'I'm sure you have, Miss Fenston,' Anna encouraged, smiling as prettily as she could.

'Theatrical, they do say. His wife. A very striking woman.'

Somebody should strike her, and no mistake, Anna thought, smiling at the idea. But she didn't have time to say anything because her father's car arrived back outside his house with a final roar of its engine that set all the net curtains twitching on all three sides of the square.

'Oh, there they are!' Miss Fenston twittered, gazing through the window with undisguised admiration at the charming Mr Pelucci, to the undisguised annoyance of his elder daughter.

And that's the woman, Anna thought. Common, of course, and nothing to look at really with all that untidy red hair. Long and skinny. Mummy's much nicer looking. And what poor taste! Fancy wearing orange and yellow with red hair. Redheads should wear blue or green. Everybody knew that. Well, the sooner she was put in her place the better.

'You've been most kind,' she said, on her feet and moving towards the door already.

'You must come again, my dear,' Miss Fenston murmured. But her guest was gone.

Her appearance stopped Albert in mid chirrup. 'Anna?' he said, staring at the unlikely colour of her hair with square-mouthed disapproval. And when she nodded, smiling at him brightly, 'Well you'd better come in, I suppose.'

They trooped into the house, and he flung his helmet and goggles onto the hallstand and turned a disagreeable expression towards her. 'What have you done to your hair? You look a sight.'

'It's *my* hair,' she said, pouting because he'd upset her. 'I can do what I like with it.' How very unwelcoming! He could at least have kissed her. 'Aren't you going to introduce me?'

'My daughter Anna,' he said brusquely, 'Queenie. I need some tea, Queenie. I suppose you'll join us, Anna.'

' 'Course she'll join us,' Queenie said, rescuing the girl because she looked so cast down. ' 'E's like a bear with a sore head,' she explained to Anna, 'all on account of 'e can't drive a car.'

'I drive perfectly,' he said and he sounded cross, although his eyes were snapping at her with what looked far too much like affection. 'What you expect when they put markets in the way? Are we having tea or not?'

'I'd better get it,' Queenie said. 'We shall never hear the end of it else.' But she was laughing at him and didn't seem to be at all concerned by what he said.

It was hard for Anna to know how to react in such an

unfamiliar exchange. Her mother would have placated him in tight-lipped silence, but this woman treated his anger like a game. She followed him into the dining room, watching him warily. Now that they were together, she wasn't really at all sure how to tackle him.

'I've been waiting with one of your neighbours,' she tried. 'A Miss Fenston. She thinks you and ...' waving a vague hand towards the kitchen because she simply couldn't bring herself to call that woman Queenie, ' ... are married.'

He was delighted! How annoying! That wasn't the effect she'd intended. 'Hear that, Queenie,' he called. 'The neighbours think we're married.'

'Quite right too,' Queenie called back. 'This ain't Paradise Street. You gotta be respectable you live round 'ere.'

Anna steeled herself for the attack. 'But you're not, are you,' she said icily and did her best to fix him with the fiercest look she could muster.

He looked at her for a long time without saying anything, biting his lips, first the top lip and then the bottom, so that his moustache dipped and tilted and to her alarmed sight his mouth looked redder and more threatening than ever. 'So that's it, is it,' he said, and he got up and called the woman into the room, but quietly now and with a new note in his voice that Anna didn't like at all. 'Leave the tea. We got a deputation.'

The woman came back, looking anxiously from one to the other, and he took her by the arm and sat her down in the chair next to his own. Anna found that she had been neatly set apart, sitting on the other side of the table with the evening sunlight dazzling her eyes. It was distinctly uncomfortable and she was sure he'd done it deliberately. There was so much hot colour all around her, the scarlet flock wallpaper blazing behind the woman's carroty hair, her father's ginger coat rubbing sleeves with the woman's orange and yellow crêpe de Chine, so tense and close that she wouldn't have been the least surprised to see sparks fly from the cloth, and, on top of everything else, that awful sun pulsing brightness from a cloud like a pool of red blood. She felt threatened by it all and antagonized. How hateful they both were, staring at her like that. As if she were the one who had done something wrong, when they were the sinners. Living in sin, demeaning her mother, and upsetting absolutely everybody.

'Well?' her father said.

'Well what?'

'Oh come on, Anna, don't beat about the bush. You got something ter say. Say it.'

Anna swallowed back the fear that was rising in her throat. He was interrogating her, the way he used to do when she was a little girl and she'd been misbehaving. 'Mother wants you to come back home,' she said baldly and her face was truculent.

'Then she must want,' he said brutally. 'She knows that. Anything else?'

'It isn't right,' she said hotly. 'You've got no business leaving her like this. She's never done anything wrong in the whole of her life. She's been a good, faithful wife …'

He cut her short, leaning across the table towards her and speaking almost gently. 'Don't keep on, lovebird,' he said. 'You don't know nothing about it. You just go on home and look after your husband and keep out of it, there's a good girl.'

'That's no answer,' she said, sneering at him because he was treating her like a child and she felt patronized and belittled. 'And why? Because you know I'm right. You've got no business leaving. You ought to come back.'

'Ought!' he roared, losing his temper. 'Ought! Who are you to tell me what I ought to do? Go home, I tell you. It's none of your business.'

'Don't shout at her, Ploo,' Queenie said, putting a hand on his arm. She felt sorry for her beleaguered opponent and was trying to calm the situation.

But Anna rounded on her with venom, her eyes blazing in the sunlight. 'Ploo!' she said scornfully. 'His name's Albert, *if* you don't mind.'

'Not ter me, it ain't, miss,' Queenie said. ' 'E's been Ploo ter me fer twenty-six years.'

'You're lying!' Anna shrieked. They couldn't have! Not for twenty-six years. '*I'm* twenty-six!'

'That's right!' her father said. 'You're twenty-six. Now you know.'

'That's filthy!' she shrieked at him. 'To leave your wife and two babies … That's disgusting.' The sun was blinding her eyes with blood. 'How could you do such a dreadful thing? My poor dear mother!'

'Shout all you like,' he said furiously. 'It won't make no difference. I stayed with your poor dear mother for twenty-nine years, I'll have you know. I didn't leave her. Or you. I stayed. An' a fat lot of good it did me. Enough is enough!'

'It's settled, Anna,' Queenie said, making another attempt to be gentle. 'Ain't a bit a' use you carrying on. Only upset yerself. Can't yer see 'e's made up 'is mind?'

'Then he must unmake it,' Anna said stubbornly. 'My mother's got the right on her side. She won't divorce him. She'll go on and on until he comes home.'

Albert stood up and leaned right across the table until his face was within inches of her butter-coloured head. 'I will *not* come back,' he said. 'Get that in your stupid head. Never. Never. Never.'

'She's your wife,' she said, holding her head steady and glaring at him even though her eyes were stinging. 'Don't you care?'

'I will not be spoken to like this by my own daughter,' he said, straightening his spine and turning to Queenie for support. He was spluttering with anger. 'God damn it!' he said, facing his daughter again. 'Queenie is more wife to me than your mother ever was or ever could be.'

'You have children too,' Anna said, encouraged by the extremity of his rage. 'I would have thought you had some responsibilities towards us. Or don't we count?'

'Children! Children!' he roared. 'Yes, I have children, and you might as well know the truth about that too. So you just listen! Queenie has a child too. A daughter. My daughter. Your sister.'

Anna went white and was too stunned to speak, but while she and her father gazed at one another across the table and Queenie pulled at Albert's coat to restrain him, a new voice joined the row in a howl of anguish and disbelief. 'No! no! It ain't true. That's a filthy, filthy thing to say.'

It was Mary Ann.

Queenie ran to her daughter at once, but Mary shook her

away. 'Say it ain't true,' she demanded. 'Say it's a lie. He's not my father.'

Queenie winced, but she told the truth. 'No,' she said. 'It ain't a lie, lovey. We should 'a' told you earlier. We was waitin' fer a good time.'

'No!' Mary said again, her face wild. 'I don't believe it. It's not true. Oh, how could you do this to me? My father was a fine, good man. A wounded soldier. A socialist. One in a million. Remember? I *know* who my father was.' She'd come home from her piano lesson with a piece of good news, feeling almost happy again, and now everything was smashed and sullied. How could they say such things? Didn't they have any pride?

Caught in the maelstrom of their emotions, Albert reacted too quickly, and thoughtless speed made him cruel. 'You're *my* daughter!' he roared angrily. 'Mine! You understand! This is your sister.'

'She ain't!' Mary said, her face wilder than ever. She couldn't be. A great, fat, painted, bottle blonde like that! The very idea was disgusting. She wouldn't allow her to be. 'She ain't! She ain't!'

'She is.'

'What does it matter?' the blonde shrieked. 'That's your dirty business. Not ours.'

How bloody insulting! 'I am *not* dirty business.'

'Not *you*! Dadda!'

'Shut up! Shut up, the pair of yer!' Albert yelled, swinging his angry face from one to the other. He was tearing at his hair, distraught with too many conflicting emotions. Anger, at himself for speaking out of turn, at them for shouting, pity for their distress, panic, regret, and a tearing sense of love for them both. 'Shut up!'

'How dare you shout at me!' Anna yelled back. The baby was squirming violently inside her and the movement was making her feel sick, but now that she'd started this row she couldn't back down. She must shout on, shout him down, shame him. 'It's not my fault. You're the one! You did it, leaving my mother for a sordid affair. You hurt us all and now you dare to shout at us.'

'You watch your mouth, my gel,' Queenie warned, rounding

on her. But Mary was shouting too.

'Go home ter yer wife! Clear off! We don't want you! Don't you understand?'

Urgent messages were flashed from Queenie's green eyes to Ploochy's brown ones, but he was too angry to respond.

'You don't tell me what ter do!' he roared. 'Remember who you are!'

'Ned Chapman's daughter! Not yours!'

'Mine! Mine! Mine! Hell's teeth, how many more times?'

'*I'm* your daughter,' Anna shrieked above the din. 'Me. Anna Maria.' But he was still glaring at the dark-haired girl.

'I won't be your daughter,' Mary blazed.

'You got no option.'

'Oh yes I have,' and there was steel in the answer. 'I'll leave home. That's what I'll do. I don't have to stay with you.'

'Don't be ridiculous.'

Fat tears were brimming from her eyes, and the sight of them made Anna feel a sudden pity for her. 'Leave her alone!' she said to her father. 'It's not her fault. You're the one.'

'Keep out of it, Anna,' Albert told her sharply. 'It none of your business.'

'She's my sister! That's what you said. My sister. I should have thought that was my business if anything was.' She was delighted by her quick answer. Try and wriggle out of that one.

The dark-haired girl was talking to her mother. 'How could you, Ma? That's what I don't understand. How could you?'

'I love him,' the redhead answered. 'One day you'll understand.'

'Call that love!' Mary mocked, and she spoke the words that were filling her sister's mind. 'That's not love! You're too old for love! That's lust, Ma.'

The word enraged Albert. 'Get out!' he roared. 'All a' you! Out! Out! This minute!' They were beyond control, beyond a joke, beyond endurance. 'Lust.' Dear God, what a thing for a child to say! He didn't care that Mary had burst into tears and rushed from the room, nor that Anna was standing before him white faced and trembling.

'Don't you yell at me!' she said with as much dignity as she could muster in her present state. 'I'm going! Don't you worry! I wouldn't stay here another minute in your rotten house with your rotten ... woman. And don't you think you've heard the last of it, because you haven't. I shall tell Mummy.'

The front door banged. Mary had taken her hat and gone. Seconds later it banged again as her sister followed her.

The silence that followed was full of shame.

'Oh God, Ploo,' Queenie said. 'That was awful!'

'They will get over it,' he said, trying to sound confident and to comfort them both, and failing to do either.

'Did we ought ter go after 'er?'

'No, no. Leave 'er be. She'll get over it. She won't go far.' But he was afraid, despite his words.

Halfway down Lyndhurst Way, Anna had to stop to get her breath back. She stood in the stabbing rays of the setting sun as the baby kicked her ribs and her heart banged uncomfortably above it. The sky over the rooftops was full of violent, rapidly changing colour. Nothing was stable or dependable any more. What a dreadful scene, she thought. Absolutely dreadful! Fancy Dadda shouting at her like that. She'd never have believed it. A chill breeze rustled the shrubs in the row of front gardens beside her. I'd better get home, she thought, I'm not doing myself any good standing around in the cold air.

There was a little group of people waiting for the tram at Peckham Road, and standing among them was the dark-haired girl, quiet and subdued, a schoolgirl in a straight blue cardigan and a panama hat. She's only a kid, Anna thought, looking at her. That must've been awful for her. And it struck her that she would really rather like this girl to be her sister. But there wasn't time to accept the idea or reject it or even consider it, because their tram had arrived and was whirring to a halt in the middle of the road.

As they climbed aboard the tram, the lights were lit, rather unnecessarily because it wasn't anywhere near dark. But they changed the mood somehow, and that cheered Anna. It was cosy now inside their crowded tin ship, and she felt easier surrounded by the undemanding intimacy of strangers. But as the new passengers settled into the remaining seats she realized with a pang that there were only two left vacant, one next to a smelly looking workman in very dirty overalls, the other next to Mary Ann.

'Sorry about this,' she explained as she lowered her bulk

into the space next to her new found sister. They were sitting so close together that when the tram swayed off along its rails, they were bumped against one another, hip touching hip. But she couldn't help it. 'It's the only seat.'

'It's all right,' Mary said stiffly. But plainly it wasn't.

The tram rattled on, and the sisters looked away from each other, busy in their thoughts.

Anna looked vaguely at the yellow light on the opposite wall. She felt she ought to offer some comfort or advice, and the feeling impelled her to speak. 'Are you really running away?'

'Yes.' Such a blunt, bleak word, and her eyes still averted, looking at the pavements and the plane trees in Peckham Road.

'I *am* sorry. I didn't mean …' Please look at me. It wasn't you I was cross with.

Mary turned her head, brown eyes looked straight at identical brown eyes, and now Anna could see that the expressionless voice was the result of too much emotion, too tightly controlled, and that now her anger was beginning to reassert itself. 'It's nothin' ter do with you, so jest keep out of it.'

'Look. I didn't mean you to get hurt. I was trying to help my mother, that's all.'

'Hum!'

'There's no need to take that tone. I didn't even know you existed. I really didn't. It's not *our* fault, any of this.'

That was true enough and the expression on Mary's face showed she accepted it. 'No,' she said. 'We're just caught up in it. It's your horrible father, that's who. *Your* father. Not mine. Well, I'm off out of it.'

What a prickly little thing she is, Anna thought. 'Where will you go?' she asked.

'Don't know, don't care.'

'Look,' Anna said, because they were running into Peckham High Street and out of time. 'Here's my address. If you get stuck …' and she opened her bag and rummaged inside it for her little address book. There was a slim pencil fitted into the spine and for once it wasn't blunt. She wrote her address as neatly as she could with the tram jerking her hand about. 'There!' she said, ripping out the page.

Mary took the scrap of paper, and tried to go on looking as though she didn't care what happened to her, but this unexpected kindness provoked tears again, and the tears made Anna feel curiously protective and maternal. But it was her stop. There wasn't time to comfort. 'Good luck!' she said.

Mary sniffed and blinked in a useless effort to clear her eyes. 'Ta!' she said, and then as she began to feel she'd been rather horrid to this woman, even if she was a great, fat, artificial blonde, she added, 'An' good luck ter yer. With the baby an' everything.'

'I shall need it,' Anna called back as she struggled along the aisle, trying to avoid as many feet as she could. Then she waved and was gone.

Chapter Twenty-Five

The Oxbury family were just finishing supper when Mary came ringing at their door. Maisie popped her head out of the kitchen window at once to see who it was. 'You heard the news?' she called, cheerfully. 'Our Tom passed his exams. Credit and two passes. We're so bucked! I'll be down in a tick.'

Mary had forgotten all about exam results in her present distress, but she knew how important they were and managed to make all the appropriately congratulatory noises as she followed Maisie up the dark staircase.

'So 'e'll go ter university now. Nothink ter stop 'im,' Maisie was saying proudly as they entered the kitchen, but then her face changed as she saw the tear stains on her visitor's cheeks. 'Why, whatever's the matter, lovey? Not yer mother, is it?'

Tom and the Ox were still sitting comfortably at the table, but now they looked up at her stricken face and were alarmed. There was no time for politeness or congratulations. The horrible facts just blurted out of her mouth. 'I've run away from home. I can't stay in that house another minute. She says Mr Ploochy's my father.'

The Ox rose to his feet. 'Nasty shock,' he said, sympathetically. 'Sit 'er down, Mother. She's 'ad a nasty shock. I got just the thing.' A small, flat-sided bottle of the best brandy was produced from the corner cupboard. 'There you are, gel,' he said. 'You jest sip that, nice an' slow. Best thing in the world fer shock. Three star, that is.'

'You know who my father was, don't you?' Mary begged. 'Ned Chapman, that's who my father was. Not that horrible Ploochy. Ned Chapman.' The first sip of brandy was warm in her throat and she sipped again so as to avoid crying. Because her head was down she missed the quick glance that passed between the Ox and his wife, but Tom saw it and thought he understood it.

'I still miss 'im, yer know,' the Ox said, sitting himself at the table again. 'Opening time I look out fer 'im. Don't seem possible 'e's gone.'

'A good man,' Maisie said, patting Mary's shoulder. 'One a' the best. D'you remember the Strike, the way 'e went round collecting fer the miners? Out all hours.' And effortlessly the talk became a paean of praise for Ned. Old times were remembered, sayings recalled, election campaigns relived, until Mary was glowing again, warmed by the combination of good brandy and skilfully evoked memory.

'They can't take my father away from me, Mr Oxbury,' she said. 'Nobody can do that, can they? He was a marvellous man and he'll always be my father, no matter what anyone says. She's forgotten him. Oh, all right, I know she's my mother and I shouldn't say things like that, but it's a fact. Five weeks he's been dead, that's all, and she's forgotten him. She went straight to that man after the funeral.'

'She was in a state, lovey,' Maisie pointed out. 'You got to admit that. You get in a state, you dunno which way ter turn. She couldn't go ter yer poor old Nan, now could she? She wanted a bit a' comfort I expect. We all need comfort, times like that. They *were* very old friends, don't forget.'

Mary shuddered. 'It's not just friendship,' she said. 'They were lovers. That's the sort of man he is. An' she can't see it. I'm sorry if I'm upsetting you and saying things I shouldn't, but it *is* the truth. I only wish it wasn't.'

'You don't upset us,' the Ox told her stolidly. 'Better ter say things than keep 'em bottled up. It won't go no further than these four walls. You get it all out a' yer system.'

'I've known all along,' Mary said, encouraged by his calm. 'The way he looks at her. You can't hide that. It makes me feel betrayed, d'you know that, every time they look at one another. She ought to have more self-respect. Specially at her age. She's lived with my father all that time and then she goes straight off with a wretched shopkeeper, a clown, a capitalist, a man on the other side. Oh, Mr Oxbury, what am I going to do? I can't go back and live with them again. Not after this. I shall have ter leave home and find somewhere of me own to live, right away from them.'

'What about Stogs?' Maisie asked. 'I thought you was gonna stay on in the sixth form and go to college, like our Tom.'

'I shall have to leave school an' all,' she said miserably. 'I can't very well go on taking his money and living in his house, can I? Not the way I feel about him.'

'No,' the Ox agreed. 'You got a point there. Be a terrible disappointment ter poor old Ned, though. 'E was always so dead set on you going ter college.'

She wept at that, saying, 'I know. I know,' between sobs. And husband and wife exchanged another significant look.

'I tell you what I'd do if I was you,' the Ox said. 'I wouldn't make no rash decision. Just in case. I'd take it one day at a time, just the way your dad always used ter say. One thing at a time, one day at a time. Remember?'

Oh, how well she remembered! One day at a time. Do what yer can. Bit by bit. She could hear his voice.

'There's always a little decision you got ter take, ain't that right?' he went on, still massively calm. 'Summink ter be done every day. Put the big one ter one side fer a bit, see how you feel later on. Now what about the little 'uns? What else 've you 'ad ter decide terday? 'Fore all this.'

She made a big effort to remember. The earlier part of the day seemed a very long way away. 'I can't think,' she said. 'I went to my piano lesson this afternoon, and Miss Hudson had to cancel because she had a sore throat. Oh yes, I remember. She wants me to join the Crystal Palace Amateur Orchestra. They've got a vacancy in the second violins.'

'But that's marvellous,' Tom said. 'You'll do it, won't you?'

'How can I if I've got to leave home?'

'First things first,' the Ox said. 'Would yer like to? Yer teacher must 'a' thought yer good enough or she wouldn't've asked yer. What d'you think?'

'Oh, I could do it. I've reached a high enough standard. It's just ...'

'So do you want to?'

'Yes,' she said. 'I do really. If only ...'

'There y'are, Mother. The first decision's made. An' I'll tell you gel, Ned'ud be thrilled. Now I got ter get going or I shall 'ave the reg'lars beatin' down the door. Ain't you got some friend or other you was going ter visit, Tom?'

He gave Mary his hideous smile and went down to the pub, and Maisie started to clear the table, and Tom, responding to his father's message, said he really ought to go and see if John Challenger had got his results too. 'We could walk through the park,' he said to Mary, 'if you'd like to, that is.'

'Take my jacket,' Maisie said. 'It gets nippy of an evening. We don't want you catching cold.'

They were living her life for her, finding things for her to do, leading her along, but she was still so numb with distress she hardly noticed it. She took Maisie's jacket, obediently, and followed Tom out of the pub into Marigold Street.

The sun had set and the sky was the clear ultramarine of early evening. All around them the strong smells of the working day were settling and diminishing like dust as the first street lights began to wink palely into action and the trams rocked and rattled along Jamaica Road. As they walked briskly towards Christ Church Gate, the regulars who passed them on their way to the pub greeted them and wanted to know how Queenie was. Mary's mind was functioning in an oddly detached way. Although she answered them politely and to all outward appearances seemed to be her confident self again, it was as though she had become two people, one greeting old friends and the other watching, and neither of them capable of feeling anything at all.

But when she and Tom were safely inside Southwark Park, and walking together under the familiar avenue of chestnut trees towards the familiar outline of the bandstand, she found her tongue again and because it was loosened by brandy and anger she spoke long and bitterly, about her mother and Ploochy and the terrible situation they'd put her in and how impossible it would be to go back and live with them. And he, being his father's son, listened patiently and let her rave.

'They're just like a couple a' kids, giggling and larking about, all the time,' she said, scornfully. 'He's over sixty, and there he is playing silly games like a six year old. Take this afternoon, for example. He would take us all off for a drive in his new car, nasty, flashy thing, sports car of course, just the sort of thing fer an old man. An' he can't drive properly, so what does he do? Crashes into a fruit stall up the market, wrecks everything and then offers the poor devil money and drives off without a care in the world. It's money, money, money, all the time with him. He thinks he can buy anything. Well, he can't buy me, Tom. I'm not for sale.'

'There's so much needs changing in this world,' Tom agreed. 'The rich have had it their own way for far too long. That's one a' the reasons I want to go to the L.S.E. and get a good degree.'

They stopped when they reached the bandstand for it was lit now and the bandsmen were arranging their music and settling down for their evening performance, and neither of them wanted to be part of the gathering crowd. They stood together well behind the audience, and she gave him her full attention, looking up at his broad shoulders and that rough-hewn, friendly face.

'You mustn't give up now, Mo,' he said, using her old school nickname. 'We shall need all the brain power we can get if we're to win next time, don't forget. And we must win next time. We can't let this terrible unemployment go on for ever. Now they can brush the ordinary working man aside. He don't count. He's not educated. He works with his hands. He's garbage. But if we're educated every bit as well as they are, they'll have to think again. They won't brush us aside. We'll be more than a match for 'em. A cabinet full of educated socialists. You think of that. There'll be no stopping us then.'

It was very, very true, and it reminded her of the passionate way her father used to talk. 'You're right,' she said. 'That *is* the way to do it. Speak their la-di-da language. Pass their exams. Latin like the nobs, Miss Clairemont says she's teaching us. Beat 'em at their own game.'

'That's it. That's exactly right.'

'But if I do that I shall 'ave ter stay with Ploochy.'

'Yes, you will. But it's only two years, Mo. And what's that in a lifetime? When there's such a lot at stake.'

It was reasonable, and praiseworthy, and unanswerable.

Behind their earnest heads the black cranes slept above the wood yards of Canada Dock, and in the sky before them the last pale colours of the sunset drained into the horizon. Then the bandsmen struck up a rousing Souza march, and a flock of starlings who were already snoozing in the dark branches on either side of the main walk rose into the air with a wooden clatter of wings.

Albert and Queenie arrived at The Red Lion half an hour later. They'd waited for over an hour and when Mary didn't come back they'd decided to go and look for her. They'd searched along every road in the vicinity of Lyndhurst Square and had driven to Bermondsey at a snail's pace, watching to right and left, and growing steadily more upset. 'I should never've gone ter Peckham,' Queenie said as they crept along Southwark Park Road, peering at the impenetrable trees. 'I shall never fergive meself if anything's happened to her, Ploo. It'll be all my fault. I should 'a' stayed where I was. Oh dear, oh dear. You can't see nothink in this light.'

He stopped the car at once and, turning in his awkward driving seat, put his hands on either side of her distraught face and held it and kissed her. 'You mussen' say that, Queenie, my dear, darling, lovely girl,' he begged, brown eyes earnest, 'not now we're together again. We've waited so long, and now we can be happy again. Really! Really! This is a bad time, a trouble. It will pass, I promise you. We will find her.'

'Oh, Ploo,' she said, 'I don't know. Perhaps it's all too late.' Since Ned's death, life had been scudding her along like some irresistible tidal wave. She no longer felt as though she was in control and that was a strange and most unfamiliar situation for her to be in. 'I can't even think straight,' she said wearily. 'It's like a bad dream.'

'I will do the thinking,' he said kissing her again. 'Just fer now. You leave it ter me.'

For the first time in her life, Queenie was tempted to let someone else take command of her affairs. 'How we gonna find 'er, Ploo?' she said.

'We find her,' Albert promised, deliberately confident. 'Bet you she's gone to Ethel's. She's a good kid. Much too sensible to do anything silly. We'll go to Ethel's.'

But Ethel hadn't the faintest idea where she was, and her newly roused anxiety increased Queenie's distress. 'We try the Ox,' Albert said firmly, and drove her quickly to The Red Lion.

279

'What a relief!' Queenie said, when she heard the good news. 'I been worried out me wits.'

'I'd 'a' been the same if it 'ud been young Tom,' Maisie commiserated. But the Ox was quiet, his little eyes assessing them shrewdly, his great jaw disapproving.

'You might ha' found her,' he said, 'But you ain't got her back.'

'Come an' 'ave a drink,' Maisie said, leading them in.

So they did, and it cheered them a little, even though the Ox's words were still echoing ominously in their minds. But he was very busy that evening and it was some time before he could come to their table and sit down with them and explain what he meant.

'Nah then,' he said, as he settled between them.

Albert, finishing his whisky, caught an expression on the Ox's ugly face that made him curious to know what this old friend of theirs had in his mind. 'You got some sort a' plan,' he said. 'Something to make her see sense, is that it?'

'Her. You. Queenie,' the Ox said seriously. 'It'll take all three of yer. She don't like your money, Ploo. She feels kept, that's about the size of it. Wants ter be independent. Go 'er own way. Change the world. You know how it is when you're young. The more you buy for 'er, the more you chain 'er. So what I suggest is this. You tell 'er you're loaning 'er the money. Say she'll 'ave ter pay you back when she's earning. Keep accounts, all level an' above board.'

'Oh Ploo!' Queenie said, remembering. 'A business arrangement. Like the sailor suit. 'E lent me the money ter buy a sailor suit, when I was just getting started on the 'alls.'

'Offered to buy it straight out, and she wouldn't, would yer?' Albert said, his face lifted into pleasure by the memory. 'An' you say she's not like you?'

They looked at each other and into the past, when their love was young and easy.

'She's like you too, Ploo,' Maisie said. 'Spit an' image. That's how we knew. First night you come 'ere.' Somehow it was easy to say these things now, with the worst of the worry over, and the cheerful racket of the pub protectively around them. But Albert was shocked just the same.

'Thanks fer not telling Ned,' Queenie said, looking away

from Albert's distress and smiling at Maisie.

'Ned told *us*,' the Ox enlightened them. 'We 'ad ideas, yer might say. Ned knew.'

'Oh, my good Gawd,' Queenie said, her hands covering her mouth. 'That's terrible! Oh, Ploo! That's terrible!'

' 'E never thought none the worse of yer,' Maisie said. 'You was a good wife, an' she was just a kid come through the side door, that's all. 'E never said nothink ter no one but us.'

It was cold comfort. For both of them felt as though the private delights of their love affair had suddenly been put on public display, and both were ashamed and demoralized.

'Cheer up, Ploo,' the Ox said compassionately. 'Least you stood by 'em an' sent our Mary through grammar school. You done the best you could.'

'No,' Albert said, heavily. 'I did the worst. D'you think they'll be long? We ought ter be getting back.' For the first time in his life he was uncomfortable in a pub and wanted to go home.

'We'll leave it up to Mary, shall we?' the Ox said. 'She can stay the night with us, if that's what she wants, or young Tom'll bring her home. I should cut off if I was you. Queenie looks all in.'

It was a strange silent journey home, with the headlights pushing the darkness ahead of them as they drove, and the engine purring, and traffic roaring down upon them from every side. Neither of them spoke, although they both knew there was a good deal that had to be said. It was as if they were convalescing.

Mary didn't come home that night, although they sat up for her till nearly three o'clock in the morning, watching the square from the vantage point of their bedroom window, as the house chilled around them. Finally, in the total silence of that dead, black hour, they talked.

'She'll be back in the morning, you'll see,' Albert tried to comfort. 'The Ox'll bring her. Or young Tom. She'll be back.'

'Then what?' Queenie said. 'What we gonna say to 'er, fer Gawd's sake?'

'Nothing,' Albert decided. 'We feed her. Sunday dinner same as always. Then she does her piano practice, same as always.'

'After all this?' Queenie doubted.

'Why not?' Albert said. Now that he'd assumed responsibility for all this, it was necessary to sound completely confident. 'We just carry on as usual. That's all. We don't talk about it. We've said too much already.'

'In front a' your Anna, don't forget.'

'No good worrying about that now. Let's go to bed.' She was drooping with fatigue, and he found that more distressing than the thought that Anna might pass on her destructive gossip to her mother.

'She'll tell Alice, sure as fate.'

'Then she tells her,' he said. 'What difference it make, eh? We got trouble enough with young Mary without worrying about Alice.'

'I wish she'd come home,' Queenie mourned, returning for one last look at the deserted square.

They didn't sleep at all well, being torn by anxious dreams and waking to worry and wonder. When day dawned they were aching with fatigue. But they got up and made coffee as if it were an ordinary Sunday and then Queenie set about cooking the joint.

It was beef. Which was unfortunate, for in Albert's household beef had to be accompanied by Yorkshire pudding, and Queenie had never made a Yorkshire pudding in her life. Oh, if only it wasn't Sunday. If only Mrs Midgeley was here. She always made superb Yorkshire puddings.

'We go without it,' Albert said, solving the problem with a wave of the hand.

But that was impossible. This dinner had to be perfect, in every way, just as usual. 'Fine thing that'ud be,' Queenie growled, ' 'ave 'er come back an' no pudding. An' where's the mustard, fer Gawd's sake?'

She was irritable with anxiety, flexing her fingers before she touched anything in the old nervous gesture that always upset Albert so much. She disorganized three cupboards and all the drawers in the dresser before she finally found a battered tin of mustard and Mary's old cookery book. Making the mustard was simplicity itself, but following the laconic instructions of the book was horribly difficult. 'What's a hot oven, fer Gawd's sake?' she howled, looking wildly from the page to Albert's amusement. 'All ovens are s'pposed ter be hot! An' it's nothink ter laugh at, neither! How am I supposed ter cook the bloomin' thing? They don't write in English.'

He caught her flailing arms and held her as she grumbled. 'You're lovely,' he said, kissing her distracted mouth. 'I don't care if you can't cook.'

'I do,' she said grimly, and shook herself free to return to her tussle with the batter.

Half an hour later, when Mary and Tom stepped quietly into the empty hall, she was easing the pudding out of the oven. It should have been cooked to fluffy perfection, but the sight of it made her howl with disappointment and anger. The edges were burnt black and the centre was as flat as a biscuit and, what was worse, the same colour and texture as rubber. 'Oh, look at it, Ploo!' she shrieked. 'Bloody awful thing! What's it done that for?'

She grabbed a fish slice and tried to hack a piece of pudding out of the tin, but it was hotter than she expected and the slice bent under her anger so that all she managed to do was to flick a rubbery chunk onto the kitchen floor and burn the side of her hand in the process. 'God damn it all!' she roared, jumping away from the heat and shaking the pain out of her fingers.

'What *are* you doing?' Mary asked coolly from the kitchen door.

'What's it look like?' her mother roared. 'Cooking a bleedin' puddin'.'

'Oh, give it 'ere, for goodness' sake,' her daughter said in exasperated affection. '*I*'ll do it. Why didntcher leave it fer me? You knew I'd be back in time ter do it.'

'Come on, Tom,' Albert said, removing him quickly before anything harmful could be said, for Queenie was scowling, and there was no knowing what might happen next. 'We open the claret, eh?'

But somehow Mary made sure that they were all too busy to argue. The table was set, and flowers picked, and a new pudding cooked, which rose most deliciously to the occasion, and the meal was served and enjoyed. Because Tom was at the table the talk was all about unemployment and hunger marches and the unforgivable treachery of Ramsay MacDonald, so Mary and Queenie were happy to agree, and Albert relaxed as he watched them grinning affection at one another.

After the meal, Tom said he had to get back and Albert, being tactful for once in his life, said he really ought to go and see how Georgie was getting on. 'Give you a lift if you like,' he offered, with a pride he didn't even try to repress, and Tom said he was honoured and off they both went.

Mary and Queenie returned to the kitchen and started on the washing up, standing side by side at the sink, close enough to hug one another should they feel like it, but undecided and still not entirely at ease with each other despite the good meal and Albert's claret.

Mary dried two dinner plates, pondering and plucking up courage. Then she gave her mother a wry grin. 'Sorry I went off the deep end like that yesterday,' she said.

Queenie put her soapy hands round her daughter's neck at once. 'You're back now, lovey. That's all that matters,' she said. 'You're too much like me, that's the trouble.'

'I meant what I said though. I ain't changed me mind. I've only come back just ter see. I might have ter leave home.'

Queenie steadied herself against the sink, her mind working fast. She couldn't leave this to Ploochy after all. It had to be handled here and now, and very, very delicately. 'Well,' she said slowly, 'if you think you've got ter leave 'ome, then you'll 'ave ter go. That's only right. I think it'ud be a pity meself, when you'll be gone in a couple of years in any case. It's up ter you really though, innit?'

'Yes,' Mary said, surprised by her mother's extraordinary calm. 'Whatcher gonna do with this burnt tin?'

'Chuck it,' Queenie said. ' 'E can buy us a new one.'

The carelessness of it brought one of Mary's grievances into sharp focus. 'That's the trouble,' she said. 'His wretched money. That's what I really can't stand, being beholden to him an' 'is wretched money.'

'I know that,' Queenie said, still marvellously calm. 'To tell the truth, I been thinkin' about it.' She paused, balancing a plate against the edge of the sink. This had to be broached very carefully. 'What would you say if 'e was ter lend yer the money for some a' the things you need? Not uniform, a' course, you gotta 'ave that, but clothes fer best, music, books, that sort of thing.'

Mary was listening intently, polishing a plate with unnecessary concentration. 'How would I pay it back?' she asked.

'When you're earning, bit by bit, all level an' above board, an' then you needn't feel beholden to anybody. Independent as yer like. Whatcher think?'

'It's a good idea, Ma. A very good idea. Yes. Yes, I think I could do that. But it wouldn't make any difference ter the way I feel about him. You know that, dontcher?'

'It's up ter you,' Queenie said. She was sensing the possibility of compromise now and it was much easier to be casual.

'You can say he's my father,' Mary said, earnestly because it was very important that her mother should really understand her. 'Anyone could say it. I could let them. *I* could say it. It wouldn't make any difference. I wouldn't *feel* he was my father. I'd still know who my father really was.' Then seeing the pain on Queenie's face, and torn to sympathy by it, she tried to soften the blow she'd delivered. 'I *am* sorry, Ma, but that *is* the truth.'

They were treating one another with more care and tenderness than had ever been possible or necessary between them before. Queenie smiled into her daughter's eyes. 'Don't say nothink to 'im,' she said conspiratorially, 'but I don't reckon it makes a ha'p'orth a' difference who yer father is. It's who you are that counts in the long run. You don't remember yer grandpa, do yer?'

'Not really.'

' 'E was great union man. You'd 'a' loved 'im fer that. Knew what was what. Took me off ter meetings a' the Federation when I was just a kid. Said 'e'd make a socialist of me. But now I look back at it, what made me a socialist was working the 'alls. Seein' a bit a' life. Bein' meself. Once I took off I could see 'im as 'e was. Good union man, strong worker, but too fond a' the drink, a scrounger. I could see how 'e bullied yer nan. Still my Dad, an' I was still me. But when it come down to it, it didn't really make no difference.'

'If I stay here,' Mary said seriously, 'will he understand all this?'

' 'E's a good bloke,' Queenie said grinning for the first time

285

in their delicate conversation. 'Give 'im a try.'

And then they were cuddling one another in earnest, and the breach was beginning to heal, and they were both in charge of their own lives again.

Chapter Twenty-Six

Anna did a lot of hard thinking on her way back to Clandon Close. She still couldn't believe half the events of that extraordinary afternoon. It wasn't possible to grasp it all. A love affair going on for twenty-six years, and a love child as tall as she was, and nobody knowing anything about it. Things like that didn't happen in real life. And yet the evidence was all there. As plain as ... the nose on Dadda's face. And hers. And Georgie's. And that girl Mary's. She was exactly like Dadda, the same colour hair, the same brown eyes, the same nose. And the same temper too, fighting back, her eyes blazing, shouting him down. She'd been jolly snooty on the tram but you couldn't help admiring her.

Nevertheless, it had put paid to the nice calm argument she'd had all worked out inside her head. So now what was she going to do? She'd promised Mummy to make him come back and all she'd actually done was to drive him further away than ever. It was always the same when she tried to do something worthwhile. 'I won't come back!' he'd said. 'Never, never, never!' And the way he'd looked at that redhead! He'd never looked at Mummy like that. And Eric had never looked at *her* like that either. The thought made her feel bleak and unloved, so she shrugged it away. A love affair going on all that time, she thought. It was very romantic.

Eric was already home from work and peeved. 'Where've you been?' he said, scowling at her. 'I've had a dreadful day and you expect me to come home and wait for my supper.'

'I've been to visit Dadda,' she said brightly. 'At Peckham,' and she started to tell him all about Queenie and Mary. 'He says she's my sister. What do you think of that?'

He wasn't the least bit interested. 'No concern of mine what dirty little tricks your family get up to,' he said disparagingly. 'Nothing to do with me, thank you very much. What's for supper?'

I'll tell Georgie tomorrow she thought. *He* won't be so beastly.

But he was absolutely horrid, taking it all so calmly, she really wondered whether he hadn't known about it all along and not told *her*.

'I've no doubt it's all quite true,' he said, 'but we won't go making a song and dance about it, will we? This is something we've got to keep to ourselves. Mother is not to know.'

'Oh, how silly!' Anna protested. 'Of course she should know. He's her husband. Besides, what am I to say when she asks me how I got on?'

But Georgie persisted, with a most unexpected and uncharacteristic strength. She couldn't argue him down no matter how hard she tried and in the end she had to agree to keep it all secret. Which was probably just as well, for on second thoughts it occurred to her that her mother would hardly thank her for bringing such awful news. If she kept quiet, Mummy could go on living in hopes for a little while longer. But that wasn't fair, because there wasn't any hope. She knew that now. Not with two families. And what would she say if Mummy asked her to go back to Peckham? She couldn't visit her father again. She simply couldn't face it. Not after that awful row. It would be too embarrassing for words. And yet he was still her father and perversely she loved him more than ever in the dreadful, muddled life he'd suddenly revealed to her. It would be too awful if she never saw him again. But fortunately that was a difficulty she could postpone. For the moment the advanced state of her pregnancy gave her a good excuse for inaction. And the move, of course, which was a fraught two weeks away.

She wasn't looking forward to the actual move one little bit, because she knew it was going to be absolutely beastly. Eric said he couldn't wait to leave their nasty, poky little flat, and yet he wouldn't do anything to help. When she dared to suggest that they simply hand the whole thing over to Pickfords and let them get on with it, he'd thrown such a temper tantrum he hadn't been able to speak to her for nearly three days afterwards. And Mummy was in too much of a state to help her, although she was grateful for the effort she'd made.

'You're a good girl, Anna,' she said when Anna finally plucked up the courage to go and tell her how she'd got on. 'You've done more for your poor old mother than any of the others. And at least you'll tell me the truth, won't you darling? What's she like? Is she pretty would you say?'

That was easy enough. 'Oh no! She's not a bit pretty. She's an absolute fright. Red hair and a long nose and all skin and bones. And terribly untidy. She had a button missing from her dress and I don't think she even knew. And awful hair. All tangles! She hadn't brushed it all day.'

'Humph!' Mummy snorted with great satisfaction. 'I knew she'd be like that. These women always are. They don't care for anything. I'll bet the house is messy.'

'Awful!' Anna agreed happily, 'newspapers on the floor and dirty cups left on the table. An absolute tip!'

'He won't like that,' Mummy said, well pleased by the answer. 'He'll soon tire of her. You'll see.'

'He's very stubborn,' Anna warned.

'He always was,' Mummy said. 'But I can be stubborn too. Oh yes! Don't you worry! You'll go and see him again soon, won't you darling?'

'After the move,' Anna promised, and hoped it would be possible. But how could she put things right after storming out of the house like that? And making Mary run away too. It seemed more awful every time she remembered it. I wonder what happened to Mary, she thought, and comforted herself that Dadda would get her back and put things right somehow or other. Dadda always knew what to do. Oh, if only he were here to help her now.

But when her moving day arrived, she found herself coping with everything all on her own, trying to pack all these nasty lumpy cases, and tea chests with the most ghastly nails sticking out of them, and all because their nasty, cheap removal men wouldn't do a thing.

Eric had been absolutely beastly of course. 'Why didn't you pack it all before?' he'd said that morning. 'You've had long enough, for heaven's sake! It's your own fault, if you will leave everything till the last moment. I'll be back at three o'clock to sign the papers. Don't fuss.' And then he'd gone off to work. Trust him! Just as if it were an ordinary day. Leaving her to cope with everything. She'd torn a hole in her stockings and bruised both her shins and she knew she looked an absolute frump. Life was so unfair.

And now there was somebody outside the flat, hooting, if you please. On and on, a perfectly dreadful row. Surely they hadn't arrived already. That really would be too bad. She lumbered across the half packed muddle of her lounge, ready to give them a piece of her mind, and discovered that it was Rollo, in his nice new M.G. Sports. Dear old Rollo, leaning on the horn and positively grinning up at her. There were two very ordinary looking girls perched on the back, with their feet in the dicky seat, but they weren't serious competition. Rollo looked positively dashing in a stunning blazer and a silk scarf trailing over his shoulder like a film star. She opened the window at once and called down to him in her most charming voice.

'Off for a teeny Martini, old thing,' he told her. 'Care to join us? Spiffing place.'

'Oh, Rollo!' she said. 'We're moving today. I'm in the middle of packing.'

'Never mind all that,' he said. 'Leave that to the removal wallahs. That's what they're for. Where's Eric? Tell him his old friend Rollo's got something to tell him.'

'He's at work,' she said bitterly. 'Won't be back till three o'clock.'

He recognized the note of martyred resignation in her voice and knew exactly what to say. 'Cat's away, eh? How about a game, mouse?'

'I don't know,' she said, tempted but anxious. 'I'd love to, really. I don't know.'

'Come on!' the girls cooed and Rollo flung his arms wide at her like Clark Gable. It was too much. 'I'll be ready in two shakes,' she said. 'Come on up.'

So Rollo and his two friends came chirruping and giggling up the stairs and wrote rude notes to the removal men and played at packing, while she changed her stockings and applied a new layer of make-up, and arranged *her* silk scarf prettily at *her* neck. Then they all went chirruping down again. It was just the tonic

290

she needed.

What fun to drive through the quiet streets, laughing and giggling and shouting at one another above the noise of the engine so that everybody looked at them and thought what jolly people they were. And the hostelry was super. Brand new, and all stainless steel and plate glass and cocktails. A ripping place. They stayed till closing time and then Rollo had another wheeze.

'You're not going back to all that wretched packing,' he said. 'Plenty of time for that. You don't have to be back till three, do you? Righto! Let's all cut off to the pictures.'

So they went to see *King Kong* and sat in the shilling seats and Rollo bought popcorn so that they could crunch it at all the most thrilling moments and annoy people. It was ripping fun.

But the aftermath was horrid.

When they finally came singing back to Raynes Park, the afternoon was nearly over, the removal van had come and gone, there was no sign of Eric and the flat was stripped bare.

'Oh my giddy aunt!' Anna wailed. 'That's torn it! Abso-bloomin'-lutely torn it! Who'll let them in at Stoneleigh Park? I was supposed to go with them. Eric'll be livid!'

'Perhaps he went with them,' Rollo said, unperturbed.

'No,' she said miserably. 'He wouldn't have. He expected me to be there. He'll be livid. What will they do if nobody's there to let them in? Oh dear, oh dear!'

'Rollo to the rescue, lovely lady!' that worthy declared. 'Soon have this sorted out. All aboard the Skylark!' So they trouped out into the road again and he drove them all to Clandon Close, at top speed and with total disregard for all other road users. But Anna's bijou residence was horribly empty and there was no sign of the van.

'Try next door, Wollo!' his girlfriend suggested, batting her eyelashes at him.

Next door turned out to be a vague young lady who'd just washed her hair and was drifting about the house with a towel wrapped round her head like a turban. She smiled amiably at their request and said she hadn't seen anything all afternoon. 'Perhaps they've gone for tea,' she offered, trying to be helpful. But Anna didn't think it likely.

'Don't you have a phone number or something?' Rollo's girl asked. She wasn't as soppy as she looked, Anna thought.

There'd been a number on the letter. She remembered it now. And where was the letter? Please let it be in her handbag.

For once the gods were kind to her and the number was found. So they piled into the car again and shot off, chirruping and giggling, to find a telephone box. Anna was beginning to feel a little frayed. It was all very well for them to laugh and make silly jokes, they didn't have to face up to Eric in a house with no furniture.

The man who answered her call was calm and horribly implacable, even though she was as sweet as she could possibly be in a vain attempt to charm him. They could bring the van back within half an hour, or she could leave it where it was, and have the goods delivered in the morning. Either way it was going to cost. Anna butted in quickly before he could tell her how much. 'Deliver it now,' she said, and added, 'please,' in a last hopeless effort to put him in a better frame of mind.

'We'll be toddling along then, old fruit,' Rollo said when he heard. 'Toodle pip!' And he was gone in a cloud of exhaust fumes before she could ask him to stay and help her.

It was absolutely dreadful. The van returned in twenty minutes, delivered at breakneck speed and left her with a house full of filth and muddle. It made her feel frantic just to look at it. Things in the wrong rooms, tea chests all packed any old how and china absolutely broken to bits. Eric would be so cross! She stood among the debris, quailing at the thought of his temper, hysteria rising into her chest like an uncontrollable fountain.

He came home as she was trying to hang the curtains in the lounge. He looked so correct in his office suit, with his respectable bowler at just the right angle and his umbrella so tightly furled that it looked like a stick, and he seemed pleased with himself, bounding along with that bouncy, straight-spined walk of his. Somehow his pleasure made her feel more afraid than ever.

'Good God!' he said when he saw the mess. 'What on earth have you been doing?'

'Oh, Itchy coo!' she tried to coax, using their baby talk in an effort to placate him. 'Your bunny wunny's done her ickle best.'

'If that's your best,' he said coldly, 'I hope I never see your worst, that's all I can say. Thank you very much! I've had a ghastly day, I hope you realize!' He looked around for the hat stand, scowling horribly, couldn't see it, and was reduced to leaving his precious umbrella in a tea chest.

'You might make allowances,' she said wearily, because her charm hadn't worked.

'Nobody makes allowances for me,' he said coldly. 'I've been buzzing about like a blue-arsed fly all day. Backwards and forwards to that bloody flat, seeing solicitors, signing papers. I had to tip the workmen, I hope you realize, you'd left the place in such a state. D'you think they care two straws about that at the Foreign Office? That's neither here nor there to them. They expect a full day's work out of me. I see no reason why you shouldn't be treated the same.' It wasn't true. His immediate superior had offered him the usual day off for removal, and he'd refused it because he wanted to appear keen. But he was so angry that truth was swallowed up in fantasy. 'What have you got for supper?'

She realized, too late, that the new cooker hadn't been delivered, and the nervous glance she shot towards the kitchen conveyed the fact to him before she could think of an excuse. He bounced into the kitchen, his spine rigid with anger. 'You lazy trollop!' he shouted. 'You bloody lazy trollop! What the hell have you been doing all day?'

'Oh, don't keep on at me,' she wailed. 'I can't stand it. I'm not well!'

'What am I supposed to eat?' he yelled. 'Bloody lazy trollop!'

'Couldn't we go out?'

'No we could not! I've spent enough money today, thank you very much.'

'I don't feel well, Eric,' she said, making a last bid for sympathy. 'The baby ...'

'Don't whine to me about how you feel,' he said heartlessly. 'You wanted the baby. I didn't. It's entirely your own fault. You wanted the baby, and you would buy this house, and you would move. You've only got yourself to blame. Serve you right. Don't whine to me.'

She put her hands over her ears, because she simply couldn't bear to hear any more. 'You're absolutely beastly!' she cried.

'Oh, I wish I were dead!' and she fled up the bare boards of the stairs, her heels making an awful clatter.

'High time we had a good strong government in this country like the one they've got in Germany,' he shouted at her retreating back. 'Be a lot less of this nonsense then.'

Upstairs in the empty shell of their bedroom, she sat on the bare springs of their bleak bed and looked at the formidable bulk of their horrible rolled up mattress and wondered how she would ever find the energy to haul it into position. She felt alone and terribly unloved. If only Dadda were here! He'd have everything sorted out in a jiffy. 'Never you mind, lovebird,' he'd say and men would appear and the furniture would be shifted, and the mattress unrolled and the bed made, and everything would be all right. Oh, why did he have to go and run off with that stupid, silly woman? Why couldn't he stay at home and look after them all? How could she possibly cope, with Eric and the baby, and Mummy on to her every day, 'You'll see him again as soon as you've moved, won't you darling?' It wasn't fair of them to expect her to take responsibility for everything like this. With the bed springs hurting her bottom and chaos hurting her eyes, and the baby wriggling and squirming inside her, she wept with despair.

Even though he would never have said so, even to Lily in the privacy of their loving bed where some of the most secret and delicate truths were dared, George was really quite glad that his father had left home and gone to live with that extraordinary redhead.

Until then, he would never have dared to question anything that either of his parents had required him to do. Despite being married and having children of his own, he had gone on considering himself as his mother's 'dear boy' and his father's obedient servant. Now he was a man in charge of his own affairs, with two off-licences to manage, and the sense to negotiate with his father for a percentage of the profits, and with a clientele who patronized his particular store because they liked to discuss books and films and the wireless with a man who shared their tastes. He and Lily had chosen a new house just round the corner, in Poplar Road, and he had already made plans to rent a bungalow at Herne Bay for two weeks in the summer and take his family away for a seaside holiday. And once a week he and Lily and the children went to Peckham to visit his father and Queenie and Mary, and he didn't even feel disloyal.

'We must let them sort their lives out for themselves,' he said to Anna, after his third visit, 'but there's no reason why we shouldn't be friendly.'

'It's all right for you,' Anna said. 'You're still on good terms. You didn't have a row. I don't think I shall ever see him again, leave alone be "friendly" as you put it.'

She looked so downcast and sighed so heavily, he gave her a hug. 'Cheer up, Sis,' he said. 'Dadda's not one to bear grudges. You just go over there and visit him as if nothing had happened. I'll bet he welcomes you in and makes a fuss of you just the same as ever.'

'I couldn't do that! You don't know how awful it was.'

'Say you've come to play duets with Mary.'

'She's home again?'

'Oh yes. She didn't go far. I think she just went for a walk round to cool off, like Dadda always used to do. They're very much alike, you know.'

'I wish this hadn't happened,' Anna sighed.

'No good wishing,' Georgie said. 'It has and that's all there is to it. We must make the best of it, that's all.'

'Still, I'm glad Mary didn't run away. At least that's one less thing for me to feel guilty about. I wouldn't have liked to have driven her out. I shall write to her tonight and tell her so.'

'I wouldn't,' Georgie said. 'It'll only go stirring everything up again. Leave well alone. That's my advice.'

But it was wasted on Anna. She sent a postcard that same evening.

'Georgie tells me that you are ...' she began. And then stopped. She could hardly say 'back at home', knowing what she knew about this new sister's feelings. So she compromised with, 'back with your mother, and that things seem to be working out. I am very glad. I wouldn't have liked to think I'd driven you out. That was never my intention. I am keeping fairly well but I shall be glad when October 20th comes and this baby is born, because I'm as big as a house. Love from Anna.'

Mary didn't know how to respond to it. At first she was very cross. 'It's no business of hers,' she said furiously to Queenie. 'Great, fat, ugly thing. I didn't run away because of her.'

'Oh, go on with yer!' Queenie said. 'She's only bein' friendly. An' she can't help bein' fat, poor beggar. That 'appens ter the best uv us.'

'I hope she don't expect me to answer.'

'Send 'er a postcard,' Queenie suggested. 'That 'ud be perlite, an' yer don't 'ave ter say much on a postcard.'

. So a grudging postcard was sent, 'Thanks for your card. No, I didn't stay away. I couldn't leave Ma. I'm very fond of my ma. I haven't changed my mind about Ploochy. Hope you continue to keep well, Mary.'

The answer came by return of post. A letter, and quite a long one. She quite understood how Mary felt, about her mother, and about Dadda. She felt the same way. He had no business starting an affair, that was the truth of it. Not at his age. And upsetting both their mothers too. It was most reprehensible. She was very very fond of him, but that didn't stop her from seeing what a terrible mistake he'd made.

This time Mary wrote back at length and with real feeling, relieved and pleased that this odd, fat blonde understood their situation, even though nobody else involved in it seemed to be able to. 'They don't seem to see what it is they're doing to us,' she wrote. And then as she'd started, she went on to other topics, how much homework she got now she was in the fifth form; and how the teachers went on and on about the School Cert, and Matric; and how little time she had for music nowadays. 'After Ma,' she wrote, 'music is the next most important thing in my life. I'm going for an audition on Thursday to see if I can get into the Crystal Palace Amateur Orchestra, and I'm sure I haven't done anywhere near enough practice.'

On Thursday morning just as she was leaving for school, a huge bunch of chrysanthemums arrived with a card to wish her luck. That evening when the audition was over, she went up to her bedroom to write a thank you letter, and this time her thanks were genuine. You couldn't go on rebuffing kindness like that.

And so their correspondence continued. And the more they

296

wrote to one another, the more they found to write. Albert's folly was thoroughly castigated, of course, but after a while his generosity was remembered too. Anna told Mary how fond of her parents she was, even though they weren't a bit alike, and could be difficult sometimes, 'but they mean well. They wouldn't hurt anyone deliberately.' And Mary told Anna how much she loved her ma and what a fine, good man her pa had been, even if Ma did have a terrible temper and Pa had been pretty boring sometimes.

When the good news came that she had been accepted as a member of the Amateur Orchestra, she sent a card to Anna at once, and after the first rehearsal she wrote a long description of all the eccentric characters she'd met and what fun they were, from the cellist who kept her knitting in her music case and mothered all the younger members of the orchestra, to the conductor who had terrified her at the audition and actually turned out to be very soft hearted. 'One of the violins is Mr Andrews, the librarian at Tom's college,' she wrote. 'What do you think of that for a coincidence? He's ever so nice, but he will have everything just so. He sets out the music before we begin, and checks attendance and things like that. I can just imagine him in a library.'

'Who is Tom?' Anna wrote back. 'You haven't mentioned him before.'

So Tom was described, as 'my oldest friend, like a big brother really.' And that led to a comparison between him and Georgie, and a discussion as to the value of brothers, in which they were both very candid and made one another laugh.

It's really extraordinary, Anna thought, as she read the latest epistle, I feel as if I've known this girl all my life and yet we've only met each other once. If only she could be a little bit older, I think I could tell her about the things that are really worrying me. I've never felt as close to any one as I do to her. Except Dadda of course.

But Mary *was* only fifteen, and you couldn't tell a fifteen year old that you were worried about giving birth. That wouldn't be fair. It might frighten her or put her off. And after a month of letters she was already too fond of her new-found sister to want to do either of those unkind things. Mummy was only too ready to talk about how awful the whole thing was, and that made matters worse. The midwife never said anything about the pain at all but her new neighbours, whether or not they'd actually given birth themselves, were all of the opinion that it would be excruciating. 'Start screaming the minute the pains start,' her next door neighbour advised. 'Then they'll have to give you something. That's what I did.'

As the October days shortened, and her girth increased, her fears grew. Oh, if only she could see Dadda! If only Mary could be a little bit older! If only she hadn't started this pregnancy in the first place!

Chapter Twenty-Seven

Anna was quite surprised when October 22nd arrived and her labour began and the pains were mild. She'd suffered a great deal more at every period. Nevertheless, she put her plan into operation immediately, and as soon as the midwife had arrived and was there to hear her she began to scream. By the time Eric got home from work, she was in full voice and could be heard at the end of the road. He was horribly embarrassed. Fancy carrying on like that and letting all the neighbours know.

'You must get the doctor,' he told the midwife crossly.

'There's nothing the matter with her,' the midwife tried to assure him. 'She's frightened, that's all it is.' But he insisted. The screams were blood-curdling.

The doctor made a brief examination, and agreed with the midwife. But by now, Eric was beginning to panic. 'You must *do* something!' he ordered. 'I can't stand this noise a minute longer. Can't you put her out or something?'

'No, Mr Barnes, not yet. Later, perhaps. Why don't you go down to the nearest pub and have a drink or two and let us get on with it? We're used to all this. It's not as bad as it sounds, you know.'

So Eric took himself off to the new pub on the estate where he told his neighbours what absolute agony his dear little wife was going through, and what amazing courage she was showing, and how terribly, terribly worried he was, and was consequently treated to rather more whisky than he'd intended to drink. He didn't leave till closing time and by then he only had a hazy idea which of the long line of identical houses actually belonged to him. There wasn't a sound. Why wasn't she screaming? How did she expect him to find his way home if she wasn't screaming? She'd been screaming loud enough when he left, hadn't she? Having a baby or something. Stupid woman.

Finally, by dint of trial, error and the examination of several letterboxes, he found the right door, and contrived to open it. The midwife put her head over the banisters, and looked down sternly upon him. 'We've had chloroform,' she whispered. 'Be very quiet.'

Anna was flat on her back and although her eyes were open she wasn't focusing them properly. There was a sickly sweet smell in the room and, lying among the elaborate frills of that ridiculous crib, a white blob of a baby. He didn't feel anything for either of them. 'Where am I supposed to sleep?' he said querulously.

' 'S a girl,' Anna said thickly. 'An' I hope you're satisfied.' She sounded as drunk as he felt.

'Talk about it in the morning,' he said.

They called the blob Marlene, and once she'd recovered from the anaesthetic Anna proclaimed herself absolutely thrilled with it. Actually she didn't feel anything for it at all, which was a terrible disappointment. It was just a baby, a small, pale, foreign creature with dark, blank eyes. Her neighbours visited with cards and flowers, her in-laws wrote a grudging letter of congratulation, and her mother and Aunt Min came to visit on the third day and brought some very pretty baby clothes, but the baby was still nothing more than a blank-eyed stranger. Try as she would she couldn't feel any emotion for it. I'm unnatural, she thought, sadly, looking down at her daughter's pale, closed face. I was an unnatural wife and now I'm an unnatural mother.

On the fifth day, her father sent a nice fat cheque, but no letter and no loving message, and the lack made her heart sink, for wasn't it proof that she'd spoiled everything with that awful row? But there wasn't time to think about it much because the new arrival dominated everything.

The midwife was rather a nuisance at first, insisting that she should feed the baby herself, but after two tearful days, while the baby screamed and screamed and she complained and wept and did everything she could to persuade everybody that the process was too painful even to be contemplated, the silly

300

woman relented and let it have a bottle. But it was a disappointing creature, always howling or sicking up milk all over its nice clean clothes or making disgusting messes in its napkins. 'We shall have to hire a nurse,' she told Eric. 'I shall be a nervous wreck if this goes on.' There didn't seem to be anything pleasant about having a baby at all.

So they hired a nurse, and prohibitively expensive she was, and the baby still howled for hours and hours and every day, but the nurse said to leave it because crying was good exercise for the lungs. But at night the noise it made was inescapable, even when they put it downstairs in the dining room and closed all the doors on it. Eric hated it more every day and couldn't bring himself to look at it, even in the daylight. If this was parenthood, he told Anna furiously, he didn't think much of it.

And Anna, allowed to get up at last on the tenth day, and struggling into a dress that simply wouldn't fit her any more, listened to the incomprehensible anger of this roaring lump of humanity she'd produced so thoughtlessly, and felt useless and demoralized. If only Dadda would come and see her. She missed him so much and he hadn't even sent her a card. And why didn't Mary write? Had she offended her in some way? She couldn't think how, but in her present depressed state it seemed very likely.

Then on the eleventh day Mary sent a letter.

'Congratulations on the birth of your daughter,' she wrote. 'You must be very pleased with yourself.' How little she knows, Anna thought. 'I've had the flu. Quite recovered now. So we've both been confined to bed, haven't we? Ma says you should be up and about any day now and will I please tell you your father would love to see you and the baby and he doesn't know how to tell you. Could you come over and see us? Once you got here he'd take you back in the car, I'm sure. And I know that's what he wants. Come on Wednesday if you can, because Ma's out then visiting Nan and that might make it all a bit easier. He'll be in all afternoon. I shall be at school, but I'll see you when I get home. Love, Mary.'

She *is* a nice girl, Anna thought. I wish she *was* my sister, really and truly. I shall answer by return of post and I shall certainly go. Wednesday was ideal. It was the nurse's afternoon off.

It was a terribly difficult journey. She hadn't realized just what a lot of clobber she'd have to cart around with her just to satisfy her awful baby. Clean nappies, and all the paraphernalia for the bottle in case it got hungry. By the time the bag was packed it was heavier than the child. She arrived at Lyndhurst Square completely exhausted.

Fortunately Dadda had been watching out for her and he rushed to the door the minute she turned into the square and took the heavy bag away from her and ushered her into the drawing room where a new pram was set waiting for the baby and the French windows were open, because although it was early November, the air was still warm. He was so full of himself, and so happy, and he smelt of cigars and his own nice salty sweat, the way he did in the summertime. For a few fluttering moments she was ashamed and didn't know what to say to him. But then he seized her in a bear hug and looked at the baby's sleeping face and told her she was the cleverest girl alive and the baby was the prettiest thing he'd ever seen and everything was all right after all. In fact she felt so welcome and so loved she was almost in tears.

'My lovebird a mother, eh?' Dadda said proudly. 'What a clever girl!'

And Anna smiled happily at him, blinking away her tears and feeling for the first time since the child was born that she'd achieved something rather special.

'A lovely baby!' he said. 'What you think a' the pram, eh?'

'It's very nice.'

'Now you tell me how you got on with the move. You comfortable in your new house, eh?'

So she told him how beastly the move had been, and he told her that next time he would organize it for her.

'There won't be a next time,' she said. 'I couldn't bear it.'

'Let me look at you,' he said, happily changing the subject. 'Beautiful as ever. You like being a mother, eh?'

What could she say? She could hardly tell him how she really felt. 'Well ...' she said. 'It's all right. Only ... none of my clothes fit.'

He was on his feet at once. 'Soon fix that,' he said. 'We go to the shops.'

'Now?' She'd almost forgotten how impulsively generous he was.

'Why not? Baby's asleep. You wheel the pram. We soon be there.'

'Oh dear,' Anna dithered, torn between desire for a nice new dress and fear that the baby would wake up while they were out buying it and disgrace her by screaming.

'Come on!' he said. So off they went.

To her mother's secret surprise, Marlene slept soundly all through the afternoon, lying in her unfamiliar pram like a cherub, pale and silent and pretty. Anna and Albert had a marvellous time looking at all the shops. They bought a full layette for the baby and some piano music for Mary and three lovely dresses for her that were a perfect fit and made her feel she'd actually begun to get her figure back after all. It took rather longer than they'd anticipated and when they got home to Lyndhurst Square it was already past four o'clock and Mary was home from school. She looked more grown-up than Anna remembered, but she came forward at once and gave her a kiss to welcome her.

'Is that the time?' Dadda said grimacing. 'I shall be late ter fetch yer ma. She'll 'ave sommink ter say then! Don't wait tea. You can have yours now, can't you?' And he was off again, cranking up his car with a great deal of noise and energy and then driving it madly out of the square.

'That's Dadda for you,' Anna said, laughing at him. 'Are we really supposed to have tea without him?'

' 'Course,' Mary said. 'I'll tell Mrs Midgeley to bring it.'

So tea was served and still the baby slept, and the sisters sat side by side and watched her.

'How did you an' – Ploo get on?' Mary asked when the tea was poured.

'It's all right,' Anna said. 'I think he's forgiven me. Well, you can see,' indicating all the parcels that her father had flung down on the sofa. Then she remembered the way she'd been invited and how much she was indebted to this girl. 'Thanks for letting me know. It's ever so good of you, really.'

Mary's motives hadn't been entirely altruistic, but she wasn't going to admit that. At least, not now. 'Think nothing of it,' she grinned. She'd felt sorry for Anna and genuinely wanted to help her if she could, but there was another and stronger motive behind her actions. If Ploochy took an interest in this new grandchild of his, he might go back to his family again and leave her and Ma in peace. 'Have a bun.'

'You're very kind,' Anna said. 'And I'm not just talking about the bun.'

They enjoyed their tea and still Marlene didn't wake up. It was miraculous. 'She's been asleep nearly four hours,' Anna said. 'I'd better make her a bottle soon, don't you think? She makes the most dreadful noise when she's hungry.'

So they made up the bottle together, and between them they managed to make sense of the instructions on the packet. And Marlene hardly had time to cry when she woke before they'd got the teat in her mouth.

'What good timing!' Mary said.

'We make a good team.'

The baby drained the bottle completely dry and then lay on Anna's lap and gazed around her. And didn't cry! It was quite astonishing. Mary sat beside them on the sofa holding one tiny hand delicately between finger and thumb. And suddenly the infant looked up at her mother and smiled, her small pink mouth stretching upwards, her cheeks plumping, her eyes alight with recognition.

'Well, look at that!' Mary said. 'She knows you.'

'Yes,' Anna said, smiling back at her baby. 'She does, doesn't she?' The smile was stirring the most extraordinary reaction in her. It was as if an iceblock was melting inside her chest. 'I think she loves me,' she said.

' 'Course she loves you,' Mary said, smiling at the baby. 'Your 'er ma.'

'Yes,' Anna said huskily. 'And I love her. Ever so, ever so much.' It was true. How extraordinary and marvellous and wonderful. 'I do love you, don't I my darling?' And the baby smiled again.

So they sat on the sofa together and were quite ridiculously happy. And Marlene went on smiling, now she'd learned the trick, and even when Dadda came crashing back with the redhead she didn't complain but continued to lie in her mother's lap like a model child, blowing bubbles.

Queenie approved of her at once. 'She's a pretty baby,' she said. 'Nice round 'ead. I like a baby with a nice round 'ead.'

'Don't they all have round heads?' Mary asked, laughing at her.

'No, they don't,' her mother said. 'Yours come to a point.'

'It didn't, did it?'

'Like a pencil. We 'avin' tea?'

After their second tea, Dadda said he'd drive her home, just as Mary had predicted, and that was a great relief because she was beginning to feel tired. It was so lovely to be petted and praised again. As they drove towards Stoneleigh Park she realized that she'd been entirely happy all afternoon. Happy in an easy way, she'd almost forgotten. Happy as she was never happy with Eric. I wish I wasn't going home, she thought. But that was childish. Nevertheless she felt depressed again when they reached her gate. It didn't feel like coming home at all.

Dadda carried her bag into the house and kissed her warmly when he said goodbye. 'I am glad you came to see us,' he said.

'Oh, so am I,' she said, thinking how dreadful it would have been if she'd lost him, and how much this visit had given her.

'See you next Wednesday, eh?'

'Oh yes!'

Later that evening, in her new-found tenderness towards her baby, she remembered her mother. Poor Mummy, waiting at home for someone to bring Dadda back to her. She knew now, in an instinctive sort of way, that he wouldn't come back, and she wasn't even sure she wanted him to, for he was so plainly and obviously happy with Mary's ma. But love for her mother nagged at her, alongside her newly discovered love for her child. I'll go and see her on Saturday, she thought. She hadn't the faintest idea how she could help, but she felt she ought to try.

Alice thought the baby was coming along beautifully. 'You can see her growing,' she said approvingly. 'A fine baby, Anna.' So for the first part of the visit they were happy enough, praising the baby and watching her smile. But then she went to sleep and it was just the two of them and Mummy asked after Dadda.

'Have you gone to visit your father?'

'Yes. On Wednesday.'

'I suppose you didn't get a chance to say anything?'

'No, not really. You know how it is with a new baby.'

'I write to him twice a week, you know. He never answers. It's very unkind.'

'Yes.' Oh dear! What could she say?

'I'm sure the neighbours are talking. You know how people

are. I'm getting so embarrassed I don't know how to face them.'

Anna had a brilliant idea. 'Why don't you tell them he's over on the other side of London building up a new chain of businesses?'

'Is he?'

'Oh yes. He's got four shops in the Peckham area now. You know Dadda.'

'Yes,' Alice said, slowly, considering it. 'I could say that.'

'Of course you could. And there's no shame in that, is there? Plenty of men spend time away from their families when they're building up businesses. Why, look at Eric today. He didn't mind driving me here, but he couldn't stay. Off to talk business with his cronies, even on a Saturday.' Actually she didn't know where he'd gone, but it sounded just right.

'I could say that,' Mummy said again, nodding her head a little.

'Much the best way,' Anna said, patting her mother's hands.

'He *will* come back to me in the end, won't he, Anna?'

'I hope so,' Anna said, feeling she ought to go on comforting, if she could. 'But you can't tell, can you? Nothing ever seems to work out the way I expect it to.'

Chapter Twenty-Eight

The Blob was howling again, 'Wah! Wah! Wah!' on and on and on and on. It was putting Eric off his breakfast. 'There's something the matter with that child,' he complained to Anna, petulantly pushing his egg to the side of his plate. 'Where's that damned nurse?'

'Late,' Anna said from the kitchen. She was making a bottle, as quickly as she could, but she was all fingers and thumbs because she was so cold.

'It's three months old, for crying out loud,' Eric said as the screaming continued. 'It shouldn't still be making a noise like that.' It was a dark, cold morning in early January and the electric fire in their modern dining room wasn't giving out nearly enough heat. He was still chilled to the bone even though he was sitting as close to it as he could get.

Anna trailed upstairs to fetch the baby. 'Mummy's coming!' she called. 'Here I come! Don't cry!'

'You'd think that damn girl could arrive on time,' Eric grumbled as Anna returned with the baby cuddled against her shoulder. 'God knows we pay her enough.'

But Anna didn't seem to hear him. She was settling herself in the armchair on the other side of the fire, and nestling the baby into her lap. 'There you are,' she said. 'There's your nice breakfast. Don't cry.'

'*Must* you feed it here?' Eric asked petulantly. Breakfast was only tolerable if he and Anna both had something to read and the Blob was asleep. But she went on ignoring him. He sighed heavily and returned to his study of the *Daily Mail*, crackling the pages fiercely as he turned them. Fortunately a strong headline caught his attention and gave him something else to think about, this time with approval and satisfaction.

' "Hurrah for the Blackshirts!" ' he read aloud, noting as he did so that the article was written by Lord Rothermere himself. ' "The British Union of Fascists is a well organized party of the right, ready to take over responsibility for natioi.al affairs with the same directness of purpose and energy of methods as Hitler and Mussolini have displayed." And quite right too. The man's got some sense. That's what we need in this country. A strong, right wing government with the power to put all these idle workers in their place. We'd have no more nonsense then. They'd soon find work for themselves then. I should say so! Instead of walking about the streets of London making a disturbance. Hunger marches!' He snorted. 'They're no more hungry than I am. It's all a load of Bolshevist propaganda. Don't you think so, Anna?'

'Um,' his wife said. Marlene was sucking greedily, her dark eyes staring up at her with passionate concentration. 'Terrible.' She had developed a new and rather useful trick of simply listening to the tone of what he was saying and ignoring the content. That way she could give him the sort of vague answer he needed, and didn't have to be bothered by understanding him.

'This man's right,' Eric said, happily and pompously. 'We should get tough with slackers. All this namby-pamby nonsense just breeds scroungers. And nobody's going to tell me that's a good system.'

Queenie knew a bad system when she saw one, and Queenie had no intention of allowing a bad system to go on for ever either. She and the Bermondsey management committee had been making plans for weeks. Early in the new year they'd been joined by a group of trade union officials from the Transport and General Workers, and to Albert's delight one of them turned out to be none other than Billy Jones, old Harry's fiery son. Soon he and Queenie were the closest allies, and he and his wife and their two young sons were frequent visitors at Lyndhurst Square. For, as Queenie said, they had a job of work to do and the more of them there were to do it the better. The marchers had to be housed and fed once they arrived in the capital, and the South Wales contingent was heading for the halls and schools of dockland. Camp beds and blankets had been gathered from every known source and the makeshift dormitories were ready. Now the committee was considering the matter of food supplies and wondering whether they could provide a hot meal somehow or other.

'Can't live on sandwiches fer ever,' Maisie Oxbury said.

'Plenty do,' her neighbour growled. 'Case of 'ave ter.'

'Not them fellers, though,' Maisie pleaded. 'They're worth more'n that, surely ter God.'

'Try old Ploochy,' Billy suggested. 'Bet you any money 'e'll help us.'

To Mary's renewed surprise, Albert had contributed handsomely to her mother's supper fund. 'I can't make him out at all,' she said to Tom one evening as the two of them set off from Lyndhurst Square on their way to a performance of *The Tempest* at the Old Vic. 'Here he is, the most blatant capitalist I've ever seen, making money hand over fist with his stocks and shares, and property all over the place, and all those wretched off-licences, and God knows what else besides, and then shelling it out to Ma for the marchers.'

'And a good job too!' Tom said grinning at her. 'At least they're a deserving cause. He'd only waste it on you else. And you'd only waste it on books and music and Woodbines, and not give me any, when I'm gasping.'

She dredged the little soft packet of cigarettes from the debris in her bag and picked out two of the least mangled for them to smoke. 'There y'are, mumper,' she said. It was nice to be able to feed him ciggies. It made her feel grown up and independent, as though she were out at work like so many of her contemporaries, instead of being stuck in the fifth form at school and still treated like a child.

'Do as much fer you some day,' he said.

'You'd better,' she told him, with something of Queenie's sharpness. 'I'm down to me last three. Here's our bus.'

Up on the top deck, as they lit up, she returned to the puzzle that was Ploochy. 'I could be a gold-digger inside a' three weeks, the things he offers to buy me, d'you know that? Top brick off the chimney if I wanted it. We're supposed to have an arrangement about money, you know. I get a clothing allowance and a grant for books and music, and we keep accounts so's I can pay him back when I'm earning. But then he goes and buys presents, and says they don't count, because it's my birthday or Christmas or something. Look at that violin he bought me when I joined the Crystal Palace Amateur. Cost the earth! And the book list I showed him at the start of term. Suggested reading, that's all it was. And what did he do? Only went straight out and bought the lot. Every single title. Downright embarrassing it was.' Her expression was stern but her eyes were gleaming with the remembered pleasure of it.

'Well, I only wish someone would embarrass me like that,' Tom said enviously. 'I have to join a queue in the college library. You don't know when you're well off.'

'It's daft,' she complained. 'And now all this money for the hunger march. He's working against his own interests.'

'He does it for Queenie,' Tom said. 'That's the long and the short of it. I don't think he thinks in political terms at all. It's Queenie he's helping, not the unemployed.'

'He's a mystery to me,' his daughter said, exhaling smoke towards the ceiling of the bus. It unsettled her that he was such an easy man to like. It would have been a great deal easier for her, in her present position, if he'd been harsh or heavy handed. 'I can't see why he lets her get her own way all the time, the way he does. I wonder whether he'll ever say no to her. She'd have a blue fit if he did.'

'No!' Albert roared. 'No! No! No! God damn it Queenie, these are black shirts, not the Boys Brigade. I not have you injured, d'you hear me!'

'You ain't bought me, Ploo,' Queenie bellowed back. 'How many times I got ter tell yer? If I want ter go, I go.'

It was a balmy morning in the middle of May and the sunlight beaming through the dining room window was a slanting white column that looked solid enough to touch. The wireless was playing a cheerful medley of sea songs, and the air was spiced with an appetizing medley of breakfast flavours, coffee and bacon and warm bread and marmalade. Outside in the back garden a blackbird was singing full throatedly among the bright clusters of the may blossom, the roses were in brightly coloured bud and the honeysuckle hung like a green mane along the full length of the fence.

It was a morning for peace and contentment, Mary thought, and yet here they were in the middle of a sudden, furious row. For the *Daily Herald* was full of information about the mass rally Oswald Mosley was planning to hold at Olympia on the seventh of June, and Ma, enraged that the British Union of Fascists was being allowed to appear in such force, had suddenly announced her intention of joining the Battersea protest march against it. Now there'll be some sport, Mary thought looking from one to the other. Their arguments were usually pretty entertaining, but this one promised to be a real humdinger. My money's on Ma.

'No you won't!' Ploochy said, his mouth square with fury at her foolhardiness.

'Yes I will. Oh, come on, Ploo, the Ox'll be there, an' most a' the management committee, an' your mate Billy Jones, an' all them fellers from the garage. I shan't exactly be on me own. There'll be thousands of us.'

Even the mention of Billy Jones wasn't enough to calm Ploochy's protective anxiety. 'They're fascists,' he said. 'They murder people!'

'All the more reason.'

'Queenie, fer God's sake!'

'Now look 'ere, Ploo,' Ma said, pointing to the front page of the paper she'd propped against the marmalade before their argument began. 'This bloody Mosley's no better'n Mussolini or Hitler or any a' that lot. We gotta stop him. Quick. You gotta see that! If we don't he'll be running the country 'fore you can turn round, a' then what'll 'appen? I'll tell you what'll 'appen. Me an' Cal an' your friend Billy Jones an' Maisie an' the Ox'll all be be'ind bars. Is that what yer want?' Her face was fierce in the early morning sunlight and horribly determined.

Ploochy was too agitated by now to finish his breakfast. 'I don't want you hurt,' he said stubbornly. 'Let Billy go and the Ox. They can stick up for themselves.'

'Not woman's work, eh?' she said and her tone was steely.

'Other women,' he said, trying to be reasonable. 'Not you. Please, Queenie.'

'Why not?'

The last of his limited patience shredded and was gone.

'Because I say so. I not allow it.'

'I'm going!' she said springing to her feet as though she fully intended to set off for Olympia that very moment. 'You ain't my keeper!'

'Quite right!' Mary said with approval. 'I'm going too!'

Queenie rounded on her daughter at once. 'No you ain't,' she scowled.

'Why not?'

'Because fer one, it's too dangerous, an' for another, yer're too young.'

'Oh, fer crying out loud, I'm sixteen. I'm as tall as you are. If it's all right for you, it's all right for me.'

'Neither of you!' Albert roared. 'D'you hear me? Neither of you! I forbid it!' And he marched furiously out of the room, slamming the door behind him. 'Damn silly women!'

'Ferbid all yer like, mate,' Queenie said to his retreating back. 'Don't make no odds ter me. I'm going.' And as Mary opened her mouth to protest her determination too, she added, 'You ain't!'

We'll see about that, Mary thought, but she didn't argue any further because she still had a healthy respect for the full power of her mother's fury, even though she *was* sixteen and nearly the same height. I'll talk it over with Tom, she thought. Perhaps he'll take me. She couldn't complain then.

But Tom was as concerned about her safety as Ploochy had been about Ma's. 'I can't take you, Mo,' he said. 'I shan't be on the march, you see. I'm going in the meeting. To heckle. I've got a ticket. It's going to be a nasty business, this. I think you ought to stay at home. Ploochy's right. People are going ter get hurt.'

'Ma's going,' she tried.

'She's tough,' he said. 'She can take it.'

That afternoon, when she came home from school, she went upstairs to her bedroom and sat down at her desk and wrote a long letter to Anna, telling her how unreasonable Ma and Tom were being, and how she just *had* to go to Olympia and oppose those awful Fascists, and how very difficult it was to be a schoolgirl when she was sixteen. 'All the other girls of my age are out at work,' she wrote. 'Adults. Nobody ever calls them children, and says they can't go to meetings because they might

312

be a bit rough. Why, even Mr Andrews of the Amateur calls me Miss Chapman. I'm sure he'd let me go if I was his daughter. Not that I could be, because he's about your age. He's terribly proper and correct about everything, and he thinks Oswald Mosley is a terrible man. Ma and Ploochy are just being ridiculous.'

The next morning a letter arrived from Anna. 'We've crossed in the post,' she said, picking it up, and laughed to think that Anna would be reading her letter at exactly the same time. But her laughter soon died, for this letter was really shocking.

'I'm afraid I shan't be coming to Peckham tomorrow,' Anna had written. 'Eric is taking me to a political rally in the evening and he says I've got to be ready spot on six thirty. It's at Olympia in the big hall, and all the best people are going. He says it will be the most stirring meeting this country has ever seen. Apparently they wear uniforms and carry flags and drums and things like that and music plays and it's all rather splendid. I'm quite looking forward to it. We haven't been out together for such a long time. It will make a nice change.'

Mary couldn't believe her eyes. ' "Rather splendid!" ' she mocked, brandishing the letter at Queenie. 'Don't she know nothing? Fascists rather splendid!' Her face was pink with indignation. 'Oh, I was right about her that first day. She's just a dumb blonde. "Rather splendid!" You got a postcard? I'm going ter give her such a piece a' my mind.'

Which she did, writing with such fury that half the words were smudged. 'The meeting at Olympia will *not* be fun or splendid. It will be *hateful*. You'll *hate* it. It is organized by *Fascists*, who are *dangerous*, *evil* people with the most *wicked* ideas. In Germany they are killing Jews. You *must* know that. How could you possibly be taken in by such *evil* people? Don't go, or you'll regret it! Mary.'

Anna was quite as upset as her sister had been when the card arrived. The first letter has made her heart sink with the awful realization that they were on different sides, and she had known then that worse was to come. 'Oh dear,' she said to Marlene, who was sitting in her high chair demolishing a rusk. 'Your aunty's ever so cross.' The anger in the card made her feel quite bleak. Politics again. That's what it was. People always got so serious and cross when it was politics. 'We'll write her a nice long letter tomorrow and tell her how lovely it all was, and how silly she was to get worried. That'll be a good idea, won't it?' After all, she's very young. I must try not to get upset even if she *has* hurt my feelings.

But she was upset, because she'd grown so close to Mary and now it looked as though they were going to quarrel. 'Politics are horrid,' she told Marlene. 'Aren't you making a mess with that rusk!'

Chapter Twenty-Nine

It was easy enough for Queenie to find Billy Jones and his friends that evening. All she had to do was to stand by the side of the road and wait as the long column of marchers came crunching across Battersea Bridge, their placards bobbing angry messages above their heads. 'Fascism means murder.' 'Down with Mosley.' It was a determined demonstration and already excessively cheerful, like an army marching into battle, each man taking courage and comfort from his neighbours, the jokes rough and smutty, the sense of solidarity intense. As she edged through the marching ranks towards her friends, Queenie was sharply aware of their open excitement and the fear that they were all holding in check. When a troup of mounted police clattered past them just as they were leaving the bridge, their passing caused a backwash of alarm and hatred.

'Don't care much fer the boys in blue,' Billy said, narrowing his eyes as though it was paining him to look at them.

'Come to 'old yer 'and, Billy,' the man beside him said. ' 'Cause, I mean ter say, they wouldn't want them blackshirts ter start cuttin' up rough.'

'That's provocation!' Queenie said, angrily. 'You don't want 'orses in a crowd this size. Askin' fer trouble, that is.'

'Should 'a' brought a packet o' marbles,' another man said. 'Unseat the buggers.'

The march was forced to slow down to crawling pace when it emerged from Warwick Road into Kensington High Street, for the Edgware contingent had already arrived and the pavements facing the long façade of the Exhibition Hall were lined with demonstrators, most of whom had come there straight from

315

work and were still in their grimy working clothes. Now Queenie could see that the police horses were already being used, their fat rumps nudging the crowds to keep them moving, even though it was little more than six o'clock and the meeting wasn't due to begin until eight. 'Pushın' us around all-a-ready, yer see,' she said to Billy, and Billy gave a cynical grimace which showed more clearly than words that it was just what he expected.

Inside the hall Eric and Anna were already in their seats and Eric was gloating about the marvellous organization of the B.U.F. 'Look at the rabble outside,' he told Anna, 'and then compare it with this. Absolutely top-hole! This is the way to run a rally, Bunny woo. Abso-bloomin'-lutely! Now aren't you glad you came?'

'Thrilling!' Anna said, fluttering her eyelashes at him automatically, and thrilling it certainly was, just as he'd predicted. The whole place was hung with flags, bright Union Jacks alternating with the bold black and yellow of the Fascist banner, and the aisles were lined with uniformed blackshirts standing proudly to attention, neat and well groomed and detached, like soldiers on parade. Seen from the distance of her seat at the back of the stalls, their close black ranks were like lines of perspective mesmerizing her eyes towards the stage, a high, still empty platform heavily draped in apricot drugget and spotlit by a long row of huge arc lamps. Powerful amplifiers all around the hall had been blasting out patriotic music ever since they arrived, and the combined effect of hard colour, strong light and heavily pulsing sound was making her feel quite dizzy. She was too excited to sit still and too overawed to move about. So when the great man finally arrived, more than half an hour late, limping slowly and nobly towards the platform and preceded by six men carrying enormous banners, as drums reverberated around the hall and the great arc lamps swung their huge, grey-blue beams to light his path, she was released into frantic emotion and cheered herself hoarse with the rest.

'Now, you listen to this,' Eric instructed as the meeting settled down again. But it was an unnecessary order. She was already quite stage struck.

The drumroll ceased, its echo rumbled away, and like Anna

the audience sat spellbound waiting for Mosley's voice. When it came it was harder than they expected, booming at them from the amplifiers above their heads, but each word was carefully enunciated and sharp as crystal. 'Ladies and gentlemen,' he said, 'this meeting, the largest indoor meeting ever held under one roof in Britain, is the culmination of a great national campaign in which audiences in every city of this land have gathered to hear the fascist case. The slow, soft days are behind us, perhaps for ever. Hard days and nights lie ahead. There will be no relaxing of the mind and will. The tents of ease are struck, and the soul of man is on the march.'

Tears began to prick Anna's ardent eyes. This was really thrilling stuff. She wouldn't have missed it for worlds. How marvellous for Britain to have a leader like this!

But then there was movement in one of the galleries, and a group of men and women were on their feet and shouting. At first she thought it was a spontaneous outcry of approval, but then the tone of the words drifted down to her and she heard the chant. 'Fascism means murder. Down with Mosley. Fascism means murder.' The great arc lamps swung round like searchlights to hold the interrupters in their beams and a pack of black uniforms burst into the gallery and sprang upon the protesters, punching and kicking with sudden and mechanical precision. Two men were felled, a woman screamed, and within seconds every single protester had been dragged out of the gallery and out of sight.

There was a ripple of applause, but it was followed almost at once by another chant. Three men were on their feet in another gallery and there was a fourth shouting in the stalls just in front of her.

Eric was scarlet with annoyance, his eyes bolting and the veins swelling on his forehead. 'Disgraceful!' he spat. 'Throw them out! Unwashed louts! No business in here with decent, law-abiding citizens.' And when the spotlights swung across the hall to reveal that these men too were being punched to the ground, he cheered aloud. 'That's it! Hit the bastards! Chuck 'em out!' He was so excited he was punching the air as the blow landed, his face suffused with hatred.

Heads turned in their direction now, and Anna felt extremely uncomfortable, but then there was another diversion as yet another group began to chant on the other side of the hall. This time the blackshirts leapt over chairs in their eagerness to get to the culprits, and several members of the audience were unseated in the rush. 'We shall not be deterred,' Mosley's voice boomed from the amplifiers. 'You are not hurting us. We are hurting you.'

But the interruptions continued and though his speech boomed intermittently on it was muffled by yells and screams, and completely upstaged by the violence all around it. Not everybody in the audience shared Eric's passion for the rough tactics of the stewards. In fact many of the more affluent were beginning to feel distinctly alarmed, and their expressions showed it. And Anna was feeling sick.

This is awful, she thought. They're being absolutely vicious. They're enjoying it. And they came prepared. They *knew* this was going to happen. Normal people don't carry knuckledusters and coshes around with them. It's horrible. I wish I hadn't come. And she remembered Mary's furious postcard. 'Fascists are evil!'

Tom Oxbury, sitting quietly in the stalls waiting his turn, watched the reactions around him with surprise and trepidation. His immediate neighbour was a middle-aged lady in a bulky fur coat who had started the evening by telling her husband loudly and confidently that the unemployment problem could easily be solved if only the government would enlist all likely young men into the army. Only Mosley, she said, could really be trusted to bring back law and order to the nation. Now she watched his henchmen spitting on their hands after a particularly vicious assault, and on a young woman too, and then looking round eagerly for their next victim, saying, 'Who's next?' She was obviously changing her mind, their perverted enjoyment being more than she'd bargained for. Now she was whispering to her husband, shaking her head and frowning, but there was so much noise in the hall that Tom couldn't hear what she was saying, no matter how hard he strained his ears.

Then, God help him, there was the signal and it was his turn to protest. He took a deep breath, stood up and yelled at the top of his voice, 'This is what fascism means. Beating up women. Silencing opposition with knuckledusters. Stop

318

Mosley now. Walk out of this meeting.' The blackshirts were galloping down the aisle towards him, fists raised, but as they ran and he began to shake with the terror of their approach, the air around him was suddenly full of leaflets and glancing up he saw that two men were running along the girders under the high gauze covered arch of the roof, shouting slogans and showering papers as they went. The spotlights swung away from him to play on the girders, and the woman in the fur coat grabbed him by the arm and gave him a shake and said, 'Run, boy! Run! Quick!' and he ran, finding speed in his legs after all, out of the hall and along the echoing corridors, hurtling towards the exit.

But before he had a chance to rejoice in his escape or to feel ashamed of it, he'd run straight into trouble again. The corridor was blocked by three blackshirts busily finishing off their latest victim, a young man who lay curled and groaning on the ground at their feet, vainly trying to protect his head with his arms as the jackboots thudded into his ribs and spine.

Anger rose in Tom Oxbury like a flame, and he remembered the way his father dealt with drunks in The Red Lion and, seizing the nearest black leg as it swung back for another kick, he twisted it rapidly so that its owner was flung violently to the ground. The second blackshirt immediately turned to punch at his face, but he ducked quickly and butted the man in the stomach as hard as he could, at the same time yelling to the man on the floor to get up and run like hell. As he straightened and stood up, he saw a knuckleduster descending and put his hand across his face to ward off the worst of the blow, and then he and the victim were running together, staggering and gasping as the walls of the corridor danced and flickered, and the exit sign advanced and receded before them like nightmare.

The evening air struck cold on their heated faces as they emerged to the ranks of police and the milling crowds of the demonstration outside. The victim sank to the pavement with an odd sighing groan and Tom suddenly realized that he felt dizzy and sick and that his legs were no longer capable of supporting him. Then there were people all around him, and he was sitting on the edge of the kerb, and rough hands were forcing his head between his knees, and blood was dripping from the tips of his fingers into the gutter, and his gorge rose into his throat and he began to vomit.

'You got someone with yer, son?' a voice asked from somewhere yards above his head.

'Needs stitching,' another voice said, and he knew that his right hand was being held and examined. But nothing was real any more.

His father was with him, wasn't he. 'Mr Oxbury,' he said thickly. 'Red Lion, Bermondsey.'

'O.K., son,' the first voice soothed. 'We'll get you to hospital, shall we?'

'Move along, *if* you please,' a policeman said. 'No loitering.'

'Where's my father?' he asked as they led him away.

Tom Oxbury senior was attending to another injury in the Portcullis Avenue, holding the gaping edges of a long cut gently together, just as he'd done all those years ago in the mud of Ypres. This was the sixth casualty he'd attended, and the worst, for this man had been unconscious for far too long and looked a bad colour. 'Better carry him down the first aid post,' he said to the men around him. 'Needs a doctor, poor bugger. Keep his head turned sideways, mind.' He could see another struggle at the other end of the passage way. 'Tell 'em I shall need more lint. An' if anyone's got such a thing as a ball a string.' Most of the young men thrown bodily and bloodily out of Olympia onto the pavement had had their braces cut so that they couldn't use their hands to defend themselves. Now, injured and in shock, they were demoralized because they couldn't keep their trousers up.

It was growing dark and at the main exit police were using torches. Here the injured sat on the kerb waiting for help or the return of enough energy to walk to the first aid post or until the police descended upon them and moved them on. Queenie and Billy Jones, down on their knees on the pavement trying to staunch the wounds of a young woman with four gashes in the back of her head, were finding it quite hard to see what they were doing. And to make matters worse the horses were on the move again, nudging and shoving, because so many of the audience had had enough and decided to leave.

'Move along! Move along!' a young policeman said peremptorily, shining his torch into Billy's eyes.

'This kid's hurt,' Billy explained. 'You'll 'ave ter move round us till we've finished.'

'Don't you get lippy with me, son,' the policeman said angrily. 'If I say move, you move.'

'I move, *son*, when I'm good an' ready,' Billy said, frowning at the young face above him. Then he turned his attention to the girl. 'Can you just lift yer head a bit, love?'

'Up! On yer feet! Shift!' the policeman said, and he seized Billy by the collar and tried to haul him to his feet.

Then a lot happened and all at once. Billy shook off the annoying hand, three more constables arrived simultaneously, and several demonstrators broke from the police cordon and ran to help. Everybody was shouting, and Queenie, still on her knees beside the injured woman, scooped her bandaged head into her lap for protection and yelled, 'Oh, fer crying out loud! Can't you see the kid's been 'urt? 'Ave a bit a sense.'

'Look, mate,' Billy said, still reasonable, 'if you want ter do sommink useful why dontcher go in there and stop them blackshirts? Bloody mayhem it is in there. That's where you oughter be.'

'You mind your business an' we'll mind ours,' an older constable said, 'otherwise I shall 'ave ter do yer.'

'Don't be so bloody silly!' Billy said. 'What for?'

'Breach a' the peace.'

'Breach a' the peace!' Billy said, pointing furiously at the hall. 'In there! That's where they're breachin' the bleedin' peace. That's where you oughter be. In there. Good God, they're beatin' us silly in there. Six ter one. Knuckledusters. Coshes. An' you stand 'ere blethering about a breach a' the peace.'

But the constable had the last word. 'You're under arrest,' he said, and while Billy was still open mouthed with surprise his arms were pinioned and he was marched away. Queenie and the injured woman were lugged to their feet, the demonstrators were manhandled back to make way for a Daimler, and three horses pranced across her line of vision, sidestepping delicately into the crowd.

'Billy!' she yelled, looking out into the muddle of waving arms, truncheons, wild white faces and steaming horse flesh. 'Billy!'

321

'Tell Dora I'm all right!' his voice rose above shouts and snorts and barking orders. 'Tell Ploo ...'

'It's like a bloody war!' Queenie said furiously, and knew as she heard the words in her mouth, and smelt the blood on her hands, that sooner or later there would be a real war, guns and all.

Chapter Thirty

The minute his determined Queenie had left for Olympia that evening, Albert had rushed Mary Ann into the car and driven her to Bermondsey before she could stamp out of the house into danger too. Eth had been forewarned, so perhaps between them they could keep at least one of his wayward women at home and safe.

'Stay with yer aunt,' he said as he left. 'If anything happen, I come straight back here and get you, I promise. Don't you go rushing off anywhere on your own.' Then he drove to Tooting and the cheerful, uncomplicated companionship of Jack Beard's. He was furious with worry.

Dickie was already at their table and had the first round ordered, but for once and uncharacteristically Harry Jones was late.

'Sorry 'bout that,' he said, scratching his head apologetically, when he finally arrived. 'Been with Em an' Dora.'

'Trouble?' Dickie asked, pushing a glass of comfort across the table towards him.

'Billy,' Harry explained when he'd drunk the edge off his anxiety. 'Gorn off ter some demonstration somewhere. Dora's worried sick.'

'She don't need ter worry,' Albert said, knowing how she felt. 'Our Billy'll take care of himself. Soldier a' the line! You don't need to worry about our Billy! An' anyway, he's with Queenie. She'll keep him out a' trouble.' It was the first time he'd spoken about Queenie here in Jack Beard's, but he needed to reassure himself as much as Harry.

'Drink up!' Dickie commanded. 'No good frettin' till it happens, I always say.'

So they got down to some serious drinking, and the spectre of the demonstration receded a little in the conviviality of the evening.

Until that night Albert had always considered that the wireless was a cheerful addition to his pub. Set on the edge of the counter, the mesh of its loudspeaker embellished with elaborate scroll work like some magical Pandora's box, it emitted popular music and variety shows whenever they were wanted, or snatches of anodyne information about football or the dogs, and when it was silent it provided a useful shelf for the return of empties. But that night it suddenly became an alarming and alien presence.

'The mass rally of the British Union of Fascists at Olympia tonight is being attended by one of the largest audiences ever seen in this country,' it told them coolly in its cultured voice. But then it went on, 'Crowds have been gathering outside Olympia since six o'clock this evening. There have been some disturbances and police say several arrests have been made.'

'Oh, my giddy aunt!' Harry said, upset at once and raking his hair with both hands. 'That'll be our Billy, sure as fate. I knew 'e never should've gone.'

Albert was already on his feet. 'I go there,' he said. 'I find out. You go home to Em. Tell Dora I look after 'im.' He was halfway to the door. He'd pick young Mary up first and then he'd go straight to Olympia.

There was very little traffic on the road so he drove well beyond the speed limit and cut corners by bumping across the edges of the pavements, but he was too angry and too worried to care. 'Damn silly woman!' he growled at the windscreen. Why couldn't she stay at home and be content with him and Mary Ann, like any other woman? All this rushing off to political meetings and demonstrations and God knows what! It wasn't natural or necessary. Damn silly woman! And he knew that he loved her to distraction and would be overwhelmed with guilt if she'd been arrested. If only he'd known how to stop her. But he recognized too, in the honesty of the driver's seat, that if she were stopped she would change, and that he didn't want to change her. He loved her as she was, headstrong and messy and passionate and unpredictable. 'Just don't let her be hurt,' he said to the windscreen and the fates.

Mary and Eth had heard the bulletin too, sitting one on each side of their wireless, ears strained to catch every word.

'I'm off!' Mary said at once, leaping to her feet. If Ma was in trouble she ought to be with her.

'Wait fer Ploo,' Eth urged. 'You promised. 'E'll come straight back. 'E said 'e would.'

'She could be arrested, injured, anything,' Mary said wildly. The very idea of waiting infuriated her. There wasn't a moment to be lost. 'She could be hurt!' she said, jamming her hat on her head.

'Quarter of an hour,' Eth urged. 'Be worth it. You jest think 'ow quick 'e'll get you there in that car of 'is.'

'All right!' Mary said fiercely. 'I'll wait a quarter of an hour. No more. Then I'm off.'

Fortunately, Ploochy arrived outside the flats well within the fifteen minutes, and with a grinding of brakes that had them both running to the window. 'Come on,' he yelled up to her. 'Get your hat, Mary. We go to Olympia!'

They drove down Jamaica Road in the pale green dusk and, turning into Abbey Street, passed the lights of The Star, where Ma made political speeches. Don't let her be hurt, she thought. And, why did she have to go there? She knew it wasn't safe. It was so dark under the long railway bridge that Ploochy had to switch on his sidelights, and by the time they reached the tangle of roads at the Elephant darkness was descending fast. They had Westminster Bridge almost to themselves, although they could see the yellow eyes of several cars that were circling Parliament Square. It was a lovely evening, calm and peaceful and rich with the deepening colours of dusk. Out in mid stream, the Thames was burnished as white as a mirror, and the golden light shining from windows all along the length of the Houses of Parliament was reflected in the darker water beneath the walls like a necklace of tangled curls. Ma's curls, Mary thought, red-gold and flecked with silver and carelessly beautiful. And now where is she? Oh, hurry up, Ploo! Hurry up and get there!

When she'd first climbed into the car she'd pulled her hat well down over her ears, so that the side of her face was partly obscured, and the gesture told Albert just a little too plainly that she was very agitated and didn't want him to know it. He was touched to see how much she loved her mother, and wished there was some way he could tell her how much he loved them both. But the distance of her denial still separated them, even now when they were both fraught with the same anxiety.

In Warwick Road they suddenly ran into a traffic jam. Albert was furious. 'God damn it!' he yelled, standing up in his seat so that the cars in front of him could get the full benefit of his abuse. 'Get a move on, fer crying out loud!' But the road was well and truly blocked and the two uniformed chauffeurs in the cars immediately ahead stared stolidly through their windscreens and refused to pay any attention to him.

'Humph!' he snorted. 'We'll soon see about that!' And he put the car into reverse quickly before anyone else could drive up behind him and block that way too. Then he shot off backwards until he found a side road, where to Mary's surprise and his own gratification he reversed neatly round the corner, crashed into first gear again and belted back the way he'd come. 'We'll nip up the side roads,' he said, suiting the action to the word. 'This will do. Should bring us out in Kensington Road somewhere.' Which it did, and this time, by dint of bullying other cars out of his way with a great deal of furious hooting and arm-waving, he barged back into the stream of moving traffic and inched his swearing way towards the Exhibition Hall, hooting every five seconds just to make his intentions abundantly clear to everybody.

He looked so fiercely extraordinary in his leather coat and his leather helmet, with his goggles black and implacable above white teeth and bristling moustaches, that it wasn't long before a policeman had been assigned to him to urge traffic and demonstrators out of his way, since the Inspector reckoned that a car that was making such a relentless noise and was being driven by such an obvious eccentric must be arriving to pick up a notable.

Mary was delighted. 'Oh, Ploo!' she said. 'You got a police escort.' Fancy a police escort to help them find someone who'd probably been arrested.

But her father had other things on his mind. 'Keep yer eyes skinned,' he told her. 'We're nearly there.' Dusk was making it almost impossible to distinguish any faces in that vast, shadowy crowd, but he had no intention of going home before he'd found Queenie. 'You watch your side, I'll watch mine.'

But in the event it was her voice that revealed where she was, loud and clear even above all the muddled noises of crowd and traffic, shouting abuse, 'Oh, my good Gawd! You got cloth ears or summink?'

'There she is!' he said happily, and the car was squealed to a halt and he was out of his seat and plunging into the crowd as though it was a surf wave.

Their escort ran back at once to see what was going on. 'You can't stop here, miss,' he said deferentially to Mary. Then he noticed that the driver's seat was empty. 'Where's 'e gorn?' he said, in disbelief.

Mary was equal to him. 'The lady we've come to collect appears to be in the crowd,' she said, and she was careful to use her most cultured, middle class voice, glad for the first time in her life that the teachers at Stogs had insisted on 'correct' speech.

It had a magical effect on the helmeted face below her. 'I see, miss,' he said. 'Will he be long, d'you think?'

'Oh no,' she assured him graciously. 'He's always very quick.'

Which was true enough. It hadn't taken him any time at all to find Queenie, and a glance had reassured him that she wasn't injured and she hadn't been arrested. But getting her back to the car was a different matter.

'Can't be done,' she said, infuriatingly. 'I got this kid 'ere, got concussion, I shouldn't wonder. They flung 'im right down a flight a' stairs. You park round the corner somewhere, an' I'll find yer soon as I can.'

'I drive all this way, worried out me wits,' he said angrily, grabbing her lovely warm arms and giving her a shake of exasperated fury. 'Now you come home, you hear.'

But she wouldn't budge. 'Leave off, Ploo,' she said and turned away from him towards that terrifying crowd.

It was too much. It couldn't be endured any longer. He seized her from behind, with one arm under her knees and the other round her shoulders and, almost before she realized what he was up to, had carried her bodily back to the car, even though she wriggled and kicked and beat his chest with her fists

327

and called him a bloody fool and ordered him to put her down *at* once. The crowd was delighted and offered Albert bawdy advice and cheerful applause, which he acknowledged with a wink and an evil grin. But the young policeman was very surprised, and watched with concern as Mary climbed into the back of the car and the unlikely 'lady' was lowered into the passenger seat.

'You all right, Ma?' Mary asked, scanning her mother's face for signs of injury. Ploochy'd rushed off to the bonnet of the car to crank the engine.

Ma gave her a grin. ' 'Course,' she said. 'Damn silly fool! What's 'e want ter go carting me off like that for?'

Because he loves you, Mary thought, and he doesn't want you to get hurt, and he's a bit frightened. Like me. But there wasn't time to say anything because Ma was out of the seat and out of the car and had dived back into the crowd like a seal returning to water.

Albert flung the starting handle to the ground with such force that it bounced up and hit the radiator. 'Bloody hell fire!' he said and set off in pursuit.

'That ain't a lady!' the policeman said, bolt-eyed with the surprise of recognition. 'That's Queenie Chapman. I seen 'er at a meeting. Well, I tell you, miss, if 'e thinks 'e can get Queenie Chapman to do somethink when she don't want to, 'e's a better man than I am Gunga Din.'

Mary laughed at him. Now that she knew her mother was safe, she felt almost lightheaded with relief. 'You watch,' she said. 'He might just surprise you. They're a good match.' She felt almost generous towards him. And it was true. They *were* a good match.

The man with concussion was gyrating like a bemused drunk. By the time Albert found Queenie again, Queenie had found him and was trying to persuade him to sit on the edge of the kerb. 'Can't afford it,' he said thickly. 'I'll go home in a jiffy. Can't afford it. I'm all right.'

'What can't he afford?' Albert asked.

' 'Ospital,' Queenie said.

'Is that all?'

'It is when yer skint.'

'Won't cost you a penny, son,' he said speaking loudly but

gently to the bewildered face between them. 'I'll take care of all the bills. Don't you worry about a thing. Just you come along with me, like a good lad. Short ride in a car and we'll have you fixed up as right as rain. Can you walk?'

' 'Course 'e can't,' Queenie said, scornfully, to show that she was still in charge of the situation even though he'd done exactly the right thing. 'Come on, some a' yer, look lively. Carry 'im to the car, if yer please.'

So the young man was carried to the car, and Mary and Queenie did their best to squeeze themselves into the narrow buggy seat, and the admiring constable retrieved the starting handle and set the engine juddering and they inched through crowd and traffic towards Hammersmith Hospital as though they had won a resounding victory. Which in many ways all of them had.

It took a long time to ensure that the young man was admitted because the casualty department was crowded with injured demonstrators, and some of their injuries were considerably more serious and gory than his appeared to be. While Ploochy was arguing with the Lady Almoner and Ma was giving particulars to a weary looking nurse, Mary remembered Tom Oxbury. He'd been at the demonstration too and nobody'd given him a thought. What if he'd been hurt? Poor Tom. What if he'd been hurt and he was all on his own, somewhere in this very hospital perhaps, with no one to look after him or comfort him or anything?

There was an admissions desk at one end of the hall, presided over by a friendly looking woman in a blue uniform. She'd know, surely. They must keep records of all the people admitted. There'd be no harm in asking.

The woman in blue consulted her book. 'Oxbury', she said, running her forefinger down the list. 'Oxbury – Oxbury. Yes, here it is. Tom Oxbury. Was that the one?'

'Yes,' Mary said, and found that her mouth was suddenly dry with fear. He *had* been hurt. 'Is he bad?'

'Twenty stitches,' the woman said. 'Fingers of his right hand. They hit him with a knuckleduster.'

'Where is he?'

'Gone home, I expect.' Then noticing how shocked Mary looked, 'He'll live, you know. It's only stitches. Right, who's

329

next?'

'Thanks,' Mary said, but the woman was already taking details from the next arrival. How brave! she thought as she wandered back to tell Ma the news. How very brave! Standing up for the cause, the way he always said he would, no matter what it cost.

'Tom's been injured,' she said proudly. 'Twenty stitches in his right hand. He was at the meeting. Inside the hall. Making a stand.'

'Good fer 'im!' Ma approved, and Ploochy beamed and looked pleased, so she decided it was safe to ask her next question. 'Can we call in at The Lion on the way home and see how he is, Ma?'

'Don't see why not, eh Ploo?'

But Albert was remembering Billy Jones and feeling rather ashamed of himself because he'd forgotten all about his original errand until that moment. 'Where did Billy get to?' he asked. He was chewing his bottom lip in distress, regretting the excitement that had caught him up and carried him along and made him forget, and the tell-tale gesture rocked Queenie into gentleness again.

'They arrested 'im,' she said.

His eyebrows knotted with anger. 'They did what?'

She explained, growing warm with remembered indignation. 'Ridiculous!' he said. 'They can't arrest you fer nothing. We find 'im. Stand bail. Get 'im out. We can't 'ave this!'

'There's a nick just round the corner,' Mary volunteered. So round the corner they went.

Hammersmith Police Station was nowhere near as welcoming as Hammersmith Hospital. They confirmed that Mr William Jones had been arrested, was now in the cells, and would come up before the magistrates at 10.15 the next morning, but they had no intention of allowing bail from any old Tom, Dick an' Harry who happened to drop by and offer it. It had been a long night and a bad one and the desk sergeant wouldn't be budged no matter how hard Albert tried. Both men were in roaring bad temper by the time it was finally established that Billy would have to stay where he was for the night.

'Tomorrow I be back!' Albert threatened, as he gathered his family around him ready for a dramatic exit.

'Very good sir!' the sergeant said, massively determined behind his important desk.

'Can we go an' see Tom now?' Mary pleaded as she and her mother ran out of the station following Albert's snorting anger.

'We should, Ploo!' Queenie urged. ' 'E might be bad, poor kid.' Anything to take his mind off this demoralizing defeat. He wasn't a man to take kindly to being pushed around by a bunch a coppers, not her Ploo.

'Damn rozzers,' he said, patting the nice warm bonnet of his car to comfort himself. 'Yes, yes, 'course we see 'im. Just let me phone the shop. Frank can nip down and tell poor old Harry 'e's not hurt.'

So Frank was phoned and given a message made unnecessarily complicated by anger and a crackling line, and then the three of them set off for Bermondsey, with Mary squashed beside her mother in the passenger seat because it was too cold now for sitting in the buggy.

Maisie Oxbury was very relieved to see them. She'd been worried sick she said, what with Tom and his poor hands and no sign of his father. 'Thank God they never done nothink ter you, Quee,' she said. 'Come on up.'

'Ravin' loonies!' Queenie said, as she followed her old friend up the stairs. 'An' the cops go an' nick our Billy.'

She and Tom were still re-living all the events of their extraordinary evening when the Ox returned with the news that the meeting had come to a rapid conclusion with over half the audience suddenly taking it into their heads to walk out. There'd been no end of a stink, he said. The nobs had had a shock.

'Good job an' all,' Queenie said trenchantly. 'High time they saw what was really goin' on. Do 'em good.'

'Don't know about you lot,' the Ox said, 'I'm starvin' 'ungry. How about some fish an' chips?'

So fish and chips it was, and presently they were all sitting happily round Maisie's kitchen table, and Mary was feeding Tom because he couldn't hold a fork in all those bandages, 'not with a hand like a bunch of bananas,' and Albert treated them all to drinks, and despite bandages and bloodstains life began to feel normal again.

Chapter Thirty-One

Although none of them knew it, at the very moment Albert's Alpha Romeo was purring along Putney Bridge Road into Wandsworth, Eric's little black Ford was rattling across Putney Bridge towards the sleeping turrets of St Mary's Church and the yellow lights of Putney Hill.

Eric was so excited he could barely contain himself. He was a man possessed, his eyes still blazing and his face so distorted with hatred that enlarged veins stood out on either side of his forehead, throbbing and swollen. He was shouting as he drove, but he hardly seemed aware of the noise he was making or the things he was saying.

'Scum!' he shouted. 'Jewish filth! Red trash! That's the way to deal with vermin. I should say so! Scum! My God, what a ripping meeting. Ripping! They won't be so quick to go shouting their mouths off the next time, thank you very much. Did you see our boys, Bunny? Weren't they ripping? That's the way to deal with scum.'

Anna sat beside him, watching the exhibition he was making of himself, her face cold with repugnance and horror. He enjoyed it, she thought. He's enjoying it now. He's absolutely vile. A monster! The knowledge that she'd married a monster made her quail, for niggling into her mind beside it came the fear that he would beat her like that if she didn't agree with every word he said. I don't like him a bit, she thought, watching his veins throb and his mouth distort ready for another tirade. Whatever did I marry him for? He's vile!

He gloated all the way home. Even the ancient calm of Wimbledon Common had no effect upon him at all, although it made Anna feel ashamed that he should be shouting obscenities in such a lovely place. She shut her ears and did her best to concentrate on something pleasant, like that darling dress she'd seen in D.H. Evans the other day, but the sound of his voice was as incessant as a hammer and far too much of what he was saying got through to her. And the more he shouted, the ranker the smell of sweat that steamed from his armpits. By the time they finally reached Clandon Close, she felt completely exhausted and distinctly nauseous.

'She's been a good little girl,' their nurse informed them. She'd woken up brightly when she heard their car at the gate and was rather pleased by the way she could instantly switch into an alert, professional stance, as though she'd been awake and watching all through the evening.

Eric wasn't the least bit interested in the behaviour of his daughter or the watchfulness of her nurse. 'Oh yes,' he said, dismissively. 'You can cut off home now. We'll settle in the morning.'

It wouldn't hurt him to drive the poor girl back to Morden just once in a while, Anna thought, especially now it's so late and dark. She must have had the most boring time looking after the baby all evening. But he never thought to offer, and she couldn't very well suggest it herself, especially tonight, considering the mood he was in. 'I'm glad she was good,' she said, trying to delay the moment when the girl had to leave them, and she'd be left on her own with the monster.

But Eric was shoving the poor girl's arms into her coat, and positively rushing her out of the house. He was so full of himself, and looked so very much like all those other dreadful bullies in their awful black shirts, that it made her feel quite pained to watch him. She had the most disagreeable sensation that he was stalking her, looking at her out of the corner of his eyes, noticing every move she made. And his breathing was really quite alarming, so tight and angry. She said goodnight to the nurse, keeping her voice deliberately light and bright. But the suspicion remained.

And of course, she was right. Eric had never felt as confident as he did that night. He was entirely sure of himself, full of a boundless, prowling energy and so horny he couldn't believe his luck. Now he had no doubt at all about the rightness of his cause, and the value of violence. That was the way to treat all subservient creatures, Jews, Commies, dagoes, queers, women. It was what they expected. You only had to see how effective it was to understand that. What they expected and what they wanted, in their nauseatingly subservient way. He'd always felt it, instinctively. And now he knew he was right. My word, he'd show Anna a thing or two tonight and no mistake!

But the stupid woman had opened the French windows and gone wandering out into the garden. What was the matter with her, brainless thing?

'Where are you going?' he called after her, crossly.

'Breath of fresh air,' she said. 'It's stifling in the house. Don't you think so?' The smell of his sweat had been quite overpowering in that hall.

He followed her out onto their newly laid lawn and stood beside her looking at the bare fence that marked the end of their bijou plot. It was a bleak, empty garden, but at least it was neat. And, of course, it was his. *His* garden to do what he liked in. He seized her by the shoulders and began to kiss her, fiercely and brutally. He was so horny he wouldn't have been a bit surprised if he'd come there and then.

His attack was so sudden and unexpected she was quite thrilled by it. 'Why, Eric!' she said, between kisses. And on a Thursday night too! Things were improving! If she could persuade him to wash they might have quite a good time.

'Come to bed,' he said, but to her disappointment it sounded more like an order than an invitation.

'Oh, not just yet,' she said. 'Let's stay out here for a little while, shall we? It's romantic in the moonlight.'

But he didn't want to be romantic. Stupid woman. He wanted to get her into bed and on her back. He kissed her again and this time with such force that her lips felt quite bruised afterwards.

'Don't be such a rough old thing,' she said trying to flirt him into being more gentle. But her plea had quite the worst effect. He kissed her again and more roughly than ever, filling her mouth with his tongue. She felt as though she was going to suffocate. 'Don't!' she said. 'Eric, please! I don't like it!'

'Liar!' he said fiercely. 'You love it! You know you love it!' And he began to pinch her breasts, tweaking her nipples painfully.

335

She struggled out of his grasp, that unpleasant fear fluttering in her throat. 'I don't like it, Eric. Really,' she said, but he was grabbing for her again, and the movement was so predatory she simply had to run away from it. She bolted back into the dining room, thinking that perhaps he'd calm down a bit once they were indoors. He looked so fierce and foreign in that white moonlight. But her flight didn't help her. Electric light revealed the flush and fear on her face, and seeing it made him crueller than ever. He pushed her violently against the fireplace, until her legs were nipped by the tiles and the back of her head crushed against the mirror.

'You love it!' he triumphed, and the smell of his sweaty armpits was right under her nostrils. She could taste blood on her lower lip and he was pinching her nipples again. 'Let's go to bed,' she said wearily. It was going to be absolutely horrid after all, so she might as well resign herself to it, and get it over with as quickly as possible.

He didn't notice her weariness or her resignation but charged up the stairs at once, dragging her by the hand, and chortling, 'That's the ticket! That's my girl! You love it!' He barely gave her a chance to get her shoes off, before he'd flung her backwards onto the bed and was ripping at her bodice with both hands. As usual he was working in the dark, and puffing and panting in the most horrible, animal way.

If I don't get out of this dress soon, she thought, he'll tear it to shreds, but she couldn't wriggle away from him, even for that. He was trying to pull her stockings off, and tugging with such force that two of the suspenders came away in his hands. He's like a wild beast, she thought, and for a brief, flickering second was almost thrilled again, but then he was on top of her and brutally inside, thrusting so hard and deep he was hurting her too much for her to be able to endure it for long. She did her best, gritting her teeth and holding on to the side of the mattress, like she'd done when Marlene was born, but he was taking a long time to come and the pain was increasing with every thrust. Soon it had become so sharp and stabbing that she knew she would simply have to stop him. 'Please, Itchy,' she said, pushing at his chest with both fists, 'stop a minute! Please.'

For answer he struck her round the side of her face with the flat of his hand, raising himself briefly to deliver the blow and then returning at once to his terrible, mechanical thrusting. The shock of it took her breath away and sent her senses into a state of panicking non-function. For a few seconds she couldn't see anything except a blotchy pattern of red shifting shapes that seemed to be pressing down onto her eyeballs. She couldn't move and she couldn't think what to do next. Then anger gave her a sudden burst of energy and she rolled her body away from that awful, hateful, hurtful cock, twisting herself until she got her hipbone under his belly, and then by heaving and kicking and struggling managed to wriggle out from underneath him and to roll off the edge of the bed so that she was sitting on the rug, with her knees under her chin and her hands clasped tightly round her shins, panting and sobbing but free.

He was still lying face downwards on the bed, and still jerking and bouncing. He's finishing it off on his own, she thought, with fascinated horror, and watched as the solitary rhythm continued until he gave his usual moaning groan and twitched to a halt. Well, thank God that's over, she thought. I was well out of *that*.

It was so quiet in the bedroom now that she could hear the little tinny tick of the bedside clock, and outside in what remained of the woods of Stoneleigh Park two owls, hooting eerily. Then the skin on the nape of her neck began to prickle and she realized with a lurch of her heart that Eric was staring at her again.

'You dirty, filthy little slut,' he said softly, spitting the words from between his teeth with the utmost venom and hatred. 'You just look what you've made me do. Nasty, unnatural thing!' He sounded as though he was crying. 'You're just a dirty, filthy slut,' he said. 'That's all. A slut! You deserve everything that's coming to you. And there's plenty coming to you.'

The threat in those soft hissing words was unmistakable. 'I don't know what you mean,' she said, trying to speak lightly, but staying where she was, with her knees under her chin.

'You know very well what I mean. Don't give me that. Working me up like that and then rejecting me, just at the very moment … Like a street walker. That's a street walker's trick. A dirty, low-grade street walker.' He was standing over her now, and threatening her with the whole of his body. Perhaps she ought to get up and run again. But where would she run to? Her heart was beating painfully and there was an odd roaring in her ears.

He grabbed her by the hair and yanked her to her feet, so that they were standing face to face in the quiet room. She was so frightened she didn't know what part of her body to try to protect first. Her stomach perhaps. He looked evil enough to hit her anywhere. But as she started to fold her arms across her chest, he brought his fist up into the side of her face, and at that she screamed and ran towards the bedroom door. He was after her in an instant, punching at her as she ran. A chair fell away from them and she made a grab at the corner of the dressing table and missed it and pulled the runner and most of her crystal vanity set crashing to the floor. He seemed to be everywhere she turned, punching and swearing, and some of his blows landed, on her face and her back and her defensive arms, but she was too far gone in fear to notice them. Only one thing mattered now. She had to get away. Into the spare room where she could lock the door against him. Or out of the house and down the road. Anywhere. Anywhere at all. Only away from his hatred.

'Stop it! Stop it!' she shrieked as she ran, and he hit her into the door with such force that the rug slipped from under his feet and nearly brought him down. His unsteadiness was the chance she needed and she took it quickly, plunging from the room and slithering along the landing into the spare room, grabbing the key from the outside of the door as she ran. For a few seconds they struggled for mastery of the door, he heaving to open it, she awkward with terror, frantically juggling with the key. But it locked at last, with the most delightful, satisfying, grating sound, and then there was a long pause while she sat on the spare bed, trying to breathe normally, and he kicked the door and called her a slut and ordered her to come out at once.

I shall stay here for ever, she thought. I shall stay here until you've gone. But she didn't dare move from the bed even though she was shivering with cold and shock and knew she ought to be under the covers. She was frightened he would kick

338

the door in. He seemed to have superhuman strength. If he does, I'll climb out of the window, she planned. I'll go to a police station and report him. He's a monster. Whatever did I marry him for? But he didn't break the door down, and at last she heard him stamp away to the bathroom. Still she didn't dare to move. She waited until the toilet flushed and the light clicked out and his footsteps passed her door and retreated into their bedroom. She listened, straining her ears as he moved about the room picking up the smashed pieces of crystal and putting them neatly back on the dressing table. Then the bed creaked as he climbed into it, and at long last she felt she was safe. She removed her crumpled clothing and, keeping her petticoat on for decency, climbed into the unfamiliar spare bed. As her head touched the cold pillow, she began to shiver and weep. I shall stay here for ever, she vowed. Oh, why did I ever leave home?

Chapter Thirty-Two

'It's going to be a beautiful day, Minnie,' Alice said as they came downstairs that Friday morning. The little front parlour was already warm, and the sunshine strong enough to project patches of colour through the stained glass of the front door to dapple the hall carpet.

Jesse was late back. 'It's gone half past seven,' Minnie grumbled. 'Where's 'e got to?'

'We'll have ours,' Alice decided, as she always did when her cantankerous cousin was late, because a slow start would put them out for the rest of the day. 'Nice little poached egg, Minnie?'

But just as Minnie was nodding her agreement there was a loud knock on the front door. A loud, foreign knock. Certainly nobody they knew or expected. 'Tut!' Alice said clicking her teeth with annoyance. 'Now who's that at this time of day?'

It was Constable Tullett, looking very out of place and shuffling his feet. 'Oh dear,' she said. 'I hope nothing's wrong.' A policeman on your doorstep always meant trouble. Not the children, she thought. Please don't let it be the children. It wouldn't be Albert. He was always so strong and healthy.

'Is Mrs Holdsworthy at home, ma'am?'

'You'd better come in,' she said, standing back to let him pass. Old Mrs Barberry opposite was twitching her net curtains already. 'If you'll just wait in here for a moment, I'll go and get her.' She'd ushered him into the dining room. It felt unused, but she could hardly show him into the parlour. She hadn't cleaned the grate.

Minnie came out of the kitchen, anxiously drying her hands

340

on her apron, and was abashed when Constable Tullett stood up to greet her. 'Yes?' she said, her face wrinkled with concern.

'Is Mr Holdsworthy home from work yet?'

'No,' she admitted. 'He's late this morning.'

'Ah!' he said ponderously. 'I see.' Then he paused, and took out his notebook, turning the pages with the end of a little brown pencil, carefully, as though he'd been given instructions that no finger prints should ever be left upon the paper. Alice found the performance irritating and alarming. 'Is something the matter?' she asked.

'Well now, ma'am,' he said at last. 'It seems a gentleman answering the description of Mr Holdsworthy met with a little – um – accident on the Embankment this morning. Now I'm not saying the gentleman *was* Mr Holdsworthy, you understand. They've just sent me down to check, as you might say.'

He's dead, Alice thought. Must be, or they'd have asked him who he was. If they haven't asked him, he must be dead, or unconscious, which is probably the same thing.

'What sort of accident?' Minnie said calmly. 'Is he hurt bad?'

It took quite a lot of umming and clearing of the throat and earnest consideration of the notebook before the constable finally confessed that the gentleman in question, who might very well turn out to be someone else, after all, had actually – um – been killed. He was sorry to say. Running across the road to catch a tram, by all accounts, and he hadn't seen the lorry until it was right on top of him.

'Poor man,' Minnie said sympathetically. The news didn't seem to have anything to do with her after all.

'Didn't linger,' the constable said. 'Nice quick death, if that's any consolation. He wouldn't've known much about it.'

'Well, that's a mercy,' Minnie said, still cheerful.

'The thing is,' the constable said carefully, 'they would like you to go along to identify the – um – body, so ter speak. On account of not being sure, you see, who it is, so ter speak.' He was very embarrassed.

'Of course,' Alice said easily, to put him out of his misery. 'We don't mind that, do we, Minnie? Where do they want us to go?'

So he left them with an address and detailed instructions about how to find the mortuary when they got there and who to ask for at the entrance, and then, settling his helmet back on a now perspiring bow, he trundled away.

'It can't be Jesse,' Minnie said confidently. 'He'd never get himself run over, not that one! He's much too fly.'

But they agreed they'd better go. Just to be sure. And they agreed that they really ought to have an escort. 'We can hardly go wandering about in a morgue on our own,' Alice said. 'It wouldn't be proper. I shall phone Albert. This is an emergency after all.' It was heaven sent. Something he simply couldn't refuse.

'Oh dear!' Minnie said. 'D'you think we should?'

But Alice was already asking for the number and wondering how she would feel to hear her husband's voice again after all this time.

It was a girl's voice, young and cool and polite, too young to belong to his woman, which was rather a relief, and too well-spoken to be a servant. 'No,' she said. 'I'm sorry, he's already gone. Are you phoning from Tooting?'

Baffled by the unexpected question Alice admitted that she was.

'Thought so,' the girl said. 'He's on his way to the court. He left in plenty of time. He said to tell you there's room in the car, if you and Mr Jones want a lift home. He'll meet Billy there, he says.'

'Thank you, dear,' Alice said, still polite although the conversation hadn't made sense to her. 'It seems he's gone off to court with Billy Jones,' she said to Minnie as she put the receiver back on its hook. 'Although what Billy Jones is doing in court I simply can't imagine. Isn't that just like Albert, rushing off to help somebody else just when we need him.'

'I'm not surprised Billy's in court,' Minnie said sagely. 'He went off on some march or other yesterday evening. Em was ever so worried. Knew there'd be trouble. She was only saying so yesterday morning in the baker's. What shall we do now?'

'We'll phone Georgie.'

'How awful!' Georgie said at once. 'Poor Aunt Min. I'll be over directly. Try not to worry.'

His concern was alarming. They'd been going along so

nicely Alice thought, not really concerning themselves with morgues or identifying bodies or anything nasty and unpleasant like that, and now somehow his seriousness had brought all these horrid things crowding back into her mind again, in nasty sharp little images that stuck like burs and couldn't be dislodged.

'We'd better get ready if we're going to this wretched hospital,' she said to Minnie.

'Should I go on my own?' Minnie asked meekly, because she could see her cousin was annoyed and was beginning to feel that all this nonsense was really rather a nuisance.

'Of course not!' Alice said. 'Whatever next?'

'It's such a nice day,' Minnie said sadly, gazing out into the temptation of the garden. 'It's a pity to spoil it.'

'We'll wait in the parlour,' Alice said briskly, 'and then we can see him the minute he arrives. The sooner we get this over with the better.'

But it wasn't Georgie's familiar cloth cap that appeared above the privet hedge twenty minutes later, it was Anna's unlikely blonde hair, swinging about her cheek, and framed by the expensive curve of her latest fashionable hat. They were both very surprised to see her, especially as she was wearing sun glasses as though it was the height of summer and a silk scarf folded tightly around her neck as though a cold wind was blowing. Alice's suspicions were aroused at once. She was up to something. You could see that with half an eye.

'Well, what a surprise,' she said as she opened the front door. 'What brings you here?' It didn't sound at all welcoming, Anna thought, but she couldn't trust herself to say anything just yet. She swept into the safety of the hall without a word, and carefully removed the dark glasses and the scarf to reveal a swollen black eye and a ridge of spectacular bruises.

'Anna! My dear child!' Minnie said, aghast. 'Whatever have you done?'

'It isn't what I've done,' Anna said wildly, 'it's what I'm going to do. Eric hit me. Isn't it awful? I'm going to leave him, Mummy. I've made up my mind. I've come home.' And she burst into tears.

'Come into the parlour,' Alice said, leading the way. 'Where's Marlene?' She was demoralizingly calm about it all.

343

'She's all right,' Anna sniffed. 'She's with her nanny. What am I to do, Mummy? I can't go back to Stoneleigh Park. He'll attack me again.'

'Well, you can't leave your baby all on her own, poor little thing, no matter what state you're in,' her mother said. 'What were you doing to drive him into such a frenzy?'

'I like that!' Anna shrieked. 'He beats me black and blue and that's all you can say! He's a monster. Don't you understand? A brute. Look at my arms,' and she rolled up her sleeve to show another batch of dark bruises all along her right forearm.

'All men are brutes, when it comes down to it,' Alice said, still perfectly calm. 'You have to learn to keep them in check. That's what marriage is about, isn't it Minnie?'

'Well ...' Minnie said doubtfully, 'you mustn't annoy 'em and that's a certain sure thing. That'ud be asking for trouble. No doubt about that.' But she spoke vaguely, her eyes still focused on the space above the privet hedge.

'You might at least give me a cup of tea,' Anna said, feeling more aggrieved by the minute.

'We're on our way out,' Alice said. 'We're just waiting for your brother and then we're off.'

'You can't leave me like this!' Anna wailed. But they were both looking at the privet hedge again. What was the matter with them? 'Don't you understand? I've walked out. I'm coming back home.'

'Well, that's up to you,' Alice said, as though they were discussing the choice of a new hat. 'You must do as you please. Just so long as you understand one thing. There's no room for you in this house.'

'Here he is,' Minnie said, trotting from the room.

'Oh, how can you say that? It's an enormous house. There's plenty of room,' Anna protested. But she was talking to the empty air. Her mother was already in the hall and opening the front door.

'Georgie, my dear,' Anna heard her say. 'You are good.'

'Are you all right, Aunt Min?' Georgie asked. He sounded unnecessarily anxious.

'Of course,' Minnie told him. 'I'll just get me coat and see Aunt Jane. We're all ready.'

'Anna's in the parlour.'

The parlour door opened and Georgie came in, still in his hat and coat. 'You coming too, Sis?' he asked. 'That's nice.'

'Coming where?' Anna said petulantly. 'What's going on, that's what I should like to know.'

'Haven't they told you?'

'Nobody tells me anything.'

'Uncle Jesse's been run over,' he said flatly. 'I've come to take them to identify the body.'

'He's not dead?' she said stupidly.

'Look's like it. Poor Aunt Min.' Then he noticed the bruises on her cheek. 'My word, you've been in the wars, haven't you!'

She opened her mouth to tell him her troubles but her mother forestalled her, returning softly into the room, with her black hat pinned firmly to her head, and her coat already buttoned. She was easing her gloves onto her hands, and watching the wrinkles disappear. She didn't bother to look at her daughter. 'We're ready,' she said.

And then they were gone. They didn't even seem to notice that they'd left her in the house on her own. She watched as they walked down the front path together, the two old ladies squat and dumpy, in their plain dark coats and old-fashioned hats, and Georgie between them, tall and quiet and contained, giving *them* all his attention and not even thinking about *her*. She was so upset she would have liked to scream. But what good would that do, with no one left to hear her?

So she began to drift about the house instead, wandering from room to quiet room, remembering and observing, like a ghost from her own childhood. The mustiness of the dining room surprised her, and so did the chill of the long drawing room. For the first time in her life she was aware of how cold the light was, blank on those elegant white walls, and realized that the room was north facing and never got any direct sunlight. That was a surprise, because she'd always remembered it as a warm, busy room, a Christmas room, with its great fire halfway up the chimney and people dancing and singing and laughing. There were no plants in the conservatory now, only empty flower pots and rusty croquet hoops and the dusty remains of an old crystal set. It looked as forlorn and deserted as she felt, and she was glad to drift away from it.

Through to the kitchen and the immediate smell of black

lead and breakfast, and, behind that the odd, familiar blend of cooking and washing, coal and kindling, soap and starch, bread and spices, flour and bacon, vegetables and dripping. She stood beside the table, trailing her fingers across the rough, ridged surface, fitting her nails into ancient knife slots, remembering the taste of her mother's food, Minnie brushing the tangles out of her hair, her father charging about roaring and teasing, she and Georgie stirring the Christmas pudding and making a wish, the smell of the orange blossom in high summer and sitting with her feet on the fender of a winter's evening. So much warmth and comfort and security. So many days and so much happiness and she'd taken them all so carelessly, and never realized how precious they were. And now here she was in a room that hadn't changed in all those years, beaten and belittled and denied. It was too bad. Tears of self-pity oozed from her eyes and fell onto the scrubbed white surface of the table, making little round dark patches like rain. The tangible evidence of her misery cheered her a little, although she couldn't have explained why, and drying her eyes she continued her tour.

Her bedroom was exactly the same as she'd left it and so was Georgie's, but that was no comfort to her at all, even though she'd hoped it might be. The library was the same too, still quiet and dusty and smelling of leather and print. She hadn't liked it much when she was a child, and she didn't like it any better now. Books were so frightfully dull. But on the other side of the landing was the door to her father's room, and that was a great deal more attractive.

All through her childhood she'd wondered what her parents' rooms were like, but as they had always been forbidden areas she'd never known for certain. Now, alone in the house with no one to stop her, she realized that she could walk in, if she wanted to, and see for herself. Greatly daring she opened the door to her father's room.

It was completely empty. There was a red Persian carpet on the floor, discoloured patches on the wall where the pictures had been, a dead bluebottle in the grate, and nothing else. She was suddenly and bitterly disappointed.

Now there was only one mystery left in the house, and that was her mother's room. That would be full of things, as she knew very well, and the knowledge deterred her for quite a long time, for she still felt she would be trespassing somehow, and trespassing on dangerously forbidden ground. But curiosity finally got the better of scruples. Her heart thumping with quite ridiculous guilt, she opened the door very quietly and crept in. And after all that, it was another disappointment. Expensive maplewood furniture, neat curtains, white bedspread, thick carpet, a well-kept, tidy room. Exactly what she ought to have expected. No mystery here.

There was an old wickerwork chair in one corner of the room, set between the bed and the window, and as it looked comfortable and inviting she wandered across to it and sat down. Until then she had been standing with her back to the fireplace and hadn't noticed that hanging on the chimney breast, dominating the room, was a large, old-fashioned studio portrait. It was a carefully posed study of a bride and groom, she in the long looped skirt and tightly buttoned bodice of Edwardian times, a small slim blonde with a fringe of short curls and the rest of her hair piled in a bun on top of her head, he in a dark suit and a high winged collar, wearing her father's bushy moustache and that unmistakable cocky expression. Good God, she thought, it's them! How young they were! I wonder why she keeps it hidden away in here? Then she realized that the picture would be the first thing her mother would see when she woke in the morning, for the bed faced it squarely, and with a sudden pang of sympathy she understood. She loves him, she thought. She still loves him. Poor mother.

She got up and went and stood in front of the picture, examining her mother's quiet young face, so still and withdrawn and contained, and her father's thick dark hair and bold eyes and air of easy confidence. I'll go and see Dadda, she decided. Even if Mary's there and still cross with me, I'll go and see Dadda. He'll know what to do. He always knew what to do. He knew it then, so I'm sure he'll know it now.

Chapter Thirty-Three

By the time Anna got to Lyndhurst Square the sun was really hot, which was quite a relief to her. For although nobody else was actually wearing sun glasses, as far as she could see from behind her darkened view, hers wouldn't look quite so terribly out of place in strong sunshine.

It wasn't her father who opened the door. It was a servant in an old-fashioned pleated apron and a dark dress that really made her very difficult to see from behind the shadow of those wretched glasses.

'No,' she said politely. 'I'm afraid Mr Ploochy's not at home this morning. Would you care to see Mrs Ploochy?'

Annoyance tightened its knot in Anna's belly. Mrs Ploochy! The effrontery of it! But she tried to push the thought out of her mind and to ignore the sensation. This wasn't the right time for annoyance. There were other, more important things.

'Oh!' Queenie said, coming to the door. 'It's you. Where's the baby?'

'I left her at home,' Anna said. 'I'm in a spot of bother. I want Dadda to help me.'

'I'm jest hanging out the clothes,' Queenie said. 'Come through.'

It was very dark indeed in the hall. Like being in a coal cellar, Anna thought. Despite her misgivings she removed her glasses and hung up her hat. Then she tried a hesitant smile at the housekeeper but that formidable lady was still correct and distant. 'This way, if you please, ma'am.'

Queenie was busy hanging up her washing. There wasn't very much of it, Anna thought, just a cotton frock and a cardigan. What a peculiar woman to be washing on a Friday.

'Right old muck this was last night,' Queenie explained, giving the frock a shake. 'All covered in bloodstains right down the side.'

'Good heavens!' Anna said. 'Were you in an accident?' Surely her father hadn't been hurt too. Or was that why he was out? Her voice was so sharp with sudden anxiety, that Queenie turned to look at her. And saw the bruises and the black eye.

'Bli' me! You been in the wars an' all, aintcher?' she said with sympathy.

'Dadda wasn't injured, was he?'

'No 'course not. 'E's gone off to 'Ammersmith. To court. Ter see justice done. I don't think! Billy got arrested last night.'

Hammersmith, Anna thought, arrests, police, and she remembered the frightening scenes of the night before. 'You were at Olympia,' she said.

'You an' all, eh?' Queenie grinned. 'Come on, mate, we'll sit out 'ere in the sun an' you can tell me all about it.'

There was a brand new, modern hammock in the garden, fatly upholstered, and shaded by a bright canopy. A lovely thing, Anna thought enviously, sinking into the thick cushions, and so comfortable, like a swinging sofa.

' 'Ave a fag,' Queenie said, offering the battered packet that was lying among the cushions.

So they sat in the sun together and smoked, and told one another the full story of the night's public events. And Anna said how horrible she thought the blackshirts were, especially Eric, and Queenie said how marvellous the Ox and Billy had been, and what a scandal it was that the meeting had ever been allowed in the first place, her eyes narrowed against the combination of smoke and sunshine and memory. 'An' your dad was a giddy marvel,' she said. 'You'd 'a' been proud a' your dad last night.'

Anna didn't doubt it. 'That's the way he always goes on,' she said when she'd heard all about his exploits. 'I wish he could have been at home this morning. He'd've known what I ought to do.' And she sighed with an unfeigned disappointment.

'Try me,' Queenie suggested. 'I seen a fair bit a' life in me time.'

But Anna wasn't sure. If her mother could reject her the way she had, then this woman would have every right to mock. 'I wouldn't know where to begin,' she said lamely.

'Start with the shiner. Who give you the shiner? Eric, was it?'

'Mummy said it was all my own fault,' Anna admitted. 'She said I must have provoked him. But I didn't. Honestly!'

Queenie's green eyes looked shrewd, but not unsympathetic. 'Your brother always reckoned 'e was a thug. Never said as much. You know Georgie. But that's what 'e thought. An' 'e's a good judge a' character, your brother.'

That's true enough, Anna thought. He is. She was encouraged by Queenie's candour. She might be Dadda's mistress, but perhaps it *was* possible to let her know some of it. After all, who else could she confide in, now? So the private story was told, hesitantly at first but then with increasing strength and passion until it was spilling from her mouth in a torrent of tears and self-pity and remembered fear.

Queenie listened to every word, watching and thinking, but she didn't say anything until the tale was over and Anna was sobbing into her handkerchief. Then she lit her last two cigarettes, handed one across, and stood up, dusting ash from her skirt. 'Now then,' she said briskly. 'First things first. We'll 'ave some dinner, 'cause I don't know about you, but I'm starvin' 'ungry, an' Mary'll be 'ome in a minute. Then we'll see what's ter be done. Mrs Midgeley can get some more chops. How'll that be?'

It was so unexpectedly kind and hospitable that it reduced Anna to helpless weeping. 'Buck up!' Queenie said, grinning at her. 'Worse things 'appen at sea. Think a' them poor beggars wiv concussion. I bet they won't get chops!'

Left on her own, Anna dried her eyes and smoked her cigarette and began to feel hopeful. It occurred to her that it was really rather extraordinary that she should be sitting here in Peckham waiting to have lunch with her father's 'other woman', and not feeling a bit guilty or embarrassed or anything like that. Even after all the things she'd been saying. Mummy would be furious if she knew. And so would Eric. Serve him jolly well right! Now and very briefly she remembered Uncle Jesse and wondered whether he really had been run over and killed. It all seemed very far away and rather unlikely, so she put the thought out of her mind. There wasn't anything she could do about it even if it was true, and anyway she had other and more important things to consider.

Mary came home just as Mrs Midgeley was dishing up the vegetables. The exam that morning had been more difficult than she'd expected and there were still concentration lines etched on her forehead.

'D'you get on all right?' Ma asked when she'd kissed her.

'I dunno. It was tricky.'

'We got company,' Ma said. 'That Anna. In a bit of a bad way. 'E's been giving 'er what for. Be nice to 'er.'

'Serve her right for marrying a Fascist,' Mary said fiercely. 'Did he hit her?'

'You'll see,' Ma said, as they walked into the dining room.

And that was true enough, Mary thought, gazing at her sister's bruises. She didn't say much more than hello, because she could see Anna had been weeping, and there was an awkwardness between them after the fury of that postcard. Nevertheless, they made a good lunch, despite the bruises and the awkwardness, limiting their conversation to exams and schools and the dreadful behaviour of the Fascists at last night's meeting. Mary told her sister all about Tom Oxbury and how bravely he'd stood up for the right, and Anna described the way the blackshirts had beaten their opponents to the ground. 'Made me feel quite sick,' she said.

'Told you they was wicked,' Mary said. 'Now you can see why I warned you not to go. They don't care who they hurt so long as they get their own way.'

'Yes,' Anna said humbly, 'you were right. I wish I'd stayed at home.'

'You two go out into the garden if you've finished,' Ma said suddenly. 'I'll make a pot of tea and bring it out.'

So they went out into the sunshine and sat down on the hammock together.

'Was it one of the blackshirts?' Mary asked, looking at the black eye.

'In a way, yes. It was Eric.'

'At the meeting?'

'No, after we got home. He got so worked up watching – and then when we got home he was like a mad thing.' She could hardly tell this girl the full story of what happened. It would put her off sex for life.

351

'Does he often …?'

'No. He's never hit me before. He yells a lot. I'm quite used to that. And has the sulks afterwards. This is the first time …' She fingered her bruises delicately, remembering.

'What'll you do?' Mary asked, pitying her.

'I don't know. I came here to see Dadda.'

'Yes,' Mary said. ' 'Course.' It was the sensible thing. He'd know what to do.

Anna sighed and gave her sister a bleak smile, thinking how sympathetic she was.

'I'd leave him if I was you,' Mary said. 'No man's got a right to do that to any woman.'

'I'm his wife.'

'All the more reason.' And she thought of Ploochy and how tender he was with Ma.

'But where would I go?' Anna said. 'Mummy won't have me. She says there isn't room.'

How unkind, Mary thought. She *is* her daughter. But there was Ma rattling out towards them with a tray full of tea things. 'Tea!' she called as she approached. 'How's that?'

'Better! Much!' Anna said. 'You're very kind.'

'My old lady always used ter say, everythink's worse on an empty stomach.'

'Yes.'

They drank their tea and enjoyed the sunshine and Anna felt cared for.

'I been telling Anna she ought ter leave him,' Mary said.

'Quite right,' Ma agreed. 'You got a wrong 'un there with that Eric. You stay with 'im, 'e'll beat you whenever the fancy takes 'im. That's the way they go on, men like that. If I was you, I'd clear out.'

'Now?' Anna said. 'Just like that?'

'Why not? Today. While the going's good. Take yer baby, an' yer clothes, an' money if you've got any, an' clear out.'

'She hasn't got anywhere to go, Ma,' Mary said. 'Her mother won't have her.'

'Quite right an' all,' Ma said. 'Never go back 'ome. Not if you want ter survive. It's the first rule a' survival, that is. No, you'll 'ave ter get a job. Support yerself. Be independent. A job, an' a little flat somewhere. There's plenty a' cheap flats if

352

you know where ter look.'

'But what about Marlene? I can't work with a baby.'

'Plenty of women work with babies. You could get a job in a pub, like I did. Work nights. There's plenty a' ways, if you mean business.'

She doesn't care for me after all, Anna thought. She's just like all the others, telling me to look after myself. She felt limp with disappointment. The sun was still shining in an absolutely flawless sky, birds were singing, and the garden was heady with roses and honeysuckle, but it was a harsh world, just the same.

'It would suit him down to the ground if I did that,' she said. 'He'd have the house and the furniture and everything. And that's not fair, because it's all my money, not his. He might have paid the mortgage for a few months, but that's all. Everything else came from my side of the family. Oh no! Why should he benefit when he's in the wrong?'

'Well, it's up ter you, ain't it? Why stay with 'im an' be a punchbag?'

'Can't she stay with us, Ma?' Mary said suddenly.

'Could if she wanted to,' Ma said, but her face wasn't welcoming as it ought to have been. It was guarded, almost as though she expected Anna to attack her. No, she was thinking, you can't come here. I've got enough problems in my life without taking you on.

'No,' Anna said, and Mary noticed that she was assessing the look too. 'I don't think that would do. Not really. There wouldn't be room, would there? Not for me and Marlene.'

'You could share my room,' Mary said impetuously. 'I wouldn't mind a bit. I could help you with the baby.'

Anna turned on the hammock and put her arms round Mary's neck and kissed her. 'You are a dear,' she said, smiling her gratitude. 'But I couldn't. Not really. Your mother's right. I've got to sort this out for myself.'

'Well, I don't think that's fair,' Mary said hotly.

'I should never have married him in the first place,' Anna [said], and now she sounded sad and resigned. 'Still, there you [are]. I made my bed. Now I must lie on it.'

[I] don't see why you should,' Mary said. But Anna was [gettin]g up.

['I'd] better go,' she said. 'The nurse'll be waiting to get off.

353

I've been away too long as it is.'

They followed her into the hall and watched as she adjusted her hat on the side of her head and arranged her hair so that it would swing across her face and cover the worst of the bruises.

'Tell him you'll leave him,' Mary urged. 'See if that'll make him behave any better.' It was dreadful to see her drifting back like this. He might beat her again. It wasn't fair.

'I'll try,' Anna said. 'It isn't easy. He doesn't like discussing things.'

'I 'ope it all works out fer yer,' Ma said. 'Come an' see yer dadda. See what 'e says, eh?'

'Yes,' Anna said vaguely.

This time she didn't bother with dark glasses. She and Mary and Queenie kissed at the doorstep as though they were old friends, and then she drifted away into the sunlight. If people wanted to look at her injuries, well let them. It wasn't her fault she'd married a thug.

Albert and Billy and Harry Jones had found a nice noisy pub not far away from the courthouse and were having a pie and a pint. Harry was dishevelled with worry and embarrassment, and ate his pie as though every mouthful was a puzzling experience, screwing up his eyes and munching cautiously. 'Can't see the justice of it,' he said. 'Don't make sense.' Billy had been found guilty of a breach of the peace and fined £25.

'Prejudice!' Billy said angrily. 'That's about the size of it. Didn't 'ave a cat in hell's chance. None of us. Breach a' the peace! I ask yer!'

'I can't understand it!' Harry said, scratching his head with both hands. 'An' you a soldier an' all.'

Billy had made a particular point of stressing his war service. 'I was at Passchendaele,' he'd declared with pride. 'I wa' wounded at the Menin Road, in the Great War. The war to en' all wars. I was one a' the ones who fought ter keep the peac' But the magistrate, who'd spent his war comfortably behin' desk, and well and safely behind the lines, hadn't been a impressed with such an irrelevant plea.

'You shouldn't 'a' paid the fine, Ploo,' Billy said. 'Not v ain't grateful, 'cause I am. I wouldn't want yer ter think grateful. It's just ... well, it ain't right. Not 'anding

354

across ter the state. I should 'a' gone ter jail.'

'An' 'ave yer mother an' Dora up the wall with worry,' Harry said, annoyed that his son should be saying such things to his old, old friend, especially when he'd just been so very generous.

'Live ter fight another day, Billy,' Albert comforted. He'd lived in Queenie's company long enough now to know the right way to handle this situation. 'Take it as a contribution ter the cause. You'll do more good outside the jail than in.'

It was late afternoon before they were all back at home after their eventful day.

Alice was still feeling shattered after identifying Jesse's body in that awful morgue. She spent the afternoon in the garden on her own, having put poor Minnie to bed and drawn all the blinds in the front of the house. It was such a nice day it seemed a pity to waste it, and anyway there was nobody around to criticize her. She was glad Anna had gone. The day had been difficult enough without her making a fuss. And in any case it wasn't as if there was anything she could do to help. Much better to keep out of it and not interfere between husband and wife. So she and the cat sat in the hammock under the cherry tree and enjoyed the sun and were peaceful together. And why not?

As Albert let himself in the front door at Lyndhurst Square, the telephone started to ring. Queenie had come out into the hall to answer it, and as she was looking an inquiry at him, he told her Billy's news before he picked up the receiver. 'A fine, that's all.'

'Bloody unfair,' she said and left him to the call.

It was Georgie making preliminary arrangements for Jesse's funeral.

'Old Jesse Holdsworthy's been knocked down by a tram and killed,' Albert said as he joined Queenie and Mary in the drawing room. And he told them what he'd heard. 'I never knew such a day!' he said. 'Everything happen at once. One bad thing after another.'

'Troubles come in threes,' Queenie said, and told him about Anna.

His response, as Mary was quick to appreciate, was

immediate and practical. 'She must leave 'im,' he said. 'She must come an' live here. We can't have our Anna knock' about.' Even though he was tired and shocked, his face was determined.

'We offered,' Queenie said, 'and she wouldn't. Wants ter be independent.'

No, Mary thought, that's not quite true. You put her off. You must know you put her off.

'I will go an' see 'er,' Albert said.

'You'll see 'er at the funeral, wontcher?' Queenie said.

'Dear God!' Albert said, his shoulders drooping with weariness. 'What a day it's been!'

But Mary was watching her mother. Why do you want to keep them apart? she thought. It was the first time she'd ever known her do anything that wasn't completely open and honest. How odd love is, if it can make Ma devious.

In Clandon Close Anna was apologizing to her nursemaid. 'I shouldn't have been out all day. You must have had a terrible time. I'm so sorry. But my uncle was run over you see. Killed outright I'm afraid, so I had to stop.'

'How dreadful!' the nursemaid said, instantly sympathetic. Then she noticed her employer's face and looked away, tactfully.

'Shocking, isn't it!' Anna said, still marvellously bright. 'Mr Barnes took me to a political meeting last night, you know, and it all got out of hand. Abso-bloomin'-lutely! Punching one another and everything. It was awful! Trust me to get in the way. Silly old me!'

The nursemaid was impressed. 'Poor you!' she said, her eyes round with awe and admiration.

Well, *that* was easy enough, Anna thought, pleased by the skill with which she'd carried it off. The excuses had come so glibly into her mind as she journeyed homewards, almost as if Fate had arranged all these events just to suit her purposes. She still hadn't made up her mind what she ought to do, but she supposed she ought to discuss it with Eric. She couldn't just walk out. Could she?

Chapter Thirty-Four

There was no discussing anything with Eric, because Eric was speechless. Not momentarily bereft of words but deliberately, perpetually, irritatingly mute. Stony faced with it, his eyes unseeing, his head as still as a snake, chill and withdrawn, as though he and the world had already parted company. Ever since Friday morning when Anna had made all that unnecessary fuss, refusing to come out of the spare room and treating him like a criminal, he had retreated into total non-communication. It was the only defence he knew.

At work he was his usual jovial self, but once he stepped through the front door in Clandon Close he folded himself into irreproachable silence. He would eat whatever Anna put in front of him, without comment or pleasure, and at bedtime he would wash and undress and apparently go to sleep as soon as he'd slid neatly into the bed. He would listen to the wireless and read the paper, but he wouldn't talk.

At first Anna found his behaviour irritating and ridiculous, and spent a lot of time berating his silent face. She told him how stupid he was, and how she didn't care if he never spoke again, and how it didn't make any difference to the way she felt about him now, not after the way he'd hit her. 'You can show off as long as you like,' she said furiously, 'you won't get any sympathy that way. You're being absolutely childish.' But the silence persisted, and after a week she relinquished the effort to break through it and just let him get on with it. It was stupid and annoying, but at least he wasn't shouting at her, and she had a feeling that while he was speechless he was less likely to hit her and his silence allowed her to sleep in the nursery with Marlene, which at least put her out of harm's way at night.

When Georgie's carefully worded letter arrived suggesting that it would be very much appreciated, especially by Mother, if she and Eric would come to support Aunt Min at Jesse's funeral, she read it aloud to him, as though he'd gone blind as well as mute.

He listened impassively, his face blank, his eyes focused on some distant, inner world.

'Well?' she asked. 'Are we going?'

Silence.

'It's no good you just sitting there. I shall have to answer it.'

Silence.

'Am I to accept or not? Don't tell me you can't answer a simple question.'

But the silence persisted.

'Oh, very well, if that's the way you want to go on,' she said. 'I shall accept for both of us, and *I* shall go. You can do what you like. See if I care.' He was impossible, showing off like that.

On the morning of the funeral he got up as usual and while she was hiding her bruises under a thick layer of make-up he shaved with his customary precision and then, rather to her surprise, and still without saying a word, put on his funeral suit. When the nursemaid had arrived and taken charge of Marlene, he switched off the wireless, put on his bowler and strutted out to the car. Anna wasn't at all sure whether she was supposed to travel with him or not, but as he didn't seem to notice when she climbed into the passenger seat, she assumed she was doing the right thing. He drove to Tooting, tight lipped and withdrawn, like a robot, and Anna, sitting beside him in their nasty, claustrophobic little car edged her body away from him and wondered how she would ever be able to explain his behaviour when they got to Longley Road.

She needn't have worried, for he became himself again the moment his feet touched the pavement outside the house, like an actor assuming his part as he walked from the wings. He greeted Georgie in appropriately hushed tones, and told Aunt Min how sorry he was to hear of her great loss, and kissed his mother-in-law like a dutifully loving son, and when he discovered that two members of Jesse's chapel had arrived he buttonholed them at once and was soon discussing the sadness of the occasion in his very best manly manner. It was quite astonishing. And horribly unnatural.

It was a blustery day and the sky above St Nicholas' church was turbulent with rain cloud. As the funeral procession arrived outside the church gate, a shower began, the falling drops scattered by intermittent gusts of wind, and rippling across the surface of the road.

They proceeded to the church hidden from one another by umbrellas. And a good job too, Anna thought, for really she'd seen enough of Eric that morning to last her a lifetime. Perhaps if she dawdled she could sit next to someone else at the service, Dadda perhaps, or poor old Aunt Min. She did look odd, poor old thing, with the most vacant expression on her face.

Minnie was certainly in a most peculiar state, vague and forgetful and oddly detached. Afterwards she said there was a moment during the ceremony when she really felt they were burying somebody else. 'The way those fellers talked,' she said, still shaking her head with disbelief, 'I had to keep pinching meself. Did you ever hear anything to equal it?'

Alice had to admit that she never had. For the Father of Jesse's chapel had spoken at the service and the things he'd said had been quite incredible. 'A fine man, Jesse Holdsworthy, a good workmate,' he began. And the two women had thought, well you'd expect something like that. But then he went on to even more fulsome praise. 'A real socialist, working for his fellow men.' Jesse? Grumbling, swearing, cynical Jesse? 'Accepting long hours, always there when he was wanted.' Because he preferred being at work to being at home, Alice thought sourly. 'A fine dry sense of humour. Always ready with a joke. A pleasure to work with.' At this, Minnie and Alice had blinked at one another in total disbelief. A joke? Why, they'd never heard Jesse make a joke in all the years they'd known him. How very, very peculiar. But they noticed that the two men looked genuinely upset as the coffin was lowered, so perhaps they'd meant what they said, unlikely though it seemed.

Albert was careful to stand with Georgie and Lily and the children at the graveside, well behind Alice and tactfully hidden by Dickie's umbrella. But he couldn't avoid the reception and so at last found himself back in the dining room at Longley Road, feeling oddly as though he'd never left it, and yet at the same time pricklingly aware that the house seemed forlorn and not so well cared for, and that the air in the dining room was faintly damp. While Anna and Eric and the two union men were walking up the path from their cars, he took Minnie to one side and kissed her and arranged for her to stay on in the house and keep Alice company.

Then Eric was in the room being suave and handing out sandwiches and saying the same unctuous things, over and over again in his unnecessary voice. 'A fine man! A great loss! Sorely missed!'

'What's the matter with him?' Minnie said to Anna. 'What's he on about?'

'Oh, don't take any notice of *him*,' Anna said. 'That's just the way he goes on. Come on over here by the fire and get comfy. It was cold in that churchyard.'

'Are they going soon?' Minnie asked querulously. 'We don't want all this lot hanging around, do we, Anna?'

'I'll get you a cup of tea and then we'll shift 'em,' Anna promised, even though Mummy's eyebrows were raised.

But before she could start throwing out hints, the two union men had walked across to say goodbye.

'A fine man,' the Father said again, shaking Minnie's hand. 'You must miss him sorely.'

'Thank you for coming,' Alice interposed, because Minnie had her mouth open and she was sure she was going to say something dreadful. 'We do appreciate it.'

'Do you think he really was as good as all that?' Minnie asked when her trade union guests were gone. The more she thought about it, the more unlikely it seemed. But Anna had gone to get her a cup of tea and people were milling about so. Nobody would stand still long enough to tell her what they thought. She held on to Dickie Chanter's arm. 'What do you think, Dickie?'

'Quite possible,' Dickie said. 'I know a lot a' blokes led double lives, one thing at home an' quite another at work.'

'Well, they certainly liked him,' Anna said, returning with the tea and giving it to Aunt Min with a special smile. Then she

360

turned her head towards her mother so that she could signal a question at her. Time to send people home? Shall we start?

But Alice was looking strained and near to tears. The smell of Albert's cigar was pervading the room, and it had roused such a rush of memories that it was paining her to receive them. I shall have to stop this funeral on my own, Anna thought. 'Goodness!' she said brightly. 'Is that the time? We shall have to be getting back, Eric. Nanny will be anxious.'

It was a strong signal and she delivered it perfectly. Suddenly they all decided that the funeral was over, and a flurry of leavetaking began. Within five minutes the room was empty, and Alice and Minnie had been left to recover alone.

Within seven minutes Eric was speechless again. But this time Anna didn't mind. Despite the bad start to the day, she felt rather pleased with herself. She had made a very good job of this funeral and the union eulogy had given her an idea. If he wanted to play dumb all the way home so much the better. It would give her a chance to think it through.

By the time they were back in Clandon Close he was totally enclosed in silence again, withdrawn and unseeing. He climbed out of the car, mechanically, and marched into the house ahead of her, his spine rigid. His briefcase was found, his tie changed and then he was out of the house again and on his way to the station. Good riddance to bad rubbish, she thought.

The kitchen smelt horribly sour and the nurse looked harassed and rather shamefaced. 'She's been a bit sick,' she explained, still washing down the high chair. Marlene was sitting on the floor in an ungainly huddle. She had a fistful of sponge fingers and was devouring them with unhealthy concentration.

'She's always eating,' Anna said, observing her. 'I'm not surprised she's sick.' She was seeing things with quite extraordinary clarity on this extraordinary day. The baby was far too fat, her flesh folded over itself like that ugly little man on the Michelin tyre advertisement. Why, she couldn't even sit up properly and at eight months she ought to have been able to do that, at the very least. And there was the reason, clear and mangled, sticking out of her gross fat hands. The nurse was feeding her to keep her quiet. 'Has she been screaming?' she asked.

'Oh no, Mrs Barnes,' the girl hastened to assure her. 'She's been ever so good. Good as gold.'

'You *do* stick to the schedule?'

'Oh yes, ma'am. Of course I do.'

She's lying, Anna thought, and she's scared half to death in case I find out and dismiss her. 'She's a greedy little thing,' she said, smiling at the nurse, 'we'll have to watch we don't overfeed her, won't we?' Her tone was light and her smile was as charming as she could make it, but the nurse still looked anxious. 'Don't worry. I'm not blaming you. Greedy babies are terribly difficult to rear.'

The smell of sick was beginning to overpower her. 'Carry on!' she said brightly and went out into the garden to see if there were any roses she could pick.

That night, when the nurse had gone home, she watered the baby's bottle, and felt quite smug when Marlene settled to sleep sucking it as she usually did and didn't seem aware of the change. 'We'll get rid of that nurse,' she said, as Marlene's white eyelids folded down into her fat cheeks. 'She's not feeding you properly, and you're my baby, aren't you? Things are going to change around here.' It gave her the most pleasant sense of decision and power.

And there was better to come.

After their silent dinner, Eric got up and walked out into the hall to collect the evening paper, which he'd left neatly folded on the hatstand, awaiting his perusal. Anna, following him, noticed with pleasure that his face revealed a momentary twitch of annoyance when he couldn't find it.

'I've put it away,' she said. 'You can have it in a minute. I've got something to say to you first.'

He didn't even bother to glance in her direction, but stalked off into the lounge. If he couldn't read the paper he would listen to the wireless. But the wireless had disappeared too. There was an empty space on the table where it ought to have stood, and the room looked odd and incomplete without it. Frowning, he turned to face his wife. She was looking insufferably smug.

'That's right,' she said. 'I've hidden all your toys. If you can't speak, you can listen. I've got something to say to you, and I want to be quite sure you hear it.'

362

He sat down in his armchair and closed his eyes. But she went on. 'Funny about Uncle Jesse, wasn't it,' she said, her tone pleasantly conversational. 'A proper Jekyll and Hyde he turned out to be. Nasty, disagreeable thing at home, always swearing and grumbling and bossing everybody about, and such a nice man at work. Made me wonder.'

He would have liked to look at her, but didn't dare. He could hardly open his eyes now he'd closed them so firmly. But his eyelids trembled and that encouraged her. 'Don't you want to know what I wondered? Oh, I'm sure you do. You don't have to say so. I wondered about you. I know what you're like at home. We both know what you're like at home. Now, I wonder what you're like at work.'

He was getting uncomfortable, his eyes rolling underneath the determined blank of their lids. She came and stood in front of him so that her body would block the light from the window and he couldn't avoid knowing she was there. Now and abruptly she changed her tone. 'So you listen to me, Eric Barnes,' she said harshly. 'I give you fair warning. You've beaten me up once, and that's once too often. If you ever lay so much as a finger on me again, I tell you what I'll do. I shall go straight up to the Foreign Office, just as I am, bruises and all, and I shall show your boss and your precious office workers just what sort of a man you really are.'

Now his eyes were open and angry and afraid. 'You bitch!' he said. 'You wouldn't dare!'

She was surprised to find that she wasn't frightened of him. 'Oh yes,' she said calmly. 'I would. Make no mistake about it.'

Tears began to spill from his eyes. 'Now I'm off to the pictures,' she said. 'Your toys are in the wardrobe.'

He jumped to his feet, the tears streaming unchecked. 'Oh no you don't, you bitch!' he shouted. 'You've got a baby to look after. Remember? You're not walking out and leaving me with the baby. Don't you think it. If anyone's going out, it'll be me.'

'Suit yourself,' she said calmly. 'I don't care what you do, just so long as you leave me alone.'

So he had to go out. It was very annoying, because he'd been looking forward to a nice quiet evening at home. Well, he wouldn't walk the streets just to satisfy that bitch, he told

363

himself as he walked jerkily along Clandon Close. Not likely! He'd go and visit his mother. That's what he'd do. She'd make him feel welcome. She knew how to treat a man. She might even put him up for the night, if he played his cards right. That would show her! Threatening to go to his work like that. The very thought of it made the pit of his stomach turn quite cold.

His mother and father were listening to the wireless when he arrived, and they weren't a bit pleased to see him.

'Well, you might have given us warning,' his mother said acidly when she opened the door.

'I thought you'd like a surprise, Mater,' he said, giving her the customary dry peck on the cheek.

'You know I don't like surprises,' she said. 'Still, I suppose as you're here you'd better come in.'

It was a very difficult evening. Eric did his best to be bright and provocative, peppering them with enviable information about his success at work and his dazzling social life in Clandon Close, but it didn't ring true even to his ears, and his mother was very cutting.

'Fancy!' she said, when he'd just finished a glowing description of a cocktail party. 'I wonder you can find the time for surprise visits, the way you live.'

'Oh well, you know me, Mater dear.'

'Yes,' she said tartly. 'I do.'

'I suppose that wife of yours is as wild as ever,' his father said.

'So vivacious!' Eric parried, trying to sound as though he meant it.

'Too extravagant for me,' his father said, 'thank you very much!'

'Just as well she's not your wife then, Pater.'

'Your father had more sense, when *he* got married,' Mrs Barnes said, scoring her point with a reptilian narrowing of the eyes and the slightest quiver of a smile. 'One flibbertigibbet in the family is quite sufficient, I should say.'

'We're thinking of joining the tennis club,' Eric tried.

'Oh!' his mother said, not giving an inch. 'Can she play?'

They didn't offer him coffee and they didn't ask him to stay, and after the late night news they started gazing pointedly at their nasty little cheap clock on the mantelpiece. But he sat it out. What else could he do? He couldn't go home. Not to that bitch. Not now. Finally his mother was forced to attack him with a hint so direct that he simply couldn't avoid it.

'I don't know about you, Eric,' she said, 'but some of us have got to get up for work in the morning.'

'Oh, it's early yet, Mater,' he said, trying to sound casual and cheerful, but hearing to his horror that the words emerged with the whine of pleading.

'Dear me!' she said. 'Haven't you got a home to go to? Surely you're not tiring of that marvellous wife of yours? Don't tell me that!' She looked so insufferably smug he would have liked to hit her.

'No! No!' he said immediately and defensively. 'I just thought you'd like a little more of my company, that's all. Ever the dutiful, you know.'

She gave him a look that was pure triumph. 'Not at this time of night,' she said firmly. 'So there's nothing to stop you from going home to your wife, is there?'

So he had to leave them. And although he said, 'Toodle-pip!' in the cheeriest way and walked away from the house as jauntily as he could, he didn't have the faintest idea where he was going.

He drifted vaguely through the dark streets, unformed thoughts revolving endlessly and uselessly somewhere underneath a throbbing headache, and after a very long time he found himself beside the small, sour enclosure of the Wandle Park. There was a bench down at one end and the sight of it made him aware that he felt very tired and that his feet were aching. He would sleep there, on that bench, that's what he'd do, and see how she liked that.

It was jolly uncomfortable and very smelly because the space underneath the slats was filled with garbage, but having folded his waistcoat into a makeshift pillow he lay down on his back with his arms across his chest and tried to will himself to sleep. An hour passed stiffly, but no matter how hard he concentrated he just couldn't drop off. His feet were cold, and his back ached, and he felt very, very sorry for himself. Then, to make matters worse, a policeman arrived, suddenly and from behind the dazzling attack of a torch.

'You can't sleep there, sir,' a deep voice said from the black void behind the glare.

Eric agreed at once. 'No, no, constable. Of course not. I was, er, waiting for my train. So tired I must have …'

'What train was that, sir?' the voice said implacably. The spotlight of that awful torch didn't waver.

'To Morden,' Eric said. 'Must be due soon.' And he made a pretence of looking at his watch. 'Yes. Yes, it is. I must be off. Thank you for reminding me, constable.'

'Every ten minutes to Morden, this time a' night,' the policeman said. 'You'd be warmer in the station.'

'Very true!' Eric agreed again. Then there was nothing for it but to take up his waistcoat and set off for the tube. Damn police! Always around where they weren't wanted. Why didn't he go and catch a few burglars or something?

It was past two o'clock when he finally crept into the back garden in Clandon Close. There was nowhere else for him to go, but he had no intention of entering the house and giving that bitch the satisfaction of knowing he'd had to come home after all. The garden shed was open and the garden shed would do for what remained of the night. It was almost as uncomfortable as the park bench, being cramped and dusty and full of earthy tools and ankle bruising piles of flower pots, but at least it was warmer and rather more private. He found a heap of sacks to sit on and after a certain amount of shuffling and wriggling eased himself into a position in which the lowest shelf would more or less support his back. Then, as sleep seemed totally impossible by now, he gave himself up to the miserable inner luxury of self-pity.

Other fellers had all the luck, he thought. Wives who doted on them and never said a word out of place, mothers who worshipped the very ground they trod on, cute, obedient, *quiet* children. And what did he get? He had to put up with all this, that bitch of a wife, that horrible Blob screaming all the time, parents … well, the less said about them the better. Nobody had ever loved him. Not in the whole of his life. Not once. Nobody had ever said, 'darling Eric,' and really meant it. And it wasn't as if he ever did anything wrong. He was always well behaved, obedient to a fault, passing all his exams, swotting and revising and God knows how difficult *that* had been, and he'd never complained or refused. Not once. He'd always done his very best. And this was how he was rewarded. Why was life so monstrously unfair? Why, even policemen were hateful to him now, and that really *was* the end. Because he'd always obeyed every authority immediately and without question. He was still trying to make sense of it when his head juddered towards his chest and he was asleep.

When Anna got up next morning and went downstairs to make a bottle for Marlene, he was still asleep, his huddled shoulders and bent head clearly visible through the little shed window. So that's where he was, she thought. Stupid fool! He must have been jolly uncomfortable stuck in there all night. Well, serve him right for showing off. She stood before the kitchen window, filling the kettle slowly and thoughtfully, and looking at his head with loathing.

I'll leave him, she thought. The very first opportunity I get, I'll walk off and leave him. Whatever did I see in him? Nasty, spiteful, dishonest thing! And a plan for self-preservation began to crystalize inside her cool morning brain. I'll save up enough money for a deposit on a really nice flat. In Peckham, perhaps. Somewhere near Dadda and Mary. She didn't have the faintest idea how she'd ever get a mortage, or ever find the money for the repayments. It was enough to dream of taking the first step. I'll sneak it out of the housekeeping, she thought, marg instead of butter, cheap cuts of meat, that sort of thing. He'll never know the difference. And that nurse can go straight away. She's just a waste of money. I won't ask Dadda. It's no good depending on other people because they can let you down. I'll do it all myself. Thoroughly independent. And the very first chance I get, off I'll go.

Chapter Thirty-Five

Saving money turned out to be a very slow business. There were always so many demands on her purse and the housekeeping was little enough to start with. Two years went by and she still hadn't reached her target, and now, to make matters worse, the target figure wasn't high enough and had to be raised because rents and deposits were going up again. It was really rather demoralizing.

Time passed slowly and there were few compensations. She'd dismissed the nursemaid and that certainly made a saving but it also meant that she was very much tied to the house and could only afford to pay a minder for one outing a week.

Marlene had grown into a rather unprepossessing toddler. She was still far too plump, with pale, rather pasty skin and lank, straight, pale brown hair. But Anna looked on all that as a challenge, for she had made up her mind that, whatever sort of life she was actually going to lead herself, her daughter was going to be a success. She'd already enrolled her at the local dancing academy, and now she was transforming her and preparing her. 'You're going to be the prettiest little girl that ever was. So pretty. Everybody will love you. They just won't be able to help themselves. And you'll marry a nice, *kind* man. I promise you. A nice, kind, *gentle* man. You'd like that, wouldn't you? Then you just sit still while I fix your pretty curls. Mind you don't get your frock in a mess. You won't look pretty with a dirty face. Stand still! Don't fidget! Keep your head up! Smile!' And the child did her best to give her mother what she wanted, learning to lisp and pose and keep clean and toss her curls, and remember to be pretty.

The pretty curls took a great deal of effort. Each one had to be soused in bay rum every night and then rolled up into a tight little sausage and fixed into position against Marlene's bewildered skull with a hair grip. The process took at least twenty minutes and the resulting mass of wedged hair and ironmongery was almost impossible to sleep on. On the first night of her uncomfortable beautification, Marlene had spent her sleepless time unpicking as many curls as she could manage. But the next morning her mother's anger had roared about her tatty head like a nightmare, and she'd soon learnt not to repeat her unwanted behaviour no matter how much the curls might hurt her.

Eric paid no attention to any of it. Children were a wife's responsibility, everybody knew that, and in any case the Blob was just an uninteresting nuisance, better avoided. He and Anna had settled into a state of subdued but perpetual warfare, a sarcastic sniping that was even sharper and more intense than his long battle with his mother. Nowadays he was very careful not to mark her if their anger reduced them to actual fighting. He would shout at her and shake her, and sometimes he would throw her about, but usually only when there was a bed handy to break her fall, and never so roughly that she had bruises to show for it.

Although there was an element of fear in these furious exchanges, in a perverted way Anna almost relished them. They gave her the opportunity to appear pale and interesting at the next tea dance she attended and to tell her partners how badly her husband treated her, so that they in their turn could advise her to leave the brute, and tell her she was much too pretty to be wasted. 'Oh,' she would say, fluttering her eyelashes at them, 'but I couldn't leave my baby.' And then they would tell her how brave she was, and what a good mother she was and, safe in the knowledge of her unshakeable fidelity, how much they would like to take care of her if only she was free. Their flattery and feigned concern gave her the most pleasurable moments of her week. Soon she was spending every penny she could spare from her savings or wheedle from her father on her self-enhancing hobby, treating herself to elaborate dance dresses and wickedly high-heeled shoes and, when she was particularly depressed, buying herself a dancing partner from the sixpenny enclosures. She knew that her blonde hair and her skilful make-up looked most attractive in the muted light of a place like the Locarno, and in the summer, when she'd acquired a healthy tan, she felt like a film star in her long, slinky gowns covered in sequins all down the front and cut daringly low at the back to reveal her nice brown skin. Eric could shout all he liked, but he couldn't take that away from her. And if she had to stay with him she'd get as much pleasure into her life as she possibly could.

She and Mary wrote to one another two or three times a week and she took Marlene to Lyndhurst Square nearly every Sunday and, that, in an odd, disjointed sort of way, was more comforting and sustaining than anything else, for at least there was one person in her life who would listen and sympathize when she spoke about how she really felt.

From time to time, when Eric had been particularly repulsive, Mary would urge her to leave him straight away. 'Never mind the flat. Just walk out.'

'One of these days I will,' she promised. 'When I've saved the deposit.'

'You an' your deposit,' Mary said, affectionately. 'Why don't you let old Ploochy buy a place for you? I know he would if you'd only tell him.'

But Anna was adamant. 'No,' she said. 'This is something I must do for myself. I'm nearly there. It won't be long now.' It was a matter of pride.

As the months passed into years, Mary knew she was growing more and more fond of this determined woman who might be her sister. Her pride was touching and admirable, and so was her capacity for endurance. She's very like me, she would think. That's what I'd do. If I had to. And it seemed to her that life was very unfair, to give her so much happiness and Anna so little.

For since Lower Schools Mary's life had been ridiculously happy. She'd just completed two years in the charmed world of the sixth form at St Olave's, studying her three favourite subjects, history, music and English, with her three favourite teachers.

She knew with her reason that human beings were capable of cruelty and torture and murder; that there were nearly two million unemployed in England alone and the National government didn't seem to care; that the Italians had been gassing unarmed tribesmen in Abyssinia; that terrible things were happening in Europe, with Hitler re-arming and moving troops into the Rhineland and persecuting the Jews and putting anyone who dared to oppose him into the most fearsome concentration camps; and that in Spain, the fascist who hadn't been elected was leading an army of thugs against the elected government, but none of it really touched her. Her study of history showed with comforting clarity that even the most brutal dictators are eventually defeated, and in the meantime there was Chaucer's subtle urbanity to enjoy and Shakespeare's incandescence, Debussy and Brahms and the inspiration of Beethoven's soaring Hymn to Joy. When her English teacher maintained that all men had the capacity for good, she nodded in happy agreement. She simply couldn't help feeling that however bad things might be at present good would ultimately prevail.

She'd even revised her opinion of old Ploochy. There was no possibility of her ever accepting him as her father. That was unthinkable. But she had to admit there was a lot of good in the man, and he'd certainly made her mother happy. Neither of them seemed to have aged since they set up house together. In fact if anything they actually looked younger now, even though they were both going grey. Queenie's hair was speckled with silver but, oddly, that only made her look softer and more loving, and there was no doubt her face was much prettier now that it had rounded out a bit. And he fairly bristled with well-being, his dark eyes snapping with pleasure and his moustache so perky and thick.

Sometimes she would watch the two of them sitting close together on the sofa, or talking directly and intimately to one another at supper time, or rushing off to the pub or the pictures as excited as children, and she would envy them. One day, she promised herself, I shall meet a man who will love me in just the same open, uninhibited way. At college perhaps. Or when I start work. But these were dreams she kept to herself. Or at least, almost to herself. She told Anna of course, because it was easy to tell Anna things these days. And she told Tom Oxbury because she and Tom had no secrets.

'He's bought her a string of pearls for Christmas,' she told him one evening as he was escorting her home from the Old Vic. He could always be depended on to take her to the theatre when there was no one else around. 'I can't wait to see her face when she opens them. She'll go potty!'

'I'd buy you a string of pearls if I had the money,' he said. Notice me, Mo. I'd do anything for you.

'Soppy thing,' she said laughing at him. 'I don't want pearls. Don't suppose I ever will. No, I shan't mind if my husband isn't rich. I'd like him a bit better looking than old Ploo, though. He's generous to a fault but he's no oil painting.'

'That lets me out then.'

'You've always been let out,' she grinned. 'You're different. You don't have to be goodlooking. You're my big brother.'

And you don't marry your big brother, he thought, no matter how much he loves you. The length and ease of their relationship was an invisible and insurmountable barrier between them, but he was the only one who could see it.

'Only six more weeks to go,' she said, changing the subject abruptly, 'and then I start college. I still don't know whether I'm looking forward to it or not.' It had been such a wrench leaving Stogs, and now two years at Goldsmiths' College training to be a teacher didn't seem as attractive as it had when she'd applied.

'Only two more weeks to go and I start work,' he reminded her. Now that he was the proud possessor of a second class degree in economics he'd taken a teaching post at a private grammar school on the Dulwich border.

'We're both in the same boat,' she said. 'Changing. I suppose things have to change. It's all to the good really. But sometimes I wish they would stay as they are.'

'I don't,' he said. 'There's lots of things I'd like to see changed.' And the way you react to me would be one of them.

But they'd reached their stop.

Dickie Chanter was feeling pleased with himself. 'Landin' a plummy new job, my time a' life,' he said to Albert with cheerful pride. 'Whatcher think a' that?' He'd been offered a contract by the B.B.C., no less, to take part in a series of programmes on the music halls, as one of four accompanyists to the old-time stars.

Albert was impressed and said so. 'How d'yer manage it?' he wanted to know.

'Ol' Florrie Entwhistle,' Dickie explained. 'She give 'em me name. First I knew of it was when the letter come.' It was an impressive paper bearing the B.B.C. crest and a polite invitation to Mr Richard Chanter to come to Broadcasting House for an audition. 'So I puts on me old bib an' tucker, an' off I goes. An' Bob's yer Uncle.'

'Lucky beggar!' Harry said cheerfully. He was genuinely pleased by Dickie's success. 'Fancy a friend a' mine on the wireless. When they gonna broadcast it?'

'Start Monday after next,' Dickie said. ' 'Alf past seven. Not bad, eh?'

' 'Ave ter lissen in ter that,' Albert said.

In October Mary started her new career at Goldsmiths' College. Ploochy was very proud of her, but to her disappointment her mother took very little notice. For in October the hunger marchers took to the road again, from Jarrow with a woman M.P. at the head of the column, and from South Wales, Merseyside and Scotland behind the N.U.W.M. banners. Provision had to be made for them, and that meant many hours in Bermondsey, and fatigue and bad temper at home when plans went astray for lack of cash or time.

But it was the Spanish civil war that concerned Queenie most passionately. In September, when the T.U.C. voted for non-intervention, she and Billy and the Ox were enraged by the folly of it. From then on, she spoke at every local trade union meeting that would invite her, urging them to put pressure on the T.U.C. to change their minds and support the beleaguered Spanish government. 'So it's only a coalition,' she said over and over again, 'but it's a coalition a' the left, an' it's led by a man who done everything 'e could ter get the unions tergether internationally. The sort a' man we ought ter support, fer cryin' out loud. Specially against a common enemy. 'Cause make no mistake about it, our government can bleat on all it likes about non-intervention, it won't stop that Hitler and his fat friend Mussolini. They'll intervene whenever they feel like it.' But her audience were afraid of another war and argued that anything was preferable to that, even placating a fascist.

'Sometimes, Ploo,' she said wearily to Albert after one particularly exhausting meeting, 'I begin ter wonder if the whole darned world ain't slowly goin' barmy.'

'You're done in,' he said. 'Give it a rest, Queenie. Let someone else go to Merton tomorrow, eh?'

But she wouldn't hear of it. 'That's 'alf the trouble,' she said, 'leavin' it ter someone else. It's up to every one of us. We all got ter do our bit. An' fer why? 'Cause if we don't them buggers'll win.'

It worried him that she was so totally and exhaustingly committed to all these causes, noble though they might be. 'She's wearing herself out,' he said to Eth the next time she came to visit them. 'I wish I knew how to get her to stop.'

'You'll never stop our Quee,' Eth said. 'Change the world singlehanded she will. Always the same. Even as a kid. You got yer work cut out with our Quee, Ploo. I could a' told yer that 'fore you started.'

'Can't get her to take time off,' he said. 'Not even five minutes!'

'You'd 'ave more chance if you was Spanish,' she said, laughing at his doleful expression.

'That's an idea,' he said.

Two days later he came down to breakfast in the full, flamboyant regalia of a Spanish matador, bearing a home-made placard on which he'd written in bold block capitals, 'Adopt a Spaniard.'

Mary got an attack of the giggles at once, because he looked so extraordinary in that unexpected uniform, all bright red and pink and orange and black, with his moustaches waxed to the sharpest of points and his eyes gleaming with devilment. But Queenie rose from the table and flinging her arms round his neck bombarded his face with kisses. 'You great, daft, darling loony,' she said, punctuating every word with a kiss. 'Didden' I adopt you years ago?'

'Adopt me again,' he said cuddling her, 'an' come to the pictures tonight.'

'It's a bargain,' she said. And then the two of them burst into song, 'He shall die, he shall die, he shall die tiddly i ty ty ty ty ty ty ty,' and Queenie, clicking her fingers like castinets, did a very fair approximation of a flamenco dance while he circled her happily, making passes with his little cloak. 'Oh, I'll raise a bunion on his Spanish onion, if I catch him bending tonight,' they sang, laughing and stamping their feet. And Mrs Midgeley, coming in inquisitively to see what all the noise was about, but with a tray to explain her presence, laughed out loud at the sight of them. 'Cabaret time, Mrs M.', Albert explained. 'We're going to the pictures!'

Despite politics and unemployment and the threat of war, it was a good life, Albert thought, this almost-marriage to Queenie. Her honesty and her lovely easy affection cast a glow over every day, no matter how much or how little of it they actually managed to share with one another. He used to think he only needed two more matters to be settled for his existence to achieve perfection. One was for Alice to agree to a divorce, but that grew more and more unlikely, and less and less necessary as the years went by. The other was for Mary Ann to accept him as her father, and although that was something he still yearned for, he was coming to accept that it too was very unlikely.

Until the evening of November 30th.

Chapter Thirty-Six

'You wouldn't be going anywhere near Crystal Palace, would you, Ploo?' Mary asked as she sorted out her music that Monday evening ready for the rehearsal of the Amateurs.

'An' what's wrong with the bus?' Queenie said.

'It's nicer in the car,' her daughter said, looking hopefully at Albert.

'Be ready in five minutes an' I'll take you,' Albert said. How could he refuse her when she looked so pretty and so exactly like her mother? He and Queenie were going up to Broadcasting House. They'd promised to meet Dickie and his old-time stars in a nearby pub after the broadcast. 'It's not far out of our way.'

'Not much! You spoil 'er,' Queenie said, as Mary rushed from the room to put on her hat and coat, but she was smiling at him. 'Great softie!'

'She *is* my …' Albert began, but then Mary was back in the room again so the conversation had to stop.

Mary liked the Crystal Palace, especially now that the Imperial War Museum had moved out of the place and all their guns and tanks had been cleared away. There was something so splendidly eccentric about it, sprawling along the length of the parade like some enormous greenhouse between its odd twin towers. In sunlight the glass shone like water, and the trees inside the nave were as green as seaweed, and by night the colonnades glimmered row upon elaborate row and the high domes were mysterious with shadow. She like the grounds too, with their lakes and fountains, and their pre-historic monsters, and their sloping lawns, and their impressive white stone staircases. A luxurious place, extravagant and Victorian and popular. And nowadays there was always plenty going on there, dog shows and cat shows, brass band festivals, dancing, firework displays, dirt-track racing, regular rehearsals, and, now and then, performances of the Crystal Palace Amateur Orchestra.

That night they were rehearsing in the Garden Hall, which was a place she particularly enjoyed because of the lovely resonant echo the strings produced in the glass dome above them. They were playing a Haydn symphony and she was waiting for the special moment in the third movement when the first violins would soar up and up in a splendid crescendo and the glass overhead would ring and sing. It made the hair on the back of her neck rise with pleasure, no matter how many times she heard it.

But that night the glass gave out a very different sound, a dull, flat, lifeless note that made the first violins look up in surprise. And as they looked the great Handel organ began to groan, long, sobbing sounds like an animal in extreme pain. The rehearsal petered out, as the players looked at one another in alarm, but then one of the cellos stood up abruptly and clumsily, knocking his music stand to the floor. 'Good God,' he yelled. 'Look at that! The place is on fire!'

And so it was. The centre transept was gushing red flame, and the piles of chairs that were usually stacked in the middle of it were burning like a bonfire.

'Everybody out!' someone shouted, needlessly. But as they were scrambling to their feet, grabbing at music cases and instruments, Mr Andrews was climbing onto a chair.

'There's no danger yet,' he said with a most authoritative calm, and Mary noticed that he was speaking, not shouting. 'If you will all make sure you've got your instruments and music cases and personal belongings, I will follow with the music. Use the two doors behind you. Straight across the lawns.' His shock of unruly hair was like a tawny halo above his head and he looked so solid and reassuring their panic was diminished by the sight of him. 'Quick as you can,' he said.

Mary tucked her violin under her arm, grabbed her case, and ran out with the rest, her heart still pounding with the suddenness of the alarm. How could the Crystal Palace be on fire? It wasn't possible. Glass didn't burn, did it? Surely not.

377

Someone would soon put the fire out. It was the chairs, that was all.

Out in the dark evening they stumbled across the grass bank together and down the steps and gathered on the pavement on the opposite side of the Parade. After a few minutes Mr Andrews arrived with a bundle of music and a list and began a methodical check to ensure that they had all got out safely and that none of their instruments had been left behind. He was splendidly calm. They stood in a stunned group all around him looking back at the blaze.

'All present and correct, Ralph?' the leader asked.

'Yes,' he said, showing the neat row of ticks beside his list. 'No casualties.'

There was a red glow of fire behind the bright glass of the centre transept and even as they watched it shot out a long spurt of flame southwards into the rest of the building. The fire took hold beneath it immediately, and spread so rapidly they could hardly believe their eyes. Black figures were running inside the building, beating at the flames. They looked frighteningly small and ineffective.

'Has anyone gone for the Fire Brigade?' the French horn wondered.

'They must have,' Ralph Andrews said, but he decided to walk down to The White Hart just to make sure.

By now crowds were beginning to drift onto the Parade and the musicians were soon surrounded by curious bystanders and found themselves telling the tale to an admiring audience. Now that she was out of the building and knew that all the members of the orchestra were safe and accounted for, Mary was really rather enjoying the excitement. Like everybody around her she had decided to stay and watch the Fire Brigade at work. 'Wonder how long it'll take them to put it out,' she said to Mrs Benwood, her fellow violinist.

'Hour or two, I should say,' Mrs Benwood estimated. 'They're very clever.'

But when the first fire engine arrived, clanging bells and driving right up to the wall, the firemen took a far more serious view. Within three minutes the crowds had been shepherded right back to the edge of the grounds and all the blackened amateur fire fighters had been called out of the inferno; within ten, more fire engines began to arrive, as the flames roared and spread in their melting glass cage, and sparks leapt high into the air from the falling timbers, and spurts of red fire fountained through the roof. The crowds grew by the minute as people came by bus and train and tram, on foot and in cars, to see for themselves. Soon the mass of watchers was so vast there was no more room on the pavements. And still they came. And Mary stayed among them, mesmerized by the strength and power of a blaze that was now clearly out of control.

But Ralph Andrews went home. 'Now you're all safe,' he said, explaining his departure, 'I'd rather not see it burn.'

'He's a funny chap sometimes,' Mrs Benwood said, watching him struggle through the crowd. 'Can't stand anything violent, you see. I knew he'd go.'

Before long the roadway was lined with a wall of fire engines, fifty or sixty at the very least, and before them the ground was tangled with hoses, coiled across and beside each other like a gigantic nest of fat grey snakes. The firemen nearest to her were busy dousing the south tower, which was still miraculously untouched, and the heat from the blaze was so intense that their faces were running sweat.

'Did you ever see the like?' Mrs Benwood said. 'It gets worse and worse.'

'It's going to burn to the ground,' Mary said, and the words made her heart contract with terror and pity. That huge, beautiful, familiar building was going to be burnt to the ground.

At that moment the great transept began to fall with a terrible roaring and grinding. 'Get back!' people yelled. And, 'Oh my God!' But their words were lost in the thunderous noise. It was a long, slow fall as the remains of the transept dropped like a great ship sinking in heavy slow motion into a sea of flames. Sparks from its fall rose so far into the sky that they couldn't see the height they reached. It was an awesome collapse.

Mary was in tears. 'It's awful, Mrs Benwood,' she said, her upturned face shining red in the unnatural light. 'It's like the end of the world.' It seemed shameful to her now that she'd been excited and happy when this fire began.

'Perhaps we ought to go home,' Mrs Benwood suggested, but she couldn't take her eyes from the blaze.

'No,' Mary said, watching intently, 'we can't go yet. We ought to see the end of it.' It would have seemed disrespectful just to walk away from such a conflagration.

So the two of them stood together arm in arm and watched as the south transept folded and buckled and fell, and the end wall crashed like a wave and the blaze grew white hot. In the silence that followed that second fall, there was a sudden gentle, whirring sound. 'Like birds,' Mary said, looking up into the smoke. And she was right. The sky above the tumbling wreckage was suddenly full of small birds, struggling upwards like black sparks, flying free and frantically from the terror of the burning air. Somebody had opened the aviaries.

News of the fire had spread all over south London. It was the main and most excited topic of conversation on Billy Jones' tram; Alice and Minnie had toiled up their four flights of stairs to the attic rooms to see the glow in the sky; and by eight o'clock people were talking about it in Broadcasting House. The programme on the music hall was over and Dickie had taken all the participants round the corner for a celebratory drink.

It had been a splendid reunion. Dickie was on form, teasing and cracking jokes, and so was Florrie Entwhistle. She was still blonde, even though her hair was as sparse as a baby's, and she still wore the brightest colours even though she was nearly sixteen stone and well over eighty. 'Come an' give us a kiss, me old cock sparrer,' she commanded Albert as soon as he arrived. 'Whatcher think a' this, eh?'

'Best thing that happen in a month a' Sundays,' he told her and was kissed resoundingly on both cheeks for his opinion.

They would have gone on till long after closing time if the producer of the programme hadn't come down to stand them all a drink. 'Big fire over Sydenham way,' he said when the round had been bought and partially consumed. 'We've been watching it from the roof. Sound engineer reckons it's the Crystal Palace.'

'Couldn't be,' Albert told him confidently. 'That's all glass, the Crystal Palace. Glass don't burn.'

'That's what I said,' the producer agreed. 'Looks exciting though, whatever it is. You can see the glow from here.'

'What say we go an' have a look, Queenie? We could pick Mary up on the way. Rehearsal must be over by now.'

'Right old rubber neck you are,' she mocked him, but she agreed to go.

'What about you, Dickie? Want a lift?'

'Be a lark,' Dickie said. 'Ta!'

So they went, and were astounded at what they found. At Tulse Hill the roads were blocked with parked cars in every direction. So they left their's behind all the others and joined the crowd, following the black silhouettes of all the caps and hats and bowlers that were bobbing along in front of them. And emerged at last into the Palace grounds to see the great Crystal Palace ablaze, the fantastic glass place that Albert had been so sure couldn't burn, incandescent with white hot fire from one end to the other, the twisting window frames black against a billowing fireball that swelled and heaved behind every colonnade. The hall of glass where they'd left their precious daughter a few careless hours ago. For a few seconds they were all so overawed by the spectacle that they couldn't move or think. But then Albert recovered and, frantic with anxiety, began to push his way through the dense crowds with Queenie in his wake, hanging on to the belt of his coat, and Dickie somewhere behind them both.

Most of the people he elbowed so roughly out of his way were annoyed and said so, but when he explained, breathlessly and with his face creased with anxiety, that his daughter was in the building, even the most aggrieved allowed him through. Soon, by dint of shoving and questioning, he found a fireman who was resting from his exertions and assured him that everybody had got clear of the building and nobody was hurt.

'Then where is she?' Queenie said.

'Gone off home most likely,' Dickie tried to comfort.

'This is dreadful,' Queenie said. 'I never thought it'ud be like this.'

'South tower's still standing,' Dickie said, glancing to his left at the firemen still dowsing the high walls of the tower.

'That's the Baird Television Company they're saving,' the man beside them said knowledgeably. 'Mr John Logie Baird keeps all his papers there, so they do say.'

The tower was glistening with moisture in the eerie light of the flames. 'It'll be the only thing left,' Queenie was saying, when Albert gave a sudden roar and began to wave his arms above his head.

'Mary!' he yelled. 'Mary! Mary!' And there she was, no more than a hundred yards away from them, standing in the crowd gazing up at the flames, perfectly safe and perfectly all right.

'It is her!' Queenie yelled. 'Thank Gawd fer that!' Then the mass of people around them moved and shifted, so that their brief view was blocked, but it was Mary, they were both quite sure of it.

'We find her!' Albert promised. 'Shout again!'

'She can't 'ear yer, Ploo,' Queenie tried to reason. 'Not in all this.' But he went on shouting and waving, his voice puny in the uproar of sounds around them. And a figure detached itself from the packed ranks to their right and turned and began to run towards them. A slim figure, carrying a music case and a violin, dodging through the crowds, running lightly, her face clearly lit by the great fire, a radiant face. And he recognized the expression and suddenly felt such an upsurge of happiness that his throat was full and he had to stop calling. She was skimming towards him just as her mother had done so often at the very start of their affair, her face shining straight at him with the same open, overwhelming affection. She loves me, he thought rapturously, she loves me after all, and he lifted his head and stretched his spine, already swaying towards her and the moment when he could catch her in his arms and tell and be told.

And she ran straight past him. She was so close there were only three people between them, but she didn't see him. His disappointment and bewilderment were so acute he was afraid he was going to cry. Then he became aware that Queenie had put her hand in the crook of his arm. 'Oh look,' she said her mouth close to his ear. 'It's Tom. Innit lovely!' Mary had run full tilt into the broad chest of young Tom Oxbury and now the two of them were actually clasped in each other's arms and he was kissing her and lifting her off her feet.

Afterwards, Mary couldn't account for the way she'd turned

her head, at just the right moment, and see Tom Oxbury looking for her in that enormous crowd. But that's what she'd done. And seen him so clearly, worried and loving and protective. Her dear, dear Tom. She ran without thought, because the sight of his face had told her so much. She knew instinctively that she had to get through to him quickly and stop him worrying and tell him she was safe.

He didn't see her until she was nearly on top of him and then he put out his arms and scooped her into the air and before either of them really knew what was happening to them he was kissing her with passion and relief in an upsurge of emotion as powerful as flame. And she was kissing him back.

'Oh my darling, darling, darling,' he said. 'I've been frightened out of my wits. I thought you were dead. Oh, I love you so much. I couldn't have borne it if anything had happened to you. Oh my darling, darling, darling.' The fire was roaring all around them and he couldn't stop kissing her. 'I love you, love you, love you!'

'Oh I know,' she said. And she did know. She'd known all along, only she hadn't realized it until that moment. 'And I love you!' She felt as though she was exploding, as though sparks were leaping from her head into the sky, as though she and the fire were one and the same, her love for him was so strong. She flung her arms round his neck, violin case and all, and kissed him again and again.

'Oh Ploo! Innit lovely!' Queenie said again, watching them.

Albert couldn't see anything lovely about it at all. But he didn't get a chance to say so because Queenie and Dickie were already pushing their way through the crush of bodies, and within seconds she was hugging Mary and kissing Tom and they were all talking at once in a babble of relief and excitement.

'I thought she was in the building,' Tom said, still cuddling Mary against his side. 'Did you hear me calling?'

'Where were yer?' Quenie asked.

'At school. We had a meeting and when Mr May came in and said ...'

'Nothink short of a miracle,' Dickie was saying.

'You been 'ere long?' Mary was asking her mother. 'Did you see the transept go? Wasn't it terrible.'

383

And then the crowd caught its communal breath and gave the long, indrawn groan that was a signal that something awful was happening. They turned to the fire again immediately, to see what it was. Streaming from the remains of the building was a sort of grey foam that rushed and tumbled down the grass embankment and scattered across the lawns. Queenie was the first to understand what it was. 'Rats!' she said. 'Hundreds and hundreds a' rats. Oh my good Gawd!' The terrified creatures swarmed into the grounds, scuttling to left and right, running over one another's bodies and across hoses and over feet. Then they were gone and a new wave was descending.

Mary's eyes were round with the horror of it. 'It's like the end of the world,' she said.

'We've seen enough fer one night,' Queenie said. 'Let's go 'ome.'

Albert was still demoralized by too many unwelcome emotions. He'd waited so long and used up such a lot of hard-earned patience trying to do the right things so that Mary would love him and now, just when he felt she had begun to accept him, that silly boy had got in the way. Fancy running past him like that. She hadn't even seen him, and they'd been so close and he'd been calling her so loudly. The fire was depressing enough, but this was worse. No, he thought, Queenie was right. They ought to go home. 'Want a lift?' he said to Dickie.

But Dickie decided he might as well stay where he was and see it out to the finish. Albert was very glad to hear it, because that meant he could take Queenie and Mary straight home in the car. But Mary had other plans now.

'I'll come home with Tom,' she said. 'Could you take me fiddle, Ma?'

'Damn ridiculous!' Albert grumbled as the car rattled down Westow Hill towards Norwood and the detour that would take them home. The night seemed very dark now that they were away from the fire. 'Why she not come home with us? Silly girl!'

'You know very well, you soppy thing,' Queenie said. ''Cause she wanted ter be with young Tom. An' quite right too.'

'A boy like that,' he growled. 'It ridiculous. She's not old enough to know her own mind.'

'Oh, Ploo!' she said laughing at him in the darkness. 'You're jealous!'

'I am not.'

'Oh, go on with yer. You got a yellow streak right down your back. You got ter let 'er go some time, you know.'

'Not now. She too young.'

'She ain't. She's the same age I was when I took up with you.'

'That,' he said angrily, 'was different.'

'That,' she said, cuddling against his side and still laughing at him, 'was exactly the same. You ain't gonna begrudge yer own daughter a bit a' love, surely ter goodness?'

'I love her,' he said stubbornly. 'Why can't she love me?' He was very hurt.

'Won't I do no more, then?' she asked teasing him, but then they drove past a street lamp and she saw how miserable he was. 'It's only natural,' she said gently. 'You wouldn't've liked it if someone 'ad disapproved of us.'

'Someone did,' he said remembering Alice. 'Someone still does.'

'Don't make no difference though, does it? Not when all's said and done.'

Tom and Mary took a very long time to get home that night. They walked part of the way, because traffic near the fire was in such chaos, and because they needed time to talk and kiss and tell one another over and over again how very much they loved one another. It was past two in the morning before they reached Lyndhurst Square and past five before they were finally able to say goodnight and part for what little remained of the night. 'You'd better sleep in the spare room,' Mary whispered as they left the drawing room, still cuddling one another. 'No point going home now.'

'This *is* home,' he said dreamily. 'Wherever *you* are. That's home.' And of course that provoked even more kisses.

And so they parted for an hour or two.

When Ma woke them, they were both pale with exhaustion, but Tom got up obediently and came down to breakfast, looking sheepish and happy. Mary stayed where she was, luxuriating in the smell of the fire on her skin and the warmth of the memories in her mind. Tom loved her. Tom, dear, old ordinary Tom had turned out to be her darling after all. It was still almost too good to be true.

'You'll be late, you don't get up directly,' Queenie warned from the foot of the stairs. And the telephone rang.

Mary listened as her mother answered it. Then she called, 'It's for you. It's Anna. *Now* will you get up?'

She skimmed down the stairs to tell her sister. 'Anna? Yes, I'm perfectly all right ... No, no one was hurt ... No, listen Anna, you'll never guess ...'

Chapter Thirty-Seven

It was the most miserable weather to be courting in, a bleak, colourless December perpetually smudged with rain. But Mary and Tom didn't mind. The rest of the world could have been washed away and they wouldn't have noticed. They were happily immersed in the most rewarding and delicious of occupations. They were falling in love, and the fact that they'd known one another for as long as either of them could remember did nothing to dispel the mystery. Quite the reverse, in fact. For now they saw each other through lover's eyes, and every meeting was a discovery.

It intrigued Mary to think that Tom had loved her for so long and never said a word about it.

'Why didntcher?' she asked.

'You'd've laughed.'

'I wouldn't.'

'You would. Look how you went on when poor old Johnny Peters wrote you that love letter at school.'

'But he was hideous.'

'See what I mean!' he crowed, laughing with delight at her lack of logic.

'But you're different,' she answered him, instantly serious. 'You're my Tom. And anyway, you're not hideous.'

'Thank you, ma'am.'

'Well, not as bad as your old man, anyway. You've got nice eyes.' He was looking at her with such melting tenderness that the fleshy nose and jutting chin he'd inherited from his father were redeemed and softened to acceptability.

'D'you really love me?'

'Um. Barmy, innit! Give us a kiss.'

He cupped her face in his hands, partly for the sheer joy of it and partly to protect her from the cold, for the rain had started again and was swooshing against their faces. They were cuddled together in the deep doorway of Mr Whiting's estate agency, but the December wind gusting from the north east threw flurries of icy droplets even into that haven.

'Lento expressivo,' she commanded dreamily, and when he'd kissed her, as languorously as if it were high summer, she approved in musical terms too. 'That was appassionato.'

'Can't help it,' he said, his cheek against hers. 'I love you too much.'

They were establishing a lovers' language for themselves and naturally enough they borrowed it from the music that had drawn them together in the first place. Both of them were pleased to think that although their love affair had begun with that extraordinary and explosive realization on the night of the fire it was now progressing at a modest and acceptable pace, allegro, certainly, but allegro assai.

There were so many occasions to share, and so many pleasures, dances at Goldsmiths', theatres and concerts, evenings cuddled together in the back row of the cinema and, as if that weren't enough, a whole lifetime to plan. On Saturday nights, when Queenie and Ploochy were at the pub, they had the house to themselves and could cook a meal and wash the dishes together as though they were already married. Afterwards they would stoke up the fire in the drawing room, and turn off the lights, and sit among the accommodating cushions of Queenie's comfortable sofa, to kiss and talk and kiss again in a languor of warmth and desire.

But however pleasurable the occasion Tom was always careful to switch on the light and rearrange the furniture long before Ploochy was due back home. There was an edge about his future father-in-law these days that rather alarmed the young man, and made him feel he ought to be on his best behaviour. Mary mocked at him and called him 'old caution', but he was convinced his instincts were right and should be followed.

'You're being too sensitive, you daft thing,' she said lovingly. 'He likes you. He's always liked you, you know that. They both have.'

388

'Better safe than sorry,' he told her, easing the sofa into its original position. 'I wouldn't want to get off to a bad start.'

'Wait till Christmas,' she said. 'Then you'll see how he feels about you.' She was looking forward to Christmas this year, now she'd given old Ploo something important to celebrate. It would be lovely for Tom to be fussed over, and if anyone knew how to make a really loving fuss, it was old Ploo.

And sure enough Christmas was a dazzling occasion, with a tree so huge that it filled the front window of the drawing room, and so many presents that they wouldn't all fit on the table and consequently had to be heaped on the floor, and so many guests on Boxing Day that Queenie said they'd have to be fed in relays. Mary was thrilled by the noise and scale of it all. She wasn't to know that her father had decided there was safety in numbers.

It was very hard for Albert to accept that this special, favourite child of his intended to marry. When Georgie and Lily got married, he'd been pleased and busy and well satisfied, with himself if not with the young couple, and when Anna planned her elaborate ceremony, he'd been pleased too, and amused by the theatricality of it all, carried along by the excitement of a good show. But with Mary it was different. This time he was aware of a tearing sense of loss. No matter how happy she might be, and she was obviously very happy indeed, he felt bleak and jealous and, consequently, guilty.

So he threw himself into the preparations for Christmas with frantic energy, organizing lavish meals and games and entertainments so there wasn't a minute between breakfast and bedtime that he hadn't filled with one diversion or another. And of course it was all very much enjoyed.

Dickie was in high good humour that Christmas. The broadcasts were going so well that he'd been signed on for a second series. He arrived on Boxing Day with two of their old friends from the music halls, Captain Cadwallader the ventriloquist and old Florrie Entwhistle, resplendent in crimson satin and with the remaining strands of her scant blonde hair tied up in unnecessary ribbon. Tilley, determined not to be outdone, brought a pork pie and her music and insisted on starting the entertainment with a bounding version of 'You can't do that there 'ere', which made them all so warm that Albert had to damp down the fire. Georgie's three children sang a carol, which old Miss Felnston declared so beautiful it brought tears to her eyes, and Marlene did a ballet dance in a white tutu and a deliberately soulful expression which, Queenie said afterwards and privately to Albert, made her look like a dying duck in a thunderstorm.

Halfway through the afternoon Harry and Em arrived with Billy and Dora and their two little boys, and there were so many for supper that the children had to have a separate table of their own in the drawing room beside the fire. And young Harry Jones switched out all the lights and told them a ghost story that was so lurid and terrifying that Marlene had hysterics and had to be resuscitated with sherry trifle.

Queenie had arranged the supper table with commendable diplomacy, setting Eric at one end between Miss Felnston and Captain Cadwallader, who were charmed by his tales of derring-do at the Foreign Office, and Tom and the Ox and Billy Jones right down at the other, where they could talk of Spain and socialism to their hearts' content without any need for polite censorship. Harry and Em and Dickie and Tilley sat in the middle with their old friend Ploochy, like a laughing barrier of jokes and tall tales and cheerful reminiscence. It was, as Tom and Mary told one another afterwards, a most harmonious occasion. Eric had been so charming he'd almost seemed happy, and Ploochy had been in his element. 'Not one jarring note!' Mary said with satisfaction. 'You see!'

There had been, of course, but she hadn't heard it, and it had been nothing to do with her and Tom. After supper, Em and Tilley and little Miss Felnston had insisted on helping Queenie with the mounds of washing up, but Queenie had drawn the line at putting the crockery away. 'Leave 'em,' she said, cheerfully piling the last clean plate on the draining board. 'They can stay where they are fer once.' So the four of them returned to the drawing room, wrinkle-handed from their massive chore, and Georgie and Anna, who had been watching for a chance to help, crept to the kitchen when Queenie wasn't looking to finish the job in secret. And as they were putting the clean china back on the dresser, they remembered their mother.

'Poor Mummy,' Anna said. 'I wonder what she's doing. I

feel fearfully mean sometimes, coming here when she's all on her own.'

'We *do* go to see her on Christmas Eve,' Georgie pointed out, as much to assuage his own conscience as hers. 'We always invite her to our place for Christmas, you know. Only she won't come.'

'D'you remember all those Christmases at Longley Road when we were little?'

'It was Dadda made them such fun,' Georgie said. 'She was always working.' Now that he had a family of his own he was ashamed of the work he'd caused when he was young.

'I wish they'd invite her here,' Anna said. And when her brother grimaced, 'Oh, I know it's not possible. I just wish, that's all. I mean, she's all on her own now, and she was good to us when we were kids. Bringing up kids is absolute hell, sometimes. Don't I know it? And it's no fun being on your own. What did she ever do to deserve that?'

'We can't do anything about it, Anna,' Georgie warned. 'You know that, don't you?'

'Oh yes,' Anna said tossing her yellow hair, 'I know that right enough. If there had been I'd have done it. I don't like to see people unhappy. I know what it's like. No, if I had my way, Georgie, everybody would be as happy as Tom and Mary, and you and Lily.'

'And Dadda and Queenie?' he suggested.

She thought for a minute and then grinned agreement. 'All right,' she said. 'Them too. Where do the vegetable dishes go?'

Alice and Minnie had had a nice quiet Christmas, and now they were sitting in the parlour beside the fire with their port and fizzy lemonade and their nice ham sandwiches, the dishes done, the curtains drawn against the world, and their two cats settled in their capacious laps like purring cushions. 'So much nicer, just the two of us,' Alice said.

And Minnie nodded, 'Time for ourselves. Don't treadmill, Noggin, there's a good puss.'

'When I think of all the work there was when the children were young, I wonder how we ever got through it. Thirteen to dinner at the very least, and heaven knows how many to prepare for at suppertime.'

'Do you remember the time your Albert bought the gramophone, and would have everybody in to see it? The Major from next door, and Harry an' Em. That was a house full and no mistake.'

'It was,' Alice said grimly. 'We were still doing the washing up next day. They never thought of all the work they were making. Not one of them. No, I tell you Minnie, it's much better as it is.'

'I s'pose I really ought to miss poor Jesse,' Minnie mused, 'but I don't, you know. Not really. Not a bit, really. Not as he was in the last years, anyway. I think of him more when he was young, you know. Young an' smart an' full of how he was going to change the world. He was all right then.'

'If you ask me,' Alice said, stroking her cat under the chin, 'they're more bother than they're worth, men. Give me a nice little cat any day of the week. Look how loving they are, and no trouble at all. Have we finished all the Turkish delight?'

'I'll open the other box, shall I?'

Albert's exuberant Christmas sustained his family well into the New Year, and even Tom had to admit he'd been royally welcomed and was probably being unnecessarily cautious after all. But then January brought freezing fogs and an outbreak of flu and reduced them all again. Even a trip to the Old Vic to see Laurence Olivier play *Hamlet* did little to dispel Tom's gloom.

'He's the most appropriate hero for our times,' he said. 'Hamlet the ditherer. Putting things off. Appeasing. Finding excuses. We're all like that. Don't intervene. Wait. Don't rock the boat. It's shameful.' The government was still committed to the policy of non-intervention in the Spanish civil war even though it was clear to everybody that Hitler and Mussolini were sending General Franco money and arms and the trained personnel to use them.

Mary gave him a hug of commiseration. 'At least we've sent men out to the International Brigade,' she said. 'We're not all callous. Some of us care.'

'Not enough of us, though,' he said seriously.

The tone of his voice chilled her into sudden apprehension. 'Not you, Tom,' she said. 'It don't have to be you.'

'We're all responsible,' he told her. 'Wasn't that what we always said?'

At that moment the bus conductor bounded up the stairs towards them, calling, 'Fez please!' so the conversation had to stop. But even the echo of it was disquieting and Mary found herself remembering it rather too often in the days that followed.

The news from Spain was very bad. With Hitler and Mussolini providing all the aid they needed, the Fascists were attacking hard. Madrid was under such pressure it looked as though it would certainly be captured, yet still the League of Nations did nothing. In fact, some nations did less than nothing. Early in January the British government decided that anyone going to Spain to fight in the International Brigade would be prosecuted under the long forgotten Foreign Enlistment Act passed way back in 1870.

Billy Jones was furious at such treachery. 'That damn fool Chamberlain, what's 'e think 'e's playin' at! Still beatin' about the bush, bleatin', about non-intervention! An' now this! Even if we're prepared to 'elp we ain't ter be allowed. Makes me spit! Well, you can see whose side 'e's really on.'

'Won't stop the Brigade,' the Ox told him stolidly. 'More ways a' killin' a cat. If people can't go open, they'll go on the quiet.'

'The Cohen boys went last week,' Maisie said proudly. 'One way ticket ter Paris. Fine pair a' boys. Trumped up threat won't stop nobody, you mark my words. They say there's more'n five hundred of our young fellers out there all-a-ready.'

And she was right. For by now volunteers knew who to approach, the *Daily Herald* or the *New Statesman* or the Spanish Medical Aid Committee, and the organizers at King Street soon learnt how to circumvent such a petty governmental obstruction. By now some of the very earliest volunteers were coming home on leave, and the tales they told made it very clear that this was an urgent and necessary war, against an enemy both ruthless and cruel. And working men, and students, and men miserably unemployed, listening at meetings up and down the country, recognized the truth of what was said. Hadn't they seen it themselves whenever Mosley and his blackshirts took to the streets? Fascism was

393

undemocratic in its very essence, government by the thugs, for the thugs. Anyone who believed in basic rights for all mankind was honour bound to oppose it. Gradually the trickle of aid and men straggling down through France towards their beleaguered allies began to increase, despite the Foreign Enlistment Act. Or perhaps because of it. And one of the new volunteers was Tom Oxbury.

He broke the news to Mary one Saturday evening at Lyndhurst Square when they had the house to themselves and were sitting by the fire in the drawing room, cuddled close together.

'I think you ought to know I gave in my notice on Monday,' he said, too casually. 'I shall be leaving the school at half term. I went up to King Street this afternoon.'

She didn't know what to say and was suddenly afraid she might cry. She was looking straight at his rugged jaw, thinking how strong and healthy and determined he looked, but she was remembering Ned's scarred face, and the way he'd managed with his one remaining arm, and the dry, insistent cough that had racked and weakened him so, and the awful day when he died. She knew it was right and noble to volunteer but she was afraid that this war might injure her Tom too, and behind that fear was another, so terrible she couldn't even think it, the fear that he might be killed.

'Oh Tom!' she said. 'You didn't!'

'I can't do anything else,' he said solemnly. 'I'd never be able to live with myself afterwards if I let this go on and just looked away and didn't do anything.'

'Yes,' she said miserably. 'I see that.'

'I knew you'd understand,' he said. But she felt bleak. As though she'd lost him already. And for the rest of the evening, while he told her of the way new recruits were smuggled across the frontier and how desperately they were needed and what a noble fight it was, the sense of loss increased.

Ma thought it was splendid news and just what she'd have expected and Ploo got excited, of course, and told Tom he'd buy him any uniform or equipment he needed. 'You just say the word.'

'Ta, Ploo, that's very good of yer,' Tom said, 'but I don't need much. We been told to travel light, you see. We're not to look as though we're going for long.'

'Pair a' boots,' Albert insisted.

So a good stout pair were bought with a heavy overcoat to match, and a shirt with two breast pockets that would look like uniform from the moment he arrived and then, unbelievable as it seemed, it was half term and he was ready, setting off for Victoria station and war, with his worldly goods wrapped in brown paper and carried under one arm, young and idealistic and unprepared and determined.

Mary went with him, holding on proudly to his unencumbered arm and glad to be seen with a man who was so obviously going to fight for his beliefs. Her chest and throat were already strained with unshed tears, but she was determined to be cheerful and supportive. It would be unseemly to make a fuss in such a public place and in any case she wouldn't have wanted to upset him for all the world. They walked towards the continental trains in silence, away from the grey pall of rain outside and into a world of strange scents and incomprehensible languages, through a concourse crowded with exotic travellers, women theatrical in capes, or snuggling into the fur collars of expensive coats, gentlemen wafting ostentatious cigars, or commandeering a trail of porters. She was excited by it all despite her worries and the impending misery of parting.

'How the other half lives!' she said to Tom, watching as a woman in a mink coat cleared a passage for herself through the crowds by the sheer arrogance of her walk.

'Another world,' he agreed, smiling at her. But they were at the barrier, and parting was only seconds away. She took a platform ticket and went with him to the door of the train, and he got into the carriage and put his brown paper parcel down on the seat. Then there was an awkward pause because neither of them knew what to say that would be adequate enough to fill the few precious minutes they had left.

'I'll write as soon as I arrive,' he promised. But she knew that.

'Tell us what you want us to send.' But they'd said that already.

'Your lady in the mink coat's going to Switzerland.' Neither of them really cared about *her*.

'We got here in good time.' Worse and worse.

'The mark of a good traveller.' How could they be spouting such silly, trite remarks when they might never see one another again?

'I hope it's a good crossing.' Doors were being banged and latecomers were running through the barrier.

He held both her hands, her long, narrow fingers beside his broad, blunt ones. Perhaps for the last time. 'I've got ter do this, Mo.'

'I know.'

' "I could not love thee, dear, so much,
    Loved I not honour more." '

'She'll 'ave 'er eye in a sling!'

'Who?'

'That Honor.'

It made them both laugh a little. 'You ain't 'alf like your Ma,' he said.

The guard was blowing his wretched whistle. A porter had closed the last door. There was only time to snatch an unsatisfactory kiss before the train began to move. 'Please don't get killed,' she said. There was no need for that engine to pick up speed quite so quickly.

'I love you,' he mouthed at her. But then he was too far away to lipread an answer and there was only the white blur of his face and his blunt hand waving. She could cry now if she wanted to, but she was too numb for such relief. God rot that foul Franco to hell and damnation, she thought coldly. If the general had suddenly appeared before her she would have killed him with her bare hands.

It was no good going home to Ma and Ploochy. They still thought it was all wonderful and wouldn't think much of her if she burst into tears. As she stood in the middle of the Victoria crowds feeling miserable and indecisive she remembered Anna. She'd go and see Anna. That's what she'd do. Anna would understand. So she took a train to Stoneleigh Park.

And Anna did understand, and was very sympathetic and let her cry on her shoulder and made her tea and told her that she had every right to grieve. 'When you love anyone as much as that, you're bound to feel awful when they're not there any more,' she said, holding Mary's hands lovingly between her own. 'But don't you worry. He'll come home safely, you'll see. I've got a sort of feeling about it. He'll come home.'

'You are a dear, Anna,' Mary said gratefully.

'Drink up your tea while it's hot,' Anna advised.

Mary sipped her tea and smiled for the first time that afternoon. 'I'm glad you're my sister,' she said.

How lovely to hear it said. 'So'm I!' Anna said rapturously, giving her a hug.

They stayed together until Eric was due to come home from work, and parted lovingly with the promise that they would see one another again on Sunday.

'Keep your pecker up!' Anna instructed as Mary left.

And for the next week while she waited for news, Mary did her best to stay cheerful. She prepared some lively music lessons for her first school practice and went to rehearsal determined to lose herself in the music. But Mrs Benwood had other ideas. 'Has he got there safely?' she asked. 'Such a brave young man. We've all been saying so, haven't we, Ralph? To go out there, all that way, when he might …' She blushed, and tried to retract what she'd nearly said, 'Well, what I mean is …'

'Might get killed,' Mary said. 'That's what you meant. Well, go on. Say it. He might get killed.'

Ralph Andrews was tuning his violin, adjusting the D string delicately. 'It's a hard fact about war, Mary,' he said seriously, 'something you have to face when someone you love is involved. I remember how it was the last time, when my father was in France.'

But she didn't want to hear about his father, or to talk about the possibility of death. It was all too horrible. 'What are we playing first?' she said stiffly and made a great business of arranging her music.

At the end of the week two cards arrived, one from Paris, and the other from Béziers, short, laconic notes simply saying where he was. Then a week went by without a word from him and despite all her efforts she grew lean with worry at the thought that he might have been captured crossing the Pyrénées. And finally a letter arrived.

'I am in a place called Madrigueras,' he wrote. 'A poor place, like Paradise Street among wheatfields and vineyards. The people are kind here and have made us very welcome.

There are only two buildings of any size in the whole place, the church, as you'd expect, and a theatre, which they've handed over to the Brigade. We sleep in the gallery and do weapon stripping where the stalls should be. Home grown entertainment on stage in the evenings. Queenie would love it. It will take six weeks to train us, so they say. The food is adequate. My love to everybody. I am kept too busy to realize how much I miss you, yet.'

She answered immediately and then locked the letter away in her dressing table, as if she could keep him safe by protecting his words.

Albert and Queenie watched over her with a concern they could only voice to each other. It was so unlike her to be pale and quiet, but it was her lack of appetite that upset them more than anything else. She was visibly losing weight. But at least the letters arrived to cheer her, and they arrived with reassuring regularity, almost as thought there wasn't a war after all.

At the end of April he sent a short and loving note to say that his training was complete and he would soon be going to the line. And then came such a long wait that Mary was privately afraid that something must have happened to him. Her relief when another letter was eventually delivered was too tearful to be hidden. He was at Jarama, he said, and had been under fire, but had not been hurt. Now he wrote like a soldier, of an anti-tank battery with 37mm guns that fired high velocity shells and had knocked out two machine gun nests; of the discomfort of flooded trenches – Dad will know what I mean; of monotonous food; but above everything else of the marvellous spirit of the Brigade. 'These are the bravest men I've ever known,' he wrote, 'and whatever the outcome of this war I shall have been privileged to serve with them.'

'You are the bravest man I've ever known,' she wrote back. 'Come home to me safely. I love you more than ever.'

On that far away Sunday evening when Tom first told them all that he was going to join the International Brigade, Albert had felt proud and excited and vaguely patriotic. But underneath these laudable emotions had been another that was really rather shameful. He couldn't help being glad that once this young man was out of the way, he could resume his care of Mary Ann, and resume it unopposed. He'd been ashamed of such unworthy thoughts immediately, of course, and had rushed to put things right by offering practical help and concentrating his mind on those other more admirable sentiments. But they'd been there just the same.

Now he realized how petty such jealousy had been. Tom wasn't out of the way at all. His absence filled the house and fear for his safety preoccupied Mary to the exclusion of almost everything else. She did her work, attending lectures patiently and writing up copious lesson notes ready for her next school practice, but her heart wasn't in it. It was a beautiful summer, too, with plenty of opportunities and excuses for enjoyment, good shows in the West End, good films at the cinemas, street parties to celebrate the Coronation. Because Queenie persuaded her, she went to the party in Bermondsey, where the banners across the narrow dark alleys read, 'Lousy but Loyal' and 'God bless the King and Queen *and* the Duke of Windsor,' but she was an obedient ghost at the feast and didn't enjoy it at all.

Anna came to see her every weekend and the two of them sat in the garden and talked head to head while Marlene played quietly and cautiously with the elaborate dolls' house that Albert had bought to entertain her.

Queenie and Albert, watching them from the drawing room window, were touched to see how fond of each other they'd grown. But even a sister's affection couldn't lift Mary from her anxiety.

'She needs summink ter take 'er right out of 'erself,' Queenie said.

'We will take 'er on holiday,' Albert decided. 'Somewhere nice an' lively. Brighton perhaps. Beginning of August. You ask her.'

She agreed. But with the same worrying docility and the quiet proviso that she would only go 'if nothing had happened to Tom'.

Chapter Thirty-Eight

'I'm so dull,' Georgie Pelucci said.

'No, you're not,' Lily told him, protectively and at once. 'You're a marvellous father, a lovely husband. I couldn't want better. You're not to say daft things.' The children were all in bed and asleep and the two of them were sitting out in their little back garden enjoying the last of the evening sun.

Georgie gave her a smile to show he appreciated what she was saying, but he wasn't comforted. He'd been thinking about his life rather a lot just lately and his thoughts all led in one direction. 'I never *do* anything,' he said, frowning at the tulips, 'and I ought to. There's Billy and the Ox and Maisie and Queenie, they all make a stand. They do things. They join things. They go off on demonstrations and get arrested. They put up a fight. Look at all the work Billy's putting into the bus strike. I'm so passive.'

'There's nothing wrong with that,' Lily said, pinning a patch onto the seat of Johnny's trousers. 'We can't all go off getting arrested all the time. Who'd look after the children?'

'I care just as much as they do,' Georgie worried. 'I can't stand Fascism, but what's the good of that when I don't do anything? Here's young Tom off to Spain to fight for his cause, and I just sit at home.'

'Good job too,' she said. 'Mary's worried sick. How d'you like that to be me?'

'I'm no better than the government really. A non-interventionist when it comes down to it. We should have intervened, Lily, the minute the Germans and the Italians started sending troops and supplies. Queenie was quite right. And now they've bombed all those poor people in Guernica, Heinkels against undefended women and children. Dreadful! And nobody to stop them. What's the good of a League of Nations if none of them ever do anything?'

'They've got to be careful though, haven't they? We don't want another war to start.'

'It's already started,' Georgie said heavily. He was very depressed about it. 'We shall have to fight Hitler in the end, you know, Lily. Appeasement only encourages him.'

'Well, I can't see any point worrying about it,' Lily said practically. The patch was in position and now she was threading her needle with tacking cotton. 'If there's a war coming, there's a war coming, an' we shall be in it whether we like it or not. Dad says if we start rearming the shipyards'll open up again, an' he'll get work out of it. So it's an ill wind blows no one any good.'

Georgie sighed deeply and returned to his paper. It seemed all wrong that he should be sitting here peacefully in his nice quiet garden thinking about war, particularly when even the idea of violence made his flesh cringe.

'I'll tell you what I think,' Lily said, tacking with deft, quick stitches. 'If there's going to be a war, we'll have two summer holidays this year, while we can. How about that? One at Herne Bay like we always do, to see the family, and another one somewhere else. On the south coast perhaps.'

It wasn't the sort of action Georgie had in mind, but it made good sense and gave him something pleasant to look forward to. So it was agreed, although neither of them had any idea which resort to choose for their new venture.

'I'll ask the customers,' he said. 'They're bound to know.'

The customers gave plenty of advice. In fact, between them they recommended or criticized every resort along the full length of the south coast. But one, a quiet librarian who came in every Friday evening for a bottle of French wine to accompany his Sunday roast, took time to tell his old friend Ploochy all about a nice little village a mile to the east of Bognor Regis. 'Lovely sands,' he said. 'Really safe for the kiddies, and there are some nice little bungalows near the beach that you can rent, or old coastguard cottages, if that's what you prefer. A lovely, sleepy place. Really old world. You'd love it. Called Felpham. You won't even find it on the map.'

So Georgie took a train to Bognor Regis the very next Saturday to give the place 'the once over' and was very taken with it. He rented a bungalow there and then, on the new beach estate, for the first two weeks of August, and bought a guide book, and came home to his family very well pleased with himself.

Unfortunately he left the guide book lying on the dresser for the children to look at, and Anna saw it. 'Don't tell me you're going somewhere else for your summer holiday!' she mocked. 'I'll never believe it.'

'We thought we'd have a change,' he said. 'It's a nice little place. Very quiet.'

'We're going to stay in a bungalow,' Johnny told her. 'With no stairs. In that road there, look. Right next to the sea.'

'I'm having a new bucket and spade,' Meg said proudly. 'I'm going to make a castle.'

'Aren't you the lucky ones!' Anna said, instantly making up her mind that if Georgie could afford to splash out on a holiday in such a classy looking place she and Marlene would go there too. She would hire a bungalow nearby. The children could all play together, and if they were all together during the day Eric would control himself and behave pleasantly, which would be a great relief even if it *was* all an act. She wouldn't say a word to Georgie. She'd just arrive at the same time as he did and give him a surprise.

Eric always left all their holiday arrangements to her anyway, so it was remarkably easy. 'Where?' he said when she told him her plans. 'Never heard of it. Whatever makes you want to go there?'

'It's near Bognor Regis. Where the king went to convalesce. You remember.'

'Oh, that's all right then.'

So she hired a bungalow with two bedrooms, one for her and Marlene and the other for Eric, and bought beach clothes for herself and her submissive daughter, and enjoyed her secret. She didn't even tell Dadda, because she really couldn't trust him not to blab. It would be such a surprise.

It was. But not quite in the way she envisaged.

She and Marlene packed their luggage neatly and economically so that there were only three cases. Eric made such a fuss if the car was overloaded and she wanted to keep him in a cheerful condition because it was very disagreeable if he was cross when he was driving. They had an early breakfast, and packed a picnic lunch and were groomed and ready long before he was, which was extremely satisfactory. By the time they reached Dorking Marlene was asleep on the back seat. The sun was pleasantly warm and the countryside pleasantly green. Everything was going according to plan.

'I like these little winding roads, don't you, Eric?' she was saying conversationally when a black shape suddenly shot across the road in front of them.

'Hell's teeth!' Eric yelled, standing on the brakes, but the two cars had already collided with a hollow thud, followed by an odd, grinding noise. The engine screamed as they careered on down the road, and Anna screamed, holding on to her hat, and Eric screamed, gripping the steering wheel for dear life. Marlene, woken abruptly by the impact and the noise, struggled to sit up and was knocked into a heap on the floor as the car slid on down the road, tyres squealing and out of control. Then there was a jolt as the two nearside wheels ran into a ditch and the car tipped over sideways, skidded on for another fifty yards, and finally juddered to a halt.

Anna found she was leaning over sideways too and jammed against the door. She knew she wasn't hurt but she went on screaming just the same. It was as if her mind had stopped like the car and couldn't move on to consider doing anything else. She recognized vaguely that Eric was still hugging the steering wheel and that now he was weeping, and somewhere behind her she could hear her daughter whimpering weakly, but it all seemed irrelevant.

'Shut your stupid row!' Eric said, raising his tear-streaked face from the steering wheel.

But it wasn't possible. She couldn't do it.

'Shut up! Shut up! Shut up!' Eric yelled, relieved that he'd found somebody to blame. The hatred in his voice was so alarming that it even penetrated her panic. She made a tremendous effort to control herself, but it was too late. He turned in his seat and slapped her viciously across the side of the face. 'Stupid, hysterical woman!'

The shock of the blow galvanized her into action. She twisted her face and her body away from him at once, and scrambled until she was kneeling in the seat and looking over it into the back of the car, where Marlene lay huddled white-faced and sobbing in an odd, juddering way. Then almost without thinking she wriggled across the top of the seat and landed in an undignified heap straddled across the back seat with her terrified baby clinging to her hair. 'It's all right,' she tried to soothe. 'Wasn't I a funny mummy climbing over that old seat?'

She sensed that Eric was glaring at them and she could hear his voice shouting, 'What are you doing now, you bloody fool?' But she was out of range so she could ignore him. Her baby was far more important than he was.

'Don' like it,' Marlene whimpered, sobbing and clinging. 'Don' like this car!'

'Neither do I, darling,' Anna said. 'Never mind. We're going to get out.' It pleased her to realize how quickly she was recovering. Rather to her surprise, the door swung open into the sky, and although the car was tilting over in the most awkward way she and Marlene managed to scramble through the gap and jump down onto the firm earth at the side of the ditch.

'That's better,' she said brightly. 'Now let's have a look at you. Didn't that silly old car go bang!' It was very quiet out in the sunshine, and very peaceful. The corn in the field beyond the ditch was rustling like silk and high overhead a skylark was shrilling as it rose. 'Did you bump yourself?' she asked gently. 'Let Mummy take your coat off and have a look.'

Now that she was out of that terrifying car and sitting in the sunshine with her mother, Marlene began to recover too, although she still kept an apprehensive eye on her father in case he started shouting again or hitting Mummy. At the moment he was circling the car, and making moaning noises. But when her mother had examined her arms and legs and put her coat on again and told her she was quite all right and wasn't that a lucky thing, he came and stood right over them, his face dark red and frowning.

'Where's the car?' he demanded.

Anna looked vaguely towards the ditch, and provoked another outburst of screaming bad temper. 'Fool!' he roared. 'The other car.' The road was empty. The other car had gone.

'Bloody road hog? He could've killed us. It's a wonder we're not all dead. Oh God, look at the state of my car! What are we going to do, Anna?' He was very near to tears.

'I don't know about you,' Anna said with icy calm, 'but I'm going to walk to the nearest railway station and catch a train the rest of the way. I'm not staying here to be a punchbag.'

'Don't be so bloody ridiculous,' he spat. 'You don't know where it is.'

'We can find out, can't we, Marlene?' she said, and she took hold of her daughter's cold hand and started to walk away from him down the long, empty curve of the road.

'You can't do this!' he roared. 'Anna! Anna! What am I supposed to do? Oh God, this is all so unfair!'

She didn't even bother to answer him. It was a nice warm day, and she and Marlene hadn't been hurt despite everything. They were bound to find a town or a village sooner or later if they just kept on walking. 'It'll be fun on a train,' she said chafing the child's fingers.

Eric was jumping up and down in the middle of the road. 'Come back! Anna, come back, please!' he yelled. 'What am I supposed to do?'

'Daddy's crying,' the child observed.

'Yes, I know,' Anna said, matter of factly. 'Isn't he a silly?'

Lily was very pleased with her seaside chalet and very impressed by the speed with which the station staff had delivered their trunk. She and Georgie had sent it off as luggage in advance, and she'd been rather worried in case it was delayed, but there it was, already standing in the porch, and they'd only just arrived. Now she could relax and take stock of her surroundings.

'It's a lovely place,' she said appreciatively to Georgie. 'Ever so seasidey!' The air was so bright and the smell of the sea so salty and strong. It was an excitement just to have arrived. And this was certainly not the sort of respectable house they were used to in Morden. There was something raffish and adventurous about it, and that pleased her and made her feel she really was on holiday this time. Board and lodging in Herne Bay had become so predictable over the years.

It was a low building with a rounded dormer window like a

porthole in the long, sloping roof and casement windows on either side of a little brick-built porch that was almost hidden by a mantle of clustered pink roses and dense dark leaves. The two flower beds beneath the windows were overcrowded too, so heaped and mounded with the curved thick roots of purple irises that there wasn't a sign of any earth left to nourish them. The little front garden was bulging with shrubs, a spotted laurel by the gate and a very tall buddleia, fluttering with brown butterflies, dropping across the left wall of the house, a cotoneaster clinging to the fence and still speckled with faded white blossom, and two thick hedges of lavender buzzingly busy with bees. There were even plants growing on the building. Algae coloured the sandy roughcast of the walls, and the tiles on the roof were dappled with olive green moss and scales of bright orange lichen. Even the keyhole was discoloured by rust, so that the key squeaked as it turned. The children were delighted with it.

'It's like the Sleeping Princess,' Johnny said, eyes shining. 'All overgrown, waiting for the Prince to come and kill the dragon.'

'What's a dragon?' Norman asked, caught between fear and curiosity.

'You don't have dragons at the seaside,' Lily told him briskly before his brother could give him nightmares. 'Come on in and let's see your bedroom. And then we'll get the trunk unpacked and find a table cloth and we can have our dinner. Aren't you hungry?'

Sea air and excitement had given them all an appetite. Soon they'd eaten all their sandwiches and demolished one of the nice new loaves they'd bought at the village bakery while Georgie was getting the key. Lily was busily cutting slices off the second loaf when there was a knock at the door. They were all very surprised.

'I'll go,' Georgie said. It was bound to be something he ought to deal with. His family listened as he walked to the front door and eased it open. 'Good heavens!' he said. 'Anna! What are you doing here? Are you all right? Come in, come in.'

'We've had such a time getting here,' Anna said as she followed him into the living room. 'You'd never believe it. Eric crashed the car, silly thing, so we had to walk, didn't we,

Marlene? Miles and miles. And then we found a nice man in a farm cart and he gave us a lift to his farm, and his cousin took us to the station in a pig van, stunk to high heaven. And we got there in the nick of time. The train was at the platform. Another minute and it would have gone without us. That was a bit of luck, wasn't it, Marlene? And we've been on a train and a bus. I'm absolutely exhausted.' She sank into a chair beside the table and looked at the remains of the food hungrily.

'You had any dinner?' Lily offered, feeling that she had to be hospitable even though she wasn't a bit pleased to see her sister-in-law.

'I packed a picnic,' Anna explained, 'but of course we had to leave it in the car.'

'Run into the kitchen, Johnny, there's a good boy, and see if you can find two more plates,' Lily said. 'It's only bread and cheese but it's better than nothing.'

'Where's Eric?' Georgie said, frowning and pushing his glasses into position with his forefinger. He was still feeling bemused by his sister's arrival.

'Don't ask me,' Anna said carelessly. 'I don't know and I don't care.' She was more interested in the bread and cheese. 'The last I saw of him he was jumping up and down in the middle of the road, screaming and shouting and making an exhibition of himself.'

'D'you mean to say you just walked off and left him?' Georgie asked.

''Course.'

'But won't it be awkward? I mean how will you ... What will he say?' The thought of the atmosphere behaviour like that would be bound to cause was making him feel horribly embarrassed.

'It'll be all right,' Anna assured him. 'It always is. He'll get the car fixed and come down here as right as rain, just as if nothing had happened. You see if he doesn't.'

'Down here? Does he know you've come down here?'

'Oh yes,' Anna said. 'We're here for a fortnight. We've booked a bungalow just round the corner. Dunroamin, it's called. Ever such a classy place. Only Eric's got the letter and everything so they won't give me the key.'

Georgie and Lily exchanged glances. A fortnight! She'd be

here all the time. How awful! And just when they were thinking they'd left all their problems behind them.

'I thought you'd be surprised,' Anna said happily. 'This is lovely bread.'

Neither of them recovered from their surprise until much later that afternoon when Georgie had gone down to the estate agent and persuaded that painstaking gentleman that Anna could be entrusted with the key to Dunroamin, and Lily had gone shopping in the village and spent a great deal of money providing food for the weekend, and the children had rushed off to the beach with their buckets and spades. Then they went down to the beach themselves and sat on the pebbles and watched their children building a sand castle at the water's edge, and told one another how upset they were.

'I thought we were going to get away from it all,' Georgie said, pushing at his glasses again. 'I'm so sorry, Lily.'

'It's not your fault,' Lily said sensibly. 'It's Anna. That's who it is.'

'We'll have trips out,' Georgie promised, 'and not tell them where we're going.'

'Do you really think he'll come down and behave as if nothing had happened?'

'Don't ask me,' Georgie said. 'I can't make head or tail of him. Never have been able to.'

'She's just like your dadda, you know. The way she rushes into things.'

Georgie gave his wry smile. 'I wish she'd rushed somewhere else,' he said, 'that's all.' But even as he spoke he knew that this reckless impulsiveness was the element that was missing in his own cautious character, and that it was the quality he most admired.

Albert's holiday wasn't going according to plan either. When he heard that Georgie and Lily were going to be on the south coast at the same time as he was he was delighted. 'It not far from Brighton,' he said, beaming. 'We'll drive over in the middle of the week and see the kids. How'll that be?' And Queenie and Mary had both said it was a very good idea.

But on the morning they were all due to leave, Mary suddenly changed her mind. She hadn't had a letter from Tom

408

for nearly six days, and although she was quite used to long delays by now, and had trained herself not to get too anxious, she wasn't prepared to go away for a whole fortnight and allow a possible letter to arrive unwelcomed and then lie unanswered on the doormat for all that time. Tom had been fighting at a place called Brunete since the beginning of July, and although he said very little about it Mary had read enough in the papers to realize that this was a terrible campaign and a very bloody one. Letters got through though, even from the front line, and it was essential they were answered right away. 'It'll be here any day now,' she said to Queenie. 'I'll stay on here and just wait for it. When it's come I'll take the first train down and join you. I promise.'

Albert was very annoyed, although he managed to control himself until he and Queenie were in the car and rattling south. 'Such a waste!' he complained. 'All this fine weather, cooped up in the house, waiting for a letter. I ask you!'

'She loves 'im, Ploo,' Queenie said. But he chewed his moustache and scowled. 'We'll go and see Georgie an' Lily anyway. Where we goin' ternight?'

He cheered up once they'd arrived at The Ship and eaten a sumptuous meal and been welcomed by all the staff who remembered them from last year. Brighton was just the sort of town they most enjoyed, and soon they were off on their first tour, rediscovering old haunts and forgetting new disappointments.

Queenie phoned home every evening, and every evening Mary said she was all right but the letter hadn't been delivered yet, so she'd wait another day. It was Wednesday before it came, but the news was good. The XVth Brigade had been taken from the line at last, and Tom had come through the long battle with nothing worse than a flesh wound, which he said would be healed in no time at all. 'I'll be down tomorrow on the first train,' Mary promised, and Queenie was glad to hear that she sounded almost lighthearted.

'We will meet you at the station,' Albert told her, taking the phone, 'and drive straight on to Felpham. How about that?'

'It sounds lovely,' she said.

Georgie was a bit put out when his father's card arrived next morning. He'd been planning to take the children to Arundel for a picnic by the river, in secret of course, so as to get away from Eric and his fatuous conversation. Now he would have to stay on the beach and endure another day of it.

'Never mind,' Lily commiserated. 'We can always go tomorrow.'

'I need to go today,' Georgie said, pushing his glasses firmly onto his nose. 'I can't take much more of that awful man. He makes my blood boil.'

Just as Anna had predicted, Eric had driven in to Felpham late that Saturday night as full of himself as if he was visiting royalty. He'd soon got everything fixed, he told them. 'The mechanic tried to cut up rough, but it didn't wash with me. Oh no! I know how to deal with your lower classes, thank you very much. Firm hand, that's all they need.'

It was the worst possible start to the holiday. And the weather was perfect too, with clear blue skies and a blue sea sparkling under the strong sunshine. The children were off to the beach every morning as soon as they'd finished their breakfast, to paddle or try to swim, or build sandcastles or gather winkles from an outcrop of harmlessly flat rocks that were marvellously exciting because they were slippery with bladder wrack and encrusted with barnacles. Even Marlene joined the adventures and got her hands dirty and was allowed to get away with it.

But the atmosphere grew tense at once as soon as Anna and Eric put in an appearance, she in an expensive bathing costume, he dapper in his holiday blazer, his shoes highly polished and his hair shiny with Brilliantine. He always brought a cushion with him, declaring that pebbles were impossible to sit on, and while Anna spread herself out on a rug to sleep and acquire a suntan, he lit a cigarette and proceeded to hold forth to his captive audience on any subject that took his fancy.

That Thursday afternoon it was the National Socialist Party of Germany. 'What any country needs is good firm leadership,' he said, narrowing his eyes against the sunshine and his own cigarette smoke. 'It stands to reason. A strong moral code. Law and order.'

'Burning books,' Georgie said, quietly. He was sitting with his back against a breakwater, facing his objectionable brother-in-law across the sleeping length of Anna's browning body.

'If they're subversive, of course. Most books are rubbish these days anyway. Deserve burning.' But the joke fell flat.

'What about free speech?'

'Twaddle. Who wants to hear a load of piffle from some Commie politician? I'm sure I don't.'

'Some people might,' Lily said, adjusting her sun-hat and trying to be reasonable. 'Dontcher think they ought to have the right if they want to? In a democracy?'

'If they want to listen to rubbish then they can't be very bright. Stands to reason,' Eric said affably, flicking ash on the pebbles. 'So that's just where strong leadership comes in. That's what strong leaders are for. To protect people like that against themselves.'

'And who's to protect the people against their strong leaders?' Georgie asked. He was beginning to feel very annoyed, the hair on the nape of his neck rising and prickling.

'What *are* you talking about?'

'Jews,' Georgie said. 'That's what I'm talking about. Jews being sent to concentration camps by your nice strong leader Adolf Hitler.'

'Oh, that's all propaganda,' Eric said, looking very superior. 'Communist propaganda. You don't want to take any notice of that. Jews are being resettled, that's all. Which is more than I'd do for 'em, I can tell you. I'd just chuck 'em out of the country. Repatriate 'em. They've no business there.'

'They were born there,' Georgie said, appalled.

'That's only what they say. Now let me tell you something before you go getting all high and mighty about a lot of Jewboys. If we repatriated all the foreigners in this country we could have our unemployment problem solved in a matter of weeks. England for the English. Germany for the Germans. It's common sense.'

His sneering expression was angering Georgie so much he forgot to be cautious. 'How would you know they were foreigners?' he asked.

'Oh, for heaven's sake, that's easy. They have foreign names. They can't speak English. They weren't born in this country. They're obvious.'

'And you'd send them all back to their own countries? No matter how long they'd been here or how hard they'd worked? Or whether they had a family here?'

'Of course. You have to be ruthless sometimes. For the good of the nation.'

'Dadda?'

'I beg your pardon?'

'Would you repatriate Dadda? He was born in Italy. Or me? I've got a foreign name. Or my children? They're called Pelucci too, don't forget.' He knew he was shouting, but he was white hot with anger and couldn't stop. Tom Oxbury was out in Spain fighting the Fascists at this very moment. How dare this jumped-up, ignorant creature come down here spouting their dreadful poisonous ideas. It wasn't to be endured.

Eric realized too late that he'd gone a bit too far. He was aware of Anna's sleepy face scowling up at him from the sandstrewn rug, and Lily's hand fluttering towards Georgie's arm, trying to placate. 'Now come on, old man. You mustn't take it personally.'

Georgie was on his feet, and shouting louder than ever. 'No? No? You come down here talking absolute rubbish day after day, insulting my father, punching my sister, and you dare tell me not to take it personally.'

'Here, steady on!' Eric warned scrambling to his feet. For quiet, unassuming Georgie had seized him by the lapels of his costly blazer and was pushing him backwards, accompanying every angry word with a little punching blow to his brother-in-law's chest.

'You're like all the rest of your awful Fascist friends. Bully, bully, bully. Mouth, mouth, mouth. You never stop to think you might be hurting people's feelings. Oh no. It's always what *you* think. What *you* want. Well, not this time. Not today. I've had enough.'

'All right, all right,' Eric said, stumbling away from the onslaught. 'I was only making conversation, for God's sake. We'll talk about something else.'

'Right!' Georgie roared. 'We'll talk about the way you treat my sister.'

'I treat her very well!' Eric squealed, and tried to run. 'If she

412

says anything else she's telling you lies.'

But the pebbles were treacherous under his uncertain feet and he slipped suddenly and fell. Anna's face was only a few inches away, and she was laughing at him. The bitch!

'Liar!' Georgie roared. 'Get up! Do you hear me? Get up and fight!' He couldn't very well hit this awful man when he was cowering on the stones, but he knew he was going to hit him, sooner or later. Anger was propelling him onwards like a great surf wave and nothing could satisfy him except a fight. As he stooped towards his enemy, his glasses slipped from his nose and fell into a sandy patch among the stones. But he wasn't deterred. He didn't even stop to pick them up. He could see well enough without them for his present furious purposes. He knew that Lily was watching him with the oddest expression on her face but he didn't even allow himself time to work out what it was. He knew, too, that he ought to feel alarmed by what he was doing, but he was actually exhilarated, even though he was very surprised at himself.

Eric scrambled to his feet again and tried to run, the stones rattling as he slithered and struggled to stay upright. Instantly Georgie was after him, pounding over the pebbles, crunch, crunch, crunch. They reached the breakwater together, and Eric had one foot on the slippery wood ready to leap over when Georgie hit him. The blow knocked him off balance again and he fell backwards over the breakwater and landed in a pool with his legs in the air.

Georgie found he was breathing hard and feeling triumphant. Then he realized that two misty shapes were running down the sand towards him, and then Anna and Lily were hanging on to his arms, and Lily was fixing his glasses back on his nose and he could see three more figures running towards him. Dadda and Queenie and Mary Ann. How awful, he thought, they must have seen it.

But Albert was laughing too and patting him on the back and saying he never thought he'd live to see the day, and Anna was peering over the breakwater at her disgruntled husband and informing him that he was terribly wet, and Queenie was declaring that you certainly saw life at the seaside, and it all seemed to be a joke somehow, and acceptable. He felt rather deflated and began to busy himself wiping the sand from his glasses. This wasn't the way to end a battle. Then he saw that the children had left the rocks and were trotting back towards them across the sands, and he felt relieved that his temper was cooling.

Eric rose from the pool and stood behind the breakwater, glaring at them all. 'I suppose you know your son's taken leave of his senses,' he said stiffly to Albert.

'Or come to 'em, mate,' Queenie said at once. 'Depends which way you look at it, don't it?'

'I don't have to stand here and be insulted,' Eric said, and he went stomping off, up the rattling pebbles towards the path. His white flannels were stained with water and his blazer smudged with sand. 'Poor old Eric,' Anna said.

'He did ask for it,' Lily said, feeling she really ought to defend her Georgie. His sudden aggressive behaviour had made her quite proud.

'Oh yes, I know,' Anna agreed. 'He looks such an idiot sometimes, that's all.'

The children were almost beside them. 'Where's Daddy going?' Marlene called.

'Home for a little rest, darling,' Anna explained brightly.

'What say we all go into Bognor for ice creams?' Albert suggested. 'An' a donkey ride. How about that?'

The tide was a long way out so they walked into Bognor along the wide expanse of firm buff sand, and the children had two donkey rides each, and they all watched the Punch and Judy show, and then Albert treated them all to a high tea, and had the restaurant reorganized so that they could all sit together at one long family table, and Marlene ate so much she gave herself hiccups and everybody, except Georgie, forgot all about Eric and the fight.

It was a pearly evening and the tide was coming in fast by the time they caught the bus back to the village. Marlene and Norman sat beside their mothers, almost asleep, as they rocked through the twisting street past thatched barns and flint cottages and the lych gate of the ancient church.

'Will Eric …?' Georgie tried to ask his sister.

'Oh, don't you worry about him,' she said. 'He'll've forgotten all about it by now. It won't 've happened. You see if I'm not right. That's the way he goes on. If anything's nasty, he

414

pretends it hasn't happened. That's why he's so thick-skinned.'

'Should 'a' took my advice long ago,' Queenie said, cuddling little Meg.

'I can handle him,' Anna said and she looked so confident it really seemed she could.

But Georgie was thinking, and his thoughts were more troubling now than they'd been before the fight. If Anna was right and Eric really did suppress any facts he didn't want to face, then he would be even more difficult to handle than any of them had realized. Or was that how all Fascists behaved? Was there such a thing as a Fascist personality? And if that was the case, was Fascism a sort of madness? Was England gradually drifting towards a war with a regime based on madness and unreality? It was a frightening thought.

Then he remembered that he owed Anna an apology. 'I'm sorry if I upset you, Sis,' he said.

'Just between you an' me an' the gatepost,' she said, 'I actually rather enjoyed it.'

They parted company cheerfully when they reached the beach estate, but Mary watched her sister walk away with considerable misgivings. What if he was in a really bad mood and she couldn't handle him this time? But she needn't have worried. Within five minutes Anna and Marlene were back. Eric had left a brusque note and gone. 'We're all on our own,' Anna chortled. 'Isn't that marvellous? Now we can have a really nice holiday without him.'

'You're priceless, mate,' Queenie said with admiration, and Albert, practical as ever, asked if she had enough money to manage.

'All the holiday money,' she said grinning. 'Every single penny.' Then another pleasant thought struck her and she turned to talk to Mary. 'I say! There's a bed vacant at my place now. How about staying here with us?'

Faces turned at once for Mary's answer. 'Yes do,' Georgie urged. 'It would be fun.'

So she stayed. And despite her worries, it was fun, for she'd never been on holiday with a brother and sister before, to say nothing of four children who all called her Aunty Mary and kept her cheerfully busy every moment of the day, swimming and digging sandcastles and eating sand-strewn picnics. They went out to Arundel Castle and took a trip to Portsmouth to see the *Victory* and the days passed quickly and for the most part easily. It was only very occasionally that she found herself with a moment for thought and then it seemed unnatural somehow that people should be bathing and dancing and buying their children ice creams and donkey rides when a few hundred miles away their countrymen were killing and being killed. But the moment passed and she went back to enjoying her days in the sun, although in an odd, anaesthetized way, like somebody enjoying a dream. It was the nights that were difficult, when she lay awake in her unfamiliar room, watching the white stars and listening to the sea sucking the shingle and wondering whether her darling was still safe and unscathed.

And Eric stayed in Stoneleigh Park for the rest of the holiday. To everybody's relief.

416

Chapter Thirty-Nine

By the end of August it was as if none of it had happened. For Mary got home to find another letter waiting for her or, to be more accurate, three letters sent by the same post. And the first one she opened brought news of another offensive. The XVth Brigade had been reinforced and now had a new Battalion Commander and a new Political Commissar and were waiting orders. 'Last night we slept in the bullring at Valencia,' he wrote in the second letter. 'I shall have so much to tell you when I come home.' 'Have faith,' the third letter said. 'I lead a charmed life. One of the Forty-two who survived Brunete.' It was meant to cheer her, but there was a chill about those figures that made her feel too closely aware of disaster. If forty-two men survived, however many had been killed?

'I'm not cut out to be a soldier's wife,' she said to Queenie as they cleared the table after their first breakfast back home.

'Who is?' Queenie said.

'You were though, werentcher.'

'Only after 'e was injured, poor beggar.'

'Oh God! Don't say things like that!' Mary begged and her expression was anguished.

'Give you a bit of advice, gel,' Queenie said, folding up the tablecloth. 'Don't do no earthly good dwellin' on things. Pertickerly when they might never 'appen. You spend most a' your day thinkin' a' the worst, dontcher? Well, that's the quickest way to the loony bin. You take my tip an' get out an' about a bit more. Take yer mind off it.'

'It'ud need to be pretty good to take *my* mind off it,' Mary said but at least, Queenie thought, she was smiling at the idea.

And, as it turned out, it was pretty good.

That Wednesday afternoon her cousin Maggie came to visit. It was early closing and her half day so there was nothing unusual about that, but she hadn't come to tea, she said. She was on her way to the Health Centre and wondered if Mary would like to come with her.

'Yes, course,' Mary said at once. If her cousin wasn't well, the very least she could do was go with her to the doctor's.

But Maggie laughed at the very idea that there might be something the matter with her. 'Not me,' she said. 'Fit as a flea, I am.'

'Then why're you going to the Health Centre?'

'That'ud be tellin',' Maggie said, grinning at her. 'Wait till you see. Me an' Sid been members fer more'n a year now. It's not like goin' ter the doctor's. It's more like … Well, wait till you see.'

The Centre was ten minutes walk away and it didn't look a bit like a doctor's surgery. It was a long, glistening, three-storey building that at first glance seemed to be made almost entirely of windows, bow-fronted windows curving gently one beside the other, columns of windows extending from the grass to the sky above a flat, unnoticeable roof. It was a most attractive place and it was drawing the crowds as easily as it drew the eye. As they stood at the gate taking it in, several women arrived, most of them with babies or toddlers. They greeted Maggie cheerfully as they passed and she answered them all, ' 'Lo Pearl. You better, Daph? How's Tony?' It was more like a club than a Health Centre.

'Come on,' Maggie ordered. 'Wait till you see inside.'

'I can't just walk in,' Mary said. But she was overruled.

'This is my cousin,' Maggie explained to the woman sitting at the reception desk. 'Can she 'ave a look round, please? I want 'er ter join, you see. When 'er young man gets back from Spain they're gonna get married an' live round 'ere.'

'You'll have to live within walking distance,' the woman explained to Mary. 'You understand that, don't you? We restrict our membership to families who live within walking distance.'

''Course,' Maggie said. 'Lyndhurst Square. How's that?'

'Welcome to the centre,' the woman said, smiling at them. 'Come and see me again if you decide to join us.'

418

'You *are* a terror!' Mary rebuked her cousin, as they walked into a wide corridor. 'I don't know where we're going to live when we get married. I don't even know whether we'll ever get married. He might …'

'Don't start talking tripe,' Maggie said briskly. 'No time fer tripe this afternoon. I got too much ter show yer.'

It was as dazzling inside this building as it was outside, for sunshine flooded in through all that glass. The place was full of people who all seemed to know where they were going, even though they all seemed to be walking in different directions. And there were so many things happening and so many different places to see. A swimming pool glimmered in the centre of the building, its blue water reflecting kaleidoscopic patterns onto the white ceiling above it. Beside it people sat in the cafeteria and watched the swimmers through a wall of windows, for the walls inside this building all seemed to be made of glass too. There were nurseries for babies, most of whom seemed to be sleeping in cots on the floor, which Mary found rather surprising, and nurseries for toddlers, and a little theatre, and a library and gym.

'Whatcher think?' Maggie asked, beaming at her cousin.

'Never seen nothing like it,' Mary admitted. 'It's … so transparent. You can see everything that's going on. And people all seem to be doing exactly as they like.'

'That's the idea,' Maggie said.

'But what if you all want to do the same things at the same time?'

'We take turns,' Maggie said. 'Simple.'

And it certainly seemed it.

'Come on,' Maggie said. 'It's my turn ter make the nursery teas. Then I'm going ter finish me frock. They got sewin' machines here an' all.' And she led the way to the kitchens, where she introduced Mary to four other women who were already aproned and busy.

So they prepared the teas and finished the frock and watched the toddlers and at four o'clock they went to the cafeteria to have some tea themselves. And were joined by a girl called Jenny who was one of the laboratory staff. By this time Mary was brimming with questions she wanted to ask, and as Jenny didn't seem to mind being the target of her curiosity the three of them plunged into a conversation that was so unusual that Mary's head was spinning with it long after she got home that evening.

'All these windows,' Mary said. 'You can see everything that's going on all over the building.'

'Do you like it?' Jenny asked.

'Yes, I do.'

'It was done deliberately.'

'Told yer!' Maggie said.

'Why?'

'To tempt people to join in. It's the natural way we extend our activities. You see something you like the look of, swimming or dancing or roller skating on the roof or something like that, and the next thing you know you're trying it out for yourself. But you have to see it first.'

'I thought it was a Health Centre.'

'There's nothing more conducive to health than a really active life.'

'You sound like my old gym teacher,' Maggie said, laughing at her, and Jenny made a grimace and laughed back.

'But what if you get people who don't want to join in?' Mary wanted to know.

'Then they don't. We wait. The moment comes, sooner or later, if you let them alone. Perhaps they need time to sit and dream.'

'The devil makes work for idle hands?'

'She's training as a teacher,' Maggie explained, sipping her tea. 'Gotta keep a class under control every minute a' the day, aintcher, Mo?'

'So they say,' Jenny said, 'but isn't that because the day is controlling the child instead of the other way round?'

'But you couldn't let children decide what they were going to do, could you?'

'Why not? They do here.'

'It would be chaos.'

'Of course. But order would evolve out of it. A natural order, growing out of trial and error. We believe that natural order is organic, you see. We don't think you can impose it. It has to grow of its own accord, first in individuals and then in groups.'

'I don't think it would grow in a school.'

'Probably not,' Jenny agreed. 'You'd have to change the way teachers thought first. We all had to rethink our own attitudes when we first came to work on the experiment. It's been pretty shattering sometimes, I can tell you.'

Mary could well believe it. It was shattering her.

It kept her awake all night, like indigestion, as she thought and re-thought and puzzled, trying to make sense of it all. For if Jenny was right, and order really was organic and would evolve naturally in groups as well as in individuals, then teaching as she understood it was not only useless but positively harmful.

The next day she ignored her studies for once and as soon as Ploochy and her mother were out of the house she sat down to write a long letter to Tom, describing the Centre and the extraordinary afternoon she'd spent there and recounting her conversation word by mind expanding word. 'If people learn and evolve towards order and an understanding of themselves and their situation through shared action, then any compulsion is tyranny,' she wrote. 'It makes a nonsense of rote learning and examinations. Even of government, if you think it through.'

The moment she'd dropped the fat envelope into the letter box, she had second thoughts about the advisability of sending it. A long disquisition on order and the education system was hardly the most appropriate thing to send to a young man fighting in the trenches. But she needn't have worried. Tom took it entirely seriously and welcomed it and answered in kind.

'Something very similar happened here at Madrigueras,' he wrote. 'Given orders always provoked arguments. A decision always had to be arrived at. We used to argue for hours. Brigaders are very independent. That's our strength. Fighting for something we believe in, you see. We certainly evolve our own order here, and chose our own leaders. Perhaps one day we can give the same freedom to everybody. I'm not sure how it would apply to education. I'm too far away from all that now. See what they say at Goldsmiths' when you go back.'

Her tutor was interested but not very encouraging. 'It *is* still an experiment,' he said. 'Only time will tell how valuable.' He didn't feel he should advise his students to put such revolutionary ideas into practice. At least not until the educational world was ready for them. But he applauded her observations.

'Why are teachers so timid?' she wrote to Tom later that day. 'I can't see why we shouldn't allow children the freedom to chose what they study. For part of the day at least. Why must we direct everything they do?'

'At Weatherby Grammar we never allowed our pupils the slightest freedom,' he wrote back. 'They couldn't even choose what desks they were to sit in. I think you're right, Mo. Perhaps we should open a private school of our own when I get home and put all these ideas into practice.'

As the months went by and autumn became winter and a new year arrived, their disjointed discussion continued and extended, despite war and worry and separation. They wrote of punishments and decided it was barbarous for anyone to impose their will on a child by hitting it; they considered rewards and wondered whether a child who had regulated its own life would actually need such things; and they decided that, whatever they were required to do to other people's children in school, their own children would be allowed as much freedom as they could possibly give them. They were talking to one another with a passion and directness that had eluded them in the careful, teasing days of their early courtship, and their closeness sustained them through all the trials of that long, hard winter.

The campaign in Aragon continued despite everything, snow and ice and biting winds, a night time temperature of twenty degrees below, ground frozen solid, and the knowledge that the Fascists were amassing an enormous army against them and the biggest air fleet that had ever been used in war. Out in the snowbound countryside the Brigaders cut headsized slits in their blankets and wore them as ponchos. Machine gun bolts and rifle locks had to be warmed against their bodies before they could be moved, and although the Quartermasters always managed to get food through to the front line, it was invariably cold when it arrived. 'I've never felt as cold as this in the whole of my life,' Tom wrote to his father. 'Still, at least the bugs don't bite, which is just as well seeing we're all lousy.'

Then at the beginning of March he sent two careful letters home, one to Mary and the other to his parents, explaining that he'd been wounded. 'Nothing serious. A leg wound. I might be invalided home. Hope not, because the Brigade needs every fighting man it can get.'

Mary was torn between relief that he'd be coming home at last and anxiety at the thought of what a leg wound might actually turn out to be. The campaign could get on very well without him, she thought. Surely he'd done enough now.

He came back to England early in April and was sent straight to the Middlesex Hospital for an operation. Mary went to visit him as soon as she got his letter.

And was bewildered and disappointed by the change she found. For this leathery stranger with the shaven head and the bulky cradle over his injured leg wasn't the gentle Tom she'd seen off to war. He didn't even smell the same, and rarely talked to her, at least not in the way she remembered and needed. The ward was full of injured Brigaders and it seemed to her that they talked to one another all the time, about their comrades back in Aragon and the horrors of a winter campaign and how iniquitous it was that none of the European governments had sent any aid to the democratically elected government in Spain. 'If it hadn't been for the Russians, we'd have been defeated months ago,' he said. 'The Germans and Italians are pouring stuff into this campaign. Non-intervention just opened the door for them. All the most up-to-date weapons, tanks and machine guns, good food, every mortal thing the Fascists could want. They're using this war as a training ground for their troups and a testing ground for their weapons. And we're letting them do it.'

'More fool us!' the man in the next bed agreed.

'I'm so glad you're home,' she said, trying to draw his attention back.

'I'm not,' he answered her at once. 'Casualties are much too heavy out there. The Brigade needs every man it can get. That's where I ought to be.' Then he noticed the expression on her face and tried to explain. 'It's not that I don't want to be with you, Mo. Of course I do. You know that. But you must understand fascism is an evil force, an ugly, evil destructive force, and if we don't defeat it in Spain this time, we shall have a world war on our hands. And I dread to think what that'll be like.'

Just one glimpse at all the pain in that crowded ward was enough to show her with chilling clarity exactly what it would be like. But the bell was ringing to mark the end of visiting time. 'See you tomorrow, Tom,' she said and kissed him briefly, and was torn to see how little her kiss meant to him now.

'I can't understand it,' she said to Queenie. 'We were so close when he went away, and we've written to one another all the time. I answered his letters the minute they arrived. You know that. We made such plans. And now it's as if I didn't exist.'

'That's what war does for yer,' Queenie sympathized. 'Takes a long time ter leave a war behind. That's all it is. All them young fellers I used ter sing to, in the Great War, they was just the same. Still in the trenches, 'alf of 'em. Used ter take 'em one a' two ways, I remember. Either they never said nothink, or they was on about it all the time. 'E'll get over it. You'll see.'

The Ox was of the same opinion. 'Leave 'im be, little Mo,' he advised. ''E's got a lot ter live through, in his mind, so ter speak.'

But it was very hard, all the same. For although his wounds seemed to be healing quite quickly, his need to talk continued unabated, and the news from Europe fuelled his anger. 'You've got to understand, Mo,' he said, 'Fascists are amoral. They don't care what they do as long as they win. I remember one time we were preparing to attack a village and a group of women and children suddenly came out onto the road and started to walk towards us. At first we thought they were refugees. Cease fire, of course, to let them get out of the way. But they weren't refugees. The fascists were right behind them, ordering them on, using them as cover so that they could lob grenades at us and we couldn't return their fire. They were a human shield, Mo, a human shield of women and children, and most of them were killed. Monsters, they are!'

How could she ask him when they were going to marry, in the face of such a story? In fact, how could she find anything to say to him at all? It was all very well for Ma and the Ox to say, 'Don't worry!' and 'wait'. They could always talk about their

424

war when they came to visit. But she felt set aside by the way he talked, as though she was no longer a part of his life.

'It's awful,' she said to Anna when she and Marlene came to Lyndhurst Square the next afternoon. 'I sit there and listen and it makes me feel like crying, it really does. And I couldn't bear that. Not to break down and cry in there, in the ward, in front of all those soldiers.'

'I tell you what,' Anna said at once. 'I'll come with you next time and keep you company. I won't come in or anything. I'll just sit outside in the corridor and then if you feel it's all getting on top of you you can come out and get me and I'll go in and keep him talking while you get over it. And no one any the wiser. How would that be?'

'You're a darling!' Mary said, and kissed her.

'Well, if you're going to do that,' Queenie said, when she heard what they were planning, 'you'd better bring young Marlene with yer an' stay 'ere the night.' 'Ave a break from your Eric, she thought.

So it was arranged, even though Eric was not impressed and wanted to know what he was supposed to have for supper.

'Fish and chips won't hurt you just once in a while,' Anna said. 'He's a wounded soldier. You wouldn't want me not to visit a wounded soldier, now would you?'

'I don't see what it's got to do with you,' he grumbled,

'I told you,' she said. 'She's my sister.'

Chapter Forty

Anna came back to Lyndhurst Square that evening in good time to get to the hospital and prepared for anything. She carried her largest shopping basket crammed with necessaries, nightclothes, flannels and sponges, Marlene's curling iron, pins and hairnet, of course, for it wouldn't have done for the child to be sent to bed uncurled, and a nice Enid Blyton to read her to sleep, a bunch of grapes for the invalid, an evening newspaper to keep him up to date and a bundle of assorted magazines to entertain him, and, tucked neatly on top of everything else, her knitting to keep her occupied while she waited.

She gossiped and chatted all the way to the hospital, determined to keep Mary's mind off her worries, and once they'd arrived she settled down in the empty corridor outside the ward and took out her knitting and began her vigil. She felt extremely happy. Virtuous and useful and sisterly.

The corridor was long and empty and antiseptic, its buff walls half tiled and the brown lino underfoot smelling of disinfectant and echoing the approach of every foot and trolley. Soon she got used to the comings and goings all around her and didn't bother to look up from her knitting when she heard footsteps approaching for the umpteenth time.

So she missed the arrival of the quiet young man, and was quite surprised to glance up from her wool and see him sitting on the opposite side of the corridor. He was a rather ordinary young man, with a pale face and untidy hair. And one of his shoelaces had come undone. In fact, he was rather an untidy man altogether, with grey flannel trousers that looked as though they could do with a good pressing and a tweedy coat

426

with large leather patches over the elbows. But patient too, she could see that from the way he sat. Very still, leaning forward, with his forearms resting on his legs and his clasped hands dangling between his knees. She wondered idly who he'd come to visit, and as he continued to gaze at the lino, and she'd reached a particularly easy patch of knitting, she went on watching him. His hair was untidy of course because he didn't use Brilliantine, but it was rather a nice colour, like straw, with sandy highlights here and there, and the thick lock that fell forward over his forehead like a fringe was oddly charming. From time to time he tried to push it back into position with his fingers, but his rough combing only made it look untidier than ever and it fell forward again as soon as his hand dropped back into his lap. I wish Eric wouldn't wear so much Brilliantine, she thought. It made such a dreadful mess of the sheets and left dark, greasy patches on the back of the armchairs. This young man wouldn't leave greasy patches anywhere. And as she was thinking it, he looked up suddenly and saw that she was staring at him and smiled at her.

She was surprised and embarrassed. How awful to be caught staring like that! But he put her at her ease, almost as though he knew what she was feeling. 'It's boring sitting around waiting, isn't it?' he said.

'Yes,' she said. 'That's why I brought my knitting.' And then as he continued to smile she thought she ought to make conversation, so she went on, 'Are you visiting someone?'

'An old friend,' he said. 'Wounded in the Spanish war. I came on the off chance, just to see how he is. Can't go in just yet. His young lady's with him.'

'Oh,' she said, thinking how tactful that was. 'Have you come far?'

'Dulwich,' he said. 'And you?'

'Stoneleigh Park.'

'That's a long way.'

'Yes,' she said. 'It is. But I shan't be living there much longer. I'm saving up for a flat, in Peckham.' It was all right to tell him. After all, he was a complete stranger, and it was rather nice to have a chance to talk about her dream. 'I've been saving for two years and I've very nearly got enough. I'm going to move as soon as I can.'

427

'That makes two of us,' he said. 'I'm saving for a deposit too. Furnished rooms are all very well but there's nothing like a home of your own.'

'Somewhere where you can do exactly as you like,' she agreed. 'That's right. That's what I want too.' And she sighed, more heavily than she realized.

'Are you … Is it someone from the war too?'

'Oh no,' she said, 'I'm not really visiting. Not what you'd really call visiting.' And then because he was looking puzzled she thought she'd better explain. 'I came with my sister. To keep her company. She finds it all a bit hard. They talk about the war all the time, you see, and it upsets her.'

They were silent for a few minutes while he stood up and took a peep round the corner into the ward. 'Still there,' he said as he sat down. 'I don't like to butt in.'

'No,' she said, reading the pattern to see what she had to do next.

'What are you making?'

'A cardigan. For my little girl.' And she showed him the pattern.

'Lucky girl,' he said. And they settled to wait again.

'I ought to get on with some work too, I suppose,' he said, touching a battered briefcase that lay on the seat beside him.

'What do you do?'

'Librarian,' he said, and there was a touch of pride in his voice. 'College librarian. That's how I met my friend. When he was a student. Fine chap. I always knew he'd do something like this. He was just the sort.'

'It seems quite extraordinary to me,' Anna confessed. 'To go off to some foreign country and fight for a foreign government. Very brave, of course, I'm not saying that, but well …'

'But they're fighting against a system,' he explained. 'A dreadful, brutal system.' And he proceeded to tell her all about Hitler and his concentration camps. 'Terrible people,' he said when he'd finished. 'If anyone opposes them, even in the slightest degree, they beat them up.'

'I've seen it here,' she said. 'I was at Oswald Mosley's rally at Olympia.'

'Were you?' He seemed interested.

So then it was her turn to tell him and in the middle of her story visiting time was over and Mary came out of the ward and found them. 'Well, hello, Ralph,' she said, 'I see you've introduced yourselves. Do you want to pop in for a minute and just say hello to him? I'm sure Sister won't mind.'

Ralph was confused and rather embarrassed. 'We haven't ... I mean ... yes, I would rather like to.' And he lolloped off into the ward, leaving his briefcase behind him.

'How funny!' Anna said. 'Fancy him being a friend of Tom's!'

'Didn't you know who he was?' Mary said. 'How funny! Ralph Andrews, plays the violin in the Amateur. I told you about him ages ago. You remember.' And then they both began to giggle.

'It was all right then,' Anna said. 'With Tom.'

'Bit tricky. I managed. Well, you can see.'

'He's left his briefcase,' Anna said.

So they waited for him. And Mary introduced them formally, 'Ralph Andrews, Anna Barnes, my sister.'

'Yes,' he said. 'I know that.' And he looked straight at Anna and gave her his nice shy smile. What blue eyes he has, she thought, and found that she was smiling back.

Then, as it was late, he insisted on seeing them home to Lyndhurst Square, and Queenie invited him in and Ploochy made coffee and they all sat round talking about the war until nearly midnight, and when he left he said he would see them again, 'outside the ward tomorrow.'

'Isn't he nice!' Anna said.

He was as good as his word and so for the second evening in succession Marlene slept at Granpa Ploochy's while her mother sat happily in her antiseptic corridor talking to Ralph Andrews, and her father ate fish and chips and listened to the wireless and felt hard done by.

On the third evening, Anna said she really ought to go home or there'd be ructions, but on the fourth she and Marlene were back again and the happy conversation continued. From then on, they spent two days at home for every three at Lyndhurst Square, and Eric allowed it even though he complained a great deal and was heavily sarcastic about her healing powers. 'Don't they have nurses in the Middlesex any more?'

429

'He'll soon be better,' Anna said coolly. 'He's coming along very well. The sister said so last night.' And it was true, although she secretly wished it wasn't, for her evenings in the corridor were so easy and so pleasurable and her nights in Peckham so peaceful.

Soon she and Marlene had settled into their new routine almost as though it were a natural pattern. 'Are we going to Granpa Ploochy's today?' Marlene would ask at breakfast, and when the answer was 'yes' her face rounded with pleasure at the prospect.

'You like it at Granpa Ploochy's, don't you?' Anna said.

'Oh yes,' Marlene said, beaming but solemn. 'We have stories.'

'Stories?'

'Granpa Ploochy tells me stories when I go to bed.'

They spoil her after I've gone out, Anna thought, and was warmed by the knowledge.

'Daddy won't come to Granpa Ploochy's with us, will he?' Marlene asked.

'No. I shouldn't think so.'

'Good,' the child said with cheerful vehemence.

'Wouldn't you like Daddy to come with us?'

'No. Daddy shouts.'

But it was too good to last and soon, oh far too soon, the doctors had signed Tom off and Mrs Oxbury had been told she could bring his clothes the next morning.

'We shan't be meeting in our corridor any more,' Ralph said that evening, and he sounded regretful to Anna's hopeful ears. 'I was going to ask you and Anna if you'd like to come to the pictures tomorrow. Last house, after visiting. Now we're not … perhaps I shouldn't.'

Mary was beaming at her good news and now she turned the full force of her delight straight at him. 'Well, not tomorrow,' said. 'Not now. But why not next week? We could make a foursome.'

Her daring took Anna's breath away. 'I can't do that!' she said.

'Why not?' Mary said, bold with happiness. 'You could stay at Lyndhurst Square. Visiting the sick, same as usual. Go on! It 'ud do you good.'

430

Ralph stood between them, waiting in his contained, patient way. 'What do you think?' she asked him. It was important to know.

He considered it for a second or so, then he said, 'I think your sister's right. It would do you good.'

'You dreadful girl!' Anna said to Mary as the two of them sat in the spare bedroom for their usual goodnight chat. 'You could've embarrassed him.'

'Didn't though, did I?'

'I wish I'd met him before,' Anna said. 'It's a bit late now.'

'Better late than never,' Mary said cheerfully, 'and you're not going ter tell me you don't like him.'

'He's the nicest man I've ever met. Make a lovely husband, and don't you dare start match-making.'

'Me?' Mary said, assuming an innocent expression. 'Would I do a thing like that?'

'If I didn't stop you, yes you would.'

'Oh, I'm so happy, Anna. Home tomorrow. Now we can start planning. D'you think he'll fix a date?'

But he didn't. He just went on talking endlessly about war and the possibility of war. Invasions, threats and complicated diplomacy had dominated the spring and now they were making the early summer neurotic. On the day after he was discharged, Tom went straight to King Street, determined to return to Spain. Fortunately for his family's peace of mind the officials there told him very firmly that he'd be more use to his fighting comrades if he spent the summer speaking at public meetings. He was, they said, just the sort of advocate they needed. He was disappointed and relieved and ashamed of his relief. But he agreed.

Now that's settled, Mary thought, perhaps we can plan our lives again. Her final exams were approaching and she knew she would soon have to start applying for jobs. 'Will you go back to teaching, do you think?' she asked him tentatively.

He didn't know. 'We could all be in the middle of a war with Germany by September,' he said. 'Hitler's playing his old game, stirring up the Sudetens. And anyway, I might be needed back in Spain.'

'There's a job going in a junior school in Balham,' she said. 'Shall I apply? What d'you think?'

'It's up to you, Mo,' he said.

431

There didn't seem to be anything she could do or say to persuade him to be interested in her or their future together. They rarely talked of the Health Centre, or any of the ideas that had occupied them all through the winter. He didn't seem the least bit interested in teaching and she was beginning to suspect that he wasn't really interested in her either. Perhaps he'll be better when we start going out together, she thought. After our foursome, perhaps.

And it was a very pleasant evening out. She'd been careful to choose a comedy and was happy to note that Tom laughed a lot and that Ralph seemed quite contented even though it was very low-brow fare. He'd bought a big box of chocolates, and that was a good sign. If her own courtship was in the doldrums, she'd just have to use up her energies aiding and abetting her sister.

When the film was over, Ralph suggested quietly to Anna that they should walk back to Lyndhurst Square and give Tom and Mary a chance to be on their own together. How could she refuse such a thoughtful and tempting offer?

So they walked home together, slowly, in the soft May night, with a romantic white moon silent above their heads and the plane trees rustling their new leaves at them as they passed. It seemed right and natural in such a setting that she should slip her hand in the crook of his nice tweedy elbow, and equally right and natural that they should talk about themselves. She explained the complicated relationships in her family and how it came about that she didn't know she had a sister until they were both grown up.

'And yet you're so fond of one another now,' he said. 'I think that's admirable.'

'Blood's thicker than water,' she smiled. 'It's funny that. Because I never used to think that was true, and yet here we are ...'

'I've bought my flat,' he said. 'It's a great improvement. Streatham Hill. Only a step away from the station. Second floor. I can see Knight's Hill quite clearly from the living room window.'

'Lucky you!' she said. And then she remembered that she'd told him how she was saving for a flat too, and wondered how on earth she was ever going to explain that if he asked her about it. It would mean telling him about Eric, and Eric was one topic of conversation she would rather avoid. Altogether too painful.

'I shall have a housewarming party,' he said. 'Do you think Mary and Tom would like to come?'

'I'm sure they would.'

'And you?' He was looking anxious and unsure of himself and the look touched her.

'Of course,' she said.

'You need friends,' he said. 'I get rather lonely sometimes, to tell the truth.'

'What about your family?'

'They're in York. I don't see them very often.'

'What about brothers and sisters?'

'Haven't got any,' he said, smiling at her ruefully in the light of the street lamp they were passing. 'Only me, I'm afraid.'

'Brothers and sisters are … nice,' she said, and realized that the word was really rather inadequate.

But he didn't correct her or laugh at her the way Eric would have done. 'They are,' he said. 'It's no fun being an only child. When I was little I used to say I'd have a really big family when I grew up. To make up for it.'

'But you're not … ' she began and then stopped, fearing that she might have been intrusive.

'Married?' he said. 'No. I nearly was once. Bought the ring. Named the day. Everything. And then she just walked out on me. After saying a few choice words. Just to bolster up my ego. You know the sort of thing. I was dull and stupid and boring and no woman in her right mind would look twice.'

How unkind! Anna thought. How awful to be hurt like that. 'Poor you!' she said.

'Yes, well,' he shrugged, 'I suppose it's just as well to learn these things young.'

'It's not true!' she said passionately, because his humble acceptance of such treatment was making her angry. 'You're not boring and dull. Not at all. I think you're the nicest man I've ever met.'

'Oh Anna!' he said. 'You *are* a dear, kind girl!'

'I'm not being kind. I mean it.'

'I know,' he said. 'You've made my day.' But they were at the gate. 'I shan't stop,' he said.

She was disappointed and her face showed it. 'Oh, all right,' she said.

'We'll go out again, shall we?'

'As a foursome?' Say no. Ask me out on my own. Can't you see how much I'd love it?

'Yes, a foursome.'

He's so nice, she thought, so correct and proper and gentle. And she went sighing into the house.

Mary was in the kitchen, making cocoa. Tom had gone home early too. 'Oh, Anna,' she said miserably. 'I think he's gone off me. He didn't even kiss me goodnight.' She looked dangerously near to tears. 'I love him more than ever and he never says anything.'

'We're a pair,' Anna commiserated. 'I think I'm in love with Ralph, only he's too much of a gentleman to give me a chance to say so.'

'What *are* we to do?' Mary said, putting the dirty saucepan in the sink to soak. Behind her head the foliage of the cherry tree etched dark blue patterns against the bright night sky. Like a romantic film set.

'If this was the films,' Anna said, 'somebody would come along and sort it all out for us and arrange two nice happy endings.'

'If this was the films!' Mary echoed sadly. 'But it ain't. Life's not like that.'

Had they known it, their father was saying much the same thing a few feet above their heads. 'If this goes on,' he told Queenie furiously, 'I will go to The Lion and give that Tom a piece a' my mind. Why he not marry her? Eh? Our lovely Mary. He want his head examined.' He'd quite forgotten his jealousy and how violently he'd been opposed to this wedding when it was first mentioned. Now his lovebird was unhappy because she should have been married and Tom was dithering. So Tom would have to be persuaded.

'You won't do nothink a' the sort,' Queenie said. 'She's a grown woman. Let 'er fight 'er own battles. I can't bear to see 'er miserable neither, but it ain't none of our business. Not this. So you just keep out of it.'

'She my daughter,' he said stubbornly.

'She's our daughter,' Queenie said gently, 'an' we both want the best for 'er. So you leave well alone. You interfere, you'll only make matters worse. Promise me, Ploo.'

He promised, with a great deal of moustache chewing and sighing. But there was another daughter to consider too. 'And what about Anna?' he grumbled on. 'Why she not leave that Eric and live with Ralph?'

'Perhaps 'e ain't asked 'er yet,' Queenie suggested, laughing at him.

'These young men! What' the matter with them? Why they all so *slow*? I don' understand it.'

'No,' Queenie said, still laughing. 'You wouldn't!'

So Anna continued to hope and Mary went on waiting, and the news from eastern Europe got worse and worse. The foursomes continued too, in their enjoyable but proper way, and on Saturdays they took Marlene out for a treat, to the Zoo, or Madame Tussauds, or the cartoon cinemas. And Ralph came with them, as though that were the natural thing to do. Soon he had become Uncle Ralph and was walking along holding Marlene's hand in what seemed to Anna a most fatherly way. But it was all pleasant and friendly and nothing more.

Mary did her last school practice, in a central school in Tooting, as Londoners were being recruited into 'barrage balloon squadrons'. And her marriage to Tom seemed to be as far away as ever.

In the end, it was Ploochy who forced a decision, or to be more accurate one of Ploochy's riotous parties. It had been Mary's twentieth birthday on May 1st and, now that Tom was well and the exams were over and there were no more excuses for delay, the occasion had to be celebrated, with friends from college and school, and Tom's friends from Spain, and everybody who was even remotely connected with her family or his. The house was full to overcrowding. Guests spilled out into the garden and sat on the stairs to eat their buffet meal and the drawing room was cleared of everything except the piano to make room for dancing. And Mary made sure that Anna and Ralph were among the guests.

To everyone's relief, Eric had pleaded a previous engagement, which Queenie said was just as well, 'otherwise ol' Georgie'ud be givin' 'im whatfor again.'

"E's the one yer want ter get ter Spain,' she told Tom. 'Never see such a fighter. Ain't that right, Ploo?'

Georgie blushed and ducked his head and looked pleased with himself. And Mary told Tom and Ralph the story.

'Good fer you!' Tom approved. Then he saw Anna looking at him quizzically. 'Perhaps I shouldn't say that?'

'Say what you like,' Anna reassured him. 'He was asking for it. I've got no sympathy for him.' She sounded harsher than usual, and Mary and Georgie glancing anxiously in her direction, noticed that there was a bruise on the side of her neck, and opened their mouths to say something about it.

But Albert had been listening and watching too, feeling protective towards the too tender feelings of both his daughters. He took the conversation over immediately, saying the first thing that came into his head. 'So when's the wedding, Tom?'

Mary winced with embarrassment, but Tom, warm with wine and dancing and the thought that a home-grown fascist had got his well deserved come-uppance, grinned and agreed. 'Ought ter be soon, didn't it,' he said.

'Fix a date,' Albert suggested happily. 'We make an announcement 'ere an' now.'

'Don't rush 'em,' Queenie said. 'They ain't engaged yet.'

'Would you like to get engaged first,' Tom asked, 'or shall we get married?'

'Are you proposing?' Mary laughed at him, hardly able to believe her ears.

'I'd get down on one knee, only it's still stiff.'

'Oh my giddy aunt!' Mary said.

'I think she means yes,' Tom said.

Albert went roaring off at once to find Maisie and the Ox. 'Tom! Tom! Where are yer. They're fixing the date.' And at that the news flew about the party like thistledown and the young guests gathered in the drawing room, giggling and bright eyed, to see if it were true.

And after all that, by the end of the party Mary and Tom had agreed that they would get married on the first Saturday in August, and Albert had invited everybody to the wedding. And Tom was happy about it.

436

But Anna was missing and in the general excitement Ralph was the only person to notice. He found her in the garden, huddled into the furthest corner of the hammock. Weeping.

'What is it?' he asked and his voice was tender.

'Nothing,' she said, flicking her fingers across her eyes. 'I'm being silly. That's all.'

'Could you tell me? Would it help?'

'I'm jealous,' she said. 'That's the long and the short of it. It's not that I'm not glad for them. Because I am. I think it's marvellous, and they've earned it, goodness knows. It's just … oh I don't know … I wish it was me, that's all. I'm jealous. Horrid, isn't it?'

'No. I'd say it was perfectly natural.'

'Would you?'

'Yes.' He was looking at her intently, his eyes bigger than usual and curiously dark in his pale, earnest face. 'Tell me if it's none of my business … What I mean is … You're not happy with your husband, are you?'

'No,' she said. It was a relief to be able to admit it. 'How did you know?'

'Well, what you said just now, for a start. And you never talk to him. Everybody else, but not him. And you've always seemed, well, vulnerable. Not in a nasty way, you understand,' because he was afraid he might have insulted her, 'just, well, I've always felt you needed protecting somehow. It's probably none of my business.'

'Oh Ralph!' she said, emboldened by his hesitation. 'It *could* be. If you wanted, it could be. Very easily.'

He took her cold hands and held them between his warm ones. 'I promised myself I wouldn't rush into things, next time,' he said. But he couldn't let this moment pass. She looked so lost and so woebegone and so pretty. 'If you weren't married and I asked you …'

'Oh yes,' she said. 'I'd say "yes".'

'You don't know what I was going to ask you.'

'Oh, I do, I do, and the answer's "yes".'

At last he leant forward and kissed her. And the kiss was slow and tender and very, very enjoyable, just as she'd always known kisses could be and should be. And having begun it was easy to continue, lovely, lingering kisses that made her lips tingle and

437

sent ripples of pleasure up across her scalp and down into her breasts. Lovely, lovely kisses. But during the third or fourth one, he let go of her hands and cradled her face with his fingers, and as he moved, he touched the bruise on her neck. She winced and drew away. She couldn't help it. 'What is it?' he asked at once and with an immediate return of anxiety.

'Nothing,' she said, because it *was* nothing and she wanted the kisses to resume.

He lifted his head until he could look into her eyes. 'You must tell me the truth, Anna,' he said. 'We can only build on truth. You flinched when I touched you. Did I hurt you? I wouldn't want to hurt you for anything in the world.'

'No,' she said. 'You didn't hurt me. It wasn't you. It was Eric, if you must know. He got a bit rough last night. It's a bit of a bruise, that's all.'

He considered this. 'May I see?'

She turned down the collar of her blouse and showed him. He considered again without a word, as though he was absorbing the information and making sense of it. 'Does this happen often? Please tell me.'

So she did, and he listened calmly until she'd finished. Then he considered again. 'I think I've known this all along in a general sort of way,' he said. 'That was what I recognized about you, that you were vulnerable. You made me feel protective. My poor, dear, darling Anna. Now you must listen to me very carefully and not say a word until you've heard everything I've got to say. Do you promise?' She nodded, hopeful and fearful as though she was in a trance. 'You will go home tomorrow, and spend Sunday just as you usually do, and then on Monday morning, after he's left for work, you will pack your things. I will order a removal van for the afternoon and you will open the door to them and tell them what furniture you want moved, Marlene's bed for instance, and her toys, things that belong to you, and you will move out and come to the flat and live with me.'

'But ...'

'Wait, please, wait. I haven't finished. I won't rush you Anna, I promise. We can live as brother and sister in separate rooms, if that's what you want. Or we can let things happen gradually, when we're ready. But whatever we decide to do, I

438

promise you I'll never leave you, and I'll never hurt you, and when you and Eric are divorced, we'll get married. Now tell me what you think.'

She flung herself passionately into his arms and covered his face with kisses. 'You're the nicest man I've ever met in my life,' she said. And burst into tears.

Chapter Forty-One

As soon as the party was over and the guests had departed and Mary and Tom had gone for a walk, Albert began to organize. 'Now,' he said triumphantly to Queenie, 'now, I fix it! Tomorrow I see the vicar, an' book the hall.'

'Not so fast!' she said. 'I know you, Ploo. You'll go rushing off without thinking. You gotta give 'em the sort a' wedding they want. I've asked Ox an' Maisie round fer supper termorrer. We'll fix it between us.'

He was very annoyed. But she was adamant. So for the first time in his life he found himself working in a committee, and a very tedious business it was. For a start the bride and groom couldn't make up their minds whether they wanted to be married in a church or a register office. After his experiences in Spain, where the Catholic church had backed the fascists even to the extent of allowing them to use their church buildings as fortresses, Tom was bitterly opposed to organized religion in any form. But Mary liked the marriage vows. 'I want to promise till death us do part,' she said, 'in sickness and health, for richer and poorer. All of it. I mean it, and I want to say it.'

'You could mean it in a register office,' he argued.

'It wouldn't be the same.'

In the end the Ox found a compromise. Marry in a church with a socialist vicar, and sing socialist hymns. And Mary immediately thought of a suitable church, St Mary Magdalene's, where Ned had been buried. What could be more appropriate than that? So Tom agreed. And the first problem was solved.

'We'll have the reception here,' Albert decided. 'Remove some a' the furniture. Plenty a' room.' That at least would be simple. But of course it wasn't. The list of guests grew longer and longer as the evening progressed, and once it had passed sixty it was obvious that they couldn't be squeezed into the house unless they removed some of the walls as well as the furniture.

'It'll 'ave ter be in a hall,' Queenie said over their third cup of tea.

'Couldn't even get that lot in The Lion,' Maisie said, looking at the list. 'We might do forty at a pinch, but not that lot. An' I bet you ain't finished yet, are yer, Ploo?' Which was true enough, for the list grew minute by minute.

This time it was Tom who found a solution. 'Perhaps we could hire The Star?'

'The Star,' Albert said, smiling his delight at Queenie. ''Course!' How right, he was thinking. The hall that had housed the strike committee during the great dock strike, where Queenie had sung in the old days, where they'd met one another again. It couldn't be anywhere else.

So plans were finally made and the vicar visited and The Star booked, and now it only remained to send out the invitations. And that posed the biggest problem of the lot, as Albert realized as soon as he examined the book of samples. How on earth was this invitation to be worded?

'Don't ask me,' Queenie said unhelpfully. 'I'm off ter the women's committee. You'll think a' somethink.' And she gave him a kiss and was gone.

As it was Wednesday, he took the problem to Jack Beard's and enlisted the aid of his two oldest friends.

Harry Jones was no help at all, although he ruffled his grey hair with both hands and did a great deal of giggling. But Dickie took it seriously and with three double brandies.

'Got yerself a problem 'ere, Ploo,' he agreed. 'I s'ppose yer can't jest say Mr and Mrs Ploochy, can yer?'

'Not with Anna and Eric coming. Be asking fer trouble.'

'*Are* they coming?'

'I don't know, to tell the truth. Haven't seen 'em fer ages. Not since the party. Three weeks nearly.'

'What about Mr Ploochy an' Mrs Whatever-she-is?'

'The neighbours think she's Mrs Pelucci.'

'Oh dear me,' Harry said, giggling again. 'What we gonna do with you, Ploo?'

'Pipe down, Harry,' Dickie instructed. "'Ow can I think wiv your row?' He picked up a beer mat and took out his fountain pen. 'Jusht jot down one a' two notesh.'

Most of the notes grew heads decorated with moustaches and glasses, but in the course of several giggling attempts at approximate writing, inspiration struck. 'Mr Ploochy an' Queenie. How about that?'

They acclaimed him as a genius. But there was still the matter of 'the wedding of their daughter'. Even in his cheerfully befuddled state Albert knew he couldn't lay public claim to this daughter, but the card had to say something.

'Weddin' a' Mary Whatchermacallit an' Tom Thingammyjig,' Dickie said, writing the words with scowling concentration. He might have slopped brandy all over the table but it was a masterly solution.

'What a mind!' Harry said, pink with admiration. Now they could settle down to the rest of the evening, all problems solved.

'My round!' Albert said. 'Don't know what I'd do without yer, Dickie.'

It was an affable evening, so affable in fact that Albert decided he could risk one of his inquiries. From time to time these days, when he thought it wouldn't embarrass his old friend too much, he would ask Harry how Alice was getting along. For even after his retirement Harry had gone on attending to her garden. It didn't take much work and earned him a bit of cash.

'She don't complain,' he told Albert that evening. 'Seems much the same ter me. Minnie 'ad a bit of a cold last week, so Em says.'

'House all right?' Albert asked, following his usual routine.

'Need decorating next year I reckon.'

'It about due,' Albert agreed.

'I wonder she don't let you 'ave your freedom,' Dickie said, made bold by his successes. 'Then you could marry ol' Queenie, an' make an honesht woman of 'er, an' we wouldn't 'ave to go writing all these cards.'

'No point,' Albert told him. 'Marriage service only make a difference at the start. Young Mary sets a lot a' store by it. Funny that! A lot a' store. With me an' Queenie it different. It not fer us. Not now.' And he realized as he spoke that what he was saying was the exact truth. It simply didn't matter any more. He and Queenie were married in everything but law. And what was the law after all these years?

As he made his euphoric way home, he remembered Anna again, and wondered how she was and what she was doing. It was most unlike her to stay away for so long. As soon as he'd got this wedding fixed he'd go down to Stoneleigh Park and see her.

But the house in Clandon Close was a well-furnished, empty shell. Anna and Marlene had gone. Anna had kept her promise. As soon as Eric had walked jerkily out of sight on that Monday morning, she and Marlene had begun to pack, in cardboard boxes filched from the grocer's and the holiday cases and anything else that came to hand, quickly and surreptitiously and trembling with excitement.

The van arrived promptly and this time the removal men were a kindly pair and very helpful. While they carried Marlene's bed out of the house, Anna put the remains of her housekeeping money in an envelope on the mantelpiece and sat down to write a short note to her husband. 'I have left you. I am going to live with someone else who is kind and loves me. I would like you to divorce me. I will give you grounds.' And she added as a satisfyingly malicious afterthought, 'happily,' and signed her name with a flourish.

She and Marlene took a taxi to Streatham Hill and felt very extravagant and adventurous.

'Aren't we going to live with Daddy any more?' Marlene asked as they passed Georgie's shop in Morden.

'No,' Anna said. 'I told you. We're going to live in Streatham with Uncle Ralph.'

'Is Daddy coming too?' Her round face was puckered with anxiety and she was fiddling with one of the buttons on her coat.

Oh dear, Anna thought, poor little thing. She's going to miss him. He *is* her father after all. 'Do you want him to?' she asked, trying to be gentle and understanding about it all.

But the answer was forthright and immediate. 'No I don't. You won't let him, will you?'

'You might not see him again,' Anna felt she had to warn.

'Good,' the child said. 'Then he can't hit me.'

'Does he … did he hit you?'

'Oh yes.'

Anna cuddled her daughter against her side, smitten with a sudden pity for her. 'You'll never be hit again, I promise you,' she said.

There was a silence as the taxi rocked them onwards towards their new life. Then the child returned to her worries again. 'Uncle Ralph doesn't hit people, does he?' It was a question and an anxious one.

'No,' Anna said happily. 'Uncle Ralph would never hit anyone. He's much too nice.'

By teatime they were settled in at Dunbarton Court and had arranged Marlene's furniture in the spare room and made a pot of tea for themselves and gone shopping. The child was still anxious so Anna was keeping her busy. They just had time to prepare a special supper before Ralph returned.

'Well!' he said as he stepped into the hall. 'What a welcome! That smells good.' And seeing Marlene standing hesitantly beside her mother tugging nervously at one straggly ringlet, 'How are my two girls? Don't I get a kiss when I come home?'

What a dear man he is, Anna thought. Just like Dadda. He's even got love to spare for poor little Marlene, and she's nothing to do with him. So they both kissed him, Anna lovingly and Marlene dutifully, and supper was served. They were beginning to feel like a family already.

After supper it was time for the evening ritual of bath, hair curling and bedtime reading, which he watched in his unobtrusive way, noticing everything and saying nothing. Then when Marlene had been settled into her familiar bed in her unfamiliar room, and had had two stories read to her, one from each of them, they sat on either side of the fireplace, just like an old married couple and listened to the wireless. He hadn't kissed her since his return, and that disappointed her, but she didn't remark on it because it occurred to her that he might be shy. Finally, at eleven o'clock, he knocked out his pipe on the fireplace, and returned it to the rack and stood before the empty grate considering. She was getting used to his long, thoughtful pauses by now, so she waited.

'You could sleep in my old bed in Marlene's room if you'd like to,' he said. 'I bought a … big bed for us. They delivered it this morning. It's very comfortable. I tried it.'

Suddenly the thought of making love to him in that new big bed was both immensely attractive and overpoweringly alarming. She was torn by these two conflicting emotions and her face showed it. 'Would you want …' she began, but how could she ask him a thing like that?

He stood looking down at her. 'I wouldn't do anything unless you wanted me to,' he assured her. 'We will take everything gradually, I promise. I'll be very careful and I won't hurt you. I'm not Eric.'

So they slept in the same bed and they made love by tender, gradual degrees, doing little more than kiss and cuddle for the first three nights, and for the next three stroking and exploring, murmuring affection all the time. But at last the moment arrived when she really felt she might like him to do *it*, and then she quailed. He'd been so loving and tender up to now, and she'd enjoyed it all so much, what if it all went wrong? What if he turned out to be rough? What if all men were rough when they did it? But he wasn't. He was gentle and gradual then, just as he'd been all the time, and soon she was enjoying their quiet rhythm together and moving her own body in time with his. Actually joining in, it was amazing, in a swooning, languorous rhythm that took her slowly and surely towards the pleasure she'd dreamed of. And it *was* pleasurable, marvellously, satisfyingly, overwhelmingly pleasurable.

When he'd got his breath back, he lifted his body to look at her. There was a question on his face but he didn't ask it. 'Yes,' she said, pulling him down close to her again. 'Yes. It was lovely.'

The next morning she woke early and completely. This was a surprise, for she was usually sluggish in the morning and liked to lie a-bed. Now she had so much energy she simply had to get up. Ralph was still sleeping peacefully, so she eased herself off the bed, put on her dressing gown and went off to the bathroom to wash her hair. I'll make myself really beautiful for today, she thought, because he's the dearest man and he is the very very best.

... ke when she was sitting at her dressing table, with her

wet hair turbaned in a white towel. They smiled at one another through the mirror. Then he watched her as she dried her face with the edge of the towel. 'What colour is your hair really?' he said.

'Dark brown.'

'Like Mary's.'

'That's right.'

'That's a lovely colour,' he said. 'Why do you dye it?' It was a straight question, there wasn't a trace of criticism in it, and he was smiling at her in the most loving way.

'To look beautiful,' she said.

'You're very beautiful now,' he said, watching her face in the mirror. 'I think you'd be gorgeous with your hair its own natural colour.'

She walked across and sat down on the bed beside him. 'Is that what you'd like?' she said.

'It's your hair, Anna,' he said. 'It's not up to me to tell you what to do with it.'

'That's what you'd like,' she said. But that was the easiest thing in the world. If that's what he wanted, that's what he should have. 'It's growing out already,' she said.

'You're so generous, Anna,' he said, and he held her hands and kissed them. 'Would you do something for Marlene too?'

'For Marlene?'

'Yes. She hates having to sleep in curlers, you know. They hurt her head.'

'How do you know that? Has she been complaining?'

'No. Poor little thing, she doesn't have to. You can see how uncomfortable they are. Look at the way she lowers her head into the pillow.'

He's so observant, she thought. I never noticed that. And the thought shamed her a little. 'What do you want me to do?' she asked.

'Let me take her to the hairdressers and have a nice ne straight cut like all the other little girls.'

'She'd hate it. She likes to look pretty.'

'No, Anna. She likes to please you.'

She thought about it for a few moments, towelling he 'All right,' she said. 'If you think that's what she war many things were changing, why not change that too?

446

He took her that very afternoon, because it was his afternoon off, and returned with a child transformed. She stood shyly beside his long legs, holding his hand and looking up apologetically at her mother. Her hair was clubbed short and straight and there was a neat fringe across her forehead.

'There!' he said triumphantly. 'What do you think of that?' And his eyes were signalling to her, most unmistakably, praise her! Tell her she's beautiful, approve of her!

'You look lovely,' she said. 'Absolutely lovely. Come and give Mummy a kiss.' And she was touched to see how eagerly the child ran to be cuddled. She *had* been worried about it. Poor little thing. And he'd known. How had he known? He really was most perceptive.

'I love you,' she said, from above Marlene's sleek head.

And as he was smiling at her, the afternoon post plopped into the letter box. 'Do you think that's Eric saying we can have a divorce?' she said. 'We deserve a reward.'

It wasn't. It was an invitation for Mr Ralph Andrews to Tom and Mary's wedding. A reminder from the outside world that they'd both been ignoring during their love-locked days.

' 'Oh dear,' she said. 'I suppose we shall have to tell people soon. What'll they think?' She didn't like the idea at all.

'We won't say anything to anybody. Not just yet,' he reassured her. 'Grow your hair out first and then we'll go visiting together and they'll all be so amazed at the new short-haired Marlene and the new dark-haired Anna they won't notice who you're with.'

'It'll take months to grow out,' she said.

'Then we'll hide away for months.'

'I shall look very weird while it's growing,' she said, realizing what she'd let herself in for.

'I shall buy you one of those nice turban hats and you can tuck it all underneath and nobody'll see anything.'

'You're very practical, aren't you?' she said. 'What do you want for your tea?'

He bought her the hat, and she wore it to go shopping. And the dark hair grew slowly. And they went on hiding away. But they couldn't hide for ever.

A bundle of letters arrived through the letter box at Lyndhurst

Square nearly every day, acceptances and congratulations and offers of gifts. It was most exciting and Mary loved it. 'Here's one from Uncle Charlie,' she told her mother at breakfast a week or two later.

'That's nice,' Ma said, licking the marmalade off her fingers. 'Who's the one underneath? Looks very official. I 'ope it ain't a bill.'

It was addressed to Mrs Eric Barnes and postmarked Central London. 'How funny!' Mary said. 'I wonder why they've sent it here.'

'Ring her up and tell 'er,' Albert said. 'High time we found out what she up to. We haven't seen 'er for three weeks.'

Was it so long? Mary thought. She'd been so busy preparing for the wedding she'd hardly noticed how the days were spinning past. Now she felt guilty and selfish to have neglected her sister for so long. 'Perhaps they're on holiday,' she suggested, hoping it was true.

'Never said nothink about it if they are,' Queenie said. 'Give 'em a ring, Mary. See what's what.'

So Mary rang Clandon Close, and couldn't get an answer. 'That's very odd,' she said. 'They can't be out this early in the morning. Perhaps they are on holiday.'

'Leave it to me,' Albert said. 'I try later. In the afternoon.' But he came home that evening, face puckered with worry, to say he hadn't got an answer either and he'd been trying off and on all day.

'Something's up,' Mary said, now thoroughly alerted. 'I shall get Tom to take me over to see Ralph this evening. See if he knows what it is.'

'He's moved house,' Tom said, when he was told. 'Sent me a card with his new address. I've got it somewhere. Hang on a tick.'

So they went to Streatham Hill.

Anna and Marlene had been very busy that afternoon, baking cakes, and when Mary rang at the door they were both spattered with flour and glowing from the heat of the oven. It would have been hard to say who was the most surprised when they opened the door.

'Anna!' Mary said. 'What 're you doing here?'

'I'm letting my hair grow out,' Anna said foolishly, her

hands fluttering up to her piebald head as though she was trying to cover it.

'What?'

'Well, aren't you going to let us in?' Tom asked.

'Oh dear! Yes,' Anna said stepping back to make room for them. 'It's just … I don't know … Oh dear!'

'You've left him!' Mary said grinning at her. 'You're living with Ralph.'

'Don't think ill of me,' Anna begged. 'I really couldn't go on with Eric another minute. I know it looks bad but I …'

But Mary wouldn't let her say any more. She grabbed her round the waist and hugged her fiercely. 'Best thing you ever did,' she said. 'Don't you think so, Tom?'

And to Mary's amazement, Tom said he thoroughly agreed, and kissed her.

'Stay to tea?' she asked, and she looked as bewildered as she felt. She'd been so sure they would disapprove, because they were so straight about things like this. And yet here they were congratulating her as if she'd got married properly, and wasn't … well … doing what she was doing. 'Ralph'll be home in a minute.' And he was.

It was a lovely tea party, and even the letter didn't upset them, although on another occasion it very well might have done. It was a disagreeable epistle from Eric saying he wouldn't divorce her under any circumstances. She had made her bed and now she must lie on it. His mother had always been right about her. She was nothing more or less than a trollop. She could live with her fancy man as long as she liked and it would serve her right.

Ralph read it aloud at the table, in such splendidly mock serious tones that it made them all laugh. 'He's even signed it "Yours sincerely",' he said.

'You're very well rid of him,' Mary said.

'And so say all of us!' Tom said. 'When are you coming to Lyndhurst Square? Ploochy's quite worried about you.'

'I thought they'd be shocked,' Anna said.

'You underestimate them,' Mary said. 'Besides, you're only doing what your dadda did, when all's said and done. It must run in the family.'

'What runs in the family?' Marlene wanted to know.

'Noses in winter,' Ralph told her, 'and then we have to keep blowing them, don't we?' And they all laughed again and the child laughed with them, although she didn't understand the joke at all.

'I think you ought to be my matron of honour,' Mary said, 'and then everybody can see we approve of you.'

'I thought you didn't want any bridesmaids,' Tom said.

'I do when it's Anna.'

'I'd love to,' Anna said, 'but what about my hair? It won't have grown out. It'll look awful.'

'Wear a hat,' her sister said practically. 'Can I have some more cake?'

'They don't seem to mind about us, after all,' Anna said when her two guests had kissed her goodbye and gone. 'I can't think what I was worried about.'

Chapter Forty-Two

The summer term came to an end, and Mary's last teaching practice was so successful that the central school offered her a job in September. Tom went to the divisional office in the same area and offered his services too and was pleased to report that although the clerk was cool he was sure there would be a job before the new term began, 'seeing you're a graduate'. Service in Spain had annoyed the headmaster of a private grammar school, but the L.C.C. had different values.

Mary and Maggie made her wedding dress, using the simplest pattern they could find, with a plain skirt and a high-necked bodice that would easily convert to a blouse afterwards, and Anna bought a suit to match her turban hat. The presents began to arrive, the wedding ring was bought, and Tom found a flat in Tooting High Street for them to rent. It was in a block called Marian Court and would suit them well enough, they said, being within walking distance of the tube and Mary's school, and an easy tram ride to Streatham Hill. Albert was delighted to think that they would be living in Tooting, and told them it was a fine place to start married life. And soon it was only five days to their wedding.

They were going to the theatre with Ralph and Anna that night, and had agreed to meet in the public bar of the Bun House in Peckham High Street. Tom was very late, and when he arrived he looked so ill that Mary was instantly alarmed.

'It's nothing,' he said, irritably shaking her hand away from his arm. 'Got a bit of a temperature, that's all. Are we ready?'

'You go on,' Mary said to Anna. 'We'll follow when he's better.'

But Anna wouldn't hear of it. 'Get a taxi,' she said to Ralph.

'He's ill. He ought to go home.'

'We'll go back to Lyndhurst Square,' Mary said. 'Come on Tom. You're in no fit state for the theatre, so don't argue.'

'You're just like your ma,' he said, but he went with her, and they noticed that he was glad to be holding on to her arm.

Queenie took one look at him and called the doctor, and the doctor, having taken his temperature, examined his wound. It was swollen and inflamed. 'How long has it been like this?' he asked.

'Two or three days,' Tom admitted, and when the doctor tutted, 'I thought it would go off.'

'Infected,' the doctor said. 'Needs hospital treatment and rather quickly I should say. When did you receive this injury?' And when Tom had told him, 'I presume you were treated at the Middlesex? May I use your phone, Mrs Pelucci?'

'We're getting married on Saturday,' Tom said weakly. There were two round patches of unnatural colour on his cheeks now and his skin was pale and shiny with sweat.

'Then we must get you in and out of hospital as quickly as we can, mustn't we,' the doctor said and went off to phone for an ambulance.

'Why didn't you tell me you were feeling ill?' Mary said fiercely as soon as the doctor was out of earshot. 'Three days and you never said a word.'

'Don't be cross with me, Mo,' he begged. 'I thought you'd think I was trying to put things off. Get out of my responsibilities, you know. After all the time I took to make up my mind when ...'

She flew to his side to kiss him and hold his hands. 'You dear, daft, silly thing,' she said. 'Don't you ever do such a thing again. Oh Ma, what are we to do with him?'

'Give 'im a chance ter breathe, poor boy,' Queenie said, practical as ever.

He was admitted to hospital that night and operated on the next morning. As the doctor had predicted, his wound was re-infected and this time it had to be drained and took far longer to heal. So the wedding had to be postponed.

For several days he was more ill than either he or Mary cared to admit, drifting in and out of a fevered, troubled sleep. Mary spent as much time at the hospital as the sister would allow and came home white-faced and anxious to report to her mother and Ploo.

This time it was Queenie who felt most upset. 'She don't eat enough ter feed a sparrer,' she worried to Albert. 'She'll be ill 'erself, if she goes on like this.'

'Soon as he turns the corner, we fix the weddin' again,' Albert promised. 'That'll make 'er feel better. You see.'

But it was a long time before the infection was finally under control, and even then the doctors said it would take months for the wound to heal as it should. 'You were very lucky not to get gangrene,' the ward sister told him. 'Whoever nursed you out in Spain did a good job.'

The mention of Spain reminded him of the war he'd left behind. When the sister moved on to another patient he asked one of the walking wounded to lend him a newspaper. Just as he'd feared in April, the Fascist attack had broken the republican line in two. Now, so the paper said, the International Brigade was being disbanded and sent home. Franco had won.

'It's dreadful, Mo,' he said when she came to visit him that night. 'All that effort for nothing. All those casualties.' He was very depressed.

She tried to cheer him. 'They've sent Lord Runciman out to Czechoslovakia to see if he can fix a settlement. He went the day you got ill. At least they're trying to stop the worst war.'

'Won't work,' he said gloomily. 'If Hitler wants part of Czechoslovakia he'll take it. Lord Runciman won't make a ha'p'orth a' difference. If you ask me, the war with Germany'll start before I can get out of here. I can't see us ever getting married this way.'

'If the worst comes to the worst,' she said, 'I'll marry you in the ward.'

'I believe you would an' all,' he said, and that cheered him up at last.

But Mary wept when she got home that night, and neither of her parents could comfort her. 'There's going to be a war,' she cried. 'I know it. An' Tom'll go back in the army an' get killed an' I shall never see him again. I don't think we'll ever get married. Oh, Ploo, I'm so miserable.'

'Don't cry, my lovebird,' he tried to comfort. 'I fix the

453

wedding day again. It all be all right. You see.' He was so distressed, he was chewing his moustache furiously.

'It's like a nightmare,' Mary said. 'Like a race in a nightmare. Which'll come first, our wedding or the war.'

'Your wedding,' Albert told her. 'I promise.'

'Oh, Ploo!' she said. 'Nobody can stop this war. Not even you.'

In the days that followed it began to look as though she was right. For the situation in Czechoslovakia got steadily worse. Egged on by their Nazi leader, Henlein, and encouraged by money from their Nazi friends in Germany, the Sudeten Germans took to the streets again, demanding autonomy. There might only be three million of them, as the British press were always pointing out, but they intended to get their own way.

'Fat lot a' good sending that fool Runciman,' Billy Jones said angrily. 'Just a sell-out that was. 'E'll give in to 'em.'

'You don't want another war, Billy, surely ter goodness,' his father protested. 'We 'ad enough with the last one. All them fellers killed.'

'Supposed ter be the war to end wars,' Em pointed out. 'Let the Czechs sort it out fer themselves. That's what I say.'

It was what a good many newspapers were saying too. At the beginning of September, the *Evening Standard* reported a speech by a French politician with the same opinion. He wished to assure the British public, the article said, that 'France will refuse to fight a war to save peace.'

'And quite right too,' Em said to Tilley when they met at the shops.

'Are we going to have a war?' Anna asked Ralph as they ate their nice peaceful breakfast in their nice sunny dining room.

'Yes,' he said seriously. 'It looks as though we are.'

'I wish Eric would let us get married.'

'We *are* married, my darling. In every sense that matters.'

'If there was a war, would they make you join the army?'

'I'm thirty-four,' he said. 'Perhaps I shall be too old.'

'Oh I *do* hope so!'

'Thanks!' he said, laughing at her.

On the 5th of September Mary started work at Ensham school,

and on the 9th Tom was finally discharged from hospital. Albert fixed the second wedding date immediately, October 1st, just three weeks away. 'There you are, my lovebird,' he said to Mary. 'They won't start their war in three weeks.'

But the very next Monday Hitler held a rally in Nuremberg and made a most belligerent speech to the accompaniment of blaring trumpets and the frenzied chanting of his followers. If the Czechoslovakian government didn't give him and the Sudetens what they wanted, he threatened, Prague would be razed to the ground.

There was a flurry of anxious diplomatic activity. Lord Runciman came home from Prague and no less a person than Neville Chamberlain, the Prime Minister, flew out to Berchtesgaden to speak directly to Adolf Hitler. The *Daily Herald* was hopeful. Surely Chamberlain would find some way of avoiding this war, close though it was, for wasn't he a man most deeply committed to maintaining the peace?

'Send them invites,' Queenie advised. 'We ain't got too long, you ask me.'

'We do 'em this afternoon,' Albert promised. 'Anna an' young Marlene can help. An' we'll get Maisie ter come too.'

'Just address the envelopes,' Queenie said as they all settled round the dining room table that afternoon. 'an' write "you" or "you both" inside. Save time. They know who they are. You can put 'em in the envelopes, cantcher, Marlene?'

Marlene nodded her nice neat head, and held out her hand for the first card to be finished.

'Tick 'em off the list as you go,' Queenie instructed. 'There's the first, Marlene.'

They worked cheerfully and rapidly, and soon Marlene had too many envelopes to manage alone and Anna had to help her. And in the middle of all their paperstrewn activity, Anna had an idea. When nobody was looking she took one of the little cards on which her father had written the word 'you both' and hid it in the pocket of her dress.

Later that evening, she teased Ralph into addressing an envelope for her, to Mrs Pelucci and Mrs Holdsworthy. He did it, but under protest. 'I hope you know what you're doing.'

'Sort of match-making,' she said. He groaned. 'Well, not really match-making,' she said, 'it's just … I don't like to think of them being lonely all by themselves in that great house. Specially now I'm so happy. It doesn't seem fair. Why shouldn't they have a bit of fun in their lives for once in a while?' And besides, she thought, it would be ripping fun to see her father's face when they turned up at the church. He could hardly refuse to let them in, not when there were two of them and not with an invitation. The combination of mischief and kindness delighted her. At last, *she'd* been able to do something to help her mother. Not Georgie, or Minnie, or Harry, or anyone else. Just her. And didn't it prove she was the best of the lot? As the days passed, she hugged her secret to herself and was warmed by it.

Alice and Minnie were surprised and puzzled by their unexpected invitation. 'Who'd have thought that?' Alice said, looking at the little card with amazement. 'He is a funny man, and no mistake. I wonder who Mary Chapman is.'

'That woman's daughter, I wouldn't mind betting,' Minnie said. 'I wonder what she's like?'

'He is a funny man,' Alice said again. She didn't quite know how she felt about this sudden approach. 'Do you think he wants to see me again, Minnie? Is that what it is?' She wasn't even sure now whether she wanted to see him. She'd grown so used to life without him. But it was flattering to be asked, nevertheless. It showed he hadn't forgotten her.

'Will you accept?' Minnie asked eagerly.

'It doesn't say R.S.V.P.,' Alice said. 'And it's very short notice. I'll see what Anna thinks on Saturday.'

Anna thought they ought to go. 'When he offers an olive branch,' she said.

'We'll answer it tonight,' Alice decided. 'I think you're right. We ought to accept.'

'Answer it now,' her helpful daughter said, 'and I'll put it in the post for you on my way home.'

'Are you staying to tea?' Alice said. 'You can take your hat off if you like, you know.' It puzzled her that Anna never removed her hat these days. And never said anything about Eric. And always seemed so happy, but in quite a new way, subdued but at the same time very intense.

'There's something going on with our Anna,' she said to

Minnie, when her daughter trotted off clutching their acceptance.

'She's very full of herself,' Minnie agreed, 'and that's a certain sure thing.' It made a good subject for speculation.

Now it was only a week to the wedding, and people in London were quite sure that the war would start at any moment. Trenches had been dug in the parks and there were piles of sandbags against the walls of all the most important buildings. On Monday the staff at Ensham school were told that plans had been made to evacuate them and their pupils 'as soon as hostilities commenced'. On Tuesday the fleet was mobilized and a state of emergency declared. And gasmasks were delivered to Lyndhurst Square and they all had to try them on, carefully adjusting the straps so that the rubber fitted tightly and didn't allow any air inside at any point. Their evil-smelling ugliness was the final sign that this war couldn't be avoided. 'We're in fer it now, Ploo,' Queenie said resignedly, fitting her mask back into its cardboard box. 'They'd never've give us these else.'

'It *is* a race,' Mary said, later that evening. 'And we're going to lose it.' She and Tom had spent the last six days decorating the living room of their flat. Now it all seemed a waste of time. 'What's the good of making it all look so nice when it might be bombed flat tomorrow.'

Tom put his arms round her as they sat together on their boxy sofa. It was a comfort to hold her close. 'They've only got to keep the peace four more days,' he said.

'I can't see it, can you?'

'No,' he agreed sadly. 'I can't.'

She kissed him hungrily, glad that he responded so quickly and passionately. 'Oh Tom, don't let's wait till Saturday. Let's go on.'

He was trembling with desire for her, but he resisted temptation, just as he'd done on every single occasion since he'd come out of hospital. 'No,' he said tenderly. 'We mustn't. We'll wait. It's only four days, Mo, that's all. We'll do the right thing. That's important.'

'Who would know?' she tempted, kissing his neck.

'We would.'

'Oh God, Tom,' she said. 'Why are you so correct? I want you. You want me. Why not?'

He took her hands gently from his neck and held them. 'When the Brigade first went into battle,' he said, 'they swore under fire. It's very easy to swear when you're scared stiff. But afterwards they had a meeting and a vote and they decided that if they were to fight Fascism with any hope of winning they had to be correct in all their behaviour. Never sinking to the lowest level. Not even to a lower one. It's important. That's what gives you moral strength, Mo. It's important.'

'It sounds right,' she sighed. 'But it doesn't feel right. I can tell you that.'

'Let's make a cup of tea and then we'll listen to the Prime Minister. Take our minds off ... things.'

So they made tea in their new, wedding present china and turned on the new radio that Georgie and Lily had given them and settled down to listen.

'However much we may sympathize with a small nation confronted by a big and powerful neighbour,' the tired, reedy voice said, 'we cannot in all circumstances undertake to involve the whole British Empire in a war simply on her account.'

'He's going to let Hitler get his own way,' Tom said. 'God help the poor Czechs!'

'Armed conflict between nations is a nightmare to me,' the voice went on, 'but if I were convinced that any nation had made up its mind to dominate the world by fear or force, I should feel that it must be resisted. Under such a domination life for people who believe in liberty would not be worth living; but war is a fearful thing, and we must be very clear, before we embark on it, that it really is the great issues that are at stake.'

The next day he flew to Munich.

Chapter Forty-Three

It was Saturday and the first day of October, 1938 and, according to the *Daily Express*, peace in Europe was assured. Mussolini had drawn up the new Czechoslovakian frontier, Hitler was to be allowed to occupy the Sudetenland, and the agreement was signed. Lord Beaverbrook was happy to headline his declaration that 'Britain will not be involved in a European war this year, or next year either.'

'Well, that's a mercy!' Minnie said as she made a last minute adjustment to the wax fruit on her new hat. 'And the weather so much nicer too.' Friday had been so cold and wet.

Alice fastened the button on her new, dove grey coat and considered her reflection. She'd taken considerable pains over her appearance for this wedding, because if Albert was going to see her again after all these years she wanted to be worth seeing. So for once in her life she'd treated herself to a completely new outfit, a coat, hat and gloves in grey, and a handbag and shoes in a quiet, complementary nut brown. It had been a long time since she'd last taken stock of her appearance, but she couldn't fault much of what she saw. Her hair had gone white so quickly it had given her quite a shock, but now the change was completed she was really quite pleased with it. It was a nice white, she thought, with a hint of pale blue about it, like snow, and it looked well between the soft grey of her new hat and the bushy fox fur of her collar. Her new teeth were an improvement too, a much better fit and not half so obtrusive as the others had been. She allowed her reflection a slight smile, to test them, and began to smooth on her grey kid gloves. The car would be here at any minute and it wouldn't do to keep it waiting.

There was consternation in Charlmont Road. Harry Jones couldn't do up the jacket of his best suit. 'Look at that, will yer?' he begged Em. 'Told you I'd put on weight. That's what comes a' retiring.'

'Jolly good job, an' all,' Em said, lovingly. 'Where did I put the confetti?'

'I can't go like this, Em.'

''Course yer can. Who's gonna look at you?'

'I wouldn't want old Ploochy ter think I was showin' disrespect,' Harry worried.

Em put her hands on his shoulders and kissed him warmly. 'You wouldn't show disrespect ter no one,' she said. 'You're an old love, Harry Jones. I'm glad I married yer.'

He was delighted by this unlooked for caress, and answered it at once, holding her about her nice plump waist, close and easy.

'You ain't so dusty yourself,' he said.

There was nostalgia in the corner shop. Tilley was putting on her make-up and remembering Lily's wedding. 'Only seems the other day,' she said, spitting into her little pad of mascara to moisten it. 'Scared stiff she was, poor kid. I never thought she'd go through with it, and now here she is, mother a' three.'

'Last wedding we was all tergether was young Anna's, poor girl,' Dickie said, fixing his tie-pin. 'Be some sport, this one, I reckon.'

There was some anxiety in Poplar Road. The children had all been dressed in their Sunday best and told to sit quietly in the hall and wait and Lily and Georgie were upstairs in their bedroom putting the finishing touches to their public appearance.

'I do hope it all goes off all right,' Georgie said, brushing his hair carefully. 'Dadda's been like a bear with a sore head, what with it being postponed and rearranged in such a rush and everything.'

'It'll be lovely,' Lily assured him, anchoring her hat firmly with two hatpins. The clouds were moving too rapidly today for the wind to be trusted. 'How do I look?'

460

'Beautiful,' he said. And so she did, with her brown hair so thick and wavy, and the blue of her new dress matching those wide blue eyes so perfectly. She was looking at him through the mirror with such affection that he simply had to bend and kiss her. 'If Mary and Tom are even half as happy as we've been, they'll be very lucky,' he said.

She stood up at once and threw her arms round his neck to return his embrace. 'I do love you, Georgie,' she said, between one kiss and the next. It was a delicious moment. So delicious that they didn't hear their children trailing up the stairs towards them.

'Are we going to this wedding or not?' Johnny asked from the doorway.

'Humph!' his sister snorted with the weary patience of the young. 'They're at it again! We shall be ages!'

In Dunbarton Court Anna was weeping. She sat on the floor of the narrow hallway with her back against the wall and Marlene anxiously attentive beside her and cried as if her heart were breaking. She knew she was being ridiculous but she couldn't help it. Suddenly, and in a way she couldn't control or understand, everything had become too much. And it *was* silly. Really silly. Why, only the day before they'd been having a little celebration of their own, and she'd felt really happy.

She'd been to the hairdresser's and the remains of those awful yellow ends had finally been cut away, leaving her, at long, long last, with a full head of short, dark curls. The effect had been quite stunning, like seeing her old, unmarried self again, as if none of the awful things had ever happened. She'd put that tatty old turban back in its box and dressed herself up in her wedding suit, which was very stylish, and suited her new colouring really well, being a cyclamen skirt and a little black jacket with huge revers striped in cyclamen and black, and a dear little pill-box hat, in cyclamen, to match. With her eyebrows grown and her hair entirely its own colour again she looked a different woman.

'So you should,' Ralph had said when she'd told him what she'd been thinking. 'You are a different woman.'

Which was true enough. So really she ought to be feeling happy still, not sitting on the floor with the tears rolling out of her eyes in this frighteningly uncontrolled way.

It was the letter that had done it. Just as she'd been putting on the kettle, the postman had arrived with a horribly official-looking letter, in a typewritten envelope, addressed to Mrs Eric Barnes. She was almost afraid to open it, because she knew it would be from Eric, and even the thought of him brought bad memories, even now when she was safely away from him. She stood in the hall for a long time just holding the envelope, plucking up courage, and when she finally unfolded the long narrow paper and began to read it her hands were shaking.

It was from Eric's solicitor. He was filing a petition for divorce on grounds of adultery. She had to read it twice before she could believe it. Then, and inexplicably, she began to cry.

'Don't cry, Mummy,' Marlene begged, dabbing at the flowing tears with her pocket handkerchief. Her eyes were strained with anxiety.

'It's all right darling,' Anna gasped between sobs. 'Don't be scared. Mummy's being silly. Be all right in a minute.'

'I'll get Uncle Ralph, shall I?'

'Oh, oh, I don't know.' This was getting worse and worse. She was sobbing aloud, and the child looked so frightened. She *must* stop herself. But she couldn't even see straight, she was crying so much.

She heard the child's feet pattering away down the hall, and her voice outside the bathroom, where Ralph was shaving. 'Uncle Ralph! Uncle Ralph! Please come. Mummy's crying.' Then there was a quick movement, swirling the enclosed air in their little hallway, and he was beside her and had his arms round her and was lifting her to her feet.

'Don't cry, my dear love,' he soothed. 'Don't cry. Tell me what it is. Anna, darling. Look at me. Tell me what it is.'

At his touch, the jumbled misery inside her mind shifted into partial focus. 'I don't want to go to the wedding,' she wailed. 'Oh Ralph, it'll be so awful. I wish I hadn't sent that invitation. It's all going to go wrong. Everything I do goes wrong. I don't want to go to the wedding!'

He walked her gently into the living room, murmuring and cuddling, with Marlene trailing behind them, pale with frightened incomprehension. Then they all sat on the sofa together and cuddled until Anna's sobs began to subdue. 'Was it the letter?' he asked.

She was still clutching the letter. How silly! 'No,' she said, handing it across, 'it's a good letter. Marvellous really. It wasn't that.'

He read it briefly and put it in the pocket of his dressing gown without comment. Then he thought, sitting patiently beside her, his right thumb absentmindedly exploring the unshaven side of his face. When he spoke, it was to Marlene, although his slow, quiet, reassuring smile was directed at both of them, one after the other.

'What a very good girl you are,' he said, 'to come and get me. So sensible. Don't you think so, Anna? A very good girl. Mummy's all right really. People do cry like this sometimes. All of us do. Think how you cried when you fell over. And that was because you thought you were terribly hurt, didn't you?' The child nodded, remembering. 'Once we knew you'd only grazed your knee, everything looked quite different, didn't it?'

'Did you fall over, Mummy?' Marlene asked.

'In a way,' Anna said, and she managed a smile, even though it was very misty-eyed.

So that was what it was. Her fears receded at once. 'Do you want a plaster?'

'Nice cup of tea,' Ralph said. 'We'll make it now, shall we? You and me. We'll be nurses. And then you can have your bath and then we'll have breakfast.'

How *normal* he is! Anna thought, normal and reasonable and patient. If anybody can cope with this, he will. But the misery went on bubbling away behind her eyes, and she didn't understand it and was afraid she would succumb again.

Tea was made and drunk, cheerfully enough, and Marlene was settled in a bath made special with Mummy's bath salts, and Ralph returned. He still hadn't finished shaving, Anna noticed, but he was calm and loving and very dear.

'Now,' he said sitting beside her. 'What is it really?'

'It's me,' she said, miserably. 'I can't tell you.' If he knew how horrid she really was, he'd stop loving her.

He looked at her seriously for several seconds. When he spoke, it was almost as though he'd read her mind. 'I love you as you are,' he said. 'All of you. Everything about you, good and bad. Not just the best, the worst too. That's what I mean by love.'

'But you don't know how bad I can be. Even when I'm making an effort to be good, I have horrid ideas. Oh, I can't go to the wedding!'

He took her hands gently and held them, caressing them with his fingers. 'Tell me what you're afraid of,' he urged. 'All of it. I promise I shall love you no matter what it is.'

She wasn't sure she could explain. Everything was so muddled. But his tenderness permitted her to try. 'It's the invitation,' she said. 'I didn't just send it because I wanted mummy to have a nice time. I *did* want that, of course. I really did. I don't like the thought of her at home all by herself. I wanted her to be part of the family again. Well, not part of the family exactly … That's silly. She *is* family. My family. Oh dear, I can't even explain it to you. But not hidden away. Happy. I meant well, you see. I really did. But it wasn't just that. It never is with me. I get this sort of tangled-up feeling, and then I want to hurt people too. Well, not exactly hurt them. That's too strong. I'm not really cruel. Pay them out. That's it. There's a nasty little part of me, wants to pay people out. I thought it would make Dadda squirm. Serve him right for leaving us. Even though I love him ever so, ever so much. Oh dear, oh dear. Now d'you see how horrible I am?'

He was still quite calm. 'Is that it?' he asked, and his voice was flat. He didn't seem shocked or curious or anything. But his eyes were smiling, and that encouraged her.

'Yes,' she admitted, shamefaced. 'That's what I'm like. And I can't help it. Everything gets mixed up. Things don't come out the way they ought to with me. Nothing ever does. Even when I'm trying to do something really nice, I know I'm nasty.'

'I love you,' he said. 'More than ever now, because you're being so honest and hurting yourself so much. You dear, dear darling.'

Her mouth fell open with surprise. 'How can you?' she asked.

'I told you how. I love you as you are.'

'You *are* good to me,' she said. And then realization entered her brain. 'I've never told anybody how horrid I am, do you know that? Only you.'

'That proves how much you love me. I'm very honoured.'

Somehow or other the mood of the day had been changed. The bleakness and desperation that had overwhelmed her when she opened that letter was fading, warmed away by the sense of being loved and cared for. She leant forward to kiss him gently. 'I *do* love you, Ralph. You can't begin to know how much.' But then guilty fear reasserted itself. 'But what if everything goes wrong? What if they have a row? It'll be all my fault. Oh, I wish I'd never sent that invitation.'

He considered this carefully. 'I don't think there will be a row,' he said. 'Your father's much too fond of you all to allow it. But if there is we will cope with it. There's usually so much going on at a wedding, a sit down meal and dancing and so many people. I don't think there'll be time for a row.'

She was remembering Georgie's wedding and the way she'd made time to inveigle Eric into a proposal. How could I have been so blind? she thought. And so utterly stupid.

'Besides you couldn't miss Mary's wedding, could you?'

'No,' she said. That was true enough. She certainly couldn't do that. Especially being matron of honour.

'Then you'll go?'

'Yes. I'm sorry I made such a fuss.'

'We'd better start getting the breakfast,' he said, hugging her to show his approval of her decision, 'otherwise we'll be late. We're going to enjoy this wedding. You'll see. Just think, we've got our own bit of good news today too. You can tell your dadda at the reception.'

But she was remembering her own wedding now and Lily's smock. 'No,' she said, 'we won't say anything. Not just yet. Good news keeps. This is Mary's day. Mary's and Tom's. We'll keep quiet about it. We can always tell them later.'

'You,' he said, hugging her again, 'are my own dear, darling tenderheart. And you say you're horrid?'

'I'm out of the bath!' Marlene called. 'Am I to get dressed?'

In Lyndhurst Square there was pandemonium. The bride was dressed and ready, cool in her well-earned white, but her parents were roaring at one another.

'Where's my umbrella?' Albert yelled, rooting about in the

465

hallstand. 'It'll rain as sure as fate! Queenie! Where's my umbrella?'

'Where you left it!' Queenie called down from their bedroom. 'Look fer it!'

'Hell's teeth!' he swore. 'How am I supposed to know where I left it?'

'It's your umbrella. Try the bathroom.'

He pounded up the stairs grumbling as he went, but the bathroom provoked further roaring. 'It's full a' stockings, fer crying out loud!'

'I'm not leaving me face 'alf done jest ter find your bloomin' umbrella,' Queenie said. 'Come in 'ere an' sit down an' give us a bit a' peace.'

'An' look at the state a' this room,' he said, blundering into the bedroom and sinking into the nearest chair. There was marmalade all over one of the pillows and a broken comb in the middle of the rug and a wreckage of discarded shoes and stockings cast all around the dressing table.

'Close yer eyes, then,' Queenie said, powdering her nose. 'You know I'm a muck-pit. Always was, always will be.'

'This is what comes a' too many people bein' involved in this wedding,' he grumbled. 'You should've let me organize it on me own. All 'a' gone like clockwork then. But would you listen? Oh no!'

'You do talk a load a' rubbish sometimes, Ploo. Nothink I ever knew ever went like clockwork,' she said, looking at him through the mirror. Then her expression changed and she swung round in her seat to face him, shrieking. 'Get up, get up, yer daft great thing! You're sittin' on me 'at.'

He leapt from the chair at once but the hat was dented, and at that her shrieks were so shrill and Albert's protestations so loud that Mary came running in to rescue them.

'Look what 'e's been an' gone an' done!' Queenie yelled, waving the hat wildly.

'Stupid woman! What you expect, you leave your 'at in a chair?'

'Give it 'ere,' Mary told her mother. 'It'll steam out.'

'A lunatic asylum!' Albert roared. 'We shall all be late, I hope you realize.'

'No we won't,' Mary comforted. 'There's plenty a' time. Anna hasn't come yet. Now give me yer hat, Ma, an' you,' turning to Albert, 'come downstairs an' I'll fix your buttonhole. The flowers 've come.' They were beaming at her, bristling with love and the passionate anger of their row. 'You're worse'n a couple a' kids,' she scolded affectionately. 'I'm glad I don't get married every day a' the week. I don't think I could stand this more than once in a lifetime.'

'You look a treat!' Queenie said admiring her. 'Don't she, Ploo?'

'She a beauty!' Albert agreed. 'Like her mother!' And he put an arm about them both, cuddling them into his sides. 'You deserve the best wedding anyone ever had,' he said to Mary, chewing his upper lip and gazing at her earnestly.

The gesture revealed his anxiety. 'It will be,' she promised. 'You'll see. It'll be a lovely wedding.'

And so it was. The simple church of St Mary Magdalene was crowded with excited guests and vibrant with flowers, arum lilies as smooth as wax, flame coloured gladioli, dahlias in all their exuberant variety, scarlet, gold, orange, white and every possible shade of pink, heaped before the high altar, massed under every window, screening the lectern, even erupting from the font. And the bride was beautiful, smiling her way down the aisle on Ploochy's arm, her face glowing above the high neckline of her bodice, her little white hat jaunty on her thick, dark curls, and her bouquet red and pink and gold against the white of her skirt.

'Charming!' Minnie whispered to Alice. And Alice whispered back, 'Yes, isn't she.' But she couldn't help thinking how very much like Anna she was. Anna when she was younger and hadn't dyed her hair and grown so hard and cynical. And then she realized that the pretty bridesmaid, in her cyclamen suit and that jaunty little pill-box hat, *was* Anna. Anna with dark hair. Anna softer and more feminine, and very pretty, and smiling at her so lovingly as she passed. So that's why she wore that turban all the time, she thought. What a change! And what a surprise! And she wondered. How very, very alike the two girls were, like sisters. But, of course, she thought, that would account for everything.

Then the first hymn was being sung, and as she didn't know it, she had to concentrate quite hard to follow the words.

'When wilt thou save the people?' What an odd choice for a wedding! And the second was even odder, although not quite so difficult to follow because at least she knew the tune this time.

'These things shall be,' they sang, 'Nation with nation, man with man, inarmed shall live as comrades free. In every heart and brain shall throb, the pulse of one fraternity.' It was more like a political meeting than a wedding. But then the service began and the church was hushed as the bride and groom gave their solemn promises, speaking so clearly that they could be heard right at the back of the church in the far corner where Minnie and Alice had prudently hidden themselves.

And then the service was over and just as the guests were tumbling out of the church, the sun came out from behind the clouds to light up the porch like a stage set. And more photographs were taken, and the happy couple were pelted with so much rice and confetti that they had to run to their car bent double beneath the onslaught, and the second car drew up to take the four parents, and Queenie discovered she'd left her handbag in the pew.

'Shan't be a tick!' she called and rushed back into the building to get it, her coat billowing behind her like a sail.

Now that the song and excitement were over the church was very quiet indeed, its ancient silence settling back upon itself in slow gentle waves. Queenie found it rather daunting and was aware that her shoes were making a terrible clatter. She felt she ought to be as unobtrusive as possible and crept carefully to her seat to retrieve her bag. But when she turned to tiptoe back, she saw that she was not alone in this quiet place after all. There were two old ladies still sitting in the last pew and as she passed they smiled at her, sensing her confusion and trying to put her at her ease.

'A lovely wedding,' the grey-haired one whispered. And the white-haired one said, 'A lovely bride.'

'My daughter,' Queenie told them proudly, but wishing her voice didn't sound so loud.

'You must be very proud of her,' the white-haired one said, smiling again.

What nice old ladies they were, Queenie thought, and she wondered who they were. 'I'm sorry,' she said, returning the smile. 'I don't know …'

'How could you, my dear?' the grey one said. 'We're friends of the bride's father. From way back, as you might say.'

'Ah!' Queenie said, feeling she understood. 'Glad ter meetcher. Are you waitin' fer a car?'

'Oh no, no, no,' white hair said, pursing her mouth into a little pout of self-deprecation. 'We're not going to the reception, dear. We only came for the wedding.'

'Nonsense,' Queenie said. 'A' course you must come ter the reception. We got cars fer everybody. I'll tell 'em to expect yer.'

'We wouldn't want to be a nuisance,' white hair said, and she looked so worried about it all that Queenie liked her even more.

'I must rush,' she explained, ''cos I'm 'oldin' 'em all up. I'll tell Fred. 'E's the third car along. Promise you'll come?'

'Well ...' white hair dithered. But grey hair said, 'You're very kind, my dear. Yes, of course we'll come.'

'However much longer?' Albert complained as she scrambled into their car.

'Didn't it go well?' Maisie said rapturously. 'They looked a proper picture, the pair of 'em.'

So there wasn't time to tell them about the two old ladies. And when they got to The Star, the reception engulfed her and carried her along on a tide of such happiness she forgot everything except the pleasure of the moment. The place was so warm and crowded and full of flowers and excited talk, and there was so much wine and such good food. And Mary and Tom were so obviously happy, sitting at the top table so close to one another that their shoulders were touching. It was all as it ought to be.

When Albert rose to his feet to make his speech, he was aware that all three of his children were watching him attentively, that Mary was smiling, and Anna was wearing her deliberately composed expression, and Georgie was looking apprehensive. For a fleeting second he wondered what his son could possibly have to worry about, but then the moment passed and the speech was begun. It was short and simple. 'I am not makin' a long speech,' he said, grinning at his guests. 'Two things I want to say, then young Tom has to speak. First I thank you all for coming here and making this such a good wedding. It is good for us to see you all here. Then I ask you to toast the bride and groom. Long life and health and happiness!'

And that was all. It was the shortest speech he'd ever made in his life. Georgie was so surprised by it he almost forgot to stand for the toast. All through the meal he'd been remembering the speech his father had made at his twenty-third birthday party, such a false, embarrassing speech, full of sentiments he was pretending to feel, and opinions he didn't really hold. The memory had disturbed him and made him feel uncomfortable in advance in case they were in for a repeat performance. Now, as he lifted his glass to his half sister, he realized that his father had been profoundly changed by his new life, that he spoke as he felt, that he wasn't putting on an act. He leant across the table to tell Lily, but couldn't because Tom was on his feet and the room was growing quiet again to hear what he had to say.

He made a much longer speech, correct and slightly formal, thanking guests for their attendance, vicar for the service, friends for their presents. Then he took two small parcels from the pocket of his jacket and set them on the table in front of him. 'Now,' he said, 'my wife and I have some presents of our own to deliver.' And Mary stood up and took the first little package in her newly ringed hand. 'These are for our mothers,' he said, 'with our love, to thank them for all the love they've given us.' And to surprise and appreciative applause, Tom and Mary took their gifts first to Queenie and then to Maisie with kisses and hugs and beaming delight, like children at Christmas. And the two mothers had to hold their presents up so that everyone could see them, and they were enamelled brooches that had to be pinned on their dresses immediately to a further outburst of claps and cheers.

Then a third packet was fished out of Mary's handbag and it was the Ox's turn. 'For you, Dad,' Tom said, 'with our love, to thank you for all the support you've given us.' And this time it was a tie pin that had to be ceremoniously put in place. And the guests clapped and cheered again, and only Alice and Queenie thought to look at Albert.

When the third present appeared, he'd felt suddenly and overwhelmingly miserable, the fourth parent, and the only one of the four who had to remain unacknowledged. She didn't mean to hurt him of course, he was sure of that. It was just something that couldn't be avoided. But rejection nipped his heart in its cruel little claws despite his attempt to be reasonable, and he had to put his hand in front of his mouth to hide his emotion. While the Ox's tie pin was admired and the guests cheered and chattered, he turned away from a happiness he couldn't share and, leaning across the table, found something to say to old Harry Jones who was sitting at the long table below him. And so he missed what was happening next.

Mary had taken a fourth parcel out of her handbag, and she and Tom were walking across the stage for the fourth time, signalling, fingers to lips so that nobody would warn him of their approach. She was behind him and had her arms round his neck before he sensed that something was going on. 'This is for you, Dad,' she said, as Tom put the little parcel into his hands, 'because we love you, and because you're the kindest dad anyone could ever have.'

He was so surprised and so overwhelmed with unexpected happiness he didn't know what to say. 'Dad', just like that, so naturally, and in public, in front of everybody there. He held the parcel unopened in his hands as Mary kissed him and Queenie kissed him and Tom thumped him on the back, and the tears sprang into his eyes and he let them fall.

'Well, open it, mate!' Harry called to him. 'If someone give me a present I'd darn soon open it.' So amid laughter and applause another tie pin was revealed and pinned in position, and then it was time for the tables to be cleared and the dancing to begin.

Still stunned, Albert sat at the high table with Queenie hanging onto his arm. 'I can't get over it, Queenie,' he said. 'Can't get over it!'

'They've 'ad it planned fer ever such a long time,' she said, hugging his arm. 'Mary an' Anna an' Tom an' Ralph. All the lot a' them. Like a lot a' kids they were!'

'Why didntcher tell me?' he asked in amazement. Fancy Queenie keeping a secret.

'An' spoil the surprise!' she said. ''Sides, I wouldn't a' 'missed the sight a' your face fer all the tea in China.'

Below them the trestles were being folded and wheeled away and the guests were arranging their chairs beside the walls so as to leave the centre of the hall free. He glanced idly across the room at the people already seated and found he was looking at Minnie Holdsworthy and Alice. Minnie had Marlene on her lap and Alice was nursing little Norman on one knee and had Johnny and Meg standing beside the other. He was so stupefied he almost forgot to breathe. This wedding was one surprise after another.

'Queenie,' he implored weakly. 'Look over there.'

Queenie looked. 'That's nice,' she said. 'They've made friends. An' with Georgie's mob, too. Now they won't feel out of it.'

'D'you know who they are?'

'Friends a' Ned's, they said. From way back. I found 'em in the church, Ploo. Ever such a nice old pair. Shy. Didn't want ter be a nuisance.'

'Who invited them?'

'I did.'

'Oh, Queenie!' he said, caught between astonishment and distress. And for the second time that afternoon, he covered his mouth with the palm of his hand.

'What's up, Ploo?'

'The one in brown is Minnie Holdsworthy,' he told her. 'The other one …'

'Is Alice! Oh, Ploochy! They said they were friends a' the bride's father.'

'So they are,' he said, beginning to giggle. 'Oh, Queenie, I shouldn't laugh. This is awful.'

'No it ain't,' she said. 'They're just a pair a' little old ladies. That's all. A pair a' little old ladies. No wonder I never recognized 'em. An' we been worried about your Alice all this time, an' what she would do, an' what she wouldn't do. It's priceless!'

'I'm glad you think so.'

'She's old an' shy, an' lonely too, if I'm any judge. Go an' talk to 'er, Ploo. You owe 'er that. They come all this way ter see your daughter married.'

He was going to say it couldn't be done, when the men arrived to clear the high table. Queenie gave him a grin and a push and rushed off to join the Ox and Maisie. He noticed that the children had gone scampering off to join their parents and that Minnie and Alice were on their own. Feeling rather

472

foolish and not at all sure what he would say, he crossed the room to speak to his wife.

'Hello, Mr P.,' Minnie said. 'It *was* good of you to invite us. We're having a lovely time. It's a lovely wedding.'

He was getting so used to surprises by now he hardly responded to this one. 'Going well, issen' it?' he asked.

'She's so like Anna,' Alice said, and she seemed to be speaking with admiration. 'Before she took to dying her hair. I'm ever so glad she's let it grow out. It makes her look so much nicer, don't you think.'

'Who's the young man she's with?' Minnie dared.

Well, why not tell them, Albert thought. 'His name's Ralph Andrews,' he said. 'He's going to marry our Anna as soon as she can get Eric to divorce her.'

'Fancy!' Alice said but she didn't sound annoyed or even disturbed by the news. 'Well, they look very happy together, I must say. Let's hope he's better for her than that Eric.'

'He's much better than Eric,' Albert said, and he drew up a chair and sat down between them like an old friend, and told them all about it. Then they discussed the children and Harry's rheumatism and Dickie's broadcasts and the state of the world. And the hall was rearranged around them.

But now the band was in position on the stage and he could see that the leader was looking round for instructions. 'I shall have to go,' he said gently. 'The band ...'

'Of course,' Alice said, smiling at him. 'It was good of you to ask us, Albert.'

'I often come to Tooting,' he said, speaking quickly and on impulse. 'To see the shops an' 'ave a quick one with Harry an' old Dickie. How would it be if I came up to Longley Road now an' then? To see how you are.'

'That would be lovely,' Alice said simply. 'We could give you tea. Or supper. Couldn't we, Minnie?'

'Wednesday after next?' he asked. And they both nodded. Queenie was right. They were just two old ladies. Two shy, rather lonely old ladies. 'I'll be there for tea,' he promised.

There was a commotion on the other side of the room where the photographer was trying to gather the guests together round the last trestle table to remain standing. In the delighted confusion of the presents the bride and groom had forgotten to cut the cake. 'Must 'ave a picture a' the cake!' he was pleading. 'Mr Ploochy! Where's Mr Ploochy?'

'Gather round everybody!' Albert boomed, happily organizing again. 'One last picture, then we dance, eh?' And the guests drifted back across the room towards the table and its huge, iced burden.

'One a' the bride an' groom,' the photographer said, setting up his camera, 'an' then one a' the whole party in a group.'

'Never get 'em all in, mate,' Dickie said, laughing at him.

'Smile!' the photographer commanded unnecessarily, as Tom and Mary balanced their hands on the knife and grinned at one another.

'Make a wish!' Maisie said.

'What've they got left ter wish for?' a voice in the crowd asked cheerfully.

'That's right!' Harry agreed.

'Long life, happiness, an' peace in our time,' Dickie suggested.

Other voices were quick to echo him. 'That's right!' 'Peace!' 'Ain't gonna be a war now.' 'We got peace in our time.' 'A long peaceful marriage!'

The bridegroom grinned at his new wife again and put his free arm about her waist to cuddle her. 'Some hopes!' he said.

Then the band struck up and the bride and groom were dragged into the centre of the room so that they could begin the dancing, and Albert rushed off to order more champagne because they couldn't eat wedding cake without champagne. And Anna, dancing cheek to cheek with her dear Ralph, wondered what she had ever been worried about. It was a lovely wedding, and both her planned surprises had gone off well.

But it couldn't last for ever, lovely though it was. Soon it was time for her to slip away with the new Mary Oxbury and help her to change, for in half an hour bride and groom would be leaving for their honeymoon.

They'd left her going away suit in one of the changing rooms behind the stage, a small stuffy box of a room made smaller by its red wallpaper and the strong glare from the battery of electric lights that surrounded the dressing table mirror. The wedding was a cheerful buzz somewhere behind them.

'Wasn't old Ploo's face a study?' Mary said happily as she pulled her wedding dress over her head.

'Dear old Dadda,' Anna said. 'Hold still, you've got your hair caught.'

Confetti showered from the folds of the dress and sprinkled the dressing table with its tiny, bright petals. Mary looked down at the new ring shining on her left hand. 'I can't believe I'm married,' she said, and to Anna's loving eyes her face seemed young and tremulous and very touching. 'Silly, isn't it?'

'You're going to be very, very happy, you an' Tom,' she said, hugging her sister. 'And it's no more than you deserve.'

Mary was stepping into her new skirt and tugging it about her waist. It was cherry red, almost exactly the same colour as the winter coat Ploochy had bought her all those years ago. She couldn't have chosen any other colour. 'I wish you could marry Ralph,' she said.

'Well ...' Anna hesitated, and when Mary looked up, brightly and hopefully and with her face full of affection, she decided to tell her the news.

'But that's marvellous!' Mary said. 'Marvellous! Both of us going to be happily married, and both of us knowing about it on the same day.'

'Here's your coat,' Anna said, holding it up as a good bridesmaid should, because she was afraid she would be weeping again if she didn't keep busy. 'How's that?'

They stood side by side, looking at their reflections in the long dazzling mirror, the same height, the same colour, bright and tender as poppies in their red suits. 'I'm so happy, it frightens me,' Mary said. 'It's too good to be true. Too good to last. This awful war'll start and knock us all for six.'

'Be happy while you can,' Anna advised. 'Where's your hat?'

'In a cardboard box somewhere.'

There was a pile of cardboard boxes in the corner. The one on top was adorned with a rough red cross. That'll be the one, Anna thought, and opened it.

It was full of gas masks, glaring up at her with their blank, ominous eyes. Now she could see that the hat box was behind the curtain, and she reached across the pile to lift it up. But her movement dislodged the gas masks so that one fell out of the

475

box, and rolled, slug black and evil, down the piles of cardboard, towards the floor. She caught it quickly and set it on the chair behind the curtain, balanced on its ugly snout. This awful war'll start and knock us all for six. Mary mustn't see it, she thought. It would upset her. 'Here's your hat,' she said, grabbing it out of its box. 'Put it on quick! I must see how you look.'

And she looked so pretty. 'Be happy while you can, Mrs Oxbury.'

'You too, Anna dear. You too.'

HEARTS & FARTHINGS

Beryl Kingston

London in the 1890s . . . a foggy city bustling with activity and bubbling with Cockney repartee.

To this alien world comes Alberto Pelucci, an early immigrant from distant Italy, dreaming of adventure and romance. Adventure enough is the verminous room of his first night's stay in London, but romance seems more rewarding when the shy Alice accepts his hand. Only on their wedding night does he realise that his bride will never share his passion for physical pleasures.

And so when Alberto meets Queenie Dawson – exuberant, sensuous star of the music halls – his ordered new life is flung into turmoil . . .

HEARTS AND FARTHINGS: the heart-warming saga of a man torn between two women, and of children born in the last, bittersweet days before the war that should have ended all wars.

Futura Publications
Fiction/Saga
0 7088 2976 7

ALWAYS A STRANGER

Margaret P. Kirk

°The tranquil Yorkshire countryside in the summer of '39 offers Lallie Wainwright, adored only child of a wealthy foundry owner, blissful happiness: as long as she has her family, dogs and Neil, her childhood friend, her life is complete.

But the war brings more than upheaval – it brings Jan Kaliski, a Polish pilot in a strange land, into Lallie's home and into her heart. Then the war, and the chaos that is war's aftermath, forces them apart. Only after heartbreak and tragedy do Lallie and Jan learn the bittersweet lesson that home is not always where the heart is. . . .

'a love story in the old, grand manner – heroic and emotionally charged. She deals with big themes in the stylish and deceptively simple manner of the born storyteller. Have your handkerchiefs ready. You won't just read. You'll care.'
Sarah Harrison, author of *A FLOWER THAT'S FREE*

'vivid and real . . . an irresistible read of passion and heartbreak. I couldn't put it down.'
Madge Swindells, author of *SUMMER HARVEST*

'a really heartwarming story with flashes of brilliance'
Cynthia Harrod-Eagles, author of the *Dynasty* series

Futura Publications
Fiction
0 7088 2723 2

SUMMER HARVEST

Madge Swindells

'a spellbinding read' Sarah Harrison

Set between 1938 and 1968 in a land where gruelling poverty rubs shoulders with remarkable opulence, and moving from the Cape to London and the West Coast of America, SUMMER HARVEST is a family saga in the finest tradition.

At the heart of the story is Anna, a woman as strong and passionate as she is ambitious, who fights her way up from near destitution to become one of the Cape's most prominent and powerful businesswomen. Only love eludes her. For Simon – a poor farmer when they marry – has too much masculine pride to stand on the sidelines while Anna plunders her way to a success that threatens tragedy and loss.

'Anna van Achtenburgh mirrors the strengths and the weaknesses of her beautiful, harsh country: the toughness, the dazzling material success, the moral dilemmas, the tragedy. I was gripped from start to finish.'
Kate Alexander, author of *Fields of Battle.*

Futura Publications
Fiction
0 7088 2528 1